Praise for the novels of Greg...

DESPERATE HEARTS

"Hinton's enthusiasm and compassion for his characters comes throug[h]
in every scene."
—*Publishers Weekly*

"A great summertime read."
—*Booklist*

"Hinton creates a modern-day *Tales of the City* with a cast of quirky,
colorful characters you'll really care about and a town that comes to life
thanks to Hinton's warm, witty writing."
—*Out Front Colorado*

CATHEDRAL CITY

"A splashy first novel . . . solid entertainment."
—*Kirkus Reviews*

"This wonderful book is as honest as it is heart-wrenching. The
intertwining lives of these diverse and unforgettable characters remind us
not of the ways we live apart, but the ways we live together."
—Greg Sarris, author of *Grand Avenue* and *Watermelon Nights*

"Hinton has an interesting sense of how people of different races, classes,
ages and ethnicities all mix in a diverse little desert town . . . Flashes of
insight . . . sharp dialogue . . . nice descriptive touches."
—*The Washington Post Book World*

"A sprawling, ambitious novel."
—*The Lambda Book Report*

"*Cathedral City* completely captures the feel of a unique place on the outskirts of Palm Springs in a way that makes the readers feel they were there.
At the same time, Gregory Hinton draws you into the lives of his offbeat
and eccentric characters and makes you care about them."
—Randal Kleiser, Director, *Grease* and *It's My Party*

"Gregory Hinton has created a colorful patchwork quilt of vibrant, passionate characters caught up in a precarious original desert world we've
rarely seen painted so romantically."
—Dirk Shafer, Writer/Director, *Man of the Year* and *Circuit*

"Gregory Hinton's *Cathedral City* chronicles the raw side of the desert
that is too quickly disappearing."
—Stewart Weiner, Editor-in-Chief, *Palm Springs Life* magazine

Books by Gregory Hinton

CATHEDRAL CITY

DESPERATE HEARTS

Published by Kensington Publishing Corp.

DESPERATE HEARTS

Gregory Hinton

KENSINGTON BOOKS
http://www.kensingtonbooks.com

KENSINGTON BOOKS are published by

Kensington Publishing Corp.
850 Third Avenue
New York, NY 10022

All Kensington titles, imprints, and distributed lines are available at special quantity discounts for bulk purchases for sales promotion, premiums, fund-raising, educational or institutional use.

Special book excerpts or customized printings can also be created to fit specific needs. For details, write or phone the office of the Kensington Special Sales Manager: Kensington Publishing Corp., 850 Third Avenue, New York, NY 10022. Attn. Special Sales Department. Phone: 1-800-221-2647.

Kensington and the K logo Reg. U.S. Pat. & TM Off.

ISBN 0-7582-0173-7

First Hardcover Printing: August 2002
First Trade Paperback Printing: July 2003
10   9   8   7   6   5   4   3   2   1

Printed in the United States of America

For Tom

For my sister, Christine

ACKNOWLEDGMENTS

I would like to offer thanks and love to fellow desert rats Pat Oygar, Stewart Weiner, Wayne Fleisher, Robert Gomer, Nancy Dolensek, Christopher Lewis, Tim Noyle, Craig Prater, Steve Rutberg, Darlene Rutberg and Harry Brent Rutberg.

To my handsome editor, John Scognamiglio, who hosts this party; my book agent, Fred Morris; my talent and literary agent, Graham Kaye; my attorney, Steve Breimer; many, many thanks.

For continuing advice and friendship, Greg Sarris, Susan Moore, Randal Kleiser, Ann Johnson, Moctesuma Esparza, Robert Katz, Kim Myers, Sev Askenazy, Monique Avila, Babs Auberger, Alva Moreno, Thelma Garcia, Cecelia Abider, Steve Cubine, and always, Dirk Shafer.

I am particularly grateful to the independent bookstores who continue to fight the good fight. Rick Anderson at Q Trading Company, Palm Springs, Bill Barker of A Different Light Bookstore in West Hollywood and San Francisco, Charles Stillwagon of the Tattered Cover Book Store, Denver. Special thanks to Steve Covington of Barnes & Noble, Palm Desert, and Roger Clements, Cathedral City Library.

For the doctors who keep me well: Phillip Musikanth, Gary Bellack, and Sy Young. My thanks to several agencies selflessly dedicated to the care of others; AIDS Assistance Program of Palm Springs, Desert AIDS Project, East Los Angeles Women's Center and Atlantis/ADAPT of Denver.

And lastly, my family, Ron Niles, John Dziadecki, Cara Campanella, Brandon Campanella, Rene Campanella, and my brother, John Scott Hinton, who inspires me and continues to live a life worth telling, retelling, and telling some more.

AUTHOR'S NOTE

Number one on a list of negative perceptions about Cathedral City compiled by the Chamber of Commerce as reported in the *Desert Sun* newspaper, 4/13/01.

- *Primarily Hispanic*

PROLOGUE

The Sex Life of the Date Palm

Since the scorched earth diaspora of old Cathedral City, the Latino residents and gay business owners of the late Sam Singer's four-block quadrant have been disbursed by the hot desert winds of progress. Without them—Kenny and Nick, the proprietors of the gay night-club; their alley neighbors, the recently naturalized Latino family of Thomas Quintero; Pablo Seladon, reformed hustler and now Stanford graduate; Maria Lourdes Castillo, the beautiful *mojada* sheltered from the INS by Kenny and Nick; and lastly, Sam Singer and his quirky, jazz-singing wife, Ruthie—the once quaint desert village seemed to not know what it wanted to be.

It was plain to any onlooker what had been torn down or allowed to slip away, but not obvious what was needed to replace it. Hence, the patient environment took over, and when the gay hangouts and tiny bungalows of the Latino barrio were torn down, the desert reclaimed them, resulting in the now empty patch of sand and cactus stretching from East Palm Canyon Drive north to the local Catholic church.

One of the few old buildings to have survived Cathedral City's renewal effort was a flat-roofed stucco structure, which, over the years, played host to a number of disparate desert eateries and watering holes, one more colorful than the next: gambling casino, USO club, jazz joint, cabaret, gay bar and most recently, a Mexican restaurant.

Cathedral City, California, counts an abundance of Mexican restaurants for a modest township. Whether one appreciates the rapidly reproducing U.S. Hispanic population has nothing to do with their love of the cuisine of Mexico.

Hence, like fresh cheese-stuffed *chiles relleno* searing in a cast-iron skillet, these joints were hopping, especially the heir apparent to Sam's historical spot: The Cathedral City Café, offering fine Mexican cuisine and drinks by its lovely proprietor, the now documented Maria Castillo.

Her landlady is desert treasure Ruth Harris Singer, a well-known and beloved local cabaret singer, and the very wealthy widow of Sam Singer—land baron and desert rat. Sam's memory adds to the colorful patina of the location because he died on the premises, a victim of a hate crime, though he himself was not homosexual. Nick, the former proprietor, was, and he nearly died that same night for being openly gay.

The negative publicity, coupled with the bona fide financial disaster that had been the Cathedral City renewal effort prompted the formation of the Cathedral City Preservation Society. The society's members quickly invited fellow residents and business owners to present possible marketing options to revamp Cathedral City's tarnished image.

In an effort to define the problem, local business owners held a secret, impromptu brainstorming session. Two lists were compiled, one positive and one negative, to identify the public's perception of Cathedral City. Second on the list of negatives, as leaked to the local newspapers: "Shady Past/Present."

Well, let's just say some fences needed mending.

"Like many residents of the culturally diverse California desert, the elegant date palm is an immigrant, its seeds and offshoots imported from Iraq and Algeria in the early 1900s. What would Southern California be without this gorgeous tree?"

The small group of city officials had gathered on the lush grounds of the famed mid-century Seven Palms Inn at the request of Scott Travers, newly designated president of the Cathedral City Preservation Society. The group included the recently elected mayor, Mr. Harry Hills; Leslie Mason, Cathedral City's controversial and outspoken city planner; and Peggy Lane, the president of Cathedral City's Chamber of Commerce. They were listening to the prepared remarks of Dominic Laneri, groundskeeper and caretaker of the Inn since the Seven Palms went into receivership a year earlier.

Dom droned on dramatically: "The date palm must live with its feet in the water and its head in the fires of heaven!"

As Dominic continued to address the group, Scott contemplated the fading wooden structure, which he was recommending be designated for historical status and therefore protected from further bastardized renovations or outright demolition. Scott knew the hotel would be a tough sell to his fellow preservation society members.

The hotel was a longtime gay establishment with a notorious reputation. Still, it was a prime example of mid-century architecture, built in the late forties, remodeled in the late eighties, but not enough to spoil the overall feeling of the place. Behind the lobby, large bar and café, the rooms of the L-shaped two-story hotel overlooked the aqua pool area. Palm trees dotted the lush, green grassy grounds, but Scott could remember how it looked before they were thinned out and sold. He lamented the demolition and relocation of many of the desert's date palm groves. Luckily, most of the old trees were moved to nearby Thermal and Mecca.

Recommending the Inn for historical status was highly controversial. As Scott perspired in the hot June sun, he pondered Dom as he continued his tour of the grounds. How old was Dom now? He had to be in his late fifties or even sixty. He was still a sexy man—tall, sleekly built; high, burnished cheekbones; a silver, buzzed crewcut; and brilliant white smile propped up by a salt and pepper goatee.

"Pollination of the female date palm can't take place without human hands. From mid-February into April, pollen is gathered from male blooms, and extracted—either inserted into the female bloom on puffs of cotton or sprayed in."

"I like it sprayed in," Scott smirked.

"Why's he lecturing to us about the sex life of the date palm? I thought we were here to evaluate the hotel," Leslie whispered to Scott. They were old friends. It was only because Leslie twisted a few arms that the mayor and the Chamber of Commerce president agreed to attend. Hills and Lane were both so conservative. This was an insane idea. To designate a structure because of its notorious sexual history.

"The sex life of this date palm grove is very important to the history of the Seven Palms Inn," Scott whispered back.

"This is so crazy! Why'd I let you talk me into this?"

"The Seven Palms is as important to Cathedral City gay history as the meat rack to Fire Island, the Christopher Street Piers to Manhattan, and the Jardin de Tuileries to Paris."

Leslie guffawed—choking it back. Everyone stared.

"She has a hair ball," Scott shrugged it off. He continued whispering to her. "Besides, it's the only prime example of mid-century architecture left inside the city limits. Let's be brave! Let's celebrate what it used to mean to the gay clientele who frequented it. Sexual identity," he pressed. "Sexual liberation!"

"To you, maybe," she cleared her throat. "But not to the mayor."

They studied him and Scott resisted the urge to laugh. Mayor Hills had come prepared by a short, detailed brief Scott had provided him about the history and reputation of the Seven Palms. He only agreed to the visit because in the past five years he'd seen millions of dollars of potential revenue flow directly into the coffers of Palm Springs from its quickly multiplying homosexual population.

"You can't continue to deny that the gay influence of Cathedral City is integral to its history. You can't have a Chamber of Commerce that doesn't recognize its huge gay and Latino population."

"How do you accurately count the gay population of Cathedral City?"

"Maybe we should."

"Sure. And while we're at it, just to be politically correct, let's not forget lesbians, bisexuals, and transgenders."

"Of course."

"*I'm talking here,*" Dom asserted irritably.

"Sorry," Scott and Leslie murmured in concert.

The debate about the framing of Cathedral City's identity had been ongoing since the city incorporated in the early eighties. There were many who long resented Cathedral City's second-class status and its maverick reputation as a haven for gay clubs and migrant housing. In the thirties and forties it was known for gambling and whorehouses. Before, no respectable family man or business wanted to claim a Cathedral City address.

The first order of business of the newly formed Cathedral City Preservation Society was to identify a list of local buildings to cite for possible preservation by the society. No one could come up with even one building until Scott pressed for the Seven Palms.

The city's downtown core had been razed in the massive renovation of Cathedral City in the late nineties. Now an enormous civic center had taken its place. With ongoing financial scandals, accusations of fraud and graft, the city hall was a Coachella Valley laughingstock and so was Cathedral City. Had Cathedral City elected to celebrate its diversity rather than homogenize it, imagine what it might be today! In a four-block quadrant opposite the civic center and stretching from East Palm Canyon Drive to the local Catholic church, Cathedral City once hosted a cultural mélange of gays, Latinos and senior citizens that could rival the most unique neighborhoods in New York or Los Angeles.

The barrio was destroyed and many residents relocated south to Indio, a desert city proud of its Latino heritage. Palm Springs, with a history of being closed to minorities, lured the gay dollar inside its city limits. Currently enjoying a majority gay population and multimillion dollar revenue infusions from events like the world famous White Party, Palms Springs' resort economy boomed and Cathedral City retained its reputation as the flawed gem in the strand of sparkling desert resort cities.

Scott and his fellow charter members decided something had to be done to chronicle Cathedral City's colorful past. He finally came up with a solution. There was one mid-century hotel, located in a date palm grove, just east of the Palm Springs city limits.

The original hotel was built inside the date palm grove for good reason. The groves provided mystery, privacy and protection. The elegant palms were phallic and sensual, the fronds rustling in the hot desert breeze. Scott loved date palm groves and had his own warm memories of the Seven Palms Inn.

As a young man Scott tended bar at the Seven Palms. Late on summer nights, when the sultry dry air wafted across the aqua pool from the date palm groves, Scott remembered the ghostly shadows of naked men undulating among the tall trees. If he stood on the terrace to have a smoke, he could hear low whistles, moaning and the soft sighs of spent ecstasy emanating from them. He could smell the odor of poppers drifting through the air, and sometimes the rank odor of Crisco emanating from the oleanders.

When his shift ended, and no other prospects loomed large, Scott—hot, short, buffed out—ripped off his tank top, stuffed it in the back pocket of his shorts and in weathered work boots topped off by heavy white socks, strode across the grassy knoll of the hotel grounds to wander among the sensual palms.

PART ONE

El Centro

1

Bambi and Madonna

The gray van passed the lumbering old produce truck at quite a clip.

They were only five minutes out of Westmoreland, south of the Salton Sea, the Superstition Mountains hulking to the west in the misty green-gray desert dawn. Scores of trucks boomed up the black-top, heading north on Highway 86 to catch eastbound I-10 just beyond the date palm groves of Thermal.

They'd just stopped for coffee and fresh Bismarcks. Madonna loved the sensation of the squirting raspberry jelly as she bit into its sugary shell. The hot Styrofoam cup of coffee between her naked thighs kept her warm. Imperial County's early mornings were typically cold; warming by eight, hot by ten, so Madonna always dressed in layers. A long sweater over short-shorts and a cute top to please Bambi—the owner of her own modest Imperial Valley produce delivery service. Madonna was tall by anybody's standards, just over six feet, with lean, tanned legs, brown-freckled arms and short, sassy blond hair—golden in certain light.

Bambi was her exact opposite—short, burly, Latina. Her daily uniform consisted of a tight black tank top, a sweat-stained weight-lifting belt, khaki, pleated shorts and scuffed Red Wing boots. Bambi was winsome as a teen-aged boy, but older by twenty years. Madonna had to fight her to be allowed to do any heavy lifting. Born and raised in El Centro, Bambi was the baby in a family of four sisters and three brothers.

Living in the Mexicali/Calexico corridor, Bambi was long accustomed to INS chases. Border jumping was commonplace. At night, on the quiet residential streets of El Centro, it seemed like the most peacefully benign place in the world, but ten miles east or west of town, the vast agricultural fields of California's verdant Imperial Valley teemed with all manner of life or death activity.

Operation Gatekeeper had forced border-jumpers east into the much more deadly California deserts surrounding Calexico and Mexicali. A thousand people a day were still being caught and turned back. Border jumpers and drug traffickers—more easily detected by INS state-of-the-art surveillance equipment like nightvision goggles and wide-ranging motion sensors—pulsed through alfalfa fields, forging deadly irrigation canals, many without success. With all the fancy equipment, the U.S. Border Patrol was limited by low morale and dwindling personnel. What good was knowing they were out there if there weren't the human resources to go out and arrest them?

Now a green and white border patrol vehicle zipped up behind Bambi's rig, followed by an identical mate.

"Shit," Bambi gripped the wheel. "Are they after us?"

The INS trucks roared past them. In the distance they disappeared around the curve, hidden by a short range of sandy hills.

"They want the gray van. I hope they get away before someone gets hurt," Madonna said.

After a thoughtful silence, Bambi commented, "You're my girl, you know that Madonna?"

"I know, baby. I know." Madonna grinned and took a bite of her Bismarck. Red jelly rolled down the side of her chin. Bambi wiped it away with her thumb, popping it into her mouth and sucking on it as though it were the most delicious thing in the world.

The produce truck groaned up the Salton Highway. They made this trip every Monday and Friday, loaded up with crates of tomatoes, cucumbers, onions and fancy lettuces. "Used to be," Bambi liked to joke, "all anybody asked for was head. Now who the heck named it head lettuce in the first place? Where's that come from, huh? I don't know, I don't know, but I built up my business providing the best head in the valley!"

Now it was different. The demand was for exotics. Endive, arugula, raddichio, romaine. Lots of call for romaine. Every house offered Caesar salad nowadays. Bambi loved a good Caesar. No end to the varieties of the dressing they came up with. Bambi had her first Caesar in T.J., where they first invented it.

"There's smoke over the ridge," Madonna commented. "Or haze."

She settled back comfortably for the drive. They'd just celebrated three wonderful years together. They were planning a commitment ceremony, once Madonna could enlist the support of her college-age daughter Laurie. Laurie was slow to come around to her mother's lifestyle change.

Bambi's family had been so accepting. How ironic. Staunch Catholics, three hulking *machista* brothers, four sisters including Bambi, her mother Florencia still undocumented after forty years living in the United States—they'd opened their arms and their hearts to Madonna without question. Florencia joked that it was only because of her name. Madonna. The Lord worked in strange ways. If he sent the Blessed Mother to her door, who was she, Florencia, to turn her away? Besides, she made Bambi happy. She'd grounded her in a way that her mother had prayed for, ever since Bambi was thirteen.

Every Sunday, after Mass, the entire family gathered for supper at Florencia's. All the brothers, their wives and girlfriends, their children and grandchildren. Florencia finished cleaning up on Tuesday and started cooking for the next Sunday on Wednesday. She was a large, gray-haired, mirthful woman. The only woman, who, when she embraced Madonna, was so big-hearted and nurturing she made her feel petite. How Madonna loved those Sundays. The fresh, homemade green corn tamales; the carnitas, marinated for days in cilantro, onion and lime; the crisp, fresh tortilla chips; and on special occasions, when Bambi made a delivery to San Diego, her ceviche—fresh cubed snapper marinated in lime juice, avocado and serrano chiles.

After years of playing the part of a Southern California Stepford Wife, no one, least of all Madonna, would be more surprised by her present circumstances. She remembered the first time she saw Bambi, in a dinner house in Cathedral City called Nick's. Nick and his boyfriend, Kenny, had been so sweet. Madonna and her husband, Burton, had been Happy Hour regulars. They both liked to drink, as did Nick. The lounge was mixed. Madonna knew that many of the regulars were gay. Madonna always caused something of a stir when she came in because she was so tall and pretty.

She laughed it off but Burton didn't think it was funny at all. On the whole, Burton had been a pretty good sport about their daily ritual at Nick's. There were certainly other desert watering holes to choose from. The lounge at Nick's was just so cheerful. It was dark and cool, with Broadway show bills adorning the walls. And autographed pictures of movie stars. And lots of pictures of Nick himself.

Plus, the clientele was diverse, and Nick was so good at keeping the conversation going. No one drank alone at Nick's, even if initially they thought they wanted to. He introduced everybody to everybody else. And he had this nice habit of talking you up, like you did important things, and he made you want to come back. So you did.

Madonna was just thirty-nine, and Burton older by twenty years. They were married as many. Her mother had been aghast by the age difference, but Madonna was looking for a father, and Burton promised her his love and security and gave it to her. They had a beautiful home high on a hill in La Jolla, overlooking the ocean. They had one girl, Laurie, who played tennis like crazy and had just transferred from San Diego State to UCLA. She was only two hours north, but the loss of her affected their marriage. They decided to buy a condo on a golf course in Rancho Mirage and winter there. They didn't want to be tired of each other so they blamed it on San Diego. They needed to spice things up.

They didn't play much golf, because Madonna preferred her afternoons at Nick's. She'd been curious about a few of the lesbians who came in. She only started noticing them because Burton pointed them out. She'd swear on Laurie's head that she never had any inclination in that direction. Not in her wildest dreams.

And the Bambi thing just hit them all like an eighteen-wheeler. She'd come up from the kitchen with Kenny, and Kenny rarely ventured into the lounge. Although he co-owned Nick's, he preferred his spot at the grill. Kenny was shy, but cultured and articulate. At first Madonna thought Bambi was a man, a very handsome Hispanic man, but his body rounded subtly, and Madonna noticed pierced earrings, and then Bambi laughed at something Kenny said, and it was definitely a woman's hearty laugh.

"You're staring," Burton had said. "Close your mouth."

And Madonna had giggled. "I thought she was a man."

"She's not, but you see what I mean."

And across the bar, Bambi winked at her. A silence came over Burton and Madonna.

"I think we come here too often," Burton said finally.

Bambi and Kenny disappeared laughing into the kitchen.

Burton and Madonna never went back, but of course they read about the terrible goings on. The violent attack on Nick by those awful kids, the murder of their landlord, Sam Singer, the self-proclaimed mayor of Cathedral City. They still hadn't caught them.

Madonna was sick when she heard about it. Sick. Burton, vindicated in his opinion about Cathedral City, had positively gloated about it, which saddened and disappointed her. How lucky it was that they'd stopped going when they did. How sordid and dangerous the place was. What if they'd been there that night?

And then they tore down old Cathedral City. The only familiar building still standing on East Palm Canyon was Nick's old bar. It re-opened a year later, under a new name, The Cathedral City Café, and Madonna impulsively stopped in one day, hoping to hear word about Kenny and Nick.

It was early in the afternoon, four years ago, and she was greeted by Maria Castillo, the lovely owner, a tall woman who smiled easily, but had sad eyes.

The room had changed, been reconfigured, Madonna noted wistfully. It was tasteful and comfortable, but lighter and frankly, new. The old bar had been moved, repadded in desert taupe. Admittedly, exquisite desert oil paintings were hung, painted apparently by Maria herself. All of Nick's old show bills and movie star memorabilia had been taken down. But behind the bar, a small candle burned in front of a beautiful *retablo,* and next to it, Madonna noticed a small photo of two men.

"Is that Kenny and Nick?" she asked.

"Yes," Maria folded her arms. "You remember them?"

"I was a regular here for a short time. My husband and me. Before . . . Well, I'm sure you know what I'm talking about."

"Yes," Maria nodded. "Are you having lunch today?" She reached briskly for a menu. She didn't seem to want to talk about Kenny and Nick.

"Do you hear from them?" Madonna pressed.

With that, a giggling, beautiful toddler, just only walking, burst through the swinging doors from the kitchen. She was being chased by a laughing baby-sitter. The baby-sitter startled Madonna, because she was deformed by a horrible birthmark, covering nearly half of her face. The baby girl stopped short at the sight of Madonna, whose considerable height scared her. She was easily a head taller than her mother.

"Don't stare."

"I'm so sorry," Madonna sputtered, thinking she was being admonished for gawking at the baby-sitter's birthmark, but Maria had been addressing her baby girl.

"Chita!" Maria motioned for her daughter. "Come here and meet the nice lady. This is my daughter, Conchita."

Chita moved shyly over to her mother.

"What an exquisite child! Look at those blue eyes!"

"Oh," Maria bent down to pick her up. "Don't give her a swelled head. And this is my best friend, her aunt, Soila Quintero." Maria reached for a reticent Soila's hand, drawing her into the circle. The birthmark was a terrible tragedy, because Madonna could see how pretty Soila was. Soila, used to the doleful, pitiful stares of well-meaning strangers, smiled at her sweetly.

"Bambi's here," Soila said. "You have a delivery."

And Bambi burst into the lounge. She took one look at Madonna and stopped in her tracks. "Whooaa."

"You know each other?" Maria commented dryly.

"We were introduced before. Only long enough to say hello. I'm Madonna. I was here with my husband. I just stopped in to ask about Kenny and Nick. To see the new place."

"I take it you've met Chita," Bambi grinned, advancing like a bogeyman on the squealing little girl. Maria gently dropped her to her feet. Chita darted behind Madonna to hide. Soon Bambi was on her knees in front of a trapped Madonna, crotch level and swatting playfully around her legs to tease the laughing little girl. For an instant Bambi succeeded in catching Conchita, and an embarrassed Madonna found herself sandwiched in a crush between the kneeling lesbian produce driver pressed into her pelvis and Maria's baby daughter wedged under her ass.

"Enough," Maria clapped her hands.

"Have *you* had enough?" Bambi gazed up at Madonna, releasing Chita to Soila.

Madonna smiled down at her.

The lumbering rig rounded the corner. The cargo van had rolled the curve, the INS pursuit cars, following too close, one rear-ending the other and plowing into the side of the now burning van.

"Shit!" Bambi slammed on her brakes, tipping Madonna's coffee cup, drenching her crotch and scalding her inner thigh. Their own groaning rig skidded toward the conflagration.

"Stop!" Madonna screamed, and brakes squealing, the produce truck fishtailed back and forth till it shuddered to a precarious halt near the burning vehicles. Bodies littered the highway, some writhing and on fire, others smoldering and still. There were kids among them. Easily six or more. Even a baby. Bambi threw her gears into reverse and backed the produce truck recklessly out of harm's way.

"Call 911!" Reaching for a compact fire extinguisher, Bambi threw open her door. "Don't follow me. It's gonna blow!" And just as she predicted, the gas tank of the second vehicle exploded into flame.

While Madonna screamed their location into her cell phone, Bambi vainly tried to extinguish the flames engulfing a crying, older Mexican lady. A stunned border patrol cop clamored from the passenger window of his overturned car, but collapsed when his palms touched the pavement, too weak from shock to hold the weight of his body. He seemed to pour from his vehicle onto the roadway.

Within fifteen minutes of Madonna's call, rescue vehicles began to arrive. Traffic was stopped going in both directions. An INS investigator began to interview witnesses, moving stiffly, stalwartly from onlooker to onlooker. Many of the passersby could only report coming upon the scene, not actually having witnessed the accident. A medic had bandaged Bambi's hands, burned as she tried to pry open the sliding door of the overturned fiery van. She would never be able to evade the stench of the burning bodies, firmly imprinted in her memory.

The bodies of maybe ten or twelve people, men, women and even a small child, smoking and charred, hair scorched from their heads, blackened eyeballs shriveled in their sockets like raisins, jaws contorted by final moments of panic—grasping fingers, scratching, clawing at the locked metal panel doors of the coyote's vehicle. They died consumed by one final bloodcurdling, unified scream.

Which one had been the coyote? The smuggler of the *mojados,* the wetbacks, Bambi wondered, scanning the carnage. All the Mexican passengers in and around the van had perished. The coyote and the van driver had certainly been killed too.

That was the good part, Bambi thought. Bambi hated coyotes.

Across the pavement, over the now blanketed dead bodies, Madonna, who was being interviewed by the INS officer, felt her girl-friend's gaze and glanced over at her. Madonna's legs were black from soot. Bambi could see where the coffee had drenched her smart white shorts. Her blouse was stained from the exploding raspberry Bismarck, which the investigator probably thought was blood. Madonna's eyes were red from crying, but she didn't seem deflated, or weakened from their ordeal. She seemed calm and resolved, and wanted to finish the interview in order to comfort her girlfriend.

The investigator followed her gaze. He'd introduced himself earlier. U.S. Border Patrol Agent Bob Roberts. Bambi considered cussing him out because she blamed the INS as much as the coyote for these daily high-speed chases. The border checkpoint was only ten miles up the road. They could have inspected the van there, when they were stopped in traffic, but she checked her temper because of his expression, which she could see when he removed his mirrored sunglasses to clean them.

She was surprised to see that Officer Bob's eyes, like Madonna's, were puffed red from crying too.

2

Brigadoon

Pablo couldn't believe the changes. The entire quadrant was gone. Now it was nothing but open desert stretching from East Palm Canyon Drive to St. Louis Catholic Church. The businesses once fronting the street were demolished and hauled away: the drive-in dairy, converted from an old gas station in the late seventies by two handsome women; Casey's Code 7, a locals' coffee shop catering to seniors, gays and cops; and the small gay bar next to it called Zak's, named, it was rumored, after the owner's cat.

And gone were all the cute little stucco houses, with Mexican tile roofs and whirling swamp coolers, comprising four blocks of Cathedral City's oldest Latino barrio. Gone also was the notorious alley separating them from the gay-owned businesses. An alley by night teeming with sexual activity and petty crime; by day a locals' thoroughfare and children's playground; a tentative fault line of demarcation between seemingly dissonant cultural plates; gay bar and Latino barrio, slamming into each other by virtue of the cultural and political dynamic of old Cathedral City. Even entire streets were missing. Glenn Avenue. Grove Street. A and B Streets. All open desert now. But for how long? At what cost?

Maria had written to Pablo about the changes. Only her club, The Cathedral City Café, formerly Nick's, remained untouched by the cultural wrecking ball of the Cathedral City Renewal Effort. It was saved due to the last ditch effort of its previous landlord, Sam Singer, who'd had it designated as a California State Historical Landmark only weeks before he died in the parking lot in the summer of ninety-eight.

The Cathedral City Café was only one in a long history of disparate desert establishments housed in the old bar. Formerly a gambling joint and a speakeasy, Al Capone, it was rumored, had played poker in basement card rooms. Then it evolved to Sam's, a desert rat gin joint and jazz club catering to mob bosses, movie stars and a discreet gay clientele till Sam passed it on to two gay guys who renamed it Nick's, after its flamboyant frontman. Kenny and Nick had been friends of Pablo's. And Maria's.

If she knew where they were she wouldn't admit to it. Maybe Pablo would ask Ruthie, Sam's widow. He was pleased to see her name on Maria's marquee: RUTH HARRIS AT THE PIANO. Ruthie had to have heard from Kenny and Nick, with so much shared history behind them.

As he contemplated the empty stretch of desert, emotion tugged at Pablo's heart. Waves of heat emanated from the desert floor, and contained within them, for a breathtaking instant, like Brigadoon, Pablo imagined he could see the old village that the desert had since reclaimed. For a minute he could see tiny Inez Quintero trudging slowly up the street on her way to St. Louis Catholic Church, where after morning Mass she'd continue up the hill toward Kenny and Nick's house in the cove section of Cathedral City, the affluent section of town where Inez and fellow Latina maids were hired to clean expensive homes.

He shook his head. It was only a mirage. Inez was happily back in Mexico. He'd spoken to her only three weeks ago to report that he'd graduated with his literature degree from Stanford and to advise her of his plans to return to Cathedral City.

"You can't leave well enough alone." Inez was her usual, hard-ass self.

"She needs me. To help with the bar. And Chita."

"Maria has Soila to help with Chita."

"Soila has to live her own life. She's using Chita as an excuse to avoid it."

"And what options does she have?"

Pablo knew what Inez meant. The port-stain birthmark that had branded Soila from birth. Inez believed it was a mark of God, intended to separate her from silly schoolgirl desires so she could focus on His work. Since they arrived in Cathedral City when Soila was a little girl, her mother had raised her in the nearby St. Louis Catholic Church.

Now Soila was nineteen and very womanly, Maria had reported, with all the natural impulses of any normal young girl. She needed to be deprogrammed from her mother's brainwashing. She was a very beautiful girl who happened to have a birthmark. Maria even believed it could be removed, but there was no talking to Inez about this issue. To remove the birthmark would condemn Soila to hell, and Soila was too frightened of her mother to ever cross her, even though she was two thousand miles away, deep in Mexico.

Pablo rubbed his eyes. It was open desert again. Up at the church, a motorcade of stretch limousines was beginning to arrive. Pablo counted at least twenty black cars. It must be someone very important. Probably famous, because press vans from local television stations also careened into the parking lot. Soon the empty parking lot was crazy with activity. Onlookers from the nearby neighborhood began to collect in the hot parking lot.

Pablo checked his watch. It was two-thirty and terribly hot. The services must be scheduled for three. He'd taken a cab from the airport. Maria promised to meet him at two, after she picked Chita up from Soila's apartment. Something must have delayed her. He wondered if she'd had trouble with the Jeep. He'd loaned it to her while he was away at school. Tomorrow he would take her to buy a new car, one more suitable for a woman with a small child.

He was looking forward to seeing the black Jeep again. It represented another time to him. Another Pablo. It would feel good to drive it across the desert tonight, back to Sky Valley and his little silver Airstream trailer under the stars.

In the distance he could hear the bleating horn of the old Jeep. He looked up, surprised to find himself standing in the center of the vacant lot. He'd wandered halfway to the church parking area. He shielded his eyes. Yes, it was Maria, beeping the horn as she four-wheeled the Jeep onto the desert floor toward him, waving happily, a laughing Chita secured firmly in the backseat, the ragtop flapping in the hot breeze.

Pablo had flirted shamelessly with her the day they first met. She was working alone in the back of the old bar. Pablo, who'd been fired by Kenny, had come to collect his final check.

"I don't know if I could trust anybody Kenny fired," she'd teased him. "You must be a very bad boy."

"You know of anybody who could use a bad boy around here? You looking?"

"No way," she smiled.

"I'm gonna make it my mission to find you a bad boy to marry."

"What about you?" she shrugged. "Why don't you marry me?" This was daring of her but it felt good.

"Oh, but you see, I'm not the marrying kind," Pablo languidly pressed against her. "But if I did marry you, we'd have very beautiful children." And Maria laughed so heartily he told himself if it could be any woman, he'd want her as lovely as this one.

The black Jeep squealed to a halt. If possible, Maria was more beautiful now, five years later, than on that fateful day. Fateful, because after years of longing for one, Pablo had just met his new best friend. He helped her down, watching as she fussed with Chita. Together they entered the café. A busboy nodded to her, disappearing into the kitchen with a plastic tub of dishes.

"Chico. I'm sorry I was late! I had to pick up Conchita at day care. Soila is helping at the funeral."

"Who died? Looked important."

"Loretta Young. A famous actress. Ever heard of her?"

Pablo shook his head.

"Your mother adored her. She won an Oscar for a movie about a farmer's daughter."

"Sounds like a joke about a traveling salesman."

"I saw her once or twice. She was very beautiful. She loved our church. And she was very kind to Soila. Soila loved her. Father Scolia asked her to assist."

"Father Scolia?"

"He's new." She shrugged. "He's no Father Gene. I don't like him much."

Pablo grinned at Maria. "You look beautiful, *mija*. You have a *novio* hidden under the table?" Playfully he peered under a tablecloth.

"No," she smiled. "Do you?"

Pablo shook his head. Still no steady boyfriends to report. Lots of dates. With San Francisco so close to Menlo Park, lots of sex. But no steady boyfriends. Would Pablo ever find true love? A love that would last longer than twelve hours? He was beginning to feel damaged. Why couldn't he commit? If he was honest with himself, he hadn't exactly been proposed to either. Had the wild years prior to Stanford taken a toll on him? He worried that he might be incapable of being intimate.

When he hustled—a dangerously rebellious period justified to punish his parents for cutting him off financially—Pablo had learned how to create a false sense of intimacy. Pablo could make any man think he loved him. He could even summon his own feelings of heightened affection for them, but as soon as Pablo or his trick climaxed, they instantly became strangers again. Pablo couldn't sustain those powerful emotions. He mostly just wanted to get dressed and out of there; back to the quiet sanctuary of his own little place. He told himself he was returning to Cathedral City to help Maria with the café and her daughter. He wondered if there was more to it. They were family to him. Was he using Maria now, to avoid intimacy? He would ask her. She'd probably accuse herself of doing the same thing with him.

"You've matured. You're a man, Pablito." They fell silent as they contemplated one another.

"How's Ruthie?"

"*Abuelita!*" Chita screamed at the mention of Ruthie's name.

"Yes," Maria nodded. "Abuelita."

In Chita's life, no relative was really as they seemed. Ruthie wasn't really her grandmother and Tia Soila not really her aunt. Tio Pablito wasn't really her uncle, and Pablo's parents in Mexico, whose house she had been born in, weren't really her grandparents either, but Chita didn't know the difference. She thought she had a wonderful extended family, though Maria had been an orphan before Chita was born.

"We're getting a younger, more Latino crowd. They don't really understand her," Maria commented. "I think it hurts her."

"You thinking of replacing her?" The thought was too terrible.

"No. But I think she guesses. It's crazy in here, every night. I don't even know the names of all my crew. It's getting to be so much to handle. Ruthie bought a new house. Her doctor told her it would be better for her. All the sad memories. Guess who used to own it?"

"I'm no good at guessing games."

Maria referred to a playbill of Ruthie, hanging near the piano, a fedora topping her head. Ruthie was famous for mimicking Frank Sinatra, a trick of Nick's she'd picked up. In his alcoholic imaginings, Nick, an orphan, sincerely believed he was the biological son of a liaison his mother had with Frank Sinatra. They looked nothing alike, but when Sinatra was alive, Nick used to devote advertised evenings to his Sinatra imitations. Because Ruthie was a better singer, she was more believable than Nick could ever hope to be. Her act grew into something camp. It drew a regular, late-night Sunday crowd, but they started wanting more of Pal Joey and less of Ruthie. She was thinking of knocking it off and Maria agreed with her.

"So whose house?"

"A house Sinatra used to own in Palm Springs."

"Really? She still taking her medication?"

Maria ignored him. "It's all been redone. All mid-century artifacts."

"Mid-century?" he mocked her. "Oh, how chic you are."

She chuckled. "Furniture from the fifties and sixties. Hey, don't make fun of me. I watch the House and Garden channel. I'm learning lots of new things. Trouble is, the house is on a tour guide's map. People are always driving by, coming up to the door. She's building a wall."

To celebrate Pablo's arrival, Chita ran screaming from the kitchen through the lounge to the dining room and back again, probably a thousand times. Pablo and Maria were seated in a booth near the window, overlooking the civic center plaza across the street. Noting it with irritation, Maria twisted the Levolor blind upward, so all they could see was blue sky.

"You still can't get over it."

"Why should I? They want to run me out of business."

"They can't touch you."

"It's horrendous," she shuddered. "I can't believe what they've done to Cathedral City. One good thing. They formed a Cathedral City Preservation Society. They came and asked a lot of questions."

"What questions?"

"You know, the history of the place."

"Old history or recent history?"

She fell silent.

"*Mija,* aren't you going to say anything about him?"

Chita roared by.

"*Chita!*" Maria cried sharply, causing the little girl to halt in her tracks. Surprised, Conchita began to cry. Maria glared at Pablo. "Now look what you made me do."

She stood up and went to comfort her baby girl. Chita allowed herself to be picked up and kissed, her large blue eyes flooding over with tears. She looked so much like Kenny. Pablo reacted.

"You see it too, huh?" Maria chucked her under the chin. She hesitated, her own chin quavering.

"What's wrong, *mija?*"

"I feel so guilty sometimes," she whispered, jostling Conchita in her arms.

"Why?"

"I feel like I'm cheating him. Like I've stolen her from him."

"Has he tried to reach you? Has he written or called?"

"No."

"Then why should you feel guilty?"

"Because I asked him not to. Because I know he wants to, every minute of every day. I *know* him."

Chita squirmed in her arms and Maria placed her gently down on the carpet. She darted off on another tear. Maria came back to the booth and sat down. Pablo reached for her hands.

"Is that the only reason you're sad?"

"What other reason would there be?" Over her shoulder Pablo could see the flickering candle next to the photograph of Kenny and Nick.

"I was just wondering," he smiled kindly, gently kissing her hands. "Just wondering, that's all."

On a small television in the kitchen, Maria's chef, Gabriel, saw a news flash on the local Spanish station about an accident involving a van loaded with *mojados* and two Migra pursuit vehicles. As many as twelve people were killed, including a baby and several small children. As he slumped against the wall in reaction to the accident, Gabrielito's cousin, Miguel, entered, kicking through the back screen door of the kitchen like he'd done for sixteen years, since Kenny first hired all of them.

When Maria returned from Mexico with her baby girl and opened up the new club, she agreed to take them back, but she refused to have Carmen, their tall, affable, outspoken cousin. Carmen had been Kenny's favorite until Maria showed up, and in her jealousy had committed unspeakable acts of revenge against her, least of which included having her deported in a Migra raid on the alley before the Anglo kids came.

For Gabriel and Miguel, and the other Latino residents of the Cathedral City barrio, time was measured before the white kids or after the white kids. This referred to the night of the raid on the alley behind Nick's old bar, when Nick was savagely beaten and nearly died, and the old landlord, Sam Singer, was murdered and Nick's doors closed forever, leaving all of them without jobs when Kenny and Nick were forced to leave the desert.

It made them glad to come back to work in the new restaurant. They didn't have anything against Maria, Carmen notwithstanding. She was fair and worked hard. By their estimation she had done quite well for herself. She arrived a *mojada,* herself a victim of an equally tragic border crossing; worked tirelessly by Kenny's side and within three years, had his baby and owned his restaurant. When Ruthie Singer died, Carmen conjectured, no doubt Maria would inherit her fortune too. One day Maria would be the richest woman in Cathedral City.

Not bad, they'd whistled respectfully.

"Not bad at all," Carmen had intoned, and wondered how she could get back in Maria's good graces.

When Miguel saw Gabriel's expression, and followed his sad gaze to the television screen, he too, was filled with despair. When Conchita made a squealing charge through the double doors to the kitchen Gabriel rebuked her, *silencio, chica!* her second admonishment by an adult in less than fifteen minutes.

Instead of crying or complaining she decided to pout, and when her mother entered the kitchen with a smiling Pablo behind her, their attention, too, turned to the television set and Chita found herself disgraced and ignored and she didn't like the feeling one bit. Later today when her Abuelita Ruthie came to pick her up, she'd tell Ruthie everything they'd done to her, and then they'd pay. Chita was certain of it.

What on the TV could be bothering them so?

She watched all of them, arms slung over each other's shoulders, propping one another up, tears rolling down her mother's cheek as her Uncle Pablito tried to console her.

"Such unnecessary tragedy."

Angrily Maria broke from the group.

"You couldn't possibly understand! You came in a plane."

"No," Pablo replied mildly, "I came in a Jeep."

"You know what I mean."

"That doesn't make me any less sympathetic. You've offended me," he chided her. "What's up with you?"

"I'm sorry," she started to cry again.

"Why are you crying?" Chita demanded, and then she started to cry. Maria quickly knelt down to hug her.

"I'm crying because people got hurt near the border. Near Mexico, where we all were born."

"How did they get hurt?"

"They were being chased by *La Migra, mija.*"

"Will we be chased?" Chita asked, her chin wavering.

"No, baby," Maria affirmed in no uncertain terms.

"She's a little young," Pablo murmured.

"She's not too young!" Maria snapped.

"Okay then," Pablo held up his hands. He'd never seen her so up-tight. So brittle.

Maria calmed herself, and then explained the facts of life to Conchita, that she, Miguel and Gabriel all came into the country illegally because they were poor and had no way to feed themselves properly in Mexico. While it was wrong to break the law, they were desperate, and all of them had worked very hard when they arrived. Now even Miguel and Gabriel were United States citizens, and she and Conchita both had green cards.

"Sometimes when people try to cross the border they get hurt, like on the TV, eh? And it just makes us sad because we aren't any different than they are. Do you understand, baby?" Conchita didn't reply, but just stared wonderingly at her pretty mother's serious face. Maria gazed up at Pablo. "She'll understand some day," Maria assured him.

"Something tells me you won't let her forget."

They shifted their attention to the tiny television set.

"I think we should light a candle," Pablo suggested. "Say a prayer."

"Yes," Maria sniffed. She grasped his hand, shaking it gently, as if to apologize. He smiled at her warmly.

Gabriel dug through a desk drawer and found a package of votive candles. He reached up to the well-worn, smoky glass candle holder and gently dropped the white votive inside.

"I want to light it," Chita whined.

"Okay, but with a wooden matchstick. Uncle Pablito will help you."

She lifted Chita up eye-view with the little altar, the same one Kenny had built and painted with boards from old wooden produce crates, ten years prior. Pablo struck a long, wooden match. While Maria held her, Pablo guided Chita's hand toward the wick of the candle. They hesitated as the small votive flickered alive. Pablo held Chita up so she could watch. Together, the group, Mexican immigrants all—Maria, Conchita, Pablo, Gabriel and Miguel—made the sign of the cross. Chita was entranced.

"Now that you're here, you'll have to set a good example as her godfather."

"I promise," Pablo whispered.

"For the travelers," Maria whispered, hugging Chita.

"For the travelers," her friends repeated.

3

The Loretta Young Show

"Poor thing," she heard them whisper.

"How sad," said another.

"Nothing could be done."

"More the pity."

"She seems peaceful."

Soila was honored to assist Father Scolia at the funeral of Loretta Young. She listened attentively to the whispered remarks of visitors as they entered the church sanctuary after signing the guest book. All the comments were the same. They startled Soila somewhat. Miss Young had lived a long, productive life. A life anyone would be grateful for. Why were they talking about her with such pity in their voices? Then it dawned on Soila.

They weren't pitying Ms. Young. It was Soila they were whispering about; felt sorry for. Because of her birthmark.

"She'd be so pretty."

"How typical of Loretta."

"What a wonderful woman Loretta was to include the child."

Chagrined, Soila kept pushing the guest book.

Cathedral City's St. Louis Church never looked so beautiful. She'd overheard that thousands of dollars had been spent on flowers. Three bishops would attend in addition to Father Scolia. Soila had been surprised when he asked her to monitor the guest book for Miss Young's family. This put her in a most conspicuous spot. Parishioners and guests would have to greet her, which to Soila would mean a thousand different faces trying to hide their distress, revulsion or sympathy over her birthmark. She'd get quite a kick out of it, actually.

Miss Young, Soila had been informed, had asked for her personally to perform this most important task. The irony didn't escape anyone, least of all Soila. The most beautiful woman in the world making a statement about inner beauty by asking the homeliest girl in the world to mind the guest book at her funeral.

Soila met Miss Young when Father Scolia first came to St. Louis, replacing the church's beloved Father Gene, who retired several years earlier. St. Louis had a bit of a celebrity reputation, given that Frank Sinatra and his family had been early patrons of the parish. It was ironic because Cathedral City was hardly a fashionable destination. There were certainly larger and more elite Catholic churches in Palm Springs and Rancho Mirage. But Old Blue Eyes, as Soila heard him referred to, loved St. Louis, and often attended midnight Mass in preference over other churches, which would have liked to have had his business.

He'd even had a statue to St. Anthony erected, emblazoned with the name Sinatra on the pedestal that guarded the entrance to the church for as long as Soila could remember. Although Soila could not name one song he was famous for, she wasn't even certain he was a singer, Frank Sinatra was to her the most famous man in the world. By the reverence his name evoked around St. Louis, she assumed he was a church deacon, maybe even a missionary of some sort.

When Father Gene was here, more attention was paid to the day-to-day ministry of the church elderly. Her poor. Her sick. Father Gene paid many home visits to the parish infirmed. He was beloved for it, and encouraged members of his congregation to follow his example. This was before so many neighboring houses had been torn down under the Cathedral City renewal plan. Many elderly residents had been promised to be relocated within at least a bus ride away from the parish.

After Father Gene retired, these promises were quickly revoked. The buses and vans were expensive to maintain and operate. It was a losing proposition, and Father Scolia quickly put a stop to it. Members who wished to attend services could put their names on a ride list, displayed prominently on a bulletin board in the church recreation hall. It would be God's will if their prayers for a ride were answered.

After they were displaced to other neighborhoods, the loss of a nearby place to worship or even sit quietly was deeply felt by those devout Cathedral City older Catholics who for so long had the luxury of simply crossing the street, or walking down the block as Soila's mother, Inez, herself had done daily for so many years.

Soila loved St. Louis Catholic Church. It was here she'd learned her catechism. When she missed her mother, which she did, every moment of every day, she could come and sit quietly in the church sanctuary and recite her rosary, just as she'd learned to do with her mother, and always felt less lonely for Inez.

How terrible those final days had been. Inez so ill. Her father so intractable. Her mother's bitterness. Her father's silly pride. So much violence in the alley behind their little house. His disappointment when Sam Singer broke his promise, that they, the Quintero family, who'd legally entered the country, worked so hard, saved up their meager earnings to buy their first little American house, would now not be able to. He was selling their house as part of a bigger parcel to the big-time Cathedral City developers. And for what?

It was still a vacant lot behind Maria's restaurant. Nothing had been built on top of it. They could have lived there another five years. It broke her father's heart and he had ignorantly blamed everything on her poor sick mother. Her father was no longer the same man, but at least, Inez now thrived in Mexico.

She missed her mother, but God had answered Soila's prayers. Inez got the medication she needed from the clinic where she volunteered. She was happy living with Soila's uncles. They spoke once a month, for a treasured three minutes. And when Soila really missed her, she could always come to St. Louis and light a candle for her. Only now, because of fire regulations, they no longer could use real votives. Soila was reduced to flipping a switch, igniting a tiny electric candle instead. Still, it was a comfort.

The timing of Father Gene's scheduled retirement, which coincided with the final assault in the alley between the gay bar and Soila's old house spared the local diocese of removing the old priest. They laid the entire tragedy at his feet, the responsibility squarely on his shoulders. They knew he privately frequented the old desert bar in plain clothes. He'd admitted to being present the night of Nick's grand reopening. Soila knew that had he not, there might have been even worse violence.

Father Gene had begun to struggle with church dogma. He could no longer be relied upon to tow the line where the needs of the homosexual community could be met. It was rumored that he'd offered Holy Communion to a gay man who'd refused to denounce his homosexual lover.

He'd left just in time. They were lucky and they knew it, as complaints, albeit only a few, started coming in. Father Scolia, apprised by church deacons of Father Gene's rather compromised approach to Church doctrine, came to St. Louis loaded for bear. Stridently conservative, his claim to fame were his intractable views about gay rights, adultery, single parenthood, abortion, divorce and the like.

Miss Young, prepared by more liberal friends inside the parish, was sent as an emissary to charm him and hopefully induce him to tone down his rhetoric. After all, she was herself not without a certain public history. She'd suffered more than her share of scandals; some of her own doing, and some not, but the church had welcomed her and provided her with so much comfort. She hoped St. Louis would remain a beacon for all desert Catholics.

She was a prime example of what a loving, understanding and forgiving church could accomplish. Besides, she had money, and when reason failed, money was always the great intercessor as it would prove with Father Scolia.

Since she was a little girl, Soila Quintero understood an important fact about human nature. People were cruel but they wanted to be kind, or at least condescend to feel better about themselves. And while growing up she'd suffered every obvious cheap shot others might take at her, Soila probably enjoyed more stature because of her deformity than if she didn't have it at all.

It started with Inez, her own mother, a small, cynical woman who pounded it into her head that the birthmark was a gift, not a curse from God. It was a mark of his love, and without it, rest assured, Soila Quintero would be nothing special. So when children made fun of her, or adults avoided her gaze, Soila had learned how to ignore the cruelty and put them at ease, because she had come to accept herself.

Other than her mother, Maria and Ruthie Singer, one other woman seemed to understand, and she was the tall, beautiful older actress Father Scolia introduced her to on a day Soila volunteered to work in his office. Actually, Father Scolia had tried to ignore Soila, but it was Miss Young who insisted on meeting her. They'd been having tea in the rectory library when Soila happened in by accident, returning a book she'd borrowed from Sister Agnes.

Soila quickly retreated, but she overheard Father Scolia's guest ask about her.

"I'd like to meet her," Miss Young had murmured.

"Soila?" he called out to her. "Come back."

And Soila politely returned, giving full credit to her birthmark. Miss Young was introduced and then requested that she join them. Soila knew the scowling Father Scolia was annoyed, but she decided to stay because she found the actress so beautiful, and frankly, calming. She had a wonderfully soothing speaking voice, and asked Soila all about herself. When Soila frankly explained that her mother had HIV and lived in Mexico because her father kicked her out, Miss Young began to cry. Did Soila's mother need anything? Was it hard for her to be away from her?

"Yes," Soila had replied matter-of-factly, but her mother, Inez, was now in good health and had lots of support. In fact, Soila reported, she worked as a counselor in a Mexican facility for women with HIV. "She loved St. Louis very much," Soila asserted. "She attended Mass every day before she got sick."

"And now she helps other unfortunate women?"

"Yes," Soila nodded beatifically, ignoring the fact that her mother was tough as nails and probably made all of them cry.

"What a beautiful story!" Miss Young dabbed at her eye with a handkerchief. When a moved Father Scolia leaned forward to help himself to a lump of sugar, Miss Young caught Soila's eye and winked. Soila stifled a giggle. When Miss Young departed she left Father Scolia charmed and Soila pledging silent allegiance to her for life.

The funeral for Loretta Young was packed; standing room only. The homily was subdued and respectful, citing her brilliant film career, her love of the Church and service to the Catholic community. Her beloved three grown children sat in the front row. Carol Channing and Jane Wyman paid respects.

It was hot, over 110 degrees. Every time the huge entry doors swung open, a furnace blast of dry desert heat overwhelmed Soila Quintero. Many of the church's regular parishioners attended but some were disappointed that more movie stars didn't come. Miss Young had outlived most of her old friends.

Soila dutifully monitored the guest book. She also kept track of the flower deliveries, recording each little gift card on a special register to be used later for thank-you cards. The flowers would all be donated to local retirement homes. Soila counted over two hundred arrangements, including President and Mrs. Gerald Ford, Barbara Sinatra and President and Mrs. Ronald Reagan. She was terribly impressed. She wanted to remember every detail to tell her mother, the next time she called.

Soila's mother didn't call often, and usually on days when she knew Soila's father, Thomas, and his fat girlfriend, Ruby, would be away. As she had been to Inez, Ruby was a thorn in Soila's side. Ruby didn't take attitude from anybody, and even someone as clever and manipulative as Soila couldn't find her way around her.

Ruby made no bones about the fact that Soila's birthmark disgusted her. Initially they all lived in a tract housing development on the windy north end of Cathedral City. Thomas, Ruby, Soila, her crazy brother, Alex, and her pretty younger sister, Anita. Only Anita got along with Ruby. The down payment had come from a life insurance policy from Ruby's husband, who died in an automobile accident five years ago. When Inez and Soila's father were still together, they rented a small Spanish bungalow behind Maria's bar, which had been called Nick's at the time.

All her father ever wanted to do was buy that little house. The house they lived in now was bigger, but his sweat hadn't tiled the bathroom. His elbow grease hadn't plastered the ceiling or repainted the walls. It was a prefab house with no character, exactly like all the other houses on their street. They'd moved from one ghetto to another, but Ruby wouldn't have it any other way.

Thomas still worked at Arte de Sonora, the same place he'd worked since the owner, Andy, had sponsored Thomas and his family to come to the United States. Soila was only a little girl. She remembered her father fondly then. He had pride. Dreams. He had his prejudices but he worked hard and wanted the best for his family.

Then Ruby entered the picture and Inez became ill. And the worst thing to Thomas, Soila knew, was when Ruthie's husband, Sam Singer, reneged on his promise to sell Thomas the little house. He was never the same after that big disappointment.

* * *

"Soila?"

Soila had been deep in thought. Startled, she glanced up. Ruthie was standing in front of her little table, signing the guest book. The services were over. Most attendees were filing out to their cars.

"It's so hot." Ruthie smiled at her. "You must be tired. Wasn't it a lovely service?"

Soila grinned. She loved Ruthie, her husband notwithstanding. Ruthie hadn't had an easy life, but you'd never know by how beautiful she was. At sixty, Ruthie could pass for early forties. She had thick red hair, a gorgeous figure and incredible legs. A local desert cabaret singer, Ruthie performed nightly at the Cathedral City Café, as she had done years ago at Sam's, then Nick's, and now Maria's.

Maria and Ruthie were bound forever by fate and history on a hot desert highway near the Salton Sea. When Maria was deported, Ruthie formally adopted her several years later to get her legally back into the United States. Maria was officially her daughter, though she would never address Ruthie as her mother, but Chita, also officially her granddaughter, delighted in calling her *Abuelita*.

"Pablito should be waiting at the restaurant," Soila smiled. "I'm finished here. Maybe we should go say hello."

"I'll drive you. It's so goddamned hot." Ruthie caught herself, just as a fuming Sister Agnes stalked up.

"I'm so sorry, Sister."

Sister Agnes waved Ruthie away. One profanity hardly would ruffle her feathers. A conservative, intractable priest was another matter. To Father Scolia, Sister Agnes was a guest who wouldn't leave. Her age and years of dedicated service to the Church as a trauma nurse in Central and South America gave her a certain stature that made her very difficult to control. He resented her attitude and her political opinions. Father Scolia's mandate was to raise money for the parish. An outspoken, liberal, left-wing nun was not conducive to such a plan. He caught her trying to form a leftist church women's group, the Radical Sisters of God, they had the gall to call themselves, and ordered her to disband them immediately.

Father Gene, while possibly sympathizing with Scolia's position would never have put it to Sister Agnes like that. She was too arrogant, would regard it as a dare to defy him, and defy was exactly what she intended to do. And now, as the little nun calculated Soila and Ruthie in the lobby of St. Louis, she decided she needed a respite. She would walk across the open desert to the Cathedral City Café and have her afternoon bourbon, which Maria, the owner, always bought for her. Would Father Scolia try to put a stop to that too?

Probably, but Sister Agnes would only take so much, and she needed her bourbon like desert cactus needed the sun.

"Good-day, ladies." Sister Agnes spun on her heels and left.

Ruthie and Soila chuckled. Soila collected the guest book and the flower registry and excused herself to leave them in Father Scolia's office, as he'd requested. He was on his way to a private reception for the family of Miss Young. Soila had been invited, but opted out. She wanted to see Pablito too.

Through the doors of St. Louis, Ruthie could see little Sister Agnes, picking her way through the desert, heading toward Maria's. What a funny place Cathedral City still was, Ruthie mused. It seemed to leach characters up to the desert surface from its very molten core.

4

A Retablo for Kenny

When Pablo greeted Soila, she hugged him for a moment longer than she thought she should have. If only Pablito were her brother, she lamented. How she missed him. How grown up he looked. How studious and mature. And still so handsome. Handsome enough to melt her mother's cold heart, that was how handsome.

Maria watched happily as her little adopted family assembled before her. They were all seated in the lounge of her restaurant, Ruthie, Pablo and Soila. Pablito was her best friend, her brother in this world. People often commented on their similar appearance. To have him back with her, bouncing Chita on his lap caused a rush of emotion. Maria got hold of herself, brushing away her tears because twice was too much for her daughter to see her cry in one day. It was hard to see all of them together without longing for the ones who were missing.

Inez, in Mexico. Sam, Ruthie's bull-in-a-china shop husband. The flamboyant, handsome and gregarious Nick, who owned this place before her, gave her sanctuary and nearly died because of it. And lastly, in Chita's face, Kenny. Chita's father.

Leave it to Pablo to stir up these emotions. Yes, she'd missed him terribly after what they went through together; all that had passed before. Soon they were laughing and reminiscing, making all kinds of plans. The little nun, Sister Agnes, sat alone at the end of the bar, though Maria had asked her to join them.

*   *   *

Sister Agnes had only recently started coming in, always late in the day.

Upon seeing Pablo and Maria together, a wave of recognition rippled across Sister Agnes' brow. Even Pablo, Maria and Sister Agnes shared a past, that was how tightly woven they all were to Cathedral City. Each threaded to the next by chance and fate. Sister Agnes never mentioned that terrible night, but Maria knew she remembered her. She longed to speak of it for only one reason, if only to assure her that Chita was not the product of violence, but love.

One afternoon, last week, Maria took the stool next to her at the bar. The little nun gazed up at her in surprise. They rarely spoke directly to one another.

"Sister Agnes . . . You know my daughter didn't come from all that sadness."

"What judgment would I make if she had? All children are innocent, the details of their conception notwithstanding. Makes no difference to me."

When she had a loftier point to make, Sister Agnes prided herself on her ability to pretend that she didn't understand what others were really driving at.

"But still, she didn't," Maria insisted gently.

Now, in the bar, Sister Agnes' hand trembled as she lifted her glass to her lips. Her hands were veined and discolored with liver spots. Maria remembered those hands vividly the night Pablo delivered her to Father Gene at St. Louis.

Sister Agnes had taken her into the rectory lavatory where she personally scrubbed every inch of Maria's trembling body until her skin felt red and purified. Then, while Maria sat huddled in a fresh blue cotton blanket, Sister Agnes washed her clothing by hand in the sink, with such ferocity Maria thought the fabric would tear.

There hadn't been any discussion that evidence was being destroyed. DNA samples lost with the fanatic scrubbing. Sister Agnes knew the traumatized young woman would never press charges. Why else had she come to the church? She was an undocumented alien in the United States of America. They could do what they liked with her here, and both of them knew it without speaking out loud.

*   *   *

"Where did this happen?" Sister Agnes had queried.

"At the festival."

"Did you know the man?"

"Yes."

"He's not the boy who brought you here."

"No. No. Pablito stopped it. He's my friend."

"He's a good friend. A miracle to be grateful for. Amidst the chaos."

A brief examination by Sister Agnes confirmed one thing. Maria had been raped, but the perpetrator would not have the opportunity to father a child. Although she herself was suspicious, even Maria hadn't known for certain she was already weeks pregnant at the time.

Sister Agnes didn't ask her who the father was, and what Maria's intentions might be. Instead she did what Catholic trauma nurses like Sister Agnes did best—master a difficult situation with utmost efficiency and tame it in the name of God.

She led her back to the kitchen, Maria having just taken a shower. Her clothing had been stitched where the rapist had torn it. She couldn't look at them. Pablo studied her with sympathy.

"Bruises. No bones broken."

"Just her heart," Pablo offered.

"God will heal her heart," the nun fired back with a scathing look of rebuke.

"Does she want to make a police report?" asked Father Gene, but he already knew the answer.

"She's adamant. She wants to be taken home. Is that something you can handle, young man?"

"Yes, Sister," Pablo nodded.

"Thank you all for everything," Maria whispered firmly. And she walked toward the exit with Pablo following.

Sister Agnes glanced up from her drink as if reading Maria's thoughts.

"Would you like another, Sister Agnes?" Maria asked her.

"I believe I would," she nodded.

Pablo stood up to go serve her. He may as well get started. After a master's degree from Stanford, he was right back where he began.

Working as a bartender in Cathedral City. His parents, though happy he was reunited with Maria and Conchita, hoped he would put his education to some use.

"Use the same glass." She tapped the lip of it. "Don't change the ice."

"Sure thing, Sister."

"I remember you," she whispered.

"And I remember you." He patted her hand, splashing Jim Beam to the brim.

"Things turned out for the best, I think. Am I right? You're no longer a shallow, silly boy. You're a man, now. There's men's work to do." Sister Agnes tossed back her drink.

"Yes," he acquiesced. God, was Sister Agnes a regular here? Did he have this to look forward to every afternoon? From her place in the booth, Maria was eavesdropping, but Chita distracted her and she looked away.

Miguel entered the dining room to tell Maria the produce delivery had arrived. Maria excused herself and followed him to the kitchen.

"Hey, girlfriend," Bambi's eyes were red from strain.

"You're late," said Maria. "You okay?"

"We stopped for an accident," she explained hesitantly.

"Where's Madonna?"

"Out back with the truck."

"I want you to meet Pablito, my friend I told you about. He's up front. We can have a drink together."

Bambi sank down on a stool. She seemed stunned. Completely out of sorts. Madonna appeared at the screen door.

"What's wrong with her?" Maria asked. "She seems upset."

Madonna rushed through the door and put her arm around Bambi's quivering shoulder. "We had a rough trip. Have you been watching the news?"

"The INS crash!" Maria gasped.

"We were the first ones on the scene. The van passed us down near Westmoreland. Two border patrol trucks came up fast behind us and went after it. We rounded the curve and they were all bunched up together, all over the road. It was awful."

"*Amigos!*" Maria cried. Pablo came rushing through the double doors. Ruthie and Soila followed, holding Chita.

"Do me a favor, baby, take Chita home for me," Maria asked Soila. "Something's come up."

Soila obliged her, taking the whining baby without any questions. Once they were gone, the group turned to face Bambi and Madonna.

"There's nothing more to say. You saw it on TV. It was awful, like Madonna said."

"What's happened?" Sister Agnes demanded. Before they could answer they heard shouts outside the kitchen door. Miguel burst through the front door.

"A girl," was all he could muster. "In the back of the truck!"

"What are you doing opening up the back of my truck?" Bambi demanded.

"I was helping," Miguel shrugged.

Maria studied Bambi quizzically. "They always unload your truck without asking."

The crowd pressed through the door to the back of the restaurant.

Gabriel stood speechless on the gate of the open truck. "I don't think she's breathing."

"Who?" Bambi demanded. "Who the hell is he talking about?"

"A girl is back there," Miguel cried.

"What girl?"

And Pablo leaped in the back of the truck to see for himself. There, lying among the crates of lettuces was a young girl, curled up as if fast asleep, but Pablo figured she was dead. He knelt beside her to pat her hand.

"Let me through!" he heard Sister Agnes insist, and in seconds she was kneeling beside him. "Call an ambulance!" she shouted over her shoulder. Maria ran inside to make the call.

"I think she's gone," Pablo whispered to Sister Agnes.

"How'd she get in there?" Bambi was demanding.

"Would you all *please* control your emotions!" Sister Agnes shouted back at them. To Pablo she gravely observed, "She is dead, but she's pregnant. Nearly full term. Get me a sharp knife if you want this baby saved."

"They're on their way," Maria called up from the back of the truck.

"I need a sharp knife!" he demanded.

"For what?"

"Quickly!" he pleaded with her, and she disappeared.

"What's going on?" he heard Ruthie query.

"Here!" he heard Maria's voice, and shortly she was crawling up into the compartment laden with three choices of knives and assorted towels.

"What are you planning to do?" Maria asked the old nun.

"I'm planning to save this little girl's baby," Sister Agnes remarked calmly. "Turn your head if you don't want to look. I need a calm person to assist me. Would that be you, young man?" she demanded of Pablo.

"Yes, Sister."

"Help me straighten her out." And together they stretched the body of the young girl outright, as Sister Agnes hacked away at her clothing. Soon her heaving belly was exposed, and Pablo and Maria could see the baby moving.

"Shouldn't you wait for an ambulance?" Madonna called. "I can hear sirens."

"I've done this procedure before," Sister Agnes assured her, but didn't care what she thought.

She picked a small sharp knife and inserted it at the base of the girl's belly. Viscous bloody liquid poured out from the cavity. Sister Agnes continued to draw the blade upward, gutting the pale body like a fish. The ambulance roared up, sirens screaming. Madonna screamed an explanation to the attendants. Soon they were pushing their way up next to Pablo and Maria. They could see that the little nun knew exactly what she was doing.

Pablo and Maria fell back.

The two attendants assisted Sister Agnes.

"I think you can remove it," they heard her say.

They all waited anxiously to hear the baby cry.

The impact on Ruthie to have observed Sister Agnes gut a child's body with little more than a hunting knife, and rip a tiny baby from a baby, in the parking lot of the restaurant where Sam had died and Nick so badly beaten, the impact of this incident, along with every other incident that informed it was too traumatic for Ruthie to accept. In that instant, as they all held their breaths, waiting for Sister Agnes to reassure them, waiting for some sign of life from the baby, it became clear to Ruthie that she would never be free from her self-inflicted demons. Her mind would never be kind to her, no matter how much Prozac and lithium she imbibed.

Sleep would never free her, nor would considerable financial freedom. She'd just today been to her attorney to work out the details of her estate. Write her new will. Sam had been so paranoid. It had been a monumental undertaking to unravel his estate. It had taken nearly five years. His furtive secrecy was never intended to hide assets from her. All their married life, Sam was pushing contracts, and escrow agreements, and bank account signature cards and tax forms at her, often while Ruthie lay comatose in her darkened bedroom on hot, blue, desert days. She had a veritable necklace of safety deposit keys, a child's diary with a ballerina adorning the cover, filled with addresses and directions and easily a hundred combinations to different safes.

Sam would claim that it had all been for her. So Ruthie could feel safe, but Ruthie knew it was his own security he feared for. As a child, Sam had been very poor. His parents were Russian immigrants. They all lived in one Detroit hotel room. A brother had died because they couldn't afford medical care. Financial security had been Sam's demon. Ruthie's chemical makeup—hers.

Performing, she had to admit, helped. When the spotlight came up, blinding her, protecting her from the living, breathing body that was her audience—singing was a rest stop—but it wasn't possible to sing twenty-four hours per day.

Plus, she knew she was losing her voice. Maria hadn't said anything, but Ruthie was having increasing trouble holding pitch and now she was forced to mike herself up. When she was young, she never needed a microphone. Her voice was so clear, so strong, she could cut through the smoky atmosphere of any nightclub. Some singers resented the low growl of a busy lounge. The waitresses taking drink orders. Someone asking for a light. The loud talking drunk. And lastly, the patron who discreetly sang along.

In her own quirky generous nature, as long as the phantom chanteuse didn't overpower her, Ruthie enjoyed the companionship, the three-minute comraderie with the stranger in the dark. Sometimes she might hear a voice that was surprisingly good. Most were little more than mediocre, valiantly trying to blend in, to not invade her performance. If they got out of hand someone would always *shush* them. The shushing was usually more distracting than the soft-voiced, innocent backup singer in the sea of cocktail tables.

While she sang, Ruthie would fantasize about whoever was so moved to join her. She'd wonder where they lived, if they had a happy marriage, how many children. She'd try to picture them waking up, what kind of room, what kind of emotional state. What were their fears? Were they ever lonely? Did they have regrets?

Now, at Maria's, Ruthie could tell she was losing her grip over her audience. They were younger, more Latin. She must seem like a dinosaur to them. With the resurgence of Palm Springs and all the new hotels in Palm Desert and Indian Wells, younger jazz singers were coming up. Diana Krall had performed to rave notices at the McCallum Theater. Ruthie had her turn. What was next? A cooking channel on a local cable access channel? She was hardly a personality like Dinah Shore used to be.

There were other venues she could try—the lounge at Lyons English Grille, or the refurbished Bamboo Room at the Racquet Club, but those acts tended to be campy. Sam would hate it if Ruthie ended up camp. That's why he never wanted her to start back here in the first place.

When Sister Agnes wrapped the tiny baby in a clean white linen napkin one of the busboys produced from the kitchen, she covered the baby's face and that was that. From the onlookers, Maria, Pablo, the boys from the kitchen, a shared sigh. From Bambi a small scream, which Madonna stifled by smothering her in a tall embrace.

Soon the coroner arrived. The Cathedral City police. Then a border patrol helicopter. There was confusion about jurisdiction. Even a few raised voices.

Ruthie didn't react. Couldn't. She waited her turn to be interviewed by the indifferent border patrol agent, conferred with Maria that it was important for her restaurant to stay open; she'd be in later to sing as scheduled and left. She was glad Soila had Chita this afternoon. She was happy for some privacy—to think things over—as much as Chita was the light of her life. They ended up closing a little earlier. Ruthie came out like the old pro that she was. She opened with a sweet rendition of '*One for My Baby.*'

That night, to distract her, Maria decided to teach Chita how to paint a *retablo*. Last month she'd found a nice flat piece of rusty tin in the desert behind the café, and with a piece of steel wool, shined it vigorously with her strong fingers until Chita could see her own muted reflection in the metal.

Chita already liked working with paints. Between Kenny and Maria, she had good artist's genes. Kenny himself was an accomplished craftsman, carving and painting wonderful wooden dolls. The doll Kenny gave her the night she came to stay with him and Nick, sat on a shelf in Maria's room, out of Chita's reach.

She'd arrived in Cathedral City with nothing. All her belongings, along with her grandmother, were lost on that scorching California highway. Kenny gave it to her, understanding that one simple possession, to have when she woke up, would at least feel like a fresh start to her and he'd been right.

A grown woman, she'd nearly strangled that doll in those first several days after she'd arrived out of love for it. For what it represented. His kindness, of course. Her obedience to her grandmother's last wish. Hope.

Luckily Pablito had saved it for her after she got deported. She'd found, staying in the opulence of his parents' home, that she wanted the doll more than any single belonging she'd left behind in Cathedral City. He'd sent it Federal Express within a day after they kicked her back into Mexico.

Why had she been so rude to him today? Poor Pablito. She'd make it up to him. He'd been so loving and patient.

When Maria opened tonight, all her regular customers were asking questions, and local reporters picked up on the angle of the dead girl found in Bambi's truck. The INS crash had been all over tonight's national news. Tomorrow they'd be asking about the girl behind the Cathedral City Café.

Judi Romero came from a very poor part of Mexicali. She was thirteen years old. She probably knew that if her baby were born in the United States, she would be entitled to benefits not available to her in Mexico.

It was a mystery to Maria how Judi found her way into the back of Bambi's truck. They still didn't know how she died, but the coroner hypothesized that she'd suffered severe internal injuries from the impact, possibly bursting organs. She may have been cushioned by the sheer volume of bodies around her, crawled out before the vans exploded, and thinking she was okay, took refuge in the back of the untended produce truck.

Early this evening, Maria, Gabrielito and Miguel erected a small cross at the edge of her parking lot, in the plot of desert where Judi and her baby came to their final rest. Then they placed votive candles and flowers in vases from the restaurant at the base of it. Soon other Cathedral City Latinos followed suit. The simple tribute was expanding hourly, with flowers and baby toys and sweet handwritten messages expressing their sorrow.

Maria was glad she had Ruthie to talk to. Ruthie had been as shaken up as she, but probably didn't know that Maria knew why. In the very kitchen where she stood staring through the back screen to the poignant little cross, Ruthie's husband, Sam, had told Maria Ruthie's sad history and explained why she could never have children.

"Chita, with a *retablo,* we tell a story."

"Tell me a story," Chita chimed in.

"No," Maria laughed. Chita's fingers were already stained with tempera. Her T-shirt streaked with all the primary colors. "You tell me a story."

"You tell me." Chita was already so willful.

"We'll make one up together. Let's ask the Blessed Virgin to help us with something. Let's paint what we need her to do for us in our *retablo.*"

"Paint money."

"No!" Maria waved her finger at Chita. "We don't need money. We're very lucky. We have everything we need." Maria contemplated Chita for a moment. "We could also paint what we're grateful for instead. We can thank the Blessed Virgin with our *retablo.* Would you like to do that? Or ask for something?"

"Ask."

Maria chuckled. So Chita was greedy, huh? They'd work on that, she silently acquiesced. "Okay. What should we ask the Blessed Virgin for?"

"My daddy."

Maria had to fight to control her reaction. "Okay, baby. You paint a picture of your daddy. We'll ask that she protect him. How about that for now?"

Chita liked this suggestion very much. Maria watched as she delicately dabbed some paint onto her *retablo.*

"Shall I tell you what he looks like?"

"I know," Chita said matter-of-factly.

"How do you know?"

"The picture."

Maria had one lone photo of Kenny which she kept framed and obscurely displayed on an upper shelf in the living room.

"He has blue eyes like mine."

"Yes," Maria hesitated. The picture was in black and white. Ruthie must have told her.

"And black hair like Tio Pablito."

"Yes, baby. Yes."

"And he's sad. I want the Virgin to make him smile," she sang. In the photo, although he looked very appealing, Kenny's eyes were clouded with apprehension.

She flashed on the first night she and Kenny sat together at his workbench, him painting the faces of his carved dolls, her delicately stitching tiny costumes.

"That's a sweet idea for a *retablo,* Conchita," Maria placed her arm around her daughter's waist, kissing the side of her sweet smelling forehead. "I think the Blessed Virgin will approve. I think your daddy would be very pleased."

Maria worked to bevel the rough edges of the small sheet of tin, not wanting Chita to cut herself. Maria found herself wanting to tell Conchita about her father. She'd debated over and over again what she should say, and had even read several child-rearing books which focused on the challenges of single-parenting. What should a child be told about the missing parent, and when? Should Maria wait till she started asking questions, or worse, when Chita's friends at day care might start asking? Should she speak of Kenny freely so Chita might feel that even if he wasn't in their daily lives, that she knew something about his character—who he was, what he looked like, that he had blue eyes like hers?

Most importantly Maria wanted Chita to know that she was the product of a lovers' union. That her mother and father loved each other, and out of that love, Maria was blessed with her wonderful little daughter. And so somewhere, was Chita's father.

"I used to sit with your papa, just like this," Maria ventured hesitantly. She could see Kenny's hands, so big for someone so delicate, gently dabbing paint on the face of one of his carved dolls. They'd sit for hours together, long into the night after Nick was helped to bed. Helped because he needed it. He was usually too drunk to walk on his own.

What a strange situation she'd landed in! Like Dorothy, in *The Wizard of Oz*. What had God been thinking? In less than twenty-four hours, her world had changed. Her precious Abuelita had died. Pitched into a river like a dead dog. Only an hour earlier Concha had squeezed her hand, urging her in some divine premonition, that whatever happened, keep going.

Suddenly Maria found herself running for her *own* life, on a deserted road in a strange country. All her important belongings gone—family photographs, papers, a scarf belonging to her mother, whatever clothing she could stuff in her small bag, her money—gone down the highway in a beat-up old van.

Where would she be without the courage and kindness of Ruthie? Of Nick? Of Kenny? Kenny—painting, whittling images out of blocks of wood, while she'd sit next to him, her stool pulled close, her foot lingering on the rung of his chair, stitching tiny garments to adorn the dolls.

How could a man be this gentle, she marveled. And still so strong.

"He's a wonderful artist, *mija*. He paints and carves."

"I want to be an artist."

"You already are, *mija*. Look how pretty your *retablo* is!" Maria smiled at her. Chita gazed up and grinned. "Chita, would you like me to put his picture on the table, next to your bed?"

"Yes," Chita nodded solemnly.

Maria thought about offering her the doll too. A rush of selfish guilt welled up in her. No, Maria decided, the doll is mine. It means too much. She shook her head and laughed gently. Let Chita get her own doll.

This had been enough reminiscing for one night. Maria had finally broken her silence about Kenny. Chita deserved to be the first. After all, he was her father.

That night, Maria slept with Chita in her arms. Tomorrow, she sleepily promised her baby, Maria would buy her anything her heart desired.

"I don't want anything," Chita advised her solemnly.

"No?"

"Well, maybe something."

"Tell me, *mi vida.*"

"My daddy," Chita whispered, and fell asleep with tiny fists knotted in Maria's luxuriant black hair.

5

Return to Sky Valley

A stubborn vestige of the old desert, Sky Valley rests peacefully in the shadow of the windy pink hills of the Little San Bernardino Mountains, due east from Desert Hot Springs. By day, across the desert floor, the majestic proscenium of the snow-capped San Jacinto mountain range takes center stage. At night, the twinkling lights of the desert cities fill the black void; the stars so bright they seem to be reflecting up from the sand.

At sunset, Pablo found himself bouncing across the open desert toward Sky Valley in his beloved black Jeep, which Maria had detailed as a thank-you for allowing her to use it while he was away at school. It wouldn't have been practical in Northern California. Too much rain, so Pablo leased an inexpensive no-frills compact car for the two years he was up there, finishing his degree. He had liked the anonymity of the little Ford sedan.

As the Jeep roared across the open desert, Pablo was pleased to find that it still did what it was supposed to do in the time he drove it—calling attention to the driver while keeping Pablo's head in the clouds.

He'd anguished about the idea of coming back to the desert, and more particularly, back to his old digs, the Airstream trailer he'd rented years before. Homesteaded by a famous seventies porn star, it sat on several acres; had privacy, running water and an excellent view of the desert floor. It also had good memories. He and Maria had lived here together in the early months of her pregnancy. In Sky

Valley they had taken care of Inez after her husband, Thomas, kicked her out when he discovered she had HIV.

The three of them, Pablo, Maria and Inez, spent summer evenings in beach chairs around a campfire, counting shooting stars and philosophizing about the meaning of life. If Pablo ever thought he'd be living with a pregnant, undocumented alien who wasn't his wife and a cynical, gay-hating hotel maid with HIV, all with his sophisticated mother's blessing—well, it was unimaginable. Now, with his master's degree completed, even his aristocratic father had come around.

Pablo's parents lived in Mexico City and commuted back and forth to Manhattan, where his father was a high-level Mexican diplomat. His mother had retired, a respected professor of literature from a Mexican university. Pablito was their only son, and with him, their branch of the family tree would come to an end.

If his mother secretly hoped that Pablo was Conchita's true father, her hopes were dashed by Chita's brilliant blue eyes. Her generosity about Maria, taking her in after she was deported, securing her the best prenatal care, and finally attending Chita's birth was a salute to Pablo's own maturity.

The fact that the family had bonded with Maria so significantly was a testament to her dignity and courage. Without her, and the influence of Inez, Pablo himself would admit he'd probably be still hustling and drugging his nights away in the seductive world of the Palm Springs gay resort life.

Now, as he roared east on Dillon Road toward Sky Valley, Pablo began to relax. The balmy desert air was having its therapeutic effect. He could smell creosote. Even the promise of a little rain. Shortly he would be home again. Maria had kept her eye on the place. She warned him that she hadn't been able to keep up with his garden, but the trailer had been well secured, no intruders had disturbed it, and she'd come earlier this week to personally tidy it up, with all that she had to worry about.

Ruthie seemed good, which pleased him. Until the thing today with the baby. She and Conchita were good companions, even though Pablito's mother, Elena, was a little jealous. Chita's surrogate grandmothers, Ruthie and Elena, had yet to meet, but Pablo was certain they'd like each other if given half a chance. His parents promised to visit later in the fall. He knew they suffered a certain trepidation to see Palm Springs, which nearly stole their only son from them. His clairvoyant mother had intuited everything there was to know about Pablo—his hustling and growing dependence on recreational drugs.

All that was behind him, thanks to Maria. And Inez Quintero.

He turned up the secret dirt road toward his Sky Valley encampment. He rounded the curve. He smiled. *Oh, mija!* This was why she was late today. She'd been over to light the Japanese lanterns. They swayed gently in the breeze as he approached, twinkling red, yellow, green and blue against the quickly muting light of day. He also saw that the skin of the metal trailer had been polished. Surely she hadn't done it all herself! And she'd lied about the garden. Bougainvillea and night-blooming jasmine had overtaken the trellis. It was paradise.

Soon he was ripping off his street clothes, thrusting his feet into thongs and emerging naked into the night desert. His body was still hard, but not pumped up like it was before. His back was brown from his two weeks in Mexico, but his ass pale. Now he looked like a white-tailed stag, mounting the hillside.

Later he pulled on a pair of shorts and built a small fire. It was warm enough to go shirtless, and he found himself growing aroused. He began to stroke the dark hair of his inner thigh. He used to wax his entire body but no more. He was moderately hairy, nothing on his back, thank God, but he liked the patch of hair on his pectoral muscles, and the line that trailed down his abdomen. His hard-on was beginning to probe the confines of his shorts.

It had been too long since he had sex. At least for Pablo. He kicked off his thongs. He hunkered down in his chair, easing the shorts down to his feet and off. He dug his heels into the sand. He began to stroke his cock, which, when he was really excited, grew so big even he could barely pry it away from the muscles of his lower abdomen. His heart began to race. Fragmented sensual images hurtled through his brain.

Lying in his beach chair, the plastic straps pressing against his skin and splaying his body up under the spectral star-filled sky, Pablo Seladon, who was home now, got himself off and had successfully avoided, even managing to block, the tragic implications of the events which had transpired in the preceding day.

Later that night as a summer rain pleasantly pelted the metal roof of his little trailer, Pablo woke up, thinking he heard the distinct intermingling sounds of popping of gunfire. Who would be target practicing on a night like this? And where? It didn't sound worrying close, but within several miles certainly.

These hills were full of desert rats. He'd never heard it before, so he probably had new neighbors, or he would be new to them. Tomorrow he'd climb the hill to investigate. Tonight he just wanted to enjoy the falling rain. Officer Bob kept coming to mind, fueling another sexual fantasy.

Today a stern, polite, sturdy looking border patrol investigator had arrived by helicopter, landing on the plot of open desert between Maria's bar and St. Louis Church. Because the dead young girl was an undocumented alien, as the Mexican ID in her wallet proved, and because her baby daughter had not survived the complicated delivery, the incident became a homicide investigation, and Maria's parking lot a crime scene.

The investigator, Bambi whispered to a shaken Maria, had been on the scene of the earlier accident. If Border Patrol Officer Bob Roberts was surprised to find Bambi and Madonna at the center of this second tragedy, he didn't let on, but they were all separated and interrogated alone. Bambi, Madonna, Miguel, Gabriel, Ruthie, Maria, Pablo and finally, a very uncooperative Sister Agnes.

Someone summoned Father Scolia, who was stunned at what he was told, that a sister of his parish had performed emergency surgery with a kitchen knife on a corpse in an apparent effort to save her baby. The events were doubly dizzying on top of the funeral for Loretta Young. Moments before the call to come rescue Sister Agnes, he had just been informed of a major bequest to the church, so substantial, well—it was a new recreation hall to say the least.

By the time he arrived, over a hundred people had assembled outside of the yellow police tape. The restaurant was temporarily closed for business, but reopened that night. All of the Latinos had been asked and proffered their green cards or citizenship papers, including Bambi and Maria.

Ruthie was the first to be dismissed. She hadn't actually seen anything but the body of the baby being passed back, still wet with amniotic fluid, the umbilical cord still attached. She reported that Sister Agnes and the ambulance crew had reacted to "something," once the baby was free of her mother's womb.

" 'Something?' " the investigator pressed. "Such as?"

"As if," Ruthie began. She closed her eyes to concentrate. "As if something was wrong with the way the baby looked. They acted . . . repulsed."

"And you didn't see for yourself."

"Frankly, I saw far more than I wanted to see," Ruthie shook her head balefully.

Once pronounced dead, the paramedics placed the baby back in the truck with the mother and ordered everyone to stand back till the authorities arrived.

While no one publicly suggested that Sister Agnes' actions had caused the death of the baby, or the mother for that matter, the matter would need to be investigated. Autopsies would be performed, the crime scene investigated. They all gave the same story. Sister Agnes had proclaimed the mother dead and while they all looked on, went into her womb with a knife to try to save her child.

Maria was released shortly thereafter. Soila had returned with Chita to find the restaurant crawling with onlookers and police cars. A helicopter in the field. Maria waved her away and Soila left without drawing attention to herself. Maria reported that she'd provided the knives and towels at Pablo's request, and saw the dead body of the girl before Sister Agnes began cutting. Plus, it was her restaurant. She'd need to be available for further questioning.

Agent Roberts, or Border Patrol Bob, as Pablo mentally nicknamed him, seemed inordinately interested in him. Any other day Pablo might have been flattered, but this muscular no-nonsense Migra cop hardly played on Pablo's team. It had all happened so fast, he explained. They thought they were saving a suffocating baby's life. There wasn't any time to think, and Sister Agnes assured them she knew what she was doing.

Pablo didn't tell them he remembered Sister Agnes from another night, years ago, when Maria was raped, and Father Gene had mentioned her experience as a trauma nurse, assuring him that she was in good hands. Agent Bob backed off. Pablo, too, was allowed to go, as were Miguel and Gabriel.

Of all those involved, it seemed that the investigation would focus primarily on Bambi, Madonna and Sister Agnes.

"What you trying to nail me for?" Bambi hollered.

"We didn't do anything," Madonna echoed.

"What was she doing in the back of your truck?"

"She musta crawled in at Westmoreland. At the crash site."

"She has no bruises. No burns to her body."

"You saw us there. You know how chaotic it was. Anything could'a happened. There might be more of 'em, hiding in the fields."

"She was obviously trying to save her baby," Madonna asserted.

"Then she should have stayed in Mexico," Officer Roberts replied.

"Fuck this!" Bambi retorted. "If you hadn't been chasing them they'd all be alive!"

"If they hadn't illegally crossed our borders, they'd still be alive too." Officer Bob searched her face. Bambi could tell he didn't believe her. Thought they were smuggling. "We need to dust your truck for prints."

"Hey, I'm an independent operator. I don't *have* another truck, man."

"Your vehicle is impounded, ma'am."

"Shit! I thought you were a good guy!"

This intrigued him because he knew she wasn't bullshitting him. "Oh? Why's that?"

"I saw you earlier," she softened.

"Earlier. Where?"

"This morning, talkin' to my girl, Madonna. When she was crying."

"And?"

"So were you, you bastard."

He smirked at her. "I think you were seeing things."

"Yeah?" Bambi folded her arms. "Well, I think you're imagining things now."

"Do you want me to fix you a plate for supper?" Florencia asked.

"No, Mamita," Bambi whispered.

"Can I do anything at all for you?"

"Tell me you love me."

"I love you, my baby girl. With all my heart. Try to sleep. I'm just outside."

"Promise me you'll tell me what she says."

"I will. Word for word." She patted her leg and withdrew.

That night, Florencia Rodriguez placed a call to her own second cousin, Josefina, to tell her where her daughter was. Florencia's friends at her church were already taking up a collection. As

Florencia made the call, Bambi lay curled in a fetal position on the bed in her childhood bedroom. In this room four sisters had slept, the two double beds taking up most of the available space in the room. They had learned to step over each other to get to the closet, change their clothes, climb through the window to sneak out with boyfriends—they were so close, so symbiotic, sleeping with women seemed the most natural thing in the world, only Bambi, of course, had a special nature that took it to another level.

Florencia would only give Josefina the barest facts. She wasn't curious by nature, and happy in her ignorance. Josefina was also religiously superstitious. To learn that a nun attended was an act of providence. She needn't hear the gory details. Nor would she ask.

Florencia herself hadn't asked any more questions than that. Bambi seemed too fragile to press. Madonna had borrowed Florencia's car to drive back to their house to feed their pets. Two cats and a dog. Bambi had asked her mother if it would be okay if she stayed with her, rather than make the trip back.

Madonna would pick her up later.

Florencia did have several questions, but would keep them to herself. It was a terrible tragedy. The poor little girl. Poor baby. *Pobrecita. Pobre Bambina.*

Weaving dangerously, the old car sputtered across the desert, the driver wending her way through the back roads to Sky Valley, till she came to the compound, just over the ridge from Pablo. She parked her car, her brights illuminating the high fence. As she staggered toward it, barking Dobermans charged her, dancing frantically on the other side of the chain-link barricade.

"Hey, fuckers!" she began screaming. "I'm on to you! Fucking murderers! Fucking skinheads. I've got you now! You'll see. I've got nothing left to lose and I'll get you!"

A muscled young Anglo with a shaved head appeared shirtless in his front door. He'd been watching her on a monitor inside the house. "Get lost, you drunken bitch. I'll sick my dogs on you."

"That would be the best thing you could do, fucking asshole. If you don't do it now, you'll wish you had, because I'm gonna get you killed! Remember that! You got greedy. You betrayed me!"

In a few minutes, a young blonde appeared, limping sleepily to the door.

"Who's that?"

"Ignore her, Misty." Logan glared into the bright headlights. "I'm warning you, sister . . ."

The old woman backed quickly into the shadows, climbed into her car and drove quickly away.

Among Logan's various businesses, he scammed credit card holders who visited his neo-Nazi web site. Logan wasn't really a neo-Nazi. He didn't really have any political aspirations at all. He just liked money. Most of 'em were just idiots and easy to get information from. Plus, they'd send envelopes stuffed with cash, small bills, mostly, any time he put out a call on the net saying they needed donations to cover this event, or that civil rights lawsuit. Folks were just too happy to help out. He didn't do it too much because he didn't want to attract FBI attention.

When he'd inherited the Sky Valley compound from his grammie, who'd raised him, he added the chain-link fence and the dogs because it looked cool, and scary. He wanted people to leave him the fuck alone. He had other businesses that interested him.

Logan was always angling for a scheme. It came up several years ago at the Salton Sea bar where he and Misty's brother Drew used to drive to play pool. A small old woman ambled over, asking him for a match in Spanish. Logan replied in Spanish that he didn't smoke. He noticed that she liked her bourbon, but didn't seem out of control. She'd been watching him intensely for an hour.

When Drew hit the can she came out with it. Would Logan ever consider a little light smuggling?

Intrigued always by anything shocking, Logan shrugged. "What contraband?"

"Mexican immigrants," she nodded seriously.

"Excuse me?"

"We need someone responsible. Capable of following orders. Compassionate. I'm proposing a mission of mercy. Too many innocents are dying at the hands of greedy coyotes." She paused, summing him up. "You'll be paid of course."

"Why me?"

"You're Anglo. Clean-cut. You won't attract attention. What good is a Hispanic-looking driver with twenty Mexicans hiding in the back of his decrepit van? We'd set you up with a high end camper, maybe even a cabin cruiser being hauled by a trailer. You'd have the right haircut, the right sunglasses, the right watch and the right rig."

"You'd teach me the business?"

"Inside and out."

"I've been looking for something new to get into."

"Then look no further." She cast a glance over toward the men's room "What about your buddy?"

"I'd have to think that through."

"You have any prior arrests. Any warrants?"

"Nah."

"We wouldn't want you taken to jail because of old parking tickets."

"I'm not stupid," Logan cracked the eight ball into the corner pocket.

"I'm betting you aren't," Sister Agnes sang. She popped a card with a beeper number in Logan's pocket, just as Drew swaggered out from the men's room.

6

Border Patrol Bob

What a bloody, bloody day. Bob pulled his green and white border patrol vehicle, a 1998 Chevy Blazer, into the parking lot of the El Centro Immigration & Naturalization Service center. He'd be up all night, writing his reports. The press was all over the crash earlier today. The El Centro information officer was screaming bloody murder for information, something to give them. They hadn't connected the Cathedral City angle yet. When they tied the gay produce driver and her girlfriend to both incidents, well, let's say nobody would have any privacy for a while.

An auto accident resulting from an INS chase brought everybody out of the woodwork. All the forces on the ground, the underground and surfing the airwaves would be set in motion. The press coverage would bring on the politicians; the political activists. And more press. They could count on a rally, just outside their gates in the morning. Maybe a hundred, two hundred protesters.

Then, with the bureau's overworked, limited personnel tapped out, the coyotes and smugglers would mobilize. Soon the Superstition Mountains and the East Mesa flanking the Imperial Valley would teem with activity. The U. S. Border Patrol would know they were out there, see them on nightvision goggles and high-tech surveillance radar and not be able to do nothing about it. They'd all be talking to the politicians and the press.

The car crash had been the worst. Luckily, no bureau lives had been lost. The two agents were shaken up but didn't suffer serious injury. The gas tanks exploded after they'd crawled away. They were taken to the El Centro Regional Medical Center, examined and released. As for the border-jumpers, another story. This had been bad, even by Bob's standards, and he'd seen it all.

With twelve years in the service, he fought the urge to quit, but daily it was growing stronger and stronger. At least two border patrol agents quit each day. Morale was lousy and life in the El Centro and nearby Calexico districts was bleak at best. His married friends argued that it was easier to be single and work in Imperial County. For the families, the quality of life was boring and downright expensive. There were no good restaurants except Mexican ones; only two movie theaters, no decent shopping centers and few job opportunities for spouses. Unless they were professionals like accountants or immigration lawyers, lots of marriages unraveled in El Centro. They just couldn't take the heat.

After a hard day's work like today, Bob was glad he didn't have to face crying kids and a pissed off wife, but he had to admit it was lonely. In this majorly Hispanic community, his choice of profession, busting Mexican immigrants "struggling for a better life," wasn't regarded too highly. A border patrol agent didn't have the same stature as a cop, but at least Bob felt valued within his own community, as much as he let them get to know him.

Bob knew he was an enigma to his fellow officers. He had a few acquaintances, but no close pals. His mother, Marilyn, lived in Prescott, Arizona, where Bob had grown up. Widowed, she lived in a mobile home park with Jo-Jo, her fat, old basset hound, and although he tried to convince her to relocate, even his homebound mother took one look at the flat, boring streets of El Centro and passed.

When Bob first transferred here, Operation Gatekeeper had forced most of the illegal immigration eastward out of San Diego and into the more dangerous Calexico corridor. Dangerous for border-jumpers because of mountain terrain and scorching desert heat. Dangerous for agents for exactly the same reason. It had been exciting, with stepped up activity and national attention focusing on the issue. Before Gatekeeper, they'd be lucky to have 800 arrests in a month. Less than a year later the number increased to a thousand per day. He worked nonstop, and because housing was at a minimum, most of the single officers were quartered in local motels.

In those days, Bob felt a keen sense of camaraderie. They'd all come home from work, play cards in their underwear, drink too many cold beers and pass out till it was morning and time to do the same damn thing all over again. The days flew by, and before he knew it, a year had passed, and then another year. Then his close buddies started to meet women, marry and move out. Now mostly everybody lived in the same housing development up in Imperial, swank by border patrol standards. Bob would be invited up for barbecue and cards, but after a while, not giving it much thought, he just stopped going. Days off he'd drive ninety miles west to San Diego, or less frequently, the same distance north to Palm Springs.

Now he rented a small new apartment in Westmoreland, just the right size for him. He was neat, liking order, and possessed few belongings. He treated himself to a 32-inch Sony XBR and a Sony DVD player. He worked out, to blow off steam, on a used Universal gym he kept in the corner of his living room. He buzzed his own hair short, gazing out into the world from piercing green eyes. He led with a thrusting square jaw that was proven to break knuckles. He had a huge knotted neck, big hard tits and thick, muscular thighs. He was nine inches erect, which made it difficult to penetrate many women, unless he was just using it as an excuse. He was hypersensitive about shit stains and always carried a packet of Wet Naps. That way, if they shot him, his shorts would be clean.

He spent most of his free time on the Internet, chatting his fair share in a few favorite X-rated locales. Coworkers stopped kidding him about his bachelor status three years ago, and stopped seriously asking about it last year.

Had he stopped going, or had they stopped asking?

He applied for promotions and got them.

His loneliness wasn't getting in the way of his career.

I thought you were a good guy. Bambi's words echoed in his mind. He *had* been crying. When he looked in the van, he saw them, melted together in a lover's embrace. Even without seeing their faces, molten then, he knew it was them. Leo and Ramon. The two young guys he'd turned back a week ago, after intercepting them in a routine sweep in the desert near the Salton Sea. They were alone, without water. They'd been separated from their group, which in turn had been dumped by their coyote five miles south of the eastern Salton Sea checkpoint. They'd been ordered to hike east into the desert from Niland, into the Chocolate Mountain Aerial Gunnery

Range. The coyote promised he'd pick them up once they circled back to the railroad tracks near Mammoth Wash.

He swore it would only take two hours. It was just before dawn. A group of twelve started walking. The sun came up. They lost their bearings in the scorching desert. Believing the coyote, they didn't conserve water. Soon they were dehydrating, throwing up. Leo and Ramon offered to walk back to find help.

They wandered in circles for the entire day. Finally they crouched under a spindly Joshua tree, a freak of nature in this part of the Mojave Desert, and passed out, kissing each other, promising to hold hands at the gates of heaven. They woke up to the *chop, chop, chop* of helicopter blades, and shortly thereafter, were cooled by the shadow of an enormous figure, gently splashing their faces with cold water. He knelt down next to them. His eyes were green as grass. He made both of them drink from his canteen.

The pilot of the helicopter trotted over to assist.

"They alive?"

"Just barely," Bob nodded.

Slowly Ramon was reviving. He attended to Leo, patting his hand, urging him to wake up.

"Where's the rest of your group?" Bob asked in Spanish.

"We don't know," Ramon wailed.

"How long have you been out here?"

"Since the sun came up. Before, even."

"How many were with you?"

"Maybe eleven. Ten."

"Coyote ditch you?"

"He said he'd meet us."

"Meet you where?"

Leo and Ramon gazed at each other. There was no point in protecting the others. They were probably dying right this very minute.

"By railroad tracks," whispered Leo.

"Near the wash."

Bob conferred with his pilot. "Let's take 'em in, call for backup."

"We don't have a spare plane. John Ashcroft is in town." The Attorney General of the United States. Inspecting the El Centro Border Patrol to get press for George W. Bush's amnesty plan. The entire office was thrown into high alert.

"Maybe the attorney general would like to save a few lives." Bob shrugged. "Call it in. You can drop me off and I'll take care of these two. Then you can go back out."

And Bob and his pilot helped the stumbling young men toward the waiting chopper.

"You saved us," Ramon whispered. "It's a miracle."

"Thank-you," Leo nodded. "Thank-you."

Once they were airlifted back, the pilot lifted up, the blades of the helicopter buffeting the metal shell of Bob's truck. The two boys were hydrating, hungrily consuming Bob's ham and cheese sandwich lunch. Bob noticed that they freely touched each other, patting a leg, grasping a hand, as if to reassure the other they were still alive.

Their gratitude to him was plain. They apologized for putting him in danger. They were worried about the others. What could they do to help? They'd tell him anything, anything he wanted to know.

He wanted to know something.

"Are you guys . . . together?"

"No," Ramon lied. "He's my cousin."

"Everybody in Mexico is everybody else's cousin."

"Second cousins," Leo corrected Ramon.

"Sorry if I offended you."

"You didn't offend us," Leo said quickly. He and Bob exchanged a knowing look.

"Life might be easier for you in the United States."

He knew they couldn't tell if he was baiting them, testing them or wanting to help them.

"Probably so," Ramon nodded agreeably.

"Culture's a little more relaxed about those things up here. Would be a good reason to make the switch. You guys ever thought of applying for a visa. Do it legally?"

They laughed. Ramon's eyes were especially warm when he laughed. "Mister, we have nothing!"

"What do you do for a living? What are your skills?"

They laughed again, chagrined.

"We're dancers," Leo admitted.

"Ah," said Bob, but he didn't press.

They drove the rest of the way in silence.

"Sorry, but I'm bound by my oath. I wish you'd think about what I suggested."

"They wouldn't want us up here either," Ramon allowed. "Thanks for picking us up."

"Yeah, thanks," added Leo. Impetuously he leaned over and kissed Bob's cheek. Bob reddened. Ramon was mortified. They quickly jumped out of the truck. They wandered over to be processed. They couldn't help touching each other. As Bob watched, Ramon turned around, saw him watching them, waved sweetly and they pushed through the turnstile to Mexico.

Bob had a theory but it was impossible to prove. The two dykes had known full well that the little girl was in the back of their truck. Not only that, they acted pretty guiltily about it. Maybe guilty wasn't the right word. Bereaved was a better word. Bob was something of an intellectual. He was a wordsmith. He'd never been beaten by a crossword puzzle. He was a junior high Arizona State Spelling Champion.

No, the ladies, whom he had nothing against personally, weren't acting guiltily, but they were actually grief-stricken. Bereaved. Hurting about the young girl and her baby in a personal way.

These distinctions were important to Bob as the helicopter lifted off. He could study the topography of Cathedral City, the layout of the town. While Cathedral City had changed, the old section torn down including a few dumpy clubs, and a good portion of the Latino barrio—the storm channels flanking the cove section of the city where he'd just left his suspects, and the Whitewater River wash that sliced the Coachella Valley in half, seemed to isolate it from neighboring Palm Springs and Rancho Mirage. If it rained, from his helicopter aerie, Cathedral City would be an island, shaped, he now noticed, like a figure in one of those old velvet Mexican paintings. Like a peasant woman knelt in prayer.

This stirred Bob's emotions as he flew away. He couldn't excuse an act of smuggling—if the dykes were guilty he'd have them prosecuted—but the remorse they had shown, without copping to anything, would be noted in his report.

What the hell. Maybe they were just bleeding-heart liberals. Or maybe they were two committed girlfriends who thought they'd help themselves to the teenage girl's baby, once it was born. They could, Bob conceived, have engineered the whole thing, but were surprised by the conflagration of today's earlier crash site. Sheer coincidence.

And what was the harm, from their point of view? What chance would a thirteen-year-old kid have with a newborn baby in Mexico? The injured party, Bob reflected, would be the American taxpayer. Giving birth to a baby on U.S. soil automatically ultimately afforded the baby and her mother hundreds of thousands of dollars in benefits, once it all got added up. Unless the two girlfriends picked up the tab. He understood that lesbians often wanted to raise kids together. They were both getting too old to find sperm donors to try to conceive themselves.

And, they'd put themselves in danger by trying to pull bodies from the burning van. Bob jotted that down. Why would they do that, with precious cargo in the back of their own rig? They couldn't have known the girl, Judi, was in any kind of danger. Otherwise one of them would have checked up on her. Both of them, the Hispanic woman and Blondie had been equally involved in the rescue effort. They hadn't given the contents of their truck a second thought. They either didn't know she was back there, or they trusted she was okay.

The Latina one had thrown him with her remark about him being a good guy. She'd been right about spotting him crying. How unprofessional. She was probably sitting around trying to figure him out now too.

As Bob lay prone in his crisp double bed, he promised himself that night that he'd put the image of Ramon and Leo in the shell of the burned out van out of his mind. Evidence from the crash site had been recovered. Of special interest, a small suitcase, thrown clear of the wreckage, stuffed with feathered costumes and big women's shoes.

As for the case of Judi Romero, Bob decided to close it. Take Bambi and Madonna's word. How could he prove it otherwise? Everybody in Mexico was somebody's cousin. If he traced her to them, which he knew he could, what did it prove?

He'd considered letting the young boys go, dropping them off with a few bucks in El Centro and looking the other way. But he had his oath. His promise to the legal citizens of the United States of America. The temptation was worrisome, however. He was fatigued, getting soft in the head. Still, he could have saved their lives.

As for the case of Judi Romero, this official INS decision, handed down by Border Patrol Investigator Bob Roberts, would unofficially be made in honor of the memory of Ramon and Leo, two of the 140 deaths caused by complicity and complications during unlawful border crossings, in the first four months of this year alone.

Bob corrected himself as he drifted off to sleep. *141 deaths,* he murmured, remembering Judi Romero's baby.

7

Twin Palms

Without the gay influence and influx, Palm Spring's own unique desert style might have been lost forever. They were fashionably late compared to preserved resort cities like Aspen or Key West, but luckily they finally showed, gobbling up all the architectural wonders of the small desert hamlet, many from poor, ignorant senior citizens, colluded against by their own shifty gay brokers, restoring them and thereby preserving them for *Vanity Fair*, the *Huell Howser Show* and centuries to come.

The depressed town (and nothing is more depressing than Palm Springs when it's depressing), soon fluttered with a small but brutal faction of mean-mouthed, tweezered, cotton-candy coifed queens, loaded with gold chains, big ugly diamond rings, pastel Gucci loafers, gold and stainless Rolexes zipping up and down Palm Canyon Drive in their red Cadillac Allante convertibles, or eighties Bentleys, lipping for AIDS charities but praying to be photographed in the society section of *Palms Springs Life Magazine* (a very fine publication) or at least *The Bottom Line*.

The only place to live was the Movie Colony section of Palm Springs, a gracious section of curving, hedge-hidden Spanish homes, nestled behind the Desert Hospital. If you were forced into a condo, only Deep Well would do. Loretta Young had a condo in Deep Well Ranch.

They relocated from San Francisco, Seattle, Atlanta and Dallas, and very quickly a bitchy class system developed. To belong, you needed the right house, the right hair, the right trophy hustler boyfriend and the right yappy little dog. You snickered about old money and new money, even if you came from no money at all. You developed a harried, pouting *tone* about you. You sighed a lot. You drank too much. You hated all the gay colors mounted on the beat-up trucks belching exhaust into your face at all the interminably long intersections.

You spoke of Mexican pavers (not Mexicans who paved, but cool terra-cotta tiles). You waxed about wall coverings, waned about the heat. You installed Greek columns to give a room much needed height. You whispered about the right section and wrong sections of town. *Honey, you don't want to live on the north end of Palm Springs. Too windy.* You freely made giggling, racist remarks about blacks and Latinos. You were terrified about your property values. If you rented, forget it.

The revival of Palm Springs was a given. In the late eighties and early nineties, as senior citizens began to die off, along with many younger men succumbing to AIDS, the market was flooded with pristine mid-century homes, decorated with integrity, and loaded with valuable modern furnishings.

For the less-affluent immigrating desert HIV community, it offered a quiet, gracious lifestyle. Companionship. Early Bird dinners for $4.95. Cheap movie tickets in ice-cold luxury theaters. Affordable housing—a two bedroom apartment with a community pool could be had on Warm Sands for $550 a month.

Palm Springs had always offered the rich and poor the same easy going way of life. Her magnificent mountain shaded everybody.

The rich, greedy, Palm Springs bitches were on their way to ruining all that.

"It was the site of probably the most spectacular fight of our young, married life," Ava Gardner wrote of the house in her autobiography, "and honey, don't think I don't know that's really saying something."

Ruthie was reading everything she could get her hands on about her new house. She was thrilled when she found Ava's book, *Ava: My Story,* because it chronicled the early years of her marriage to Frank Sinatra. Although he built it in 1946 for his first wife and children, this was the only home he and Ava really had together.

Reading it late at night, Ruthie felt like a trespasser.

Within a week of Ruthie moving in, by opening and closing it probably a thousand times, Chita managed to burn out the motorized sliding glass door which opened the entire living area of Ruthie's new house to her swimming pool. Ruthie had it repaired and Maria had a discussion with Chita.

The swimming pool was shaped in the form of a grand piano. At noon, the sunlight cast a shadow in the form of piano keys along the covered walkway flanking the pool. The house could boast that even the reclusive Greta Garbo once slept there. A flag was hoisted at sunset to let the neighbors know it was ' 'tini time.'

Ruthie was surprised that owing to her avowed obsession with Frank Sinatra that her therapist had encouraged her to buy Twin Palms, Mr. Sinatra's first desert home, located in the fashionable Movie Colony of Palm Springs. The fact that it was even available defines the nature of the sleeping giant that was the Southern California rebirth of mid-century art, furniture and architecture.

The office of the gay psychiatrist was loaded with mid-century artifacts. An Eames chair, a Danish Modern sofa. A Frank Gehry cardboard desk. For many of his middle-aged clients, it must have been as cozy as a sixties sitcom living room. It certainly was to Ruthie.

Later she found out from her realtor that her own shrink tried to outbid her. The house had been offered for a song by the owner who'd bought it from Sinatra, after his move to Tamarisk Country Club in Rancho Mirage. The seller accepted Ruthie's bid because it was all cash and she agreed to a three-day escrow. It was time to give up the old house in Las Palmas. It was time to really say goodbye to Sam; to Kenny and Nick, and all that sad, sad past.

It was also time to unload the shrink. Partly because of the matter of the house and mostly because she wanted her privacy back. Unbeknownst to anyone, Ruthie had detoxed herself off her lithium. Then the Prozac followed and in two carefully monitored months, Ruthie was flying solo. What a relief it was to feel like herself again! She didn't sleep as well, true, but she was happy to get up in the morning, and her old energy level roared back.

Singing on lithium had been like painting with warm milk. The songs felt bland, she felt bland and she hated the *levelness* of it all. When Sam would chastise her to get out of bed, she'd always reply that nobody ever got into trouble sleeping too much. She had the blues, she sang the blues and without the blues she wasn't really herself, was she?

She certainly hadn't felt herself in the last several months. And the lithium had bloated her. A woman in the market asked her if she had cancer, and how long had she been on chemotherapy.

That was it. No more medication. While she knew that certain risks were involved, she could also safely claim that she'd dealt with her secrets, her psychological demons. Sam had given her the gift of his honesty in the market when she tried to steal that poor woman's baby. The mother had been on to her, but Sam bullied her away. All things considered, Ruthie had been lucky. Luckier than Sammy.

Poor Sam. Ruthie had been such a burden to him, but she forgave herself because he loved her. And she, too, had compromised her dreams when she agreed to marry him.

As Ruthie wandered through the rooms of her new house, she marveled at the changed woman she was. She loved Maria and Chita. Although Maria rented a cute house in the cove section of Cathedral City, only blocks from Kenny and Nick's old place, Ruthie assigned a guest room for her and Chita, and filled it with toys.

The house was childproof. There was a locked fence around the pool area, though Chita could already swim like a fish. Ruthie's modern *objet* was secured with earthquake putty, and if Chita broke it, so what?

Maria spent her mornings and early evenings with Chita till she fell asleep. That way she could accommodate her heavy workload at the café. Soila and Ruthie took turns taking care of the little girl, but Soila happily bore the brunt of it. Soila once confided to Ruthie that she thanked God for Chita, because she'd certainly never get to have a child of her own.

When Ruthie pressed for an explanation, Soila had simply replied that men found her ugly, and besides, she'd probably join a convent like her mother always wanted.

"Is that what you want?" Ruthie had asked her.

"What does it matter what I want?" Soila had answered, folding Chita's blanket and putting it neatly away. "I'm marked by God. I have a destiny, a predetermined fate. What I want doesn't change that."

"I think fate has a surprise or two in store for you."

And Soila simply smiled and continued folding.

Bipolar disorder is often referred to as manic depression, but symptoms tend toward one extreme or the other, not typically both. In Ruthie's case, her optimism and general good cheer began to erode several weeks into her third month off the medication. Because she lived alone, with exception to her semiweekly afternoons with Chita, Maria and Soila would not see any noticeable difference in her mood or behavior for months.

Chita was a different story. Her *abuelita* seemed sad to her. Because Chita napped, Ruthie often laid down too. What Maria didn't know is that sometimes, when Maria dropped Chita off just after noon, Ruthie had only just gotten up an hour before.

Before, Abuelita would read to her, or play games. She loved to take Chita shopping. Maria gently asked that Ruthie not spoil her, but some days Ruthie cheated, hiding the gifts and guiltily inveigling Chita to keep them a secret. Ruthie's happiest moments, other than when she was singing, were roaring down the aisles of the local Jurgenson's Market with Chita in tow. People always stopped to ask about her.

"This is my granddaughter!" Ruthie would exclaim. "Isn't she the most gorgeous little girl in the world?"

At her monthly poker game, Ruthie's only organized social activity, it was finally Ruthie's turn to bring out photographs of her grandchild. Chita was far more beautiful than those pale, uncooked bow buns her poker buddies were trying to pawn off in conversation between hands.

"Can I bring out my pictures?"

Norma, a longtime poker buddy was still miffed about the time five years ago when Ruthie, admittedly suffering a mild psychotic breakdown, upon inspecting photographs of Norma's grandchildren, had, to everyone's shock and dismay, ripped them in half, after, mind you, deriding their physical appearance. (The children had Norma's very broad forehead. They looked like changelings.)

"This is Chita in the pool with her water-wings."

"Hmm . . ."

"This is Chita playing in the Cathedral City Civic Center fountain."

"You let her wade in there?" Several of the women were shocked.

"Well," Ruthie said, "Sure. It's across the street from the club. I wait with her till Maria picks her up. It gives her a chance to play with the other children. Plus, it's cool."

"What kind of children are forced to wade in a public fountain to be cool?"

"I don't know!" Ruthie glanced up. "Why don't you tell me?"

Uncomfortable, Norma glanced at her cards.

Carolyn, an old girlfriend from Ruthie's younger days, intervened. "Let's play!"

"I understand neighborhood women do their laundry in that fountain," Norma sniffed.

"I do my hand washables," Ruthie eyed her. "Saves me the time it takes to drive to the river."

"Girls."

"Well, really," Ruthie snapped. "She's made a stupid remark and she should just apologize for it. Nobody I ever saw washes their laundry in the wading pool."

"I certainly wasn't referring to Chica."

"It's *Chita.*"

"I'm sorry, I'm sorry." The cards fluttered from Norma's hands. They could all see her hand. "Now look what you made me do."

"We'll just re-deal."

Ruthie continued to scowl at Norma.

"Ruthie?" A look from Carolyn. "Can you let it go?"

"She makes me terribly nervous," Norma fought back tears. "She's getting like she was before."

Ruthie took a deep breath, forcing herself to compose herself. "I'm sorry if I overreacted. You know how much I love my little girl."

"I'd never purposely say anything against your granddaughter," Norma insisted. "There's just so much bad publicity about Cathedral City."

"Well, then." Ruthie sorted her new cards. On every face card she saw the image of Chita grinning out at her. This was certainly new.

"We went to see the new Follie's last night." Norma referred to the *Palm Springs Follies.* A very popular review which featured old Vegas dancers. Many in their eighties. "Have you ever considered auditioning?"

"Norma! You're picking on her. Ruthie is twenty-five years younger than the youngest dancer in the show!"

"Well," sniffed Norma. "At least she has it to look forward to."

Ruthie ignored the remark. She was too busy being distracted by Chita telling her what cards everybody was holding.

That afternoon she went for her first drive in years. It was on just such a drive she'd found Maria.

The adoption of Maria had been very important to Ruthie. She wanted official and legal status in Chita's life. Otherwise these women would only nod sympathetically and patronize her till it was time for their turn to brag about their families. Ruthie had spent too many years in Palm Springs to not know what a status symbol a grandchild was for a woman of a certain age.

At first, Maria had been put off by the gentle suggestion that she allow herself to be formally adopted by Ruthie. Even though she lost her mother and father at a very early age, she remembered them distinctly. Social workers and political activists, they'd been killed in an uprising in a mountain village in Central Mexico when Maria was only eight. Maria's grandmother Concha had raised her, and died while attempting to illegally cross the border near Mexicali with Maria. Ruthie had rescued her in the traumatic moments following Concha's death, literally saving Maria's life.

When Ruthie's offer came, Maria had been living in Mexico in a guest house owned by Pablo's mother and father. Chita was only six months old. Abuelita Elena, Pablo's mother, had been so kind, but Maria sensed resentment from Señor Seladon. Knowing that it had everything to do with Pablo's sexual orientation, and the Mexican class system, Maria's situation in their household was no better than the one she had in Nick and Kenny's house in Cathedral City. She didn't really belong there. Their dysfunction made room for her, but it wasn't ever going to be her true home. She would never have a "face" as she explained to Sam Singer. A legal status.

The same was now true in Cuernavaca. The Seladons would most likely never have a grandchild from Pablo. Señora Seladon refused to allow her to work thinking that Maria needed to devote her time to her newborn baby girl. In the truest sense of the word, Maria rightfully felt used, but the kindness had been so overwhelming and poignant, she didn't know how to extricate herself.

Pablito had understood. She didn't even have to finish her sentence. Why did she think he was studying in Northern California? Why did she think he'd come to Cathedral City in the first place? They were smothering him with their expectations. And in Mexico, especially with the status of his family, he could never really come out, be who he was. When Ruthie made her proposal, Pablo advised Maria to accept on her own terms.

Ruthie could not expect Maria to take her last name. She was a grown woman. Maria would never think of her as her mother, or ever be expected to address her that way. But because Conchita had no living relatives other than Maria, Ruthie could be her *abuelita*, her grandmother. In exchange, Maria could return to Cathedral City to run the new restaurant with legal resident status. Ruthie didn't want any management responsibility at all. She wanted to sing three nights a week, enjoy Chita and decorate her new house.

They would all benefit. No strings attached.

So Maria went for it, and thus far, it was going great. Most importantly, Chita loved Ruthie and would always have financial security. Without Ruthie, Maria's circumstances would be vastly different. But hadn't she, too, saved Ruthie's life that day on the dusty desert highway when fate intervened, crossing their paths?

Wasn't that the day Ruthie had been reborn? Wasn't that what immigrants do for countries? Shake things up? Create change?

The room full of drunken Latino drag queens dressed as Vickie Carr was probably the last straw. She tried to be good-natured about it, but was so dismayed she could barely finish the set. Where she normally sang Johnny Mercer, Harold Arlen, Rogers and Hart, the "ladies" were screaming for her to sing 'Let It Please Be Him' in Spanish. When she begged off, saying she didn't speak Spanish, they booed her off the stage.

Maria had been so angry, she took the microphone and told them all off. Back in the kitchen, as her crew sympathetically looked on, a tearful Ruthie told Maria that enough was enough. She was finished, and should have admitted it sooner. The new clientele didn't appreciate her. Her voice was going. She couldn't remember her lyrics. The club wanted to be something else and Ruthie wouldn't stand in the way.

Crestfallen, Maria tried to argue with her, and Ruthie got angry.

"Don't patronize me. You've wanted to tell me for months."

"Ruthie! That's not true. I'm no expert. I love your voice."

"Well you must be tone deaf! The busboys can hear when my voice cracks."

"How do you know?" Maria glared at a busboy, cowering in the pantry.

"I hear them laughing. Do you know what Sam would have done if he caught the crew laughing at me?"

Maria didn't know how to respond. Ruthie was trying to pick a fight. Attacking her. They'd never had bad words between them in five years. "I'll speak to them," Maria stammered.

"Sam was right. I never should have lowered myself. I had good memories of Cathedral City. Now they're spoiled."

Maria shot a glance at her crew. "What are you all staring at? Give us some privacy. Go close the dining room." Miguel and Gabriel shot out of the kitchen. "You're probably tired," Maria told her. "Do you want me to drive you home?"

"I hate the new house. I miss my old house."

Maria decided to just listen.

"I can't find my way around. I go to a drawer in the kitchen for a measuring tape and instead it's full of silverware. Why didn't you stop me?"

"What?"

"You should have said something."

"You wanted the house."

"Well, now I don't."

"I have to put Chita to bed," Maria checked her watch. "Shall we go together? You can spend the night with us."

"I suppose you don't trust me with my own granddaughter, now." Tears were streaming down her face. Her mascara was running.

"Ruthie!"

"I—"

"This is all nonsense," Maria shouted. "I'll call Soila and ask her to stay. Then I'm driving you to my house. We'll all stay together."

"Why would I want to stay with you?"

"Because you're my daughter's grandmother. Because you make her happy. Because we love you. We're family. If you're hurting, I'll sit with you till you feel better."

And then Ruthie began to cry softly. She allowed Maria to hold her till she calmed down. "I'm sorry," she whispered. "It's time we think about changing the lounge act. That's what this is all about. I've had my comeback. You and Chita are enough for me now."

Maria kissed the side of her face. "We'll talk about that another day. Let me drive you home."

"No. You go home and tuck Chita in. I can get myself home."

"Call me when you get there."

"I'll wake the baby."

"If you do, you can say good night to her."

And Ruthie called several minutes after Maria kissed Chita good night.

"I made it," Ruthie sang. Her voice was surprisingly strong and clear.

"Good night, Mamita . . ." Maria whispered. "I love you. I'll always love you."

And Ruthie, who had never been called "Mother" before, told Maria that she loved her too.

"Abuelita, I'm hungry." Chita was standing next to Ruthie's bed, just having wakened from her nap. It was two-thirty in the afternoon. When Chita had been dropped off two hours ago by her mother, Ruthie put her down for her nap instead of making her lunch as usual. Chita was tired so she fell asleep. Now she was hungry.

Ruthie didn't stir. The drapes were drawn and the dark room made Chita uneasy. "Abuelita?" She stared at her. She was sleeping so deeply. *"Abuelita!"* she shrieked, stamping her feet. Still, nothing.

She wandered down the hall toward the kitchen. She'd fix her own lunch, she decided. She was never allowed to open cupboards at home. This felt so naughty. She shivered with excitement. Opening the pantry she spied a package of cookies. She reached for the bag, sank to the floor and began eating them.

Outside, the aqua pool shimmered. The yard was filled with flowers. Then Chita noticed something. The gate to the fence hadn't been closed. Chita didn't have a pool at home. She knew how to swim, but she didn't know it was dangerous to go into the cold water after eating.

Her tummy full from the Oreos, Chita made her way through the sliding glass door and across the tiled patio to the pool gate. She trotted to the water's edge. Kneeling at the deep end, she peered in, and seeing her reflection amused her. Chita had a strong connection to water. She'd taken to it quickly. Maria had signed up for swimming lessons when Chita was only nine months old. Elena Seladon loved to watch Chita and Maria swim together in the family pool.

For as long as Chita could remember, Maria had told her that her great-grandmother Concha's spirit lived in the water. Often, as Maria or Ruthie watched, Chita liked to lay on her stomach on the warm patio surface and gaze into the water, looking for Concha. At night her mother often lit floating candles and as Chita watched, carefully placed them on the surface of the water. It amazed Chita that they didn't sink. They might fizzle and pitch, but the brave little flames always stayed lit, until long after Chita was put to bed, they went out by themselves.

Now as Chita knelt over the water's edge, she could hear her mother's voice, giving a name to each candle as she lit it and sent it to the center of the pool's surface. This is for my mother, Pia, this is for my father, Hector, this is for my grandmother Concha, this is for Abuelita Ruthie, this is for Tio Pablo, this is for Tio Nick, and:

"This one is for Kenny."

"Kenny," Conchita mused. Kenny was her daddy.

Was he in the water? She perched on the pool's tiled ledge and leaned out over the water for a closer look.

8

Ruby

"What's wrong with you?" Sister Agnes asked Soila as she listlessly licked stamps for the new church food drive mailer.

"I couldn't sleep last night."

"You probably have a guilty conscience," the little nun observed. Even to a girl as sweet as Soila, Sister Agnes could push to her limit.

"I was just at confession. Father Scolia has absolved me for all my impure thoughts and deeds."

"You confessed to everything?"

Soila just kept licking. She was sitting in the church office, staring through the window. Heat steamed up from the newly paved blacktop of the church parking lot. Ground had already been broken for the new church recreation hall. Soila found herself intrigued by the muscular brown backs of the construction workers. She wondered what it would be like to press herself against their chests. To her utter humiliation, she'd had to confess the feelings she'd felt when she'd hugged Pablo upon his return to Cathedral City.

"Bless me Father, for I have sinned. It's been seven days since my last confession."

Father Scolia waited for her to continue.

"I'm guilty of lusting after my mother's friend."

"What friend?"

"Her friend Pablo. He's my friend now too."

"I thought your mother lived in Mexico. She has a boyfriend in

Cathedral City?" Father Scolia was very judgmental, unlike Father Gene.

"Not a boyfriend, no. Just a friend."

"She's still married to your father."

"Yes," Soila grimaced. Now he'd start in on Ruby. He'd rail against their ungodly union. Ruby and Thomas'. Her poor father. God had really punished Thomas for his poor treatment of Soila's mother, Inez.

"Have you reconsidered moving into the rectory?"

Soila shuddered. Once they had her, next stop, the nunnery. Soila, they knew, would be a status symbol for the rectory staff. Look how generous they were. How kind. Who else would take her in? So pitifully ugly. The birthmark, after all. Wasn't that a true Catholic for you? Celebrating inner beauty? Eschewing shallow, earthly vanities?

Besides, Soila was clever and good at numbers. She was cheaper than a bookkeeper.

"No. My father isn't feeling well," she finally answered his question. "Ruby isn't . . ."

"It's a sin to judge her."

"But I didn't finish my sentence."

"Ruby's soul is suffering because of the sinful contract she's entered into with your father. They're adulterers. Their spiritual malaise is making them physically ill."

"She hasn't lost her appetite." Why were they talking about Ruby? She wanted to talk to someone about these strong feelings she was having. The workman's big arms. The way she felt when she pressed her breasts into Pablo's strong chest. She would be better off to talk to Maria. Even Ruby would understand. Suddenly Soila was filled with terror. What if she became obsessed about men when she knew no man would ever want her? What kind of living hell would life become for her? Despair overtook her.

"Father, I'm going to be sick."

"Three Hail Mary's and sin no more. Get some air." Father Scolia had had parishioners vomit in confessionals before, and it was hell to air them out. Soila exited as stealthily as she'd come in.

She couldn't sleep because Thomas and Ruby had another fight last night. Soila hated living with them. The fights were always about the same thing. Thomas Quintero had no interest in making love anymore. Where were his balls? True, Ruby had gotten very fat after they moved in together. She ate one burrito for every one she served at her job as a waitress in Cathedral City's best Mexican restaurant. And unless Soila was imagining things, her once imperious and physically fit father seemed emaciated to her. He'd not only lost weight, but muscle mass and tone.

Soila thought he was sick and wanted him to go see a doctor. Thomas refused. He said he didn't believe in doctors. Soila was imagining things. Who wouldn't lose weight living with such a whining bitch like Ruby, who broke things when she got mad, and on occasion, physically assaulted him?

When Thomas and Ruby moved in together, his son, Alex, never came around, mostly because of her. In Ruby's house, if you drank a beer, or ate a sandwich, you had to sign for it on a blackboard next to the refrigerator. If you didn't show up with twice what you consumed, you got billed. If you didn't pay your bill, you got banned.

Thomas hadn't seen him now in over a year. His youngest daughter Anita, now eleven, was the only one who showed him, or Ruby, who doted on her, any respect. As for Soila, she floated above the household, devoting all her free time to Father Scolia at St. Louis Catholic Church, and to baby-sitting the little daughter of *la puta* who owned The Cathedral City Café. Thomas and Alex called Maria a whore for an interesting reason, justifiable only to them.

Early one morning, four years ago, when Thomas was living in the old house behind Nick's, before they cheated him out of buying it and tore it down, Alex had come home, badly beaten up. Thomas and his wife, Inez, who Thomas had traded in for Ruby, listened in amazement that Alex, after making love to Maria at the Indio Date Palm Festival, had been accused of raping her. An intercessor had intervened, *un maricon*, a homosexual *friend* of Inez, as it was later revealed, savagely beating his son, leaving him for dead, although sitting before them Alex had seemed cheerful and well.

The girl had been *una mojada,* a wetback, and lived with Kenny and Nick, who owned the bar across the alley from Thomas' beloved house. She was certainly beautiful, and Alex, Thomas reasoned privately, could not have been expected to control himself, though Thomas would certainly have never sanctioned rape.

Out of this situation came several undeniable factors, all which contributed to the incredible change sweeping old Cathedral City. The homosexuals were overrunning the community. They were becoming too blatant, as Thomas knew only too well when they openly propositioned him with blow jobs in the date palm groves behind the Seven Palms Inn. Yes, he might participate, either there or in the dark alley behind his little house, but he was never a receptacle for their ardor. Thomas Quintero was *un machista,* only penetrating their mouths or their assholes, and the latter, only when he was really drunk.

Since living with Ruby, who liked taking it up her rear end, his need for other activity had positively diminished. Ruby was passionate in every way, and sexually insatiable. They made love three times a day when they moved to this new stucco house, but now Thomas was tired all the time, and needed his energy for work.

Ruby chose Soila to complain to. "He doesn't wanna fuck me anymore! What am I supposed to do here, huh? Why should I have to put up with this shit? I should send him back to Mexico to your mother! What good is he to me?"

"He's sick," Soila advised her solemnly. "Make him go to the doctor."

Thomas had insurance from his job. All he had to do was go to Kaiser for a checkup.

"You have to help me more around the house. This place is a pigsty. You can't keep freeloading around here."

"I give everything I earn to you, Ruby. And I make dinner every night."

"You spend too much time with that baby! You know, Maria's stealing business from us. Our business is way down, thanks to her! You shouldn't work for her. It's disloyal, that's what it is."

But Soila knew she was just jealous because Maria and Soila's mother had been good friends. They had lived together with Pablo in his trailer over in Sky Valley and had all moved back to Mexico together so Maria's baby could be a Mexican citizen.

Sometimes Soila missed her mother so desperately. Ruby was nothing compared to her, her mother who worked so hard, sacrificing everything so Thomas could buy his little house. And when she got sick, he threw her out.

And now he was sick, Soila was sure of it. Did he have the same thing?

"You've got to get him to see the doctor," Pablo admonished her. Soila had come to Sky Valley to visit him. They were seated on a picnic table, studying the clouds as they moved across the parched blue desert sky. Below them, cars zipped silently back and forth on Interstate 10.

"He won't go."

"Will Ruby?"

"Ruby?" Soila blinked.

"Doesn't she know?"

"Know what?"

Pablo was appalled. "You understand what your mother has, right?"

"She has La SIDA."

"Yes. Do you know how she got it?"

Soila shrugged. It was bad enough that she had it. Soila hadn't even considered how. She didn't think in sexual terms. She supposed it had just been her mother's bad luck. Or God's will.

"You don't know that La SIDA is transmitted by the exchange of blood and certain other bodily fluids?"

Soila blushed. When she did, her birthmark turned crimson, darkening to a deep, ruby red stain.

"*Mija,* you get it from having unprotected sex."

When was sex protected? she wondered. How do you protect sex?

Exasperated, he clapped his palm to his forehead.

"Your mother got the virus from your father."

"How did he get it?"

"That's his business. The important thing is this. We tried to get him to go to the clinic and he wouldn't. Now he's probably getting sick. He has to face it. And so does Ruby. Somebody has to talk to her."

"Well, I can't." Soila wrenched her fingers. She hesitated.

"What's wrong?"

"Can you die from La SIDA?"

A burst of profanity erupted from Pablo's mouth. "How can you be so naïve? What do they teach you at that Catholic Church? Of course you can die from it!"

"Do you mean my mother might die?" Soila began to tremble.

Pablo read her anguish and caught himself. "Your mother takes pills, so she won't get sick. You've talked to her, right? She's doing fine, okay?"

"Okay," Soila repeated softly, but tears were forming in the corners of her almond eyes. Pablo leaned across the table and held her head in his hands. Tenderly he kissed her forehead.

"Let's call her," he suggested. "Let's call and ask her how she is so you'll feel better. Would you like that?"

Soila nodded. Tears were streaming down her face. Pablo felt terrible. How could a nineteen-year-old girl be this sheltered? He went inside his trailer to make the call to Mexico.

"*Bueno,*" the familiar crusty voice answered.

"*Bueno* to you," Pablo grinned into the receiver. Outside he could see a forlorn Soila, tugging at a strand of hair. "I'm sitting with your daughter. She seems to think her father is getting sick like you were. Is it possible he never did anything about it?"

"*Si,*" he could picture Inez shrug. "Very possible."

"Is it possible he never told his girlfriend?" Pablo didn't know Ruby. He was just learning about her now.

"*Si.* Very possible."

"Not the clinic?"

"They could get sued." She spoke from experience, because she now worked at a SIDA clinic for poor women in her town. She relocated there to live with two of her six brothers, the two gay ones, that is. "He never got tested and if he had, the tests are confidential. What are his symptoms?"

"He's losing weight. He's always tired."

He could hear Inez take a deep breath. "Something else, *novia.*"

"What more?"

"Soila is upset."

"Upset about her father," Inez observed.

"That too. She's more upset about you. She's very naïve," Pablo told her. He studied Soila through the screen of his galley kitchen. "You need to talk to her. Tell her the facts of life. She didn't know that AIDS can be fatal. How's that possible?"

"It's possible," Inez observed. "Put her on."

"Soila?" Pablo called out into the yard. "It's your mother!" he held up the phone. A fearful Soila Quintero walked cautiously toward the trailer.

Because it sheltered battered women and children, the two-story Guadalajara structure, which housed Avance, necessitated bars on its windows, a tall iron fence surrounding its perimeter, allowing volunteers to easily see who was buzzing to get in before they pushed the button to unlock the front gate.

Earlier today Inez peered through the lace curtain fluttering in the side window of the strong wooden door of the reception room. A short figure stood at the gate, frantically pressing the buzzer to be allowed inside. At first Inez couldn't tell if it was a man or woman, because a brown paper bag had been placed over the face and head. She was also wearing a very baggy, dirty sweatshirt. Inspecting more thoroughly, small breasts and rounded hips revealed that some poor woman was hiding her face. Her arms and legs were either bruised or covered with Kaposi's sarcoma, KS, the skin cancer associated with La SIDA.

She also seemed desperate to be allowed inside. Inez pressed the button. The woman charged through the gate, which slammed shut behind her. Another security door awaited her at the front of the house. Behind it stood Inez Quintero. AIDS survivor and orientation counselor for Avance.

The women pounded at the front door. A locked, heavy steel screen door separated Inez and the woman when Inez opened up from inside.

"Please," the woman begged.

"Calm down," Inez ordered her. "Tell me what's wrong with you."

"My husband wants to kill me!"

Inez quickly scanned the street. "Is he following you?"

"He was. I think I lost him."

"Why are you wearing that bag over your head?"

"Because of the marks. He makes me. So our neighbors can't see my face."

"What marks? Are they bruises?"

"Please. Can't I come in?"

"How do you know about us?" Inez demanded.

"A neighbor heard about you."

"You live around here? If you do, I'd send you to a clinic out of this area, away from your husband."

"I've ridden for two hours around the city already!"

Inez could see that she was crying. The paper bag was stained with tears where she'd torn holes in it to allow her to see.

"What's your name?"

"Graciela. Graciela Romero."

"Gracie? I remember you. We've processed you before. You disappeared. You never came back. Take the bag off your head!"

"Please don't make me," she pleaded. "I'm so ugly."

"I'll close this door in your face if you don't!"

Slowly Graciela removed the bad. Inez, who figured she'd seen it all, began to involuntarily wretch. Gracie's bloodied face was covered with fresh bruises. Where her husband hadn't savaged her, KS lesions were finishing her off. Her front teeth were broken and bleeding. One eye was completely swollen shut, the size of an egg under her split eyebrow. Her nose had been smashed.

"We need help!" Inez screamed over her shoulder. Several aides heard her and came rushing from the kitchen through to the reception foyer. They too reacted, but fell quickly into emergency mode. Quickly they unlocked the screen door and Gracie rushed in. Inez scanned the fenced grounds and slammed the wooden door, locking it twice—as much for Gracie's psychological benefit as for her physical safety.

"We need her file. We've processed her before," Inez ordered a wide-eyed young volunteer. "Her name is Graciela Romero. I need her address, her husband's name. Then call the police. He's a monster and they have to arrest him."

"No! My daughters! They won't have anyone to take care of them."

"You want this to happen to your daughters?"

"They'll be placed with agencies. I won't ever find them again."

"Look!" Inez grabbed her wrist. "I'm breaking the rules by letting you in here again. Did you see those sick women hanging around in the alley across the street? They broke the rules. We kicked them out. We only give *one* chance. There are too many women to help. You want me to put you out? We can't waste our time with you!"

She began to grab Gracie's arm and drag her toward the door.

"*No!* I'll do what you want. No! Please, anything."

"She's in terrible pain," whispered a young aide. The aides were college students, many affluent, who volunteered their time at the center for college credit.

"Yes, and in another hour, someone worse off will come knocking and because of her, we won't have a bed." Inez gazed fiercely into Gracie's one good eye. "What's it gonna be?"

"I'll stay! I'll do what you say."

Inez opened her arms and reached out and hugged her. Gracie sobbed into her shoulder. "There, there, *mija*. He can't hurt you again. We won't allow it, even if you think you deserve it. I know how you feel. I've been through it too."

Her volunteers stared at her. How, they tried to imagine, could someone so fierce as Mrs. Quintero ever allow herself to be battered and abused? How could she have changed from what they speculated she once was, to the fierce warrior who now stood between Graciela Romero and her evil husband.

"I've been in her position," Inez shrugged. "With each knock on the door, I relive it."

They didn't understand that he'd changed.

The Sun Tours bus driver noticed him right off because of his dilated pupils, the perspiration dripping down the side of his face and the fact that occasionally, in some kind of Pentecostal religious rapture, he'd cry out something in Spanish that a passenger translated as a threat from the Book of Revelations.

With that, the driver told Alex Quintero to pipe down or get off her bus, which he did, since the bus was in front of the fancy house that compelled Alex to take this particular tour in the first place. This was where his baby daughter lived, and Alex had come to visit her.

The Pentecostal church Alex had discovered in Indio, had indeed been his salvation army, because instead of running with his gang, smoking crack and robbing Thermal liquor stores, Alex Quintero had been saved. In the six short months since he experienced his rapture, Alex had witnessed the salvation of countless souls, could now speak in the tongues of angels, and had experienced firsthand the exorcism of a sinful woman whose soul had been abducted by evil spirits. The hot nights on the metal folding chairs in the tiny converted storefront meeting halls had miraculously transformed Alex Quintero from an arrogant, woman-beating, drug-addicted hoodlum into the loving son of God who now stood on the edge of the immaculately manicured double lot where Ruthie Singer lived, and often took care of his little daughter.

It was love for her that caused him to wander first into the little church. It was the love of Jesus which had washed over him, the Holy Spirit cleansing him of his impure thoughts, flooding him with forgiveness for his many sins and teaching him the sacred language of angels.

Within days of his salvation he had dropped all of his old friends, and moved in with a family from his newfound congregation. They lived near his father in Cathedral City.

Alex often saw his sister Soila, waiting at a bus stop on Date Palm near Ramon Road, for the bus that would transport her south to St. Louis Catholic Church. He sought council about approaching her, and the elders of his church, believing that all Catholics were going to hell, decided it was worth risking Alex's salvation by exposing him to her evil. Perhaps he could witness to her and save her soul.

At first she didn't recognize him. She'd been sitting under a shaded kiosk, waiting for the Cathedral City bus, which was late again. She felt a presence behind her, assuming it was another rider waiting to be picked up, but she sensed something familiar about him, turned, and saw her own brother standing behind her, with a strange glint in his eye.

Alex had always been handsome, but his beauty had been supplanted by a distinctly fervored tenor. His eyes were ablaze, ecstatic even, and his young brow was furrowed like a middle-aged man. Instead of a skin-tight T-shirt and baggy, low riding jeans, he wore a polyester Hawaiian shirt and khakis, and new white sneakers. His hair was greasy, and he seemed unkempt, unheard of for someone as vain as Alex could be.

"What do you want?" she'd uttered. Not hello, how are you, but what did he want of her.

"I want to share good news with you," he smiled.

And Soila knew what would follow. She'd been proselytized more than once by these evangelists. Her nuns had warned her about them. They bitterly hated Catholics, would rob her of her soul if they got their hands on it. She should resist them with prayer.

Now here stood her brother, one of them, and if they'd managed to snare him, what chance did she have but to run, which she did. She fled the kiosk and ran back to her house, because she knew Alex wouldn't dare to cross Ruby, who'd kicked him out over a year ago for refusing to contribute his share of expenses.

Since that day, she noticed him watching her, always from a safe distance, not approaching but not going away either. He'd wait till her bus rolled up, watch her climb on and linger until it pulled away.

One day, in frustration, she demanded to know what he wanted.

"I want to see my baby girl."

"What baby girl?" Soila asked him.

"The one you take care of," he smiled beatifically.

"Conchita?"

"Is that her name?" he grinned. "Is that my little girl's name?"

"She's not your daughter," Soila exclaimed.

"Yes," he affirmed, "she is."

This was unbelievable. Soila always assumed that Chita was the product of a union between Maria and Kenny. Only Kenny had eyes that blue, and in the year that Maria arrived, they were inseparable. Alex had only been on one date with her.

"She has blue eyes," Soila advised him. "She can't be yours."

"A mark from God," Alex shook his head at her simplicity.

"No. Kenny's eyes."

"Impossible. He was a homosexual."

Soila didn't understand all this intrigue. What did that have to do with anything?

"I want to see her. I want you to arrange it."

"I can't!" Soila told him. "No."

"Yes, you can."

"No, I can't."

"Then I'll see her on my own."

"Leave the baby alone."

"She's my daughter."

"Go away!"

And he did. Soila didn't see him waiting across the street for her again.

When Alex unlatched the side gate to Ruthie's house, he never expected to see his sweet little girl floating calmly, face down in the pool, with no one attending her. A moment later screams could be heard, coming from the house and a hysterical older woman with red hair came flying outside toward the pool, exactly at the same time Alex was surveying the surface of the water.

He ran to help her, diving into the pool and pushing the limp body of the little girl up to the surface and into Ruthie's arms. CPR had been required in his high school gym course, and Alex scrambled out of the pool, grabbed Chita from a panicked Ruthie and quickly began to administer mouth-to-mouth resuscitation.

Chita was already conscious, because she was never really drowning. She knew how to float. She was simply searching the pool floor for this mysterious Kenny her mother was always lighting candles for.

To be grabbed from underneath the water by a stranger was frightening enough, but to be thrust into the hands of her screaming, terrified *abuelita* was the most terrifying moment of her young life, until the following instant, when the stranger from the water grabbed her, threw her on the ground and started to kiss her.

"No, don't cry. I'm your daddy, I'm your daddy."

She resisted and started crying, clearly alive.

And then on top of everything, she heard her mother's voice. *"Chita!"* Maria screamed. *"Chita!"*

And all Chita wanted was for everybody to calm down. She was fine, no harm done, and now could she have her lunch?

"She fell in the pool!" Ruthie stammered an explanation.

"What are you doing with my daughter?!" Maria screamed at the stranger.

"She was drowning," Alex smiled at her.

"No," Chita shook her head. "I was swimming."

"Get away from her!" Maria lunged at him, knocking him away from Chita, and backward into the water. Snatching a screaming Chita, Maria turned to Ruthie. "Get the gun! I know him."

"What?"

"Get the gun! Get the gun! Get the gun!"

And Ruthie ran for the house.

"I'll kill you!" Maria screamed at Alex, floundering in the pool as Chita wailed. *"I'll kill you!"* And then neighbors began to arrive and sirens could be heard and by the time Ruthie returned with the 9-mm Glock Sam had given her, which had been padlocked in a hiding place high in her closet, the yard was filled with strangers, and Alex was pinned, hands behind his back, facedown on the wet pavement by Lars, her neighbor's burly personal trainer.

9

The Exquisite Child

"Beauty. Beauty . . ."

"Hey, *chica.*"

"Baby, you need a man in your life?"

Maria ignored them.

"Stuck-up bitch."

Maria shook her head and laughed ruefully. She had come to drop Chita off at the church to Soila. The construction workers, upon seeing her striding down the sidewalk with her daughter started catcalling. As soon as Chita was safely behind the sanctuary doors, she intended to go back to have a word with them.

"Mind your aunt," Maria admonished Chita.

"Stuck-up bitch," Chita mimicked the workman.

A shocked Maria leaned down and slapped her tiny hand. "That was a very ugly thing to say to me!"

Chita was so surprised she didn't even cry. So was Soila.

"Apologize to me, Chita."

Chita refused.

Soila nudged her. Chita always sucked up to Soila. "I'm sorry."

"I'm sorry I slapped your hand. I want you to watch what happens when men call women bad names like you just called me."

Maria took Chita by her reddened little hand and led her to the open sanctuary door. A nervous Soila followed her. A curious Sister Agnes appeared in the foyer, obviously overhearing the whole exchange.

Maria boldly strolled into the center of the construction site. The catcalls swelled up. A nervous Latino laborer came over. "Help you, lady?"

"I want to talk to your foreman."

"She's up on the scaffold."

"Tell her to come here to me, at once."

The construction crew fell silent as they watched him ascend a ladder to a platform where several figures in hard hats were having a discussion. He said something and pointed to where Maria stood, below.

He and the athletic woman foreman nimbly came down the ladder.

"Yes?" the woman greeted Maria. "You wanted to talk to me?"

"A crew member just insulted me in front of my daughter. That one, over there."

"Hey," the crew chief grinned. "They're just kiddin' around. I get it all day long."

"That's my daughter standing in the doorway of the church with Sister Agnes. I want him to apologize to me in front of her." Maria folded her arms.

The construction foreman smirked at her.

"I own the Cathedral City Café. If you don't move quickly, I'll hit you, your construction company and the church with a sexual harassment suit that will break your financial backs to defend. This kind of behavior is unconscionable. Sanctioned by a woman in charge, *despicable.*"

Sister Agnes, Soila and Chita had wandered up behind Maria.

"Oh, another thing. My daughter repeated what he said. That's contributing to the delinquency of a child. A felony."

The foreman began to perspire. She'd probably worked for years perfecting control over her mostly male crew. How should she handle this? They were all waiting for her to do something.

"I think an apology would be cheaper in the long run," Sister Agnes smirked. "Father Scolia wants his recreation hall."

The foreman nodded. "Okay, okay. We need to do the right thing here. Who made the remark to this lady?"

A slow-witted doughy redhead ambled forward. "I did, ma'am."

"Why?" Maria asked him.

"Because you're pretty. And you'd never look at a guy like me. Plus, I was showing off a little. I'm sorry I said what I said in front of your daughter." He was an idiot, with no more than an IQ of 89. "Sorry, miss," he added to Soila.

Maria glanced down at Conchita, who was gaily watching a hawk sail overhead.

"Thank-you," Maria said briskly. "Come to my bar, and I'll buy you a drink. I'm not looking for a boyfriend, but it took guts to apologize." She scanned the construction team. "I'm not what he called me. I only want to raise my daughter to have self-respect. And to know how to say she's sorry. Conchita."

"Sorry," Conchita repeated.

"Come along." She took Chita's hand and together they strolled back to the church. A mortified Soila accompanied a chuckling Sister Agnes.

"They're always calling me names," Soila whispered wistfully to the old nun. "I didn't know I could complain."

Every day of Maria's life, one man, if not five, acknowledged her. Some made crude innuendo, usually younger *cholos* in groups, hanging off each other in the shade of the Ralph's market in Cathedral City. Some flirted good-naturedly, joking around with her with bright happy eyes, and others sincerely wanted to get to know her, to ask her out.

At thirty-two, Maria Castillo had taken herself out of the running, off the romance market. She doubted she'd ever fall in love again. The day after the incident with Alex Quintero, she stood in the mirror of her tiny little house in the hills of Cathedral City and brushed her hair a hundred strokes. It was too long, she decided, and the style was immature for a woman of her age.

Her features had set; her cheekbones were more pronounced, her lips wide and full, and her nose, slightly aquiline, her most exotic and attractive feature, perfectly complemented her big, wide-set brown eyes. She was tall, with large breasts and a tiny waist. Her daily uniform consisted of a pair of jeans and a colored tank top, and blue-collar men went crazy when she passed, but until today, she pretended not to notice.

Ruthie complained that Maria never dressed up, that the hot desert temperatures were no excuse not to dress nicely. She could wear simple cotton shifts, a little makeup, and modest jewelry, maybe a bracelet or a gold necklace. She could make an effort, but Maria always laughed her off.

Maria knew Ruthie never left the house without looking her best; always in a dress, her red hair colored and cut every two weeks.

Since Sam died, she'd let her look go a little more natural. Ruthie complained to Maria she'd overheard someone once remark, "There goes the mobster's wife."

Ruthie had been mistaken more than once for Ann-Margret, or, when Nick cut her hair, vaguely reminiscent of Jill St. John. These similarities were flattering to Sam. He loved to show her off, but Ruthie wanted to be more modern, not feel like an artifact, so she wore her hair softer and more natural, changing her high heels for pretty sandals, and people still smiled approvingly when she passed.

With Sam gone, so went the persona of danger that followed them wherever they went. Sam liked his gruff image, the Jewish godfather of Cathedral City who was licensed to carry a pistol but in thirty years never used it until the night the kids came back.

Maria was aware that Ruthie kept Sam's gun, but had been assured that it was childproof, locked in her safe in the back closet of her dressing room. The vision of Alex Quintero hunched over the body of her baby girl would haunt her forever. Maria could never survive the loss of one more precious family member, let alone in a violent fashion. If she'd gotten her hands on the loaded gun, Alex Quintero would not be a worry today.

The police had taken him away, even though he calmly explained that he only entered the yard when he heard Ruthie's screams. Lars, the trainer, disputed his story, having observed him hanging around in front of the house, as did the tour bus driver, who remembered that he'd been nervous-making enough to expel him from the bus.

"You should press charges," Pablo urged her.

"I already did. For trespassing."

"No. I mean for assault."

"You mean rape," she corrected him.

"You're a legal resident. You have rights. They can't deport you."

"I don't want everybody thinking there's a chance he might be Chita's father."

She promised she would think it over. Pablo was a witness, and so now was Sister Agnes. They could get this guy thrown away for good.

As it was now, all they could charge Alex with was simple trespassing. A lawyer could make a case that he'd only come running when he heard Ruthie scream, and had he not, Chita would have drowned. He saved Chita's life, locals would think, and this is how the mother repaid him?

A tearful Soila also arrived, admitting that her brother had asked about Chita, claiming that she was his daughter and all he wanted to do was meet her. Soila was conflicted. Alex's transformation, while unusual, didn't seem dangerous or violent to Soila. She privately speculated that he felt so guilty about his past with Maria that his religious conversion was the only way he had to deal with it.

It was possibly a good thing, though not the part about stalking Chita or assuming that he was her natural father. Soila planned to beg him to stay away. Even though he'd been so cruel to her, he was still her brother and she didn't want him to get into more trouble. Besides, Maria might not allow her to take care of Chita, thinking that Alex would persuade his sister to let him see her. It was all such a mess.

They all loved Chita, which wasn't surprising. She was an exquisite child, possessing a strong personality. Witty and cunning, Chita also displayed moments of sweetness that were so painful, Maria thought she'd die of love for her. She was such good company everybody wanted to spend time with her.

The subject of Ruthie's continuing ability to take care of Chita was the more major issue at hand. Devastated by the fact that Chita had found her way into the pool, Ruthie couldn't explain exactly why the gate was unlocked, unless Alex unlocked it and also, why had she decided to take a nap so soon after Maria dropped her off? Normally Ruthie took Chita shopping, to the market or one of the air-conditioned malls in Palm Desert.

Chita didn't usually nap till after they came home. Why would Ruthie put Chita down for a nap and need one herself so early in the day? Chita could be a handful, Maria mused, and Ruthie wasn't the first grandmother in the world who found herself tired out by an energetic toddler. But if she didn't feel well, why not admit it? It wasn't impossible for Maria to rearrange her schedule. She was the boss, she had staff to cover for her. The café practically ran itself.

How would they proceed from here on out? How could she deny Ruthie her precious time alone with Chita? Maybe this had taught them all a lesson. No matter how careful, how much control they all thought they had, sometimes it would be impossible to protect a child. Chita had survived. Alex had played his hand. Ruthie needed to be watched more carefully. Maria was better served by knowing than not.

All these other concerns, on top of the issue of Alex Quintero avowing that he was really Chita's father were grave and must be seriously considered. Maria filed a restraining order against him, helped with the testimony of his own sister. He swore he never intended any harm to Chita, that he loved her, and now that he'd seen her, promised never to bother them again. He was certain he had been sent by God to save her life. That was clear. He felt no other impulse to make contact.

He spent three days in the Palm Springs jail, agreed to plead guilty to trespassing and got released.

Maria and Pablo conferred with a lawyer about pressing charges for the rape, but the lawyer advised her that for something that happened years ago it would be difficult to make a case. She could have found him long before the incident with Chita. It would appear vindictive, and he doubted they could get a conviction.

And now, as Maria continued to brush her hair, one last thing haunted her. Last night, when she put Chita to bed, Chita hugged her good night as she always did. When Maria turned off the light, she heard Chita whisper the following:

"My daddy in the pool."

"What did you say?"

"Daddy in the pool."

"That day at Abuelita's?"

"Yes."

"No, Conchita. That wasn't your daddy."

"Daddy in the pool."

"No, no."

"*Yes.*" And her answer was so firm, Maria thought she'd better drop it. For that reason, she also decided not to pursue any other action against Alex. The business about saving her from drowning. Maria had little doubt, given the extraordinary coincidence and chain of events, that he probably had.

She should accept this ironic gift from God and move on. Her dreams, unfortunately, would not be so forgiving. Alex Quintero was back in her mind, and so was his treacherous memory.

10

Badlands

Pablo was starting to have doubts about his decision to come back to Cathedral City. First the incident with the dead girl found in Bambi's truck. Then Conchita nearly drowning. And Maria so dour. And the matter of his neighbors. In Sky Valley, if anyone lived a mile away, that person qualified as a neighbor. The homesteads were interspersed among the rolling high desert, and the main reason most residents lived there was for privacy.

It was interesting, Pablo hypothesized, that members of the far left and the far right both ultimately wanted the same thing. The right to be self-determining without any compromise at all. There were lots of extremists living in the hills of Desert Hot Springs and Sky Valley. Desert Hot Springs had the highest per capita population of the witness program in the United States.

Conversely, at one time, it could probably boast as many male porn stars as a major city. That's what made the desert so funky. So delightfully weird. But the nightly shotgun blasts from over the ridge were beginning to concern him. Night after night, just when he'd settled into his bed he would hear them. The distinct pop-popping of submachine gun firing, intermingling with the high-pitched yelping of coyotes.

Pablo had yet to go investigate, deciding that he didn't want to know. The way his luck was running, he'd probably encounter a compound of skinheads, an enclave of Branch Davidians—his own desert-style Waco. Pablo thought it best to mind his own business.

Tonight he planned another evening of smoking joints by the fire and jacking-off, but just as he lit up the joint he reconsidered. He should go out. Make new friends. Get laid—as much as he was growing to love his own right hand.

With no clubs left in Cathedral City, Pablo decided to drive to Arenas Road, the West Hollywood of Palm Springs. In the past Pablo would have known exactly what to wear, but tonight, he didn't have a clue. It was warm, probably still in the mid-seventies. He doubted he'd be doing any dancing. He felt silly in a tank top at his age. He pulled on a black T-shirt and an old pair of jeans and took off.

Pablo drove west on Dillon Road till he reached Indian Canyon Avenue and turned south toward Palm Springs. The Santa Ana winds were blowing earlier today, and all the summer haze had dissipated. The sky was jet black. The Big Dipper seemed close enough to touch. As a kid in Mexico City, he rarely saw stars, because the air quality had been so bad. Now he found himself mesmerized by the night sky. He planned to buy a telescope as soon as his trust fund kicked in.

Pablo had always known that a small fortune lay accruing interest for him, and would become available to him on his thirtieth birthday if he received his master's degree. If not, he'd have to wait another ten years. It had already been delayed five years because he'd dropped out of school when he first moved to Cathedral City.

Pablito had grown up in opulent surroundings. His parents were very wealthy, his mother perhaps wealthier than his father when they'd married. This was why she wasn't looking for a husband. An intellectual, Elena had her doctorate. Political and bohemian, she loved to travel. She was also extremely beautiful, but too radical for most men's taste. When she turned thirty-eight, she found herself with the urge to have a child. She didn't want to marry only for that reason, but within months found herself at a dinner given by the President of Mexico and his wife, and was seated next to Jorge Seladon, Mexico's ambassador to the United Nations.

Jorge was twelve years older than her and had recently lost his wife to cancer. She had been unable to have children. They were married in a year and had Pablito nine months to the day after. With homes in Mexico City, Cuernavaca and Manhattan, Pablo had been raised on private jets. He skied in Gstaad, climbed mountains in Nepal, and later, camped on Fire Island. Pablo always knew he was gay, and so did his astute mother. After the surprise return to their

East Side apartment, catching Pablo in bed with the sexy night doorman, so finally did his father.

Pablo loved his sexuality, and if offered a magic pill to change, he'd never take it. At twenty-nine he'd yet to have a lover, not even a relationship lasting longer than three weeks, and he was lately intrigued that he found himself longing for one. The break at Stanford was profound for Pablo. The scholarly environment was radically different from his privileged upbringing. His family money couldn't buy good grades. He had to perform or he was gone.

His ass wasn't going to save him either. If there were many gay grad students, he never met them. His pouting lower lip and his six-pack of abs meant nothing to his old English professors. If he couldn't apply critical thinking to paper, he would fail. It was astonishing, and invigorating, to find himself without any tricks up his sleeve. He didn't graduate with honors, true, but he hadn't flunked out either, which his father probably expected. Thankfully, his mother privately expressed to him, he wasn't spoiled either.

She had no problem with him living in a little trailer overlooking the living desert as long as he wasn't polluting his body with drugs and anonymous sex. A career in the arts would mean more tenacity and discipline than would ever be expected of him in a more conventional career. Education was its own reward.

She cried when he gave her his diploma.

Pablo found a parking space just west of Arenas Boulevard. He walked a block back to Arenas and happily, the street was promisingly busy. Gay businesses lined the short street; gift shops, a video store, the MCC Church, a coffeehouse and three bars. Hunters, Street Bar and Badlands. The gay flag flew everywhere. Pablo had noticed more and more of the multicolored decals and bumper stickers. Palm Springs was truly a gay city. Nick had lamented the fact that the gay community had deserted, or been kicked out of Cathedral City. Palm Springs, with its closed history, was not the rightful heir to the gay dollar, but a gay newcomer wouldn't feel anything but welcome on this street.

Pablo decided to try Badlands, a club located at the intersection of Arenas and Indian Canyon. He wondered if he'd see anybody he knew from before. Pablo lingered in the frame of the door, allowing his eyes to adjust to the light. Nobody he recognized, but judging by the fact that many handsome men were staring at him, the room would soon be filled with a new set of old friends.

As much as Pablito didn't want to trade on his old cachet, it was nice to know he could if he wanted to. He reminded himself he was here to find a lover, someone to grow old with. Why were they all staring? A grinning Pablo decided to bask in the attention a moment longer.

"Hey, buddy, can you step aside?"

It was a polite resonant voice, one that sounded familiar. Pablo turned. Backlit by the headlights of a car, parking in the lot outside, a powerfully built man with piercing eyes and a strong buzzed head gazed frankly at Pablo. He had the physique of a professional wrestler. Pablo was not short, just under six feet, but this fellow's stature made him appear much taller, though they were probably the same height. Easing past Pablo, he entered the room, and every eye Pablo thought was staring at him, followed this giant as he moved toward the bar.

Pablo began to laugh. So much for great entrances.

"Hey buddy, don't be sad. I think you're just as cute," someone offered sweetly from the darkness. Pablo nodded sheepishly and headed over to buy a beer. The monster man had already been served a frosty Corona, waving off attempts to be bought his drinks. He was neither friendly or unfriendly. He looked slightly uncomfortable, and as Pablo studied him, he wondered if he might be straight. Had he blundered in here by mistake? He wasn't looking at anyone in particular, but seemed to possess a terminator kind of cognition, as though he'd already mapped out the configuration of each and every patron, and could reliably testify later who he saw in here, where they stood, who they were talking to and what they drank.

Was he a cop?

Pablo, like the others, openly gawked at him now, but when he finally glanced up, he didn't survey the room. Instead he lifted his beer bottle and nodded to Pablo, but this time Pablo didn't feel the need to check over his shoulder to be certain he was gazing at him.

Pablo ambled easily down the bar toward him.

He drove an immaculate Toyota 4-Runner, and followed Pablo across the desert toward Sky Valley. He kept his brights on, so whenever Pablo shot a glance in the rearview mirror of the Jeep, it was too brilliant to see anything more than the outline of his buzzed head. He wondered if he was doing this purposely, and if so, why?

This was a lot of man following Pablo. The two vehicles raced toward the dimmed lights of Desert Hot Springs, their high beams impaling the darkness of the open desert floor. They had only exchanged a few brief remarks before Pablo suggested they leave.

It wasn't that Pablo was so horny. He wanted to escape the scrutiny of the others in the bar. They were all staring, watching their preliminary exchange. Those closest eavesdropped on their conversation.

"You wanna get out of here?"

"Sure," he said. They ambled out the door.

"I live across the desert in Sky Valley," Pablo told him on the street. "Unless you want to go to your place."

"I live in El Centro."

"Maybe my place then," Pablo asserted. "I'm Pablo."

"I know," and for the first time, the big man smiled.

"How do you know me? What's your name?"

"It'll come to you. I want to see how long it takes." He nodded to Pablo's Jeep. By coincidence, they were parked a car away from each other. "I'll follow you."

"No, tell me your name."

"It's Bob. I was the investigating border patrol agent who came to the scene of the dead girl in the produce truck. Behind your girlfriend's café."

Pablo drew a deep breath. Of course it was him. Border Patrol Bob. He was shocked that he hadn't recognized him. "Am I a suspect?"

"Depends on how tonight's interview goes," Bob replied.

"Do I need to show you my green card, Migra?"

"I'm off duty."

"I'm not totally sympathetic about what you do for a living," Pablo asserted.

Bob sighed, deflating somewhat. If possible, Pablo would swear that he'd hurt his feelings.

"Maybe this isn't such a good idea."

"You don't go out much."

"I don't have the time. I rarely get enough time off. I work hard."

"How many *Mexicanos* did you arrest today, Migra?

"As many whose lives I possibly saved."

"That how you see it?"

"Today I dragged a woman and two small babies out of the New Canal. You ever heard of it?"

Pablo had heard of it. A river of white, bubbling, toxic waste. People died after trying to swim across it.

"She hugged me when I pulled her out. One of her babies was drowning. I drove them to an American hospital where she was treated."

"I guess there's your side of it."

"It's a complex issue. Not very sexy."

"Then you've changed your mind?"

"About?"

"Coming back to my place."

"I'm proud of what I do."

"Bambi told me she remembered you from earlier that day."

"I remembered her and her girlfriend."

"She said she thought she saw you brush away a tear or two. Why?"

"They were in my eyes. I couldn't see."

"Why were you crying? You must see tragedy all day long."

"I was crying because I recognized two young guys in the hold of the overturned cargo van. They were burned up but I recognized them."

"How?"

"They were boyfriends. I'd caught 'em a week before. They pretended to be cousins but I knew they were together. They were only eighteen. I'd considered letting them go, but I consider letting everybody go who's polite or scared."

"But you didn't this time?"

"No. I never do."

"Why not?"

"I'm paid to protect our borders. I can't break the rules. Too many people do things properly, wait their turn. As you did."

"You pulled my file?"

"Yes. I abused my power. I liked you. I was hoping to see you again."

"Why didn't you call me back for another interrogation?"

"We call them interviews."

"Interview then."

"That would have been unprofessional. I decided to come look for you here instead."

"You came all the way to Badlands to look for me?"

"I told you I was an investigator. I found you didn't I?"

"Did you follow me in there?"

"No. That part was sheer luck. I thought it was pretty neat."

"I have a problem with guys who have an ethnic bias."

"What the hell are you talking about now?"

"I don't like guys to be into me because I'm Latin. I'm a man. Not a type."

"I don't like guys to be into me because I wear a uniform."

"Okay, then."

"Okay."

"Any more complaints before we go?"

"No," Pablo smiled sheepishly. And Bob smiled back.

Pablo built a small fire and laid a ground cloth on the sand and a soft red blanket on top of that. He disappeared inside the trailer and lit the lanterns and a few inside lights. He knew how beautiful it looked against the night desert sky. When he came back Bob had already pulled off his clothes and lay prone on the blanket with his arms folded behind his neck, staring calmly up at the sky. Firelight danced on his pale skin.

Everything about this large naked man was calm and considered. Pablo, who'd slept with hundreds of different men, always searched for something unique every time he encountered someone new. Bob already had an erection, and it throbbed slightly as Pablo padded barefoot across the sand. Pablo had stripped to a pair of sweats, and his own hard-on pressed against the inside of the pilling fabric as he got nearer.

Pablo gulped when he saw how big Bob really was. His body was beautiful, his cock, perfectly formed. Museum quality, Pablo thought. Pablo dropped to Bob's side. Bob rolled over lazily and gazed into Pablo's eyes. Then he kissed him tentatively. Pablo kicked off his sweat pants. His belly was already wet with pre-cum. Pablo slid down Bob's side to his groin, tasting the silky tip. He teased the hole of Bob's penis with his tongue for an hour.

Then they got into other things.

*   *   *

About three, Pablo awakened to the same staccato sounds of rifle fire he'd noted for the past several weeks. He wasn't surprised to find Bob awake, too, gazing attentively up the ridge in the direction of the sound.

"It happens almost every night."

Bob reached for his jeans.

"You taking off?"

"No. I want to hike to the top of the ridge to see what's going on."

"I've been avoiding it."

"Better to know." Bob tossed Pablo his sweats. "Go get some sneakers. Let's take a hike."

A few moments later, they had stealthily mounted the hillside. Pablo was sorry he'd come along. Below them, maybe five hundred yards, a brightly lit compound, a sullen newer stucco house and two small outbuildings, stood surrounded by a high chain-link fence. Guard dogs, Dobermans, calmly patrolled the outermost parameter, but oddly enough, Pablo had yet to hear them bark. An SUV was parked inside the fence, a white 1997 Blazer.

"They're well-trained dogs," Bob commented, reading Pablo's thoughts. "When they bark, the owners really know intruders are nearby."

"Should we move closer?"

"Definitely not."

The popping was audible again, and seemed to be coming from a long, narrow outbuilding closest to the house.

"They have an indoor firing range," Bob whispered. "Let's go back."

"Now?"

"They most likely know we're here."

"How?"

"These survivalists have the same high-tech detection equipment the government has. Move. Now."

They trotted down the hillside toward Pablo's encampment.

They slept inside Pablo's tiny paneled bedroom, tangled up in each other's arms. As a general rule, Pablo didn't like sleeping with his sex buddies, but tonight he hadn't given it a second thought. Bob did. This was the first time he'd ever had sex with a man laying down. To sleep with a man, unthinkable, unless you counted the beer nights in El Centro, when they all played poker in their Jockeys and passed out together. He dozed off in minutes, with Pablo gently tracing the creases in his forehead with his forefinger.

The next morning Bob woke up to brilliant blue sky overhead, visible through the hatch in the ceiling that Pablo popped up to vent the room. Bob woke up with a piss hard-on, and Pablo was already giving it his best shot. He swallowed Bob up furiously, and in moments, Bob's semen came gushing across his belly.

Pablo straddled him, grinning down into his peaceful face. A shadow of a beard was beginning to darken Bob's square jaw. He'd shaved last night before driving north to Palm Springs. Bob opened his eyes.

"Your eyes! They're so green!"

"So I'm told."

"I never saw eyes so green." He slid down Bob's torso and kissed him. Bob gently tugged at Pablo's hair till he laid his head on his chest. Outside, desert birds were singing. Bob could smell coffee brewing. It felt very domestic.

"This place isn't big enough to swing a cat." He traced the tendrils of hair at the base of Pablo's neck. "Why doesn't it feel cramped with two big guys like us?"

"I can't speak for you, but it must have something to do with how comfortable we feel with each other." Pablo opened one eye, to survey Bob's reaction.

"I haven't ever been with anyone," Bob gazed up at the ceiling. "More than once. It's a new impulse."

"What impulse?"

"To want to see you again." He caught Pablo's eye. "You were pretty direct last night on the street outside the bar. You said some things about my profession. I'm a square guy. That won't change."

Pablo mused. "Gee, are we negotiating a second date or a long-term relationship?"

"What are you ultimately looking for?"

Pablo sat up, sliding his legs over the side of the bed. He gazed down the narrow corridor through the trailer to the windows in the front compartment. He could see the pink mountain range of the high desert in the distance.

"Before last night, Migra, I couldn't have told you." He stood up, and Bob followed his naked ass into the kitchen and watched him pour a cup of coffee.

"And this morning?"

"This morning? Well, let me put it this way. What do you take in your coffee? If you like cream and sugar, I'll have to bring some in."

Conchita liked to wade in the plaza fountain in front of the Cathedral City Civic Center, across the street from her mother's restaurant. On evenings when Ruthie had to sing, she'd bring Chita there a little earlier. The shallow fountain, with its spongy foam floor, had been designed exactly for that purpose—a safe cool play area for small kids. It was frequented mostly by local children, many Latino, who lived in houses that had survived the diaspora of 1998, when the Cathedral City cultural core had been eradicated by the Cathedral City renewal effort. The barrio had been leveled, with exception to a small neighborhood east toward Date Palm Drive.

Because the evening was so warm, Maria decided rather than wait for Chita at the café, she'd cross the street and surprise her. It was six-thirty. Ruthie's first set started at seven. Maria customarily took Chita home, made her supper and spent the evenings with her. Pablo's return to Cathedral City had been a godsend. He would become the new night manager, which luckily he looked forward to. Pablo was a night person whereas Maria liked to be in bed by ten. Tonight was his first night.

He'd come in at four, humming.

"Why so happy, *chico?*" She sat at her desk, signing checks. In the summer, business fell off. The snowbirds always flew back to Canada and the northwest in May. Luckily the desert was a year round destination.

"Why so blue?" he retorted. She was always so severe, except when Chita was around.

"I'm paying bills, and business is slow. We only did twenty dinners last night."

"But the bar business is bound to pick up," he grinned, "now that I'm here."

"You're pretty sure of yourself." She glanced up from her desk. He was beaming, checking grins. His face looked slightly burnished, especially his chin. He seemed very happy. Very self-satisfied. "Why are you acting this way?"

"It's been a long time, *chica.*" He sank to a folding chair opposite her desk.

"A long time since what?" she asked irritably. Then it occurred to her. "Oh."

"Oh, what?"

"You've met someone."

He smiled.

"Who is he?"

"You're never gonna believe it."

"I know him?" Was he one of her waiters? A customer? Who else did she have time to know?

"Remember the border patrol guy? Who interviewed us after the thing with Bambi and Madonna?"

"It was more than a thing," she chided him quietly.

"I know."

"What about him?" Maria asked. Her mind was racing. It had all started that day. The funeral of Loretta Young. The dead girl in the back of the truck. Sister Agnes' attempt to save her. The pale dead baby. Then Chita nearly drowns. Alex Quintero's crazy idea. Business being slow was nothing compared to that list. "What about him?" Maria asked again, somewhat impatient.

"It's him."

"Who?"

"*Mija,* if you aren't gonna listen, I'm not talking to you." He stood up.

"Okay, okay. Just tell me *chico.* Who?"

"Border Patrol Bob. I ran into him last night in a club in Palm Springs. We had a great night. We're gonna see each other again this weekend. He lives in El Centro. I'm gonna drive down there," Pablo babbled on, caught up in his excitement.

"Your new boyfriend is a Migra *cop?*"

"Well, I told him I didn't like what he does—"

"He's investigating Bambi and Madonna. Did he tell you that?"

"He has to close out the case. It's only procedural."

"Are you fucking *insane?*" She stood up. "They think they have to hire a lawyer. A *Mexicano* dating a Migra spy?"

"No," Pablo held out his hand. "He's a good guy!"

A stream of angry words burst from Maria's lips as she screamed at him in Spanish. The blood drained from her face. Where were his loyalties? It was no different than a Jewish woman dating a German guard in a concentration camp. He arrested hundreds of people every day, just like her and Conchita, and kicked them back across the border with nothing. Because of his privileged background, Pablo couldn't see that Bob was the enemy. And Pablo was sleeping with him.

"*Mi amor,*" he replied softly. Veins in the side of her head were coursing, and she breathed so heavily he thought she might pass out. "Sit down."

"I'm waiting for Chita. I'll go across to the fountain. They're probably over there."

"You've never been this angry. And you direct it at me?"

Disappointment flickered in her eyes. "You don't understand at all."

"It's his job. If it wasn't him, it would be someone else who had to do it. He cares about people. I can feel it."

"You spend one night with him and you know all about him? What kind of man he is?" A tear rolled down her cheek. Angrily she brushed it away. She collected herself, steeling herself in front of him. "I'm going across the street to wait for Chita. If Ruthie brings her here, send a busboy to get me."

"*Mija—*"

But she pushed past him, banging out through the kitchen screen door. She hesitated for a moment as she contemplated the small white wooden cross at the edge of the parking lot. The flowers had stopped coming for Judi and her dead baby. Empty votive holders remained behind, with weathered-looking notes and prayers stuffed inside them. She turned to go around to the front of the building. Pablo stood in the frame of the kitchen door.

Ashamed, he studied her. She felt bad, but didn't stay to talk it over. She rounded the corner of the café and made her way across the busy street to the plaza.

11

Bad Weather

As Maria waited for Ruthie, she contemplated the evening sky, noting thunderheads gathering in the west as they poured into the Coachella Valley basin. Even in August, snow still capped Mt. San Jacinto. Last spring she and Ruthie had taken Chita for her first ride up the Palm Springs Aerial Tramway. Maria wanted her to see snow for the first time. She looked so cute in her tiny coat and boots. She'd been so startled by the coldness of it. Ruthie threw a snowball at Maria, which amused Chita to no end. The three of them played and laughed for over an hour. Ruthie taught Chita how to make a snow angel. How grateful Maria was to God for Ruthie. What a wonderful grandmother she was making for Chita.

As she watched them play in the snow, Maria realized how much she'd missed by not having her mother to watch her grow up. She'd be close to Ruthie's age, maybe a little younger. She'd had red hair too.

Maria and Chita were close. The café took more time than she might have liked, but with Ruthie's help, and Soila's, her schedule was manageable. She had the evenings with Chita, and her mornings. Now with Pablo's help, she wouldn't have to come in at night to close. Even with Soila watching her, she hated the idea of Chita waking up and not finding her home.

She felt bad about Pablito. She'd have to apologize. She wondered if she wasn't a little jealous for his happiness. That he'd finally met someone he liked. He never talked this way the day after he met anybody. She hoped she hadn't spoiled it for him.

She looked at her watch. It was a little after seven o'clock. She scanned the Civic Center parking lot. Ruthie's big new white Volvo station wagon was nowhere to be found. She got rid of the Cadillac when she let her look go more natural. The futuristic Volvo was more practical for Chita, and probably safer.

Where were they? A few cars were turning into the café parking lot across the street, but she didn't see Ruthie's car either. Ruthie wouldn't bring Chita to the fountain this late. The sun had nearly set. She'd go straight to the restaurant to start her set.

The clientele and character of the café was changing. Maria altered the menu to fine Mexican cuisine because so many customers asked for it, and it was a change from Kenny and Nick's old fashioned continental menu. She could still serve simple steak and pork and fish if they wanted it. They made an excellent baked chicken, but now they offered fresh salsa cruda or mole sauce. They also offered green corn tamales.

Instead of the old desert rats, many of her regular customers were now affluent Latinos. They drove north to Cathedral City because of Maria's food. There was a grim fascination about the place because of its history. Formerly a gambling hideout, a gay bar, and now, an upscale Mexican bistro. Nobody drank like they used to. Happy Hour at Nick's had been his mainstay. Due to lack of support, Maria stopped pushing Happy Hour a year ago.

Ruthie, while glad the café was successful, had mentioned again she didn't feel she was connecting with the new clientele. She felt oldfashioned, like a fifties relic when she came out singing Cole Porter to people nursing margaritas and munching on chips. They listened politely, clapped after each song, but no one made requests. This was unheard of in cabaret. She felt like she was intruding on their conversations. Plus, many of them brought their children. It had become a central gathering place for the desert Latino intellectual and political community.

Cathedral City was after all, at the center of all the desert cities. Many of these customers had grown up here, to migrant parents who were undocumented when they arrived. The proximity to St. Louis also helped. St. Louis always had a large Latino congregation. The eradication of the little barrio hadn't changed that.

As Maria left the plaza and crossed the parking lot, she wondered what Kenny would think of everything. Of Chita. The new restaurant. Of her? When he wanted to come to her in Mexico, she had refused him, telling him he had to stay with Nick on some high moral pretext. After the savage attack, Nick needed Kenny more than ever now. Had the attack not happened, and Kenny felt freer to leave, she now admitted to herself that she would have been forced to stop him for another reason.

There it was. Had she really loved him at all, or had she just used him? It had all been so complicated. The three of them, Nick, Kenny and Maria, living in the house up the hill together. How could it ever have worked?

She had arrived with nothing and Kenny had taken her in. Now she had his baby and his business. She was affluent, if not wealthy. How must this look to the others? Not to Pablo or Ruthie, but to Gabriel and Miguel. The other Latinos in Cathedral City. Certainly Carmen's mind had been made up.

Her look had become very anglicized. Some of the other young women who came to her café braided their hair and wore clothing that celebrated their Latino heritage. They spoke almost exclusively in Spanish, eschewing English except when it was necessary to communicate with Anglos.

Chita's Spanish was not as good as her English. Maria wondered if she should speak more Spanish to her. She should tell Soila to do so also. Pablo, the traitor, probably wouldn't cooperate.

A break in the traffic allowed her to trot across Palm Canyon. Just as she reached her parking lot, a huge raindrop fell, striking her squarely on the forehead. It shocked her into reality. She looked up. More drops began to fall, perfuming the air with the smell of rain and the fecund desert floor.

She scanned the cars parked next to her building.

Where was Ruthie?

She'd go inside. Maybe she called.

Her *abuelita* was talking crazy today, but when she did, Chita knew they'd have fun. Now Chita was strapped in her car seat in the back of Ruthie's white station wagon, and they were driving across the desert in the rain. Ruthie had gotten dressed up, more dressed up than usual. Chita had helped her with her makeup. Fascinated with lipstick because her mother rarely wore it, Chita was allowed to smear a dab on her own lips, and she stood on a small wooden step stool Ruthie placed next to her makeup table, for exactly this reason.

"We have to look our prettiest, Chita. We're going for our audition at the studios."

Chita smacked her pink lips, perfectly imitating Ruthie.

Ruthie had been digging in her closet till she found the blue cocktail dress she'd worn the night she opened at the Chi Chi. The Chi Chi was a Palm Springs nightclub, headlining major fifties' and sixties' nightclub acts. The manager was the brother of her best friend, and because his main singer was late, offered to give his kid sister's friend a break. He'd heard her sing at a recent wedding in Santa Monica. Ruthie was elegant looking, surprising him with her voice.

On a weekend visit to Palm Springs, his sister Carolyn reintroduced them. When the main act didn't show, he offered Ruth Harris the mike to get her feet wet. She sang *Tenderly,* just as the booked singer walked in, a jealous middle-aged jazz act from Denver. The woman overtook the microphone without so much as an introduction, thanking Ruthie and killing her chance to sing another song, but the impressed clientele wouldn't stop applauding till Ruthie sang one more.

Her future husband, a local desert tough named Sam Singer, had been sitting in the bar. Sam was good-looking and felt a little dangerous. He told a disappointed Ruthie he had his own nightclub out in Cathedral City and not to worry. She could sing there whenever she wanted.

Looking back, Ruthie regretted never giving Los Angeles a try. She'd come all the way from Cincinnati to see the ocean and stopped a hundred miles short. There were great clubs to sing at in Hollywood, and she'd been told she was pretty enough to be in pictures. Doris Day and Dinah Shore had been her heroes. It was time to give it a try. The incident with Chita in the pool had convinced her of that.

She couldn't admit to Maria that she'd stopped taking her medication, that she'd been asleep when Chita found her way through the unlocked pool gate. That part hadn't been her fault, she was sure of it. The pool man had been careless. That, or the strange brother of Soila's had opened it and lied to protect himself. Luckily, it all ended okay. Chita was safe and sound in her car seat in the back, dozing with her stuffed animal.

Chita was such good company. And cute enough to be in pictures.

My, wasn't it raining hard? Luckily the Swedish car was heavy. They'd never get washed away in this station wagon. It was too heavy. They'd sink like a stone.

Ruthie merged onto the westbound freeway at the Indian Canyon on-ramp. A slow line of cars crushed slowly up the hill toward the Banning pass. Warm rain pounded the desert floor, and Ruthie started thinking she should turn back. Only five minutes up the highway, a wave of sanity overtook Ruthie and she decided to exit at the Highway 62 off-ramp, the road to the high desert cities of Morongo Valley, Joshua Tree and 29 Palms. She'd drive as far north as Dillon Road and head back to Indian Canyon and cut south to Palm Springs. She'd have to wait for her big break till another day.

She heard ringing, like a telephone, only more insistent and shrill. She studied the gauges in her car dash. She couldn't figure out what it was. Chita had awakened. She stared at Ruthie expectantly.

"It sounds like a phone but it can't be. There aren't telephones in cars."

"Cell phone," Chita informed her. "Cell phone."

"What's a cell phone, baby?"

The bell stopped ringing. On the passenger seat next to her, Ruthie's cell phone registered that she'd missed one call. The white station wagon forged its way up the highway, past Dillon Road. DESERT HOT SPRINGS 4 MILES, the sign read. Ruthie forgot that she planned to turn.

The good traction of her tires and the weight of the car, built for Swedish winters, were an easy match for this high desert highway. Ruthie switched on her CD player. Aretha Franklin belched "I Say a Little Prayer for You" into the warm compartment. Her windows had started to steam, but Ruthie managed to see out of the tiny semi-circle of clear windshield just above her dash. She didn't think to turn on her windshield wipers. Chita had fallen asleep. Ruthie drove for another twenty miles, passing through the town of Morongo Valley till finally she stopped at an intersection in Yucca Valley. She noticed a street sign: PIONEERTOWN ROAD. Built in the mid-forties by movie studios as a permanent movie set for westerns, Pioneertown was abandoned when it became too costly to supply water, which had to be trucked in. Desert rats had moved into the old Western buildings of the set.

Ruthie took the turn. Pioneertown to her meant they had to be that much closer to Hollywood.

The wet, winding road climbed through a rocky canyon, awash with rain. It was pitch black and the Volvo was the only car on the road. Rivulets of water washed under her tires. Occasionally the rear end of the car fishtailed slightly. Ruthie kept pushing forward.

Lights from a few cabins in the hills to her left beckoned in the storm. It comforted her when she saw them. The canyon was only twelve miles long, but it seemed they'd been climbing forever. The lights twinkled and disappeared. Then Ruthie came to a sign. 1946— PIONEERTOWN.

"Good, it won't be long now, Chita. Nicky, give her a sip of water. She's thirsty."

In the backseat of the car, Chita continued to doze.

The first establishment Ruthie came to was a rustic wooden bar, Pappy and Harriet's Pioneertown Palace. Even through the pouring rain, Ruthie could smell the odor of barbecued pork ribs. She was hungry.

"How about we all stop for a plate of ribs? Then we'll go to the studio. Nicky? Sam? You hungry?"

The car lurched to a halt against a concrete block.

When a drenched redhead in a blue dress entered the bar carrying a wet and crying toddler in her arms, a grizzled local looked up in surprise from a crossword puzzle. The crew had just been sent home. Who'd be out on a night like this? There were already flash flood warnings in Palm Springs.

"Please," Ruthie cried. "My daughter's very cold."

"Where'd you come from?"

"It's raining like crazy," Ruthie affirmed.

"Let me get towels and blankets for you and the little girl."

"Oh, you work here?" Ruthie queried.

"I got my own cabin up in the hills. I eat supper here, most Sundays. When it rains, I stay put. The owners, they're real nice."

He disappeared through the back door. Moments later he returned. Ruthie and Chita were shivering near the fire.

"You wanna get her out of her wet clothes? They have a dryer out back."

Chita stopped crying, she was so intrigued by the person in the bar. "Are you a lady?" she asked bluntly.

"Chita!" Aghast, Ruthie turned apologetically to their host. Then she saw why Chita asked. The face was haggard, with a thousand tiny lines cracking the leathered surface of her skin. She wore a man's plaid shirt, faded Lee jeans and cowboy boots. Her long hair was steel gray, and tied back with only a string. She had clear blue eyes, which searched Ruthie's face with recognition.

"I know you," the face spoke in wonder. "You're Ruth Harris. My name is Gloria. Gloria Graham."

Ruthie self-consciously touched her wet hair. She must look like a drenched cat. She toweled off Chita's head. "Hold up your arms." Chita obliged, still staring frankly at Gloria. Ruthie dried her off. "Put this around you. Give me your shorts." Covered by the blanket, Chita chastely removed her wet shoes and her shorts.

"I have a robe you can borrow. Or a clean shirt and a pair of pants. I don't think we should dry your dress. It's in perfect condition. Vintage, eh?"

"No, it's brand new. I bought it at Desmond's." Desmond's was a Palm Springs dress shop. Ruthie had worked there, thirty years ago.

"Let me find you something to wear." Gloria disappeared again through the swinging door. She came back with a simple white blouse and a pair of khakis. "These should fit. You're the same size as my friend Jeanne. You can change back there if you like."

"You're being very kind. Isn't she, Chita?"

"Cocoa," Chita suggested hopefully.

Ruthie shook her head but Gloria smiled.

"I can fix her up, straightaway. Would you like something, Ruth? A brandy? An Irish coffee? You won't be driving for hours. It might warm you up."

"I haven't had an Irish Coffee since Sam and I went to San Francisco last spring."

"Sam Singer," Gloria shook her head. "How is he?"

"Haven't you heard, Gloria?"

"I don't follow much local news," Gloria apologized. "I'm afraid I'm a bit of a hermit."

"Sam and I were married last year."

Gloria studied Chita and smiled. Chita looked close to four years old. "Well I'm glad he made an honest woman of you."

"Oh, Chita isn't Sam's. She's Nick's."

"Daddy in the pool."

"No," Ruthie laughed. "Daddy isn't in the pool."

"You'd better change out of those wet things," Gloria smiled. Outside, the rain really started coming down.

12

Gloria

"The cops are looking for your boyfriend's son."

"Whaaa?" Ruby looked up from her plate of refried beans and cheese. "What'd he do now?"

Her friend, Monique, was pulling off her raincoat. She'd just come back from the corner to buy tampons.

"You know Maria Castillo? The owner of the Cathedral City Café?"

"She's a snotty bitch."

"The cops are crawling all over her place. Her little girl is missing."

"What's Alex got to do with it?"

"I dunno. You tell me."

Ruby stood up and trudged to the front door of the restaurant and surveyed the raining street. Monique was right. Three Cathedral City police cars were blocking the parking lot to Maria's café.

"They had this thing," Ruby murmured.

"What thing?" Monique pressed her.

"I dunno. I heard something about it. It was bad. I don't let Alex in my house. He's loco, that one."

"Shouldn't you call his dad?"

"If they're looking for him, they already have. Besides, Thomas won't know where he is. He's so out of it, he doesn't even know where I am. Her kid's missing?"

"Yeah. Isn't that sad?"

"He probably took her to Mexico."

*   *   *

It was after eleven P.M. and Ruthie and Chita were still missing. Maria and Pablo didn't know if they should wait at the café, at her house or Ruthie's house. The slick streets were nearly impassable. A flash flood warning had been issued for the Whitewater River. Torrents of water now thundered down the wash, slicing the desert cities in half.

When Chita and Ruthie hadn't appeared by seven-thirty, Maria asked Pablo to drive to Palm Springs to see if they were home and not answering the telephone. Pablo obliged, calling from his Jeep twenty minutes later. There was no sign of them. The lights were off. Using Maria's key he searched the house. He was careful not to touch anything more than he had to.

Maria called Soila. "Have you heard from Ruthie? She and Chita were due here an hour ago. I haven't heard from them. Can you check my house while I wait here?"

Soila called ten minutes later. "No sign. Do you want me to come to the café?"

"Can you locate your brother?"

Soila fell silent.

"This is Chita we're talking about!" Maria railed.

"I'll call my dad."

Soila called back in five minutes.

"He hasn't heard from him. We don't have his number in Indio. He may not even have a telephone."

"What about his friends? Who might know where he is?"

"I don't think he's involved."

"Then save him some trouble and find him. Get him over here. I'm calling the police." And Maria hung up on her.

Before Pablo left Ruthie's he decided to call Border Patrol Bob. He figured the Cathedral City police would already alert the border patrol, but he wanted Bob to know it involved people he loved. Bob was very businesslike on the phone. Pablo could picture him in his uniform, sitting at a desk, surrounded by serious fellow investigators. Only twenty-four hours earlier, Pablo and Bob were fucking under the open desert sky.

Bob offered to go personally to the United States Border Inspection Station to alert them that a potential kidnapping had taken place. He took a brief description of Ruthie, Chita and Alex Quintero.

"This is very common," Bob warned Pablo. "It happens a lot."

"Do you recover the stolen kids?"

"Not very often, but we have a head start. The suspect perpetrator. He dangerous?"

"Very," Pablo whispered. "Please find them. Bob?"

"Yes?"

Pablo hesitated. Whatever he wanted to say was inappropriate. Not official business.

"Yes?" Bob repeated himself.

Pablo stared at the receiver of Ruthie's telephone.

"Call us at the restaurant if you find anything."

Maria was under fierce interrogation at a table near the window when he arrived. A trembling Soila observed her from her vantage point in the bar. Once again Maria's café was closed for police activity. It didn't really matter. No sane person would be driving in this weather. Maria told the officers every suspicion she could muster about Ruthie and Chita's whereabouts. Maybe they'd been cut off by rising floodwaters. Maybe Alex Quintero had kidnapped them. She didn't mention that Ruthie had flipped out. And why, they would wonder, might she suspect that? If she was worried, why did she allow Ruthie to baby-sit her little girl?

A guilty Maria didn't have a good answer for that.

"And what about the mental state of Mrs. Singer?"

"She's the baby's grandmother. She loves her."

"But do you think she might have lapses in judgment?"

"It can't be her. It's him. He's kidnapped them!" The horror overwhelmed her.

"What about the father of your little girl?"

"I haven't spoken with him for years."

The detective paused. "Are you at odds with him?"

"No," she stammered. "Not at all. He agreed, at my request, that I would raise my daughter on my own."

"Were you on close terms?"

"Yes. But not in that way. We were friends," Maria struggled to explain. "Look, please don't divert your attention away from finding Ruthie or Alex Quintero. I'm certain Kenny has nothing to do with my daughter's disappearance."

"I need his name and his last known address."

Maria reluctantly gave him Kenny's full name. "I have no idea where he is. He left California before my daughter was born. He contacted me in Mexico shortly after her birth."

"And?"

"He wanted to help and I refused him. I asked him to stay away."

"Were you afraid of him?"

"You're wasting time!" Maria pleaded. "Look, he was involved with someone else. I just wanted a baby. I wasn't looking for a husband!"

They studied her suspiciously. Pablo, overhearing, stepped forward.

"He was gay. They were friends. It was a one-time thing. He's a good guy."

The detective relaxed. "His name is on her birth certificate. He deserves to be notified. "

"I couldn't begin to guess where he might be . . ." she shook her head.

On top of everything, now this. Maria could imagine a police car pulling up in front of Kenny's house, a belligerent officer demanding to know the whereabouts of Conchita, if he had anything to do with her disappearance. He would think Maria was accusing him! How could she possibly betray him more than she already had? Maria shuddered with grief. Pablo placed his arm around her.

"I know what you're thinking," Pablo whispered to her, kissing the side of her head. "He'd understand. Besides, they'll find Chita before they find him. She's too ornery."

It would rain heavily for twenty-four hours. The power went off around midnight. Much of Cathedral City and Palm Springs lay in watery darkness. Pablo and Soila lit candles, as Maria sat forlornly in the dark booth by the window. Where had her faith gone? Maria wondered. It had been over a year since she'd been to Mass. Nobody cared for the new priest. He seemed arrogant and intractable. She missed Father Gene.

Please, she whispered, but her heart felt so cold with dread she couldn't formulate the necessary words to pray. The investigating officer called. They searched Ruthie's house. Unused bottles of lithium and Prozac were found in her medicine cabinet.

"Did you know Mrs. Singer was bipolar?"

"She drives when she goes off her pills." The acknowledgment jumped from Maria's lips.

"Drives?"

"Her husband once told me when she gets really depressed, that she relives a traumatic event in her life."

"What event?"

"She had an abortion in Mexicali when she was very young. She nearly died. She could no longer have children. It made her very sad."

"Where would she drive?"

"It varied. He said she went looking for her lost baby."

"We already have a description of her car. If she's on a main highway, they'll see her."

"She prefers side roads."

"How would you know?"

And Maria recounted how they first met.

"I didn't know until later why she was driving in such a remote location," Maria told the officers. "Out in the middle of the desert, on such a hot, lonely day. She was out looking for her lost child."

"Do you think that's what she's doing now?"

"Perhaps," Maria whispered.

"Have you ever known her to be violent? Suicidal?"

"Never."

"Is the baby sleeping?" Ruthie had successfully managed to navigate Highway 62, which rapidly descended in altitude from four thousand feet above sea level to zero within ten miles. "Nicky? Sam? Is the baby sleeping?"

No answer, but she could see Chita's car seat in the dark backseat. They all must be napping. She was exhausted herself.

Gloria had been fun. A wonderful hostess. The baby had been so intrigued with her.

"Smart baby," Ruthie affirmed merrily. "Nothing gets by you!"

Ruthie remembered Gloria after all. She'd been a true fan, among many gay men and women who frequented Sam's in the last year before they got married. Gloria wore beautifully tailored gabardine suits, smoked thin cigars and drank bourbon and water with Nick at the bar.

She'd heard about Nick, and the incident in the alley, and she was sorry to hear that Sam had died.

"Gloria was sad to hear," Ruthie called to the rear of the car. "She says it's part of the reason she's become a hermit. She remembered us, Nicky. She remembered those days like they were yesterday. I'd like to be a hermit someday. She doesn't get lonely, she says. She fills up her days, puttering around. My, look at all this rain."

When she looked down at her feet she was amazed to find them immersed in several inches of water. Rain was gushing from up under the heavy car.

"Chita?" Ruthie spoke soothingly to her cherished granddaughter. "Lift your legs when the water gets to you. Just like in the pool, okay honey? I love you baby. I love you so."

Gloria's neighbors kept an eye on her. In Pioneertown, that's how neighbors were. At eighty-one, Gloria could feed and bathe herself. She could walk from her tiny cabin to the local general store and buy TV dinners or cans of spaghetti. She squeaked by on Social Security.

As her memory continued to fail her, she withdrew more and more each day. She didn't like to be engaged in conversation. Compassionately, they let her do her business as long as she wasn't a danger to herself.

Her routine was predictable. Every Friday she ambled the half mile from her front porch down the hill to the center of Pioneertown. From a distance she favored Willie Nelson. She'd check her post office box which had been empty for years. The only mail she ever got was her Social Security check. Several years ago the local post mistress arranged for it to be direct deposited to Gloria's checking account. Her groceries and rent were deducted automatically. Her landlord paid her utilities. She didn't have a phone.

Ruthie's car was found on a sparkling summer morning, partially buried by mud and debris in a flooded Cathedral City wash. An officer arrived at Maria's café, only a half a mile away and knocked politely on the door to the lounge.

Inside, Pablo and Maria lay dozing in each other's arms. Soila was asleep on the opposite side of the booth. They heard knocking, but Pablo thought he imagined it.

They all woke up at the same instant.

"There's a cop at the door," Pablo murmured.

"Are they with him?" Soila asked pleadingly.

Maria sat up, backing as far against the corner of the booth as she could wedge herself. As Pablo padded like a cat to open the door, she began to quiver. Soila noticed and moved into the booth next to her.

Soila began to pray her rosary. Maria's thick hair fell across her eyes. She looked wild, like a feral animal when Pablo returned. The officer remained at his post at the front door. Maria could see him study the front of the building. He held up his hands and placed them firmly against the wall as if anticipating that he might be the only force which could keep it standing.

Pablo stood gravely in the center of the room, his face flooding with tears.

"Ruthie's car has been recovered in the wash. They found her body a mile away."

"Chita?" Soila queried.

"They haven't found her yet. But her car seat was found near Ruthie."

"Alex?"

"They picked him up in Thermal. He has an alibi."

"What?" Maria demanded. "Those crazy Pentecostals?"

"No. He's been in jail for the last week." Pablo moved toward her, to comfort her. "They're sending out dogs."

"Rescue dogs," Soila offered sweetly. "Good."

"No, *mija*. These dogs are trained to find . . . Well . . ." His voice trailed away.

"Dead bodies. Cadaver dogs." Maria finished his sentence.

Outside, the stucco walls seemed to reverberate, causing the police officer to quickly step back from the building. He hated this part of his job.

The tension was so high; the sadness so great. The walls of a mother's heart were breaking.

PART TWO

The Apparitions

13

Nevada Gratis

Last night Kenny was dreaming about making love with her again. Nick could tell. His face changed when he slept. He could see the longing in the lines drawing out from the creases in Kenny's forehead, the occasional quivering of his chin. She appeared in ghostly sketches Nick would find, hidden under the clutter of colored fabrics, carving tools and unfinished whittled images in wood, placed haphazardly on shelves above Kenny's workbench.

Nick must have reached for the telephone a hundred times. He was overwhelmed with the urge to call Ruthie. He wondered why he was thinking so much about her. The only thing that stopped him was his deal with Kenny. The call would have appeared on the phone bill. He would have been caught.

The tacit deal was as follows. If Nick started calling Ruthie, or anybody else in Palm Springs, then Kenny might feel entitled to call Maria, although Ruthie hadn't barred anyone from calling her. They left California to leave California behind. Why else had they sacrificed so much? It would only lead to more heartache. Nick talked himself out of it. Besides, if Nick were to make the call at all, it would have to be from a pay phone.

Nick was listening to his *Funny Lady* recording of Barbra Streisand singing Kander and Ebb's, *Isn't This Better?* Kenny wouldn't be home for hours.

Nick spent most nights in their tiny Reno apartment, candles burning, game shows blaring, or, if he was feeling sentimental, listening to his favorite CDs, which he ordered from his secret golden oldies account. Secret, because Kenny would worry about the money. Kenny always worried about money. Not Nick. Nick had his secret about money too.

Nick gazed at the digital clock. 9:38.00 Another day shot. Kenny was frying hamburgers at a local truck stop on Interstate 80. He didn't get off till midnight.

As for Nick, he hadn't gotten off with Kenny for a year. "It ain't better," Nick snarled up at the ceiling. "Not by a long shot." He pounded his pillow and tried to fall back asleep.

Maria was everywhere in the apartment. In his artwork, his waking thoughts, his dreams. It was an issue they silently agreed never to visit. Not that Nick wouldn't hear him out. Kenny's anxiety about the child—was she safe? Did she look like Kenny or more like Maria? Kenny only knew she was a girl, now over four years old. And that her eyes were blue like his. At least they were when she was born.

Maria had written him. In the same letter where she pleaded with him to stay away. To stay with Nick who needed him more than she did. She and the baby were fine, well-cared for, living with Pablo's family in Cuernavaca, Mexico, high in the mountains above Mexico City. She named the baby, without asking Kenny, Conchita-Inez, after her grandmother, who Kenny had known, and Inez—Kenny's longtime cantankerous neighbor; friend of Pablo; mother of Soila. Inez had once been Nick and Kenny's maid, in a time and place, a million miles, a million years away from now.

Nick's recovery had been miraculous. His doctors thought, in addition to the severe trauma to his face—a shattered jaw, broken cheekbones, teeth imbedded in the back of his throat—that Nick had most likely suffered severe brain hemorrhaging. For a critical forty-eight hours in ICU, Kenny had been told to prepare for the worst, and had even been advised by one nurse to consider removing life support. Kenny had refused. Five ribs were broken, his kneecap shattered. The bone in his forearm had been snapped in two.

You can't leave him, she'd written. *I could never trust you if you did.* He was in her prayers. Slowly Nick began to recover.

He blamed Nick now, Nick could feel it. The first year was exciting. Driving away together had been exciting, that first night, escaping the clutches of the California border. The Nevada state line.

Their lowly belongings spilling out onto the freeway. Kenny at first trying to salvage what he could of their old life, not for himself, certainly. He wasn't sentimental about a single thing. He was doing it for Nick. Just like Kenny did everything. For Nick.

And Nick had surprised him by climbing up on the other side of the truck and tossing it all back onto the desert floor again. If Kenny didn't need it, neither did he. He could start fresh, if that meant they were starting fresh together. And for the hours and days and months that passed, that's how it felt. They had eight hundred bucks in slot machine winnings to build a new life. They had the money, their old truck and each other. They had history. They'd survived.

They'd bypassed Las Vegas—Kenny was afraid Nick would squander their winnings. Instead they flipped a coin and veered northwest on Highway 95, through Indian Springs, past Amargosa Valley and finally spent several days in a cheap motel in Scotty's Junction. Kenny even applied for a job as a fry cook in the motel/casino all-night coffee shop. They turned him down because of Nick. Nick's fault again. The manager was a born-again Christian, and she thought something was 'funny' about the both of them. Nick had fading scars all over his face. He looked like rough trade. She told them over bifocals and a red-beaked nose that she didn't need any of that.

So they checked out, drove on. A little less lighthearted. Their optimism checked, just a tiny bit. One thing was plain. Wherever they went, Nick would be there too. No longer a drunk, but still with the attitude. The flipped-up lapels. The tapered slacks. The red espadrilles, à la seventies' *After Dark* photographer Kenn Duncan, Nick's photographer idol. The red shoes were always a dead giveaway and he refused to ever give them up. Then, too, had been the Blackgama mink ads Nick had had made up, his image replacing Angela Lansbury—*What becomes a legend the most?*

Some legend. Look where he was now.

Ruthie's little suitcase was empty, sitting on the top shelf of the tiny bedroom closet they shared. The secret contents had been dumped into a Merrill Lynch account in Nick's name only, with Kenny as his beneficiary. He had the broker hold the statements for pickup. He didn't want any paperwork coming to the house.

The subject of Ruthie's money would always be a tricky one. Recently Nick was fighting the urge to tell Kenny about it, but he was equally fighting the urge to have a drink. Had he continued to attend AA after he left Betty Ford, he would have learned, or least been warned, that an alcoholic's secrets can get him drunk.

What would be the harm in sitting Kenny down and admitting that the day they drove away from Cathedral City, Ruthie, who'd been terribly worried about the both of them, had handed Nick a suitcase filled with stacks of tens, twenties, fifties and hundreds—over a hundred thousand dollars—money that she had ferreted away from Sam's rent cash, saying only that the contents contained memorabilia from Sam to remember him by?

Kenny hadn't even been interested in the little case, not asking about it once. If he opened it and found it empty, he probably assumed that Nick had disposed of whatever Ruthie wanted them to have because it wasn't anything of major importance. For anything to be interesting to Nick, it had to have glitter, glamour or resale value.

Nick, the pack rat, thought he'd eschewed those habits on that lonely California highway, along with his love for vodka. The tiny, furnished, one-bedroom apartment was once again crammed with secondhand belongings. For entertainment, Nick hobbled on his cane through Reno thrift stores and pawn shops, only a half a block from their apartment. Reno had a great Sunday swap meet on the south side of the town. Everybody knew Nick, amazing Kenny. Some remembered him from Laguna, some from Nick's. Some from the weekend before. Nick was like them. Off the grid. Perfect for Reno. He was easy to spot. Who else would wear red espadrilles in the dead of winter?

"It isn't that I'm ashamed we're gay," Kenny complained. "I get upset because it looks like you have no sense!"

And Nick would refuse to change them. He was still painfully thin. Kenny had gained a little weight, still well-distributed. He worked hard, often twelve-hour shifts. He did more grunt work than he'd had to in his own kitchen. Nightly he carried pails of dirty grease to the barrels out back by the dumpsters. He personally scrubbed out the refrigerated walk-ins because he knew they were the first place the health inspectors started grading down a restaurant.

They'd allowed themselves one luxury—a premium cable package. Nick had to have something to do when Kenny was working. They bought a secondhand widescreen TV with Kenny's first check. The TV proved to be good cognitive therapy. Nick had suffered head trauma from the assault in the alley, which had permanently affected his short-term memory. He might forget a question, or remark, and since his principal contact was Kenny, a rhythm had developed between them. The first year conversations had been laden with thousands of "I'm sorry, honey's" and Kenny would gently repeat what he'd said, or had heard on the television.

And although he didn't really want to admit it, Nick thought his condition had improved, if not completely, nearly all the way. He was addicted to game shows, his great passion, and found himself remembering the questions on *Jeopardy* and *Wheel of Fortune* and answering them correctly. The shows had actually been therapeutic. If Nick hadn't gone into the restaurant business, he would have loved to have been a game show host. Now he studied himself in the mirrored wall behind the dinette. No chance now. Not with his broken face. Not at his age.

The scarring in his face had muted—luckily Eisenhower Memorial had a good trauma plastic surgeon, Dr. Tim Hansen—because apparently no one had much hope for Nicky at all. It was a miracle he'd survived. He didn't remember anything about the assault. With Sam dead, there were no other witnesses, though the cops assumed at least one of the occupants living behind the barricade fences lining the alley probably saw everything.

When Kenny had returned, Soila Quintero was cradling Nick in her arms, her lap soaked with his blood. Old Sam Singer lay in a heap nearby. Soila had always loved Nicky. An ardent schoolgirl crush. Nicky, Soila knew, was one person who never saw her birthmark at all. Kenny would never tell Nick what he looked like. Fortunately, he had no memory of it whatsoever.

If it hadn't happened, Nick now reflected, they probably wouldn't be together at all. Kenny might have gone down to Mexico, invited or not. Nick would have taken his share of the proceeds from Sam's allotment for the business and moved back to Laguna.

Nick never felt sorry for himself, not after he got sober and not after the assault. They assumed it was probably the same kids who'd been marauding the alley all along. Ralph Zola, the Cathedral City renewal attorney, had been perfunctorily interviewed. The city wanted to put the whole incident behind them. If Zola was implicated, the entire renewal would be called into question. There was no public support to pursue it. With Sam Singer dead, the last obstacle had been removed. Only he would have been strong enough to keep the investigation alive.

His wife was incapacitated. So was Nick. Kenny could have fought for the truth. But he was more broken than the rest of them.

So now Nick was left to wonder. Who did this to him and why? This question, along with the question about admitting they had more money than Kenny could have dreamed of, enough to start a new business, to live in a decent place; and lastly that nasty compulsion to start drinking. Contemplating all these things night after night, waiting for Kenny to come home, for the click of his key in the lock—the soft turning of the doorknob—enough warning for Nick to pretend he was asleep. For all this, for all his desire to remain married to Kenny, Nick found himself bored by him.

Living with Kenny—who came home smelling of grease, onions and cigarettes, without the distraction of his bar crowd—was simply not enough. This possibility had never occurred to Nick.

He had to find courage to go out into the world again. He decided to call the automated teller at Merrill Lynch. He punched in his security code. The value of his money market was close to three hundred thousand dollars. Tech stocks had been good for him. And Nick, even in his diminished capacity, had been smart enough to know when to get out.

He was hankering to start a business, maybe buy a small restaurant with a liquor license. Nothing big, enough for the two of them, with one waiter, a busboy and an honest bartender to free Nick up to do what he did best. Work the room. Make friends of his regulars. Sing a song or two.

He'd even picked out a possible location. Only three blocks over. He could walk. They wouldn't need a second car. It was a rundown neighborhood, but then, so was Cathedral City. There were ten leather booths, in great condition. A mural of old downtown Reno with a backdrop of the Sierra Nevada mountain range ran the length of the bar—only slightly in need of repair, which Kenny could fix with his eyes closed.

Scraping several inches of old paint from the corner of the front window revealed beveled stained glass, decorated with playing cards, authentic to the Victorian period, which the broker placed to be the age of the building. The mildewed, moth-bitten carpet revealed beautiful, planked wooden floors. The cracking old leather bar would probably have to be reupholstered. Nick fantasized about buying one, secondhand, from the same period. He'd ask one of his cronies at the swap meet.

Dreaming again. Kenny was dreaming of Maria. Nick was just dreaming. How wonderful it felt! An idea taking hold, floating around the top of his brain, just like the good old days. This was his gift, and since that bloody night in the alley behind Nick's, cradled in the arms of that sweet little Soila Quintero, he'd felt her love for him, heard her prayers.

Whereas Kenny was saved from drowning in the river after Maria's grandmother begged God to spare him, God, Nick was certain, had heard the prayers of Soila Quintero. Nick mused on this, as memory rushed back to him. Before now, he remembered nothing about his attackers.

When Nick stepped into the alley and stood fumbling to lock the door, he turned around to find a beautiful young girl smiling at him.

"Hello," she grinned.

"Hello, young lady! It's a lovely night, isn't it?"

Behind her a white Blazer rolled into view. Two young men hopped stealthily to the ground and formed a semicircle behind her. One resembled the girl. Had the same smile. The other was older. Had a bat.

Nick took a deep breath. He could see them as distinctly as his ten fingers. Oh, this was so big, so important. He'd need someone to concur. Sam was dead. He'd seen them. Kenny came after they were gone.

In ICU, Nick couldn't tell the police anything. Privately, he was grateful. Who'd want to relive such hatred? Soila had been there, but denied seeing them. Was she telling the truth, he wondered? Had she really come from her gate, after they'd taken off? Or had she witnessed the entire, horrible event?

Soila had been the eyes and ears of the alley. How could she not have heard something, peeking through a hole in her fence to see what was going on? Maybe hearing Sam threatening to shoot forced her to flee to the safety of her house. Sam himself hadn't been attacked. He'd died from a heart attack, probably in defense of Nick. But Nick's eyes had fluttered open, only momentarily. He could see Soila's face, smiling at him kindly. He remembered thinking what a pity her birthmark was. He knew how much it humiliated her.

Nick picked up the telephone. He'd once made a promise to himself. Drunken, yes, but still worthwhile. He dialed information for Palm Springs, California. He asked for the telephone number of Dr. Tim Hansen.

Then, without talking to Kenny, Nick opened escrow on the bar that afternoon.

Kenny, also, was fighting his urge to make a call, and Ruthie was top on his list of ideas too. He figured his crew had disbursed, moved on. Gabriel and Miguel wanted to go back to Mexico. Carmen probably had resituated. Tonight, as he stood sweating over the grill, he'd steal glances at his fellow crew members. Instead of their boss, he was now their coworker. He knew he was considered something of an oddball here. They probably even thought he was a little slow. He didn't gossip with them. Didn't talk about his nights, days or weekends off. They didn't know if he had a wife. Or if he was gay. They didn't know where he came from.

Early on, when he'd made the modest suggestion about placing a lighted votive candle in the kitchen on top of the walk-in, the Latino crew, (he thought they'd get it) reacted like he was loco. These weren't the same sweet men and women he was used to working with. Though all of them, as far as he could tell, were native to Mexico, they were all U.S. citizens and completely anglicized. This, too, included a complete and total rejection of their old superstitions and religious mores.

He'd been working as a fry cook at the Second Chance now for over two years. They always promoted younger workers over him, even though he had more experience, always showed up on time and never griped about working overtime. He guessed he was a threat to the manager, Margie, who didn't want him angling for her job. Kenny laughed. He never wanted to supervise any living thing again in his life. And as long as he did his job, nobody ever told him what to do.

Nick was safely stashed in the Donner Apartments, an eighteen-unit building built in the sixties and named in honor of Donner Pass. Only forty miles west into the Sierra Nevada Mountains, the Donner Party, stranded in a gold rush blizzard, resorted to cannibalism to survive.

Kenny knew he and Nick would chew each other up too, if they continued on as they had in Cathedral City. He had achieved what he set out to do. Kenny had punished them. Brought them into another desert, assumed he heard God talking to him, laying down several ground rules. First and foremost, Nick would not be allowed to fuck them up again financially. In order to keep him in check, Kenny would earn the money and pay the bills. Nick could have his small allowance for spending money and groceries. He could lay around and watch television night and day for all Kenny cared. Kenny just didn't want to be subjected to more wild imaginings—crazy, alcoholic whims, though of course Nick didn't drink anymore. If he wanted to, he didn't say anything.

Yes, Kenny saw to it they both were punished for their sins, but what good was it doing either of them? Kenny's faith had faded fast when they moved out of California. His belief system had more to do with Father Gene's Cathedral City. He missed Father Gene too. He wondered how he was.

Tonight they were busy, and time passed quickly. One day blended into the next. More often than not, Nick would be fast asleep when he got home. Those were the times he was most tempted to pick up the phone and call. But Kenny was beyond kidding himself. Although he loved Ruthie, he knew he wouldn't be really calling her. He'd be using her to hear about Maria. And Conchita.

What kind of man abandoned his own child? Why had he listened to her? He fell to thinking about this more and more. He had rights, but realistically, what could he have done under the circumstances? Nick in the shape he was in and with no money? At least he'd been assured they were okay—in better circumstances any of them might have imagined. Still, had she wanted him to, he would have come. She was too smart for that. What did he really have to offer her? In fantasy, Kenny reordered fate.

Every night, Maria came to him in his dreams, as he floated naked on the raft in the pool.

The pool glowing with candlelight. All the candles lit and floating on the warm blue surface of the water.

Kenny not moving when she approaches the water—pretending to be sleeping. Palm trees shimmer in the distance, silhouetted against the backdrop of the moonlit desert.

She hesitates at the water's edge, removing her robe and diving under the surface of the water. When she breaks the surface, many of the floating candles pitch, hissing angrily but righting themselves and bursting up with self-righteous flame. She surveys the raft which she sees overturned. Has she thrown him into the water?

Frantically she searches the surface of the pool, and not finding him, dives deep underwater. He waits for her, dancing on the pool floor. She swims to him and together they burst to the surface. They huddle together along the wall of the pool, heads barely above the surface. Because she is slightly shorter than he, Kenny grasps her hands and guides her up to the tops of his feet so her chin can clear the lapping blue water.

To steady her stance he supports her at the small of her back. Her waist is tiny as he presses her against him, her breasts swelling up against his chest. With his other hand he smoothes her hair back, cupping her jaw in the palm of his hand. They study each other solemnly. For the first time since they met, neither look away.

Kenny teases her cheek with his lips, grazing over it till he finds the corner of her mouth, always so beautiful. Brushing his lips over hers, lightly, barely touching them, over and over till he heard her sigh, Kenny kisses her passionately.

He pulls her along the wall to the shallow end of the pool, in a dark corner with underwater steps leading up to the terrace. He sits, legs splayed open on the middle step, and pulls Maria inside the circle of his body. There he gently examines her, kissing her neck and her shoulders. Fearful of her resistance and his growing excitement, he begins to gently test her limits. He kisses the globe of her breast, gently at first, but when her head falls back, he presses his face into them, greedily tasting her nipples.

Maria, too, begins to test Kenny, kissing his neck, tracing her tongue up to the lobe of his ear. He reacts, groaning deeply. She extends her reach around his sturdy back. His lateral muscles expand and tighten. Maria always loved Kenny's back. She runs her hands down to his waist, lightly tracing the outer cleft of his buttocks with her fingers.

"Kenny," she whispers.

And he lifts her up out of the pool and they make love.

Tonight when Kenny climbed the stairs, he figured it would be just another night. He'd make dinner and they'd watch TV. Luckily the little apartment had a fireplace. Nick would light candles. He'd always smile up from the sofa, genuinely pleased to see Kenny.

When Kenny came in, he was surprised to find the lamps ablaze, with Nick fully dressed, staring at the telephone, which sat on the coffee table opposite him.

When Kenny saw this, he surprised Nick with the following acknowledgment:

"I want to call, too," and they felt like lovers again.

They decided to wait, to make it an event. First they made love, after such a long estrangement. The lovemaking was passionate, wild, because they were about to embark on a critical, illicit course. They were flirting with the past, in a manner that could disrupt their carefully conceived, dogmatically executed, self-imposed exile. With one call, they were putting their civil, humorless, joyless lives on the line. They were whistling at memory. They showered together. Nick trimmed Kenny's hair. They sat scrubbed and clean and stared at the telephone.

"You do it."

"No, you do it."

"Okay," Nick nodded. "I will."

They shared a long, vulnerable, important kiss. Nick started dialing. Ruthie's line began to ring. Kenny watched in grinning anticipation.

14

A New Face on Everything

"Hello. Is Soila Quintero available please?"

The call came late one afternoon from a nurse. Ruby answered, jumping for the cordless telephone, no doubt, Soila suspected, because she had a boyfriend on the side. She always answered all syrupy and sweet. Then she'd giggle, receiver tucked under her double chin, and Ruby would peruse the open refrigerator for leftovers.

Today when she answered, Ruby scowled. "For you. Don't tie up the line!"

Glaring at Soila, Ruby tossed her the phone. Soila, caught unawares, allowed it to bounce off her body and clatter to the carpeted floor.

"It's for you, you clumsy bitch!"

Unless it was Maria or Father Scolia, Soila never got phone calls. She stared stupidly at the bent antenna of the gray receiver.

"Who is it?"

"Pick it up!" Ruby railed.

Soila knelt gracefully and retrieved it. "Hello?"

"Is this Soila Quintero?"

"Yes."

"I'm a nurse for Dr. Tim Hansen. I'm calling to schedule an appointment for you . . ."

Soila stared stupidly into the receiver. It was smudged with Ruby's hot pink lipstick, like a dirty glass in a restaurant.

"Hello?"

"I don't need a doctor. I didn't call you."

"No, someone else is arranging for the consultation. Let's see, I have a ten o'clock next Wednesday. Would that be convenient?"

"Who's arranging for this consultation? What kind of doctor is he?"

"He's a renowned plastic surgeon."

It was someone playing a cruel joke on her. She moved to hang up.

"Hey! Miss?" The woman was very good. She actually sounded angry at Soila. Probably some waitress friend where Ruby worked.

"Who is this?" Soila whimpered. "I think you're being very mean." She glanced up. Ruby's skeptical, curious reaction changed her mind. She apparently didn't know anything about it.

"I'm just following orders," the nurse insisted. "The session is free of charge. The doctor will explain when you come in. Is next Wednesday at ten o'clock okay?"

"Yes."

"Do you know where we're located?"

"No."

"We're in Palm Springs at the medical offices of the Desert Medical Center on Indian Canyon. Suite 405."

"I don't have insurance."

"You won't need it here anyway." And the nurse hung up on her.

Ruby studied Soila suspiciously. "What was that about?'

Soila shrugged. It certainly was mysterious. Who would make an appointment with a plastic surgeon for Soila? And why? Soila shrugged.

"She had the wrong Soila Quintero."

"So do I," Ruby stated hatefully. "I'll never have a baby with your father. It might come out as ugly as you."

Soila surveyed herself in the mirror over the fireplace. There were days when her birthmark looked angrier than others. Ruby sank into her leatherette Barcalounger and reached for the TV remote. It was one o'clock, and time for her stories.

"Thomas? You feeling okay?" Thomas' boss, Andy, was a very caring man. Andy had discovered Thomas while visiting Mexico. He was touring Mexican antique districts. When a dealer nearly passed off a new armoire as a hundred-year-old antique, Andy sneaked around the back of the shop only to find Thomas Quintero, with ten identical new armoires lined up, hand-finishing each one to look authentically old, just like the piece Andy had nearly purchased in the front of the showroom.

Thomas was an artist. Andy, who spoke fluent Spanish, asked to meet with him after he got off work. Thomas's normal workday began at six A.M. and didn't finish until nine that evening. They met for *cervezas*. Within an hour, Andy offered Thomas a job at his store, Arte de Sonora, in the small California community of Cathedral City. He would sponsor Thomas and his family for green cards. The cost of living was reasonable and Thomas would make a truly fair living wage. He would have accepted for far less than what Andy had offered. He went home to discuss it with his family.

Inez Quintero was not a pretty or affectionate wife. When they met he'd been hired to refinish some fine antiques left to the family by an old maid aunt when she died. Thomas was impressed by the gracious home. His own family had been very poor. Whereas Thomas was very handsome and already had many girlfriends, Captain Sanchez' daughter, though plain, had been quietly sweet and adoring. She'd make a good match, but was far too young.

Thomas set out to seduce her. A devout Inez attended Mass twice a day. Thomas began to accompany her, whispering to her with sweet flattery into the church choir loft. There, in a quiet struggle among the missals, the mourning doves cooing in the polished eves of the cathedral roof, Thomas prevailed. Inez Quintero lost her most precious gift, all in view of the magnificent crucifix, looming over the sanctuary of her childhood church. She would forever associate sexual intercourse with the hurting disappointment she saw in the eyes of the Son of God, hanging in agony on that cross.

Thomas expected threats when her pregnancy was revealed. He even planned for them. They had been forced to marry when she was very young, only fifteen, and pregnant with their first son, Alexio. Inez' father, Captain Sanchez, was the local police captain. Inez his only daughter. He and her six brothers had offered Thomas two choices. He could marry her, or be dragged out of town by a mule and shot.

What he hadn't anticipated was Captain Sanchez' refusal to allow Thomas to move from his poor house in with them. Because Inez had disgraced her father, she would be obliged to move in with Thomas' family.

* * *

So Inez, who grew up with servants, in a comfortable, lovely home, was forced, at fifteen and pregnant, to relocate into her mother-in-law's squalid little house in a barrio in the hills overlooking the town. They were never invited to her father's house except for Christmas Eve dinner. At midnight Mass, Thomas and Inez were relegated to the choir loft. Their marriage was cold and loveless. Thomas relished his long workdays. He turned his wages over to his bitter mother, who treated Inez as little more than her personal maid. Old Senora Quintero had worked as a hotel maid all her life. Now, in Inez, she had a servant of her own to wait on her when she came home.

So after the interview with the Americano, Thomas came home to Inez with a plan. He outlined Andy's proposal. They would leave his mother's house and her father's jurisdiction. They had been handed an opportunity. They would turn their backs on Mexico forever, and legally, once the paperwork was settled, cross the border into California. Because of him, because of his skills, Thomas Quintero and his family were elevated to a class structure he never might have dreamed of.

Unlike the millions of illegal Mexicans who lived and worked in the United States, they had been invited. He trusted the young man who was offering to help them. Inez could see for herself. What he didn't tell her was the innocent struggle that ensued in Andy's car after their drunken business dinner.

"I've had too much tequila," Thomas admitted.

"Me too," Andy chuckled. "Tequila always makes me horny."

"I'm always horny," Thomas laughed, his hand flexing over his crotch.

"That so? What do you do about it?"

When Thomas removed his hand, the soft mushroom tip of his penis was protruding through the zipper of his trousers.

"This has nothing to do with my offer. It's just extra," Andy whispered. He was always so ethical. "Nothing to ever talk about again."

Thomas rested his head against the passenger headrest of Andy's rented car. While sifting Andy's silky blond hair through his callused fingertips, Thomas allowed Andy to finish unzipping his trousers; to greedily gulp the juices from Thomas' thick papaya of a cock.

*   *   *

Since his wife, Inez, moved back to Mexico and they took up housekeeping with Ruby, Thomas Quintero had withdrawn from his children, possibly with the exception of Anita, who Ruby seemed to genuinely enjoy. His old aunt had died shortly after the move, which was fine by Ruby. It also meant that Soila didn't have to share a room. He continued to work very hard. The real estate boom in the desert had been very good for the business of Arte de Sonora, the Mexican import–export business where he'd worked since they moved to California.

His boss, Andy, continued to pay Thomas a fair wage. Thomas now supervised six furniture refinishers. The business had expanded to three storefronts. They dealt in faux antique pine finishes. Tables, chairs, dressers and armoires that were made to look old, but could accommodate big televisions and DVD players.

Thomas had recently lost weight, and gazed out in the world through amber eyes. His libido had been shot for over a year, and Ruby retaliated by overeating and cheating on the side. Thomas was bewildered and unfortunately had no one he could discuss it with.

It had been his dream to move from northern Mexico to the Southern California desert. So much success awaited anyone with skill and a strong work ethic. Hadn't his talents been so apparent Andy had sponsored him and his family? Thomas was a master with his hands and tools. He gave new life and history to any piece of wood he touched. He was an artisan, that rare man with a unique, desirable skill. His kind would be welcome in any country. His family entered with green cards in place, unlike so many other *mojados* who came illegally, hoping to squeeze into the rich economy undetected.

These very *mojados* had been rewarded for their dishonesty as far as he could see. How many amnesty programs had been proffered by the American government? It had been so unfair, Thomas thought. Many of his Mexican American friends shared his views. He had crossed the border legitimately, fulfilling his part of the bargain. He was an asset to Arte de Sonora.

Andy had even recently rewarded him with shares in the business, a profit-sharing plan and health insurance, but only for him and little Anita, because Ruby refused to marry him. Soila and Alex were both over eighteen. He and Ruby had been happy at first. They reveled in their new house. It wasn't the sweet little Spanish bungalow he'd been cheated out of in old Cathedral City, but so much unhappiness had ensued from those walls, he'd been just as happy to move.

It reminded him of his sick wife and all the violence in the alley behind it; the sordid comings and goings of the homosexuals who frequented the gay bar across the alley of his little house. Now he felt ill, but not in a way he understood or could try to describe. First of all, he was always tired, the fatigue seeming to permeate his body. He'd get up and in an hour, need to take a deep nap before he went to work. Once he was there, he made excuses to go off in his truck and sneak home again, for a second nap before lunch.

His brain felt too heavy for his skull. It felt damp and sodden. So full it forced his eyelids to close. Andy noticed and urged him to see a doctor, but Thomas Quintero hated doctors.

"You might have hepatitis," Andy warned him. "I really have to insist. You might be endangering me and the others. You go."

Thomas nodded wearily. "Okay, I'll go."

The earnest young physician was Mexican American, like Thomas. He joked around, thumping him on his back and chest. He listened to his heart, and asked Thomas to cough several times. He grew quiet when he listened to Thomas' lungs.

"I think a blood test is in order. I'll send in the nurse. Are you afraid of needles?"

"Can't you give me a pill?" Thomas asked him in Spanish. "I need to get my strength back."

"I think you might have pneumonia, but to find out what kind, I'll need to arrange for a bronchoscopy."

Thomas stared blankly.

"I need to biopsy fluid in your lungs."

"Cancer?" Thomas drew back.

The doctor shook his head. "Let me do a few tests. While we're at it, have you ever been checked for HIV? It's very routine."

And Thomas reared up. "I can't get HIV!"

Taken aback, the doctor asked why.

"Because I'm not one of them. *Un maricon.*"

The doctor was aghast. So many of his male Latino patients still suffered from the same dangerous assumption. Sexually active, many outside of their marriages, with steady girlfriends or regular encounters with prostitutes; refusing to wear condoms. It was an assault to their masculinity. Secondly, if he could ever get any of them to admit to same-sex encounters, he often encountered the same closely held belief that Thomas espoused. An innocent blow-job, or quickly occasional male-on-male ass-fucking, as long as the active position was adhered to, didn't make any Latin man a homosexual. Any Latino who would allow himself to be penetrated by another male was not a man at all. They were homosexuals.

It was difficult enough to get many Latino men in for a standard medical checkup. This was partly due to lack of insurance if they were undocumented immigrants, or general suspicion of the American medical community. Even the Hispanic medical community wasn't above the paranoia with many factions of the Latino population.

"You don't have to be a homosexual to contract HIV. Besides, it's standard. I just want to rule it out."

"I don't have la SIDA!"

The doctor studied him curiously. He took off his glasses nonchalantly. He didn't want to scare him away, but Thomas was already dressing, buttoning up his shirt.

"Aren't you going to stay for your blood test?"

"No!"

"Señor Quintero, it's possible you have a serious illness. Let me treat it and you'll feel better. You might possibly be infecting your wife."

His wife. Heart pounding, Thomas Quintero ignored him and fled his office. After a long drive in the desert he drove home. Ruby was out. Anita was at school. The house was empty. Thomas went directly to bed and allowed sleep to overcome him. These sleeps, while perplexing, felt wonderful when he gave himself up to them. By the time his head hit the pillow he was out. He felt guilty to be in bed in the afternoon. His father never took a nap his entire life.

The doctor hadn't told him anything he hadn't suspected. He knew what the warning signs were, had in fact, been expecting them. He read the Spanish pamphlets Inez had recently sent his daughter. Anyone can contract HIV, the brochure had cautioned. It had nothing to do with his potency as a man. It didn't make him a homosexual. In his dreams, Thomas was not allowed to forget. Anyone could contract HIV.

He watched Inez wake to the sight of him looming over their bed. His eyes dead with fear and disappointment. Suspicion. Then, without warning, scooping her swiftly up in his arms.

"What are you doing?" she'd asked him wearily.

"Quiet," Thomas growled.

He carried her into the living room where the old aunt slept in her customary place on the sofa. Soila and Alex heard the commotion. They both appeared from their respective rooms and gathered behind Thomas holding their tiny mother aloft in the darkness.

"What are you doing with her, Pop?" asked Alex.

Thomas placed Inez on the sofa.

"Papa, what are you doing?" Soila asked him again.

"She's leaving this house in the morning!"

Inez looked up at him incredulously. Soila moved to comfort her.

He turned, the shocked eyes of his family trained on him like cowering animals. Alex started to say something but Thomas held one finger up and he fell silent. Grimacing, he disappeared into the dark hallway and slammed the door to their bedroom behind him.

Anyone, he muttered, as once again, Thomas Quintero succumbed to sleep.

"Nevi flammeus," Dr. Tim Hansen proclaimed as he strode confidently through the examining room door. He was tall and blond, something extreme about his own perfect extreme, but Soila couldn't explain why.

"My name is Soila," she corrected him.

"I *know* your name is Soila. Soila Quintero to be exact."

Soila sat primly at the edge of her chair. The office was very opulent, with a large mahogany desk, recessed lighting and photographs of beautiful men and women, adorning the walls. It looked more like a movie producer's office than a place where sick people came.

He took the liberty of switching on bright vanity lights, and taking the back of her chair, spun her around to face a large oval mirror behind her. Firmly tweaking her chin and drawing her hair away from her face, he brutishly examined the outline of her birthmark and the contours of her cheek.

"I could do this blindfolded."

"Do what blindfolded?"

"Remove your birthmark. *Nevi flammeus*. It's nothing more than a port-wine stain. How long have you had it?"

Soila struggled out of his grasp. "Since I was born."

"This is exceptionally large, but I see nothing complicated about getting rid of it. It's a simple laser procedure. Same method we remove tattoos. My nurse will schedule you."

"I don't understand."

"You don't need to worry about the expense. It's been taken care of."

"By who?" Soila rarely allowed herself to get impatient, but now her limits were being tested.

"The donor wishes to remain anonymous."

"How much will this cost?"

"Twelve thousand dollars." He snapped off the lights and spun her around to face his desk. He took his seat opposite her and reached for a photograph album. "Here, this might be very interesting to you. These are a few patients who suffered from the same condition as you. Before and after."

She was about to refuse the book, but intrigued, instead began to study the photos, turning page after page of faces blighted by the ruby-stained birthmark she had been afflicted with since her birth. Some of the stains were barely noticeable. Others more severe than her own. Soila found herself moved by the relief in the eyes of the patients after the procedure.

All ages, male and female, some ordinary, some winsome, but all perfectly normal after this miracle procedure.

"It doesn't hurt. It's painless," he smiled at her. "Impressive, aren't they? The treatments are performed in my offices. Each one takes about an hour. What do you say?"

"Who arranged for this?"

"Anonymity is a stipulation of the bequest. I can't tell you, but I can't stop you from guessing, can I? Who do you know who has this kind of bread?"

He was a funny man, gleeful and somewhat prissy. Over his shoulder she noticed a certificate from Doctor's Without Borders awarded for work in Guatemala in 1999.

"I spend so many days with spoiled clients. Your benefactor described you perfectly. You're sweet and humble, aren't you? You're pretty with or without the procedure. What do you say? Can we go ahead? Let me show you how you'll look."

He positioned her in her chair, and reached for a digital camera from the top drawer of his desk. He snapped her photograph. Then he connected his camera to his computer. Several seconds later, Soila's image filled the screen. She winced, averting her eyes.

"No, wait. Let me show you some magic."

An eraser appeared on the computer's monitor which Dr. Hansen began to manipulate on a keypad, as if by magic. Slowly, half of Soila's face began to disappear, the half with the birthmark. Then he captured portions of skin color on the clear cheek and filled in the missing portion of the other, blending them in with the remainder of her face.

"Okay. You can look now . . ."

Soila nodded as she turned to study her face in the mirror. She gasped.

"Who do you look like?"

Soila was speechless.

"That's right. Jennifer Lopez!"

"Do it." Soila whispered.

"Part of the deal includes hair, makeup and wardrobe. Honey, I think your luck has changed."

In the next several weeks prior to her operation, Soila tied her hair back and went everywhere in broad daylight. She didn't avoid the harsh glare of the supermarket overhead lights. She waited outside for Mass to begin at St. Louis, in the bright desert morning sunshine. She accompanied Anita to her dance lessons in Rancho Mirage.

She held the gaze of passersby, instead of quickly glancing away. She could always predict a stranger's reaction to her. First a wincing look of disgust, and then, depending on the character of the onlooker, the expression might shift to empathetic concern. Then a quick aversion of eyes. The exaggerated shift of the head. A certain, not very discreet comment to a companion, and then the same reaction by the companion; pity, sometimes repulsion, sometimes, in the case of young boys, even jeers.

When she'd been young her mother had been known to lunge for the cruel ones, a response so startling that boys had been driven away howling from fear. Her tiny mother was no beauty, but carried herself with such defiant ferocity she always had her way. A housekeeper by profession, Inez Quintero's clients were so intimidated by her they left their homes for the entire day when she came to clean, rather than face her huffing and puffing wrath.

Ironically, in her own nuclear family, Alex and Anita had inherited their father's handsome good looks. How many times had well-intentioned strangers remarked, "You'd be so pretty if it wasn't for that birthmark."

Although both of her parents were relatively short, Soila towered over them by a head, a fact which doubly called attention to her deformity. Not only was she ugly, she was an ugly giant, though she and Maria were both about the same height. Many onlookers assumed they were sisters, which Soila loved, because Maria was regarded by many Cathedral City residents as the most beautiful woman in town. Ironically, Maria's beauty was lost on her and ugliness lost on Soila. They made their way through life on their wits. Keeping up appearances weren't luxuries they indulged themselves in.

She wished she could ask Maria's opinion, but Maria wasn't in any mood to talk with anyone these days.

15

Phantom Pain

It felt familiar, but more intense. She'd heard that amputees, suffering from advanced diabetes, or an accident of some sort, even a shark attack, continued to feel the limb as though it were still attached, but cruelly, not the healthy arm or leg or foot or hand, but the limb in agony, the teeth of the shark still embedded, seconds prior to the amputation.

Was her baby in agony when God took her from Maria? Had she cried out, *Mamita!* when water began to rush up under the car, rising in the backseat, up to the soles of Conchita's little pink sneakers? Had she screamed for Maria when Ruthie, probably after scrambling to unbuckle her seat belt, had twisted in the driver's seat, impeded by the steering wheel, water now up to her neck, to her chin, desperately tried to unfasten Chita's child seat, while Chita was underwater?

To even imagine such a vision caused Maria to stagger through the rooms of her little house, her breathing as labored as the final ten feet of a marathon—or the last few moments of delivery, *breathe, breathe, breathe.* The pain had breached inside of her, high under her rib cage, so acutely she swore she could trace the outline of it in her bathroom mirror. So these were her nights. Stomping through the house, pounding her fist, *breathe, breathe, breathe,* but her Lamaze exercises were no match for this. Drowning was supposed to be peaceful. Absurd. How could any last moments be more chaotic?

Ruthie's body had been recovered. Maria held a small, nondenominational service for her at the restaurant. Mostly fans attended.

Her cardplaying pals. Ruthie was Jewish, but not practicing. She didn't even have a service for Sam. She always said she wanted the same thing for herself. Nothing. The service for Ruthie was Maria's way of sending a message about Chita.

Her daughter wasn't dead. Hence, no words needed to be spoken over any empty baby's coffin. She was defying them all to ask. No one did. Not even Pablo. Certainly not Soila. When Pablo's parents offered to come, she politely refused. Come when we find Chita, she told them. Come when you can celebrate.

Elena Seladon insisted that she see a therapist. Out of courtesy— Elena had been present when Chita was born—Maria agreed to one visit. The psychiatrist had been sympathetic, but unable to transfer Maria's stalwart grief, began to cry in the session, infuriating Maria. She gave Maria some sample prescriptions, and Maria dumped them in the toilet when she came home.

Although her circumstances were known to the community, few felt comfortable enough to approach and console Maria directly. News of Ruthie's drowning and the disappearance and presumed death of her young daughter had been on every front page desert publication. Everyone knew who she was. Curiosity seekers even came to her café and were ghoulishly delighted to get a glance at her, but she didn't play the part of the grieving mother to their satisfaction. She wasn't pitiful or hysterical. Instead she was growing formidably more beautiful. In some faces, grieving heightens beauty, as was the case with Maria Castillo.

Maria no longer seated her patrons as she had in the past, but she came early every morning to prep with her crew and remained through the evening till closing time. She tried to stay behind the scenes, working at her cluttered desk in the kitchen. Sometimes she might glance up, half expecting to see Ruthie at the screen door with Chita giggling at her side. These visions were only wistful mirages. It bothered her that Chita's image accompanied the apparition of Ruthie. She feared it meant that Chita too, had perished, lost in the flooding wash, and that God was trying to tell her something.

Other times it might be Kenny at the door, standing behind the shimmering steel mesh of the screen, peering through it, his hand shading his blue eyes, *Chita's blue eyes,* looking for Maria with a hint of a smile as if to say, I've found her, here she is, here I am. The first time Maria shot to her feet in disbelief, but the light changed, the mirage dissipated and she sank back to her chair with a thudding, hurting heart.

Another day brought her grandmother Concha, arms crossed, chuckling merrily, eyes calmly assuring Maria that her family was waiting for her. The last vision was that of her mother and father, Pia and Hector, holding hands, luminous in white linen.

These experiences were so real, so deeply true that instead of recoiling, Maria began to look forward to them. They only occurred early in the morning, when Maria was alone. Unfortunately, they stopped as quickly as they started. These were her loved ones, coming to urge her to move on with her life.

How, after all her loss, would such a thing be possible?

Across the parking lot and beyond the decrepit shrine to Judi and her lost baby, the sloping rooftop of St. Louis Catholic Church beckoned to Maria. Father Scolia, at Soila's request, said a polite Mass for Chita and Ruthie, but Maria's unmarried status and Chita's unconventional baptism, in this very kitchen where she now sat, were sore points with the grim priest.

Soila had written to Father Gene, who had since retired to a mission in Arizona, but didn't hear back until months later, from a nurse at a Catholic hospital advising her that he'd recently suffered a debilitating stroke. He was very distressed, the nurse had written. When advised of Maria's tragedy, he required sedation. Was Maria seeking comfort from the local Catholic clergy?

When the parade of apparitions stopped coming to Maria's kitchen door, Maria decided to try St. Louis again, trudging stalwartly across the empty desert floor to its doors for morning Mass. The parishioners were more of an ethnic mix than she remembered. Famous funerals like Loretta Young's attracted new blood to Cathedral City's only Catholic Church. She must have known something nobody else did.

As Maria sat in the center of a solitary pew toward the rear of the sanctuary, she allowed that she hadn't come to Mass without a sad heart since she'd arrived in Cathedral City. Then it had been the loss of her grandmother Concha in such an evil, cruel way. Later she had to come to terms with her feelings for Kenny, who loved her, which she couldn't allow without hurting Nick.

And now Chita. What could God be thinking? she wanted to scream as Father Scolia officiated at the altar below her. What kind of a God takes a loving and happy little girl away from a mother who loves her so?

"This is the lamb of God who takes away the innocent children of this world!"

Suddenly the entire congregation swung around and stared at her.

Behind her, a firm, withered hand patted her shoulder. "Come with me."

Had she actually cried out? She turned and found the wise, stern eyes of Sister Agnes staring into her own. At the altar, the priest began to prepare the host.

"Lord," the congregation repeated after the priest, *"I am not worthy to receive you but say the word and I shall be healed."*

Maria stood up and followed Sister Agnes to a side exit door.

"I'll make us some tea."

Sister Agnes left Maria in a small living area in the church rectory designated for clergy to meet with visiting family members. The furnishings were sparse, a simple wooden table with four plastic chairs and a short sofa with worn brown plaid upholstery. The rectory windows opened up the hill to the cove section of Cathedral City where Maria once lived with Kenny and Nick. Behind the houses loomed the somber brown foothills of the Santa Rosa Mountains.

Sister Agnes returned with two steaming chipped cups teetering on a warped plastic tray. Maria stood to assist her but the old lady waved her away. She pushed a cup toward Maria's place at the table. Instead of dunking her Lipton tea bag by the tag and string, Sister Agnes dipped hers into the scalding water with her bare fingers.

Maria, surprised at first, succumbed to a nervous chuckle, the first time she'd laughed in months. So the old nun wanted to prove how tough she was. Maria studied her as she sipped her tea. She was always trying to guess her age. Sister Agnes looked to be in her late sixties, her head draped with a coarse blue burlap shawl. Her uniform consisted of a long-sleeved, short blue tunic dress, navy stockings that wrinkled at her ankles and sturdy walking shoes with crepe soles.

As Maria studied her, she certainly felt tied to her now.

"Sister, why did they all stare at me? Did I shout at the priest?"

"You didn't utter a sound. They simply felt your grief and turned in your direction." The old lady studied her frankly. "You're angry at God."

"Yes."

"You don't have it as bad as some."

"I know."

"I've held mothers down as soldiers murdered their entire families. Shot tiny babies in the head for no other purpose than cruelty; men who enjoy feasting on a woman's pain. You were raped by one man," Sister Agnes admonished Maria. "I've sutured prepubescent girls who were raped by twelve men and then flogged and tossed into a ditch. Left for dead."

"Yes, Sister," Maria nodded, but she wasn't interested in this particular lecture.

"You feel guilty. Good. Your conscience is working."

Maria stared at her hands.

"It's all your fault, you know. You put them all in harm's way. All of them. Your grandmother. Your daughter. Your friends."

Maria glanced up. This wasn't going to be any ordinary pep talk. She listened while the old nun quietly accused her of causing all the sadness she'd experienced in the last five years.

"Selfish," Sister Agnes charged.

"I want my daughter back."

"Your daughter is lost."

"I don't believe it."

"No?" A smile curled at the corner of her thin lips. "What would you give to get her back?"

"Anything," Maria replied.

"I don't profess to know God's mind. But from the look of things, I think you owe him much more than He owes you."

"I want my daughter back."

"I have a few women I think you might enjoy meeting."

Several days later, Maria was notified by Ruthie's attorney that it was time to discuss the details of Ruthie's will. He wondered if he might take her to lunch. He picked her up at the café and drove her to Melvyn's Ingleside Inn, one of Palm Springs' glamorous old hotels.

When Maria entered with him, heads turned. She had dressed for the occasion and wore a simple sleeveless black dress with black heels. Her hair was longer now, curling generously down to her shoulders. All the men in the room had noted her. The maitre'd ushered them to a prominent table overlooking the sumptuous garden.

Several men dining at a nearby table noticed her and she saw them whispering about her.

"Mrs. Singer's assets have been somewhat difficult to amass, but I think I have a clearer picture now. As you know, you were her sole heir."

"Me and my daughter," Maria corrected him. "We both have equal shares."

"Yes."

"Conchita is not dead until they produce her body."

"I just think for the purpose of expediting Mrs. Singer's estate, it would be more prudent to apply for her death certificate."

"Absolutely not."

"Fine, fine," he tittered, shuffling his paperwork. The table of men who watched her responded as if they thought she was magnificent. A waiter rushed over to pour her more iced tea. "In that case, I'll give you the bottom line. Your share of Mrs. Singer's estate, including her new home, the restaurant property in Cathedral City, her other real estate holdings, her bank accounts, her stocks and bonds," he scrawled a figure on a napkin and divided it into two. "Your share comes to four million, eight hundred and seventy-two thousand dollars. An equal share will be held in an estate for your daughter, with you as the suggested trustee."

"Oh God," Maria whispered. "Oh, God. Poor Ruthie," she began to cry. "What a wonderful woman. I never dreamed it would be so much. Poor thing."

"Mr. Singer was a very shrewd businessman."

"He never thought he had enough. She said he was always afraid of being poor."

"That's because as a boy he was poor. Once you're poor, no matter how much money you have, you're always poor."

Maria wept quietly into her napkin. God was having another laugh at her expense. So much money, and no one she loved to share it with.

Her attorney collected his thoughts, waiting for her to compose herself. "This makes you a very wealthy woman. If you wanted to be, it could also make you very powerful."

Maria glanced up. "Powerful?"

"That's right. As it stands, I'd venture to point out that you're probably the richest woman in Cathedral City. Do you think you'll move into your house in Palm Springs?"

"I plan to stay where I am. Sell it."

"You could afford pretty much anything you wanted."

"I don't need any more room. I'm alone. My little house is already too lonely as it is."

"Maybe you might consider moving. Less painful memories."

"No. It's my daughter's home. I want it to be there for her when she finds her way home."

He nodded. They finished their lunch making small talk. The table of curious onlookers paid their check. A tall, good-looking man approached their table. He smiled affably. "I'm in the fashion industry. My friends and I think we recognize you. Are you a model?"

"No," she shook her head. She was annoyed by his interruption. Men were always gawking at her. "I'm older than I look."

"Well," he said, pushing his card at her. "If you ever want to be in the fashion industry, call this number." She glanced at his card. He was a photographer. He smiled and walked away.

Later that night, Maria studied herself critically in her bathroom mirror. Tonight she'd brushed her hair a hundred strokes and pretended that Chita was watching the way she always liked to.

Maria studied the business card of the silly photographer. She tossed it in the wastebasket. Then she reached for a pair of scissors. Taking a thick strand of hair she began cutting, close to the crown of her scalp. The hair easily detached in her grasp. Shocking her at first, she now had no choice but to continue. Over the course of the next hour, Maria continued to cut her hair, strands at a time until finally it lay clotted in her sink.

In Mexico she could have sold lustrous hair like this for many pesos. Money now wasn't the issue here. She studied herself in the mirror, taking pains to even out the job. She knew she was still pretty, but she liked the effect. She stepped into the shower to wash her head and body free of the loose hair.

When she stepped out, she didn't apply lipstick or eye shadow. She wasn't about feminine trappings now. Grief was abating to anger. These weren't peaceful times.

16

The Radical Sisters of God

"I'm taking my evening walk," Sister Agnes announced.

"You mean your regular *Thursday* evening walk," observed Father Scolia.

"It's been my habit to stroll exactly at this time ever since I came to this parish. Even Father Gene occasionally accompanied me. I like to climb into the hills above Cathedral City. It reminds me of our Lord's path to Gethsemane."

"He had a cross to carry," Father Scolia muttered. He didn't give a hoot where she went. The new recreation hall was nearly completed. He was planning a christening ceremony. He was hoping Carol Channing might officiate.

"I have my cross to bear, also," Sister Agnes chided him.

Father Scolia angrily removed his bifocals. "Sister, you've been barely civil to me since I arrived at St. Louis. What's your problem?"

"I was fond of Father Gene."

"And how, may I ask, is that any fault of mine?"

"You concentrate too much on finances. You pay little attention to the spiritual maladies of individual members of this parish. Particularly the impoverished ones. You seem to be overly impressed with fame and wealth."

"Without the fame and wealth that has attached itself to this parish, you might not have been served a sixteen-ounce porterhouse as your entree this evening."

"I've always been blessed by a healthy appetite."

"You have an appetite for controversy, I've noticed."

"Jesus raised his voice."

"And for what cause do you feel your voice needs to be heard above the throngs?"

"For impoverished women who are daily mistreated as they attempt to cross our borders from Mexico. Women who are raped, beaten, enslaved, kidnapped, separated from their small children, abandoned in the desert to die and murdered at the hands of coyotes and smuggling cartels. All because they wish to escape the miserable poverty that has had a lifetime stranglehold around their throats."

"We don't exactly have the type of congregation here which can relate to that kind of suffering."

"You underestimate them. They would relate if they were inspired and educated to do so. Had Father Gene been a younger man—"

"This parish would have risked being ousted from the main body of the world Catholic order. His reputation was infamous."

"He loved his congregation and they loved him in return."

"Are you suggesting that I am unloved by my parishioners?"

Sister Agnes didn't reply. "You're fulfilling your mandate. You've raised money for the parish. The barrio is gone. The per capita income of each church member has risen tenfold, now that it's safe to park outside the cathedral."

"You're a reverse snob, Sister."

"If I have that reputation, I'm happy," she replied. "I'm certain everyone will enjoy the new recreation hall. I think I'll take my walk, now."

"I hope you aren't breaching our agreement, Sister Agnes."

"I'm an old woman," she replied, turning her back on him. "My conscience is clean."

"I certainly hope so," Father Scolia called after her.

She turned back with such ferocity in her eyes she forced him to wince in her presence.

Sister Agnes commenced with her constitutional. Father Scolia was growing increasingly suspicious of her behavior, but figured her time at St. Louis was coming to an end shortly anyway. He noticed that she was frequenting the lounge across from the Civic Center on an almost daily basis. When she returned she often smelled of alcohol.

But tonight Sister Agnes strolled east of the church, toward the remaining barrio houses on the opposite side of Van Fleet. On this sultry desert night trudging slowly along D Street, she noticed small children playing in barren yards, littered with old tires and broken appliances. Many of their mothers, sweating and grave, nodded to her in acknowledgment. If their husbands and boyfriends, leaning into the engines of their old junky pickups, noticed her, they said nothing. Sister Agnes was a woman's woman.

She was born in New Jersey, the daughter of Italian parents, but her father died when she was very young. Agnes Angotti and her mother moved in with her grandmother in upstate New York. When Agnes was seven, her grandmother had a stroke. The house had to be sold to pay for a nursing home. Her mother, unable to support them, was forced to move in with her mother's unmarried brother Alvy, in a cramped apartment in Queens, where they slept on the floor of his living room.

Several months after they moved, her mother disappeared with no explanation. Her uncle, a fanatic Catholic, deposited her at the local church on days he worked. It was there that a sister informed her that her mother had left because she was pregnant with a baby brother. The father could not have been Agnes'. She left Agnes with Alvy to avoid disgracing her.

Agnes, rebellious at first, responded to the affections of the nuns who pitied her. It was never explained to her where her mother went. When she asked if she could see her brother, she was told that he, too, had been given away by their mother. He lived in an orphanage in California. It was unlikely that they'd ever see each other again.

Strangely, the sense of relief that she had a brother somewhere, who had also been abandoned by her mother made her the happiest young girl in the world. Somewhere someone probably understood her. She prayed for him every night.

Alvy was a recluse—agoraphobic as she now understood the condition—but he didn't seem to mind the company of his little niece. Agnes, heartbroken at being separated from her brother and the unexplained disappearance of her mother, demanded nothing from him for fear he'd send her away to another strange place.

As his condition worsened and she grew older, he could no longer leave the apartment and survived on a small disability pension from the government. It was up to Agnes to fend for them, selecting food and clothing from the local Catholic charity and when he was up to it, reading to him, or saying her prayers.

It was wonderful preparation for the life ahead of her. She had learned to survive a broken heart. Broken hearts would come with the territory, loneliness and poverty the life of an aesthete would often-times require. Because of her vulnerability, a young woman with no family and no future prospects to speak of, the sisters of the local order subtly and steadfastly groomed her for a life in the church. Agnes would become a bride of Christ. Ultimately, she would see more of the world, experience greater adventure than she or those sisters could have ever foreseen.

After Alvy died, every choice she'd make would be reactionary to his sorrowful loneliness. Agnes would leave her room, her borough, her state and her country. By the time she arrived in Cathedral City, she'd served God and the church on all seven continents. She was old now, had witnessed much suffering; seen many miracles. Her service had been in exchange for one immutable fact. The heavy aching heart of the first days and weeks after her mother disappeared had never returned.

Since that time, God removed her ability to experience the emotion of love. How much easier, more efficient, her life had been as a result of being delivered of that wretched monkey on her back.

It was a small group of women, no more than eight or nine, each handpicked by Sister Agnes. She hadn't been wrong yet, and wasn't particularly concerned about any of them because even in their grief, they moved with the same mechanical efficiency that Sister Agnes had observed in other true survivors of great tragedy.

They met in an air-conditioned garage behind a small stucco house at the outer edge of the remaining barrio. Behind the property was a rocky ravine and then open desert, cresting up above Cathedral City. A card table with iced tea and a plate of ginger snaps, Sister Agnes' favorites, always lay waiting prior to the meeting.

Folding chairs were placed in a circle. A shade was drawn in the little portal window of the side door entrance into the garage. The main garage door had been bolted closed and rusty for years. The meeting only convened after the sun had long since set. The women never came in pairs. They all arrived alone, staggering their appearance in intervals of seven to ten minutes apart. It took slightly over an hour for the entire group to convene. Those arriving first made the room ready. They came on foot, approaching the meeting place from behind the property, coming up behind it from the ravine. Although insuring privacy necessitated their stealth, it was equal parts ceremonial. Most had penetrated the U.S. border under cover of darkness, traversing ravines such as this, but for miles instead of minutes.

The short trek in the ravine was meant to remind them of how many had crossed the border into the United States. It was also an act of solidarity for other women like them, this very night, running desert ravines in *La Frontera,* two hours south at the Calexico/Mexicali border. These women were spiritual border-jumpers. They believed in the dissolution of all international borders between Mexico and the United States.

Although most were now American citizens, they also believed that anybody wanting to live and work in the United States had a God-given right to do so without fear of deportation and punishment. They believed, as Sister Agnes had proselytized, that poverty justified any means, except murder in cases other than self-defense, and most importantly, the safety and protection of poor women seeking asylum on either side of the border was sacrosanct, more important than any international or national law.

These were the Radical Sisters of God. They had all been violently victimized personally or in close association by coyote smuggling cartels. Several had been dragged off from their groups and raped, some multiple times. Others had watched loved ones, usually husbands or brothers, separated out and murdered for challenging a cruel or inept coyote; and some had been forced to continue at gunpoint while friends and family members too weak to continue got left behind, ultimately to die alone in the desert.

This year, in the first four months of the year, over 140 bodies had been found in the desert by border patrol agents, picked clean by animals. That number represented only the bodies they were able to find in the hundreds of square miles patrolled between the Salton Sea and Calexico. Too many were young children, even babies. Too many had been outright murdered, as if dehydration wasn't bad enough.

One woman's life lost is too many. One woman's life saved justifies all.

This was the credo of the Radical Sisters of God. They formed to protect other women like them.

Tonight as Sister Agnes mentally took roll, all but the last member of the group had arrived, and was expected at promptly 9:10 P.M. Surveying the women gathered, Sister Agnes noted with satisfaction how confident the weaker ones had grown by associating with the stronger ones. They all knew to expect a new member, but didn't know who she might be.

Tonight they were huddled over a large topographical map of the Imperial County quadrant of the southern California desert. Detailed in red magic marker were commonly traveled smuggling routes, hundreds of them. Behind them the door swung slowly open.

A tall grave woman with short cropped hair, a slightly aquiline nose and a luminous complexion stood in its frame. She wore a khaki green tank top, green army surplus fatigues and shiny black boots. She surveyed the occupants of the secret meeting room.

"Hey, girlfriend," a woman greeted her from the shadows.

Maria squinted into the direction of her voice. It was Bambi. Sitting next to her, arm thrown over her shoulder sat Madonna. Next to her nodded Soila Quintero. Sister Agnes moved to kiss a surprised Maria's hand.

"We're glad you've joined us," Madonna smiled.

"We're planning our first mission," Sister Agnes nodded. "We've set our sights on a local coyote. He smuggles drugs. He's a rapist and a murderer. We can use your help."

"What's expected?"

"Risk capital," Sister Agnes replied. "More than you think."

"I'll need a sign from God before this goes any further."

"Keep your eyes open," the little nun grinned.

It was Pablo's first sleepaway with Bob. As agreed, he would spend Sunday and Monday night in El Centro, Pablo's nights off from the café. Privately Pablo had been dismayed by the spartan living quarters Bob called home.

"You don't like it."

Pablo dropped his duffel bag. "No, it's . . . very clean."

"I'm pretty anal," Bob grinned, sweeping up Pablo's bag and trotting it into his bedroom. Pablo followed him inside.

"My, you have a very big TV set," Pablo called after him. He had tricked with guys who lived like this. Basic furnishings. The big black wide-screen Sony XBR with enormously huge extra speakers.

Bob returned. "I unpacked for you. I cleared you my top left drawer. You have a small hole in one of your left socks. I can mend that for you. I didn't go through your kit bag. Kinda personal, I figured. But I stowed it under the sink next to mine. We could get some toiletries, later on," he offered. "If you think you might come back."

Agape, Pablo found himself growing aroused. Usually such talk made him impotent for twenty-four hours. This time it really turned him on.

Clad only in a T-shirt and a pair of gray gym shorts, Bob leaned against the frame of the bedroom door and searched Pablo's face with a wondering expression in his eyes. Was he coming on too strong? Being too forward? He'd never done this before, had a guy sleep over. No one had ever been willing to drive all the way to El Centro, or had he ever actually asked?

He couldn't remember. All he knew for certain was that he liked this man. He liked Pablo's company and the feeling made him nervous; nervous and greedy. He too, was getting excited. It was mid-evening. Pablo had called before he left, and given that he hadn't been to El Centro, Bob figured it might take him longer than expected to arrive.

He wanted tonight to be memorable. He thought he'd take him to dinner in Mexicali. They could cut across the border and have dinner in Mexico. He knew of a good seafood restaurant with a subtly mixed clientele. They could hold hands if they liked. Would it offend Pablo if Bob wanted them to eat Mexican food?

He was so nervous.

Pablo laughed at him across the room. Then he rushed toward him, full force, knocking Bob back into the bedroom, onto the bed. They crashed, kissing and fondling, onto the mattress. Pablo—fully dressed and fumbling with his zipper, removed Bob's shorts, yanking his T-shirt over his head—fucked him with his boots and the lights on.

Later that night, while Pablo lay curled on his side, snoring softly, the soft white cotton blanket rising and falling with every hushed breath, Bob had yet to fall asleep. It was new, sleeping with the same person. Since the night at Badlands, he'd returned twice to Sky Valley, once arriving unannounced, which he'd never do again, and the second time a planned Sunday day trip, which included brunch, a word he hated, at a gay place in Palm Springs, and a hike up to Tahquitz Falls, which had been surprisingly cruisy. Hot men were nude sunbathing on the flat sun-drenched surfaces of high distant rock formations. Others frolicked under the tepid waterfall. The only thing spoiling it momentarily had been a guy who'd been tailing them for several minutes, looking for a threesome. Pablo teasingly queried Bob to test his interest. Bob rebuffed him coolly, hurt by the suggestion.

"Baby, I was joking. Do you want me to throw a rock at him? Make him go away?" He turned to their stalker. "You're wasting your time! I'm not sharing my boyfriend with anyone. Ever," he winked at Bob, forcing a relieved smile. Then Pablo pulled him behind a rock and kissed him for an hour.

"Am I really your boyfriend?' Bob queried uncertainly.

"I'm certainly asking," Pablo smiled. "Are you?"

"Yes," Bob replied. "Yes. But I'm not as experienced as you. Not as open."

"I know," Pablo replied breezily. This was it. He didn't want to discuss his past, as much as he liked Bob. His sexual history might be a problem to their growing relationship. It had all been drug related. Fun, yes, but meaningless. He didn't party anymore. He'd outgrown it since he went to Stanford.

Bob started to speak, but the look in Pablo's eyes caused him to change his tack. Now he found himself formulating the question once again, and once again decided to drop the issue. Differences in their past, and their political values would eventually have to be addressed, but not now. Not yet.

The handsome sleeping boy was too sweet to disturb. Bob wanted to allow Pablo his sweet dreams.

The night before her first treatment, Soila Quintero awoke to a warming sensation on her deformed cheek. It didn't hurt really, but tingled so noticeably she felt forced to climb out of bed to study herself in the mirror. Her sister Anita was fast asleep. Soila feared waking her. Anita had grown quite spoiled under Ruby's tutelage. She didn't respect her older sister. She'd be mad if Soila woke her out of a sound sleep.

Soila crept to her bureau to reach for her hand mirror. It was a full moon tonight, and light, almost bright as day pierced the curtain window. What could be wrong with her cheek? It almost felt like it was vibrating from within. She held up the mirror and gasped.

"What's wrong with your cheek?" her younger sister demanded from the darkness. Soila had awakened her, but she didn't seem angry. She was sitting up in bed, staring at Soila as if she was confronted with an apparition. Whining, Anita backed away from her, huddling in the corner with her sheet pulled up to her chin. "What is it?" Anita asked again.

"I don't know," Soila replied, tenderly touching the surface of her skin. "It feels so strange."

"I'm getting Ruby."

"No. Don't wake Ruby," Soila admonished her, with a confidence both of them were surprised by. "Turn on the light, now that you're awake."

Anita switched on her lamp. She climbed from her bed and cautiously approached her sister. "Put down the mirror. Let me see."

Slowly Soila lowered the looking glass. Anita's hands flew to her face in disbelief. Then she fell to her knees.

"What is it? What are you doing?"

"It's the Virgin! The Virgin of Guadalupe!"

"What?" Soila raised the mirror. The birthmark on her face had slightly reorganized itself. It did slightly resemble a robed feminine figure. Why tonight? Soila lamented. It was her mother, haunting her from Mexico. This was too impossible, even for someone as devout as Soila.

"*I can see her eyes!*" Anita shrieked.

"*Quiet!*"

"And her mouth. She's speaking to us. Her mouth is moving!"

"*What the fuck is going on in there?*" Ruby began pounding on her side of the wall. "Shut up, you goddamned bitches, or I'll send you both back to Mexico!"

"Be quiet!" Soila advanced on her sister. "Please!"

And Anita quieted instantly, her face filled with prayerful rapture. She lowered her head, bowing to Soila's birthmark. "It's her," she affirmed.

Embedded in Soila's cheek, the Virgin of Guadalupe, the patron saint of travelers.

17

Betty B

She started coming in late afternoons. Always ordered a Coke or a Calistoga water. She didn't say much, just ordered something nonalcoholic and seemed inordinately interested in Maria's little shrine to Kenny and Nick. She'd usually only sit for as long as it took to drink her beverage. Occasionally, she'd nod to Sister Agnes and glance shyly away.

Today she surprised both Pablo and Sister Agnes by greeting the little nun by name. "Hello, Sister Agnes." Focusing again on Maria's votive altar, she noticed two new photos. "Why the new pictures?"

"A local tragedy," Sister Agnes said gravely.

"What happened?"

"Lost recently in the flood," the Sister replied, nearly a whisper.

Betty's eyes widened, and she shot a glance in Pablo's direction, as if to confirm the little drinking nun's observation. He nodded.

"Who was the little girl? She's so beautiful."

"The owner's daughter."

"And the woman?"

"She used to sing here. Nights," Sister Agnes cut in. "God's will must be done."

"I have a hard time understanding God's will sometimes."

"That's your problem," Sister Agnes muttered. It was so rude, Pablo had to choke back a chuckle.

"Lots of senseless things have happened around here, Sister," Pablo asserted, coming to the newcomer's defense. "Let's be nice."

"Nice," Sister Agnes nodded. "Okay, I'll try to be nice."

Pablo smiled at the woman. "I'm Pablo. This tipsy little bride of Christ is Sister Agnes."

"My name is Betty," the shy woman replied.

"Hello, Betty," Sister Agnes growled. "My friend is correct. I am drinking more than I used to. Perhaps for the very reason you mentioned. As I get older, I understand less and less. But to complain about it is impractical, don't you think?"

"Have you known personal tragedy, Betty?" Pablo liked to get to the heart of things. It made bartending more interesting.

"Yes," she replied primly.

"Illuminate us," Sister Agnes slurred.

Pablo shook his head. "Sister, I'm going to be forced to cut you off. You're being horrible."

"No, she's not. I'll tell you. I lost my husband in a plane crash when my children were very young. He was a commercial pilot. His jet went down in the San Jacinto Mountains. It was big news. All eighty passengers were killed. They blamed him. Pilot error. I lost everything. Most of all, control over my children."

"They took them away?"

"No. Emotionally, I just gave up on them. I've been a problem drinker. Hence, my daily soft drinks."

"How old are they now?"

"Nineteen and twenty."

"Adults, then."

"They still live with me."

"You're a woman who could use a drink."

Agape, Betty and Pablo turned to Sister Agnes.

"Look at you. You're a mousy thing. You have no stature. No dignity. I think you have a secret. It's sapping you of your morale. That's what big secrets do to weak people."

"Sister!" Pablo reprimanded her. He reached for her half-empty glass, but she clutched it with both hands and he withdrew. "I won't arm wrestle you for it."

"You'd lose," she replied.

Betty grew ashen. At first Pablo thought she was going to cry, but she composed herself. If anything, she seemed to find Sister Agnes' brutal honesty somewhat refreshing. She focused again on Maria's shrine.

"Do you ever hear from him?"

"Who?"

"Nick. The previous owner."

"No. They left the desert four years ago."

She became emotional. "It was awful what happened to them. To Cathedral City."

"Yes," Sister Agnes observed. "And it won't stop till we all confess our secrets. Tell God our sins."

Betty reached for her purse.

"It's on me," Pablo told her. "Come back earlier, next time. She can't sneak away from the church till after four."

"On the contrary, the conversation with both of you has been most enlightening. First honest talk I've had in years. Thank you for the drink."

She crept down the back hallway of the lounge to the exit opening out onto Maria's parking lot.

"Why were you riding her?" Pablo snatched her empty glass away.

"Give me one more. I'm sad today."

He shook his head and splashed her ice with half a shot of bourbon.

"Why are you sad, Sister Agnes?"

"That woman made me sad. She knows something terrible about her children. She's debating whether to turn them in."

"Are you clairvoyant now too?" Pablo patted her hand. "Relax, Sister. When Maria returns, I'll walk you back to the rectory."

"I can walk back alone. I've walked in jungles alone."

"I know, Sister. But the difference is, tonight you won't have to. I'll be with you."

When they left Maria's café, Pablo steered a forlorn Sister Agnes across the desert floor. Across the highway, the bell tower of the Cathedral City Civic Center began to chime. The stained glass windows of the church glowed in the distance. In the gently sloping hills above Cathedral City, stars began to appear. It was a timeless moment for Pablo. He felt a rush of affection for Sister Agnes.

"I never see you at Mass," she murmured.

"I'm afraid I'm not Kenny." Pablo gently steadied her elbow with his fingertips.

"I didn't know him," she observed. "Father Gene was obsessed with him."

"Hmm . . ."

"Not in the way you're thinking!" she snapped at Pablo.

"Sister," he chided her boldly. "Why else would a priest be interested in someone like Kenny?"

"What's that supposed to mean? 'Someone like Kenny.'"

"I mean his sexual orientation."

"Out of concern for his salvation," she replied, but without rancor. "Father Gene was very devout. Is that so hard to believe? Are you really so cynical?" She posed the question with such sadness, Pablo struggled to compose a respectful, truthful reply.

"I don't want to be," Pablo ventured.

"That's a start. You're further along than I am, if that's really the case."

"I'm sorry if I offended you."

"You didn't offend me," she acknowledged. They had nearly reached the edge of the church parking lot. "I'll tell you a little secret."

"What's that?"

"The life I've chosen. It's been easier in the long run. Fewer options. Fewer decisions to make. For someone as stubborn as I am, it would be much harder to be a civilian."

"Civilian?"

Sister Agnes chuckled.

"Why were you really sad tonight?"

"I was wishing I was in touch with my brother. As I've gotten older, I've become too sentimental."

"You don't know where he is?"

"I never met him. All I was told was that a brother was born after me, but he was adopted from an orphanage in California. I wish, some days, that I could locate him."

"We could hire a service."

"No," she said firmly. "Well, young man. I'm home." She gazed up at the church spire. "Now you have to hike back through the desert alone. Do you want me to walk you back?"

Pablo smiled and waited till she disappeared through the door to her quarters.

After Pablito escorted Sister Agnes home, he hopped in his Jeep and raced across the night desert toward his Sky Valley encampment. He liked Sister Agnes' gruff demeanor. She reminded him of his cantankerous little friend Inez. In a fair fight, even Inez would have a hard time holding her own against Sister Agnes.

Inez reported that her health was stable, that the monthly supply of AIDS medications she received gratis from Mexican charities continued to keep her virus undetectable. She suffered from several maladies as side effects. Fatigue was a serious problem. Even her iron will could not master the malaise, which overcame her in the early afternoon, when a deep nap was required if she was going to do herself any good the remainder of the day. Also, neuropathy plagued her. Her feet often hurt, as did her hands and fingers. Her regimen of free pills unfortunately didn't include medications which were known to be helpful for sufferers of those symptoms. She'd also reported lipodistrophy, or buffalo hump, which were unsightly fat deposits at the base of her neck and accumulating in her abdomen.

Never vain, she was still bothered by this phenomenon. Her body was now deformed by HIV medications. Still, Pablo wrote back, what were her options? She would continue to take her pills and be thankful God had made them available to her.

Inez wrote back to ask if Pablo had seen her husband Thomas around Cathedral City lately. Soila continued to express grave doubts about his health. He had lost considerable weight and she reported seeing swelling in the lymph nodes on his neck.

Ruby, apparently, was a holy terror. Daily she was growing fatter and fatter, and impugned his masculinity in front of Soila and Anita. He never wanted to make love to her anymore. Although they weren't married, they co-owned the new house. Soila suspected that Thomas missed her mother, but he'd never admit to it. Ruby, too, proved to be a grave disappointment to Thomas. Fiery, sensual and affectionate, shortly after they moved in together she quickly grew cynical and bored. His *machista* bullshit wouldn't work on her.

If his wife let him get away with it, Ruby never went to that old school. She was raised in Cathedral City in a matriarchal family. All the women were tigers—the men, weak-in-the-knees little goats. Plus, she didn't want to continue working. She wanted to stay home and watch *Telemundo* all day long. Inez had been such a hard worker and without question always turned over her paycheck to Thomas. Because Ruby worked for tips, he could never be safely assured that she wasn't holding out on him.

Would Pablito please go to Arte de Sonora and see if he could spy on Thomas long enough to ascertain his health? Inez no longer hated him. Her work at the clinic had eradicated most of those negative emotions. He was still her husband in the eyes of God. The father of her children. Anita needed a father, as did Alex. Soila, not so much. She was already betrothed to Jesus, at least in Inez' eyes.

That night, Pablo decided to climb the hill to assess his separatist neighbors. He was surprised to see activity brimming in the brightly illuminated fenced yard of the compound. A white Blazer and a black Mustang were parked inside the fence. Several figures stood talking between the vehicles. He could see that one was a hard-looking blonde girl, maybe late teens, who needed a cane to walk. The other two were men.

He could hear bits and pieces of conversation, but not make anything out. He wished Bob were here. Bob probably had listening devices that could detect sound, a complement to his nightvision surveillance equipment. Suddenly, another figure bolted from the house, carrying a rifle. He shouted at the people in the yard, and all turned to scan the hillside, the hillside sloping up to where Pablo lay hidden.

After a hushed, urgent exchange, the lights to the compound went dark.

They clearly knew he was up there. It took Pablo's eyes a moment to adjust. When they did, he could see that the yard was now empty, and he could hear footfalls scaling the hillside toward him.

He remembered Bob's warning. He turned, bolting down his side of the ridge toward his trailer. Luckily the lights were off. If he hurried, he could scurry down his path and inside. All would look benign when they scaled the crest of the hill. That night Pablo lay huddled in his bed, annoyed that he'd called attention to himself. If they were paranoid, and believed he spied on them on a regular basis, it placed him in serious jeopardy.

He was furious with himself. Why hadn't he listened to Bob? This meant that they'd start watching him. Every time he wandered naked from his trailer, or made love with Bob outside by the fire, they might have camera equipment trained on them.

Damn.

Pablo didn't fall asleep till dawn.

*   *   *

She heard Misty's cane clattering to the tiled floor of the service porch. They were home.

Misty and Drew were accosted by their mother, Betty Barnes, waiting in the dark by the unlocked laundry room window they customarily crawled through to slither back to their rooms before dawn. This routine was completely unnecessary, because they were over eighteen and had been doing exactly as they pleased for the last five years. If they wanted to come in late, they knew where the doors were, but they liked to sneak around just to bug her.

They learned self-sufficiency as children after their father died when they were toddlers. Her response was years of alcohol and pills till she sobered up seven years ago. A reformed parent doesn't have the luxury of turning back time. As children they took care of her emotional needs; they acted like adults and when their puberty collided with her newfound sobriety, they turned into minister's kids. In other words, they were hardly going to listen now, not after the years she virtually ignored every need they expressed as small children. She may be their mother, and she might be more interested in them now, but to Misty and Drew, Betty B was only a sober moonie, begging to make amends, begging to take back the control she had long since relinquished years ago.

"Don't wake Betty B," Misty giggled as she wriggled through the window over a box of laundry soap.

The light snapped on.

"Uh-oh Mist. Bustola."

"Take us to Betty Ford, Mom," Misty held out her wrists. *"Please.* We need help." They dropped to the floor from the washing machine. Misty knelt for her cane, and wielding it, shoved past her mother into the kitchen.

"Where have you been? It's three-thirty in the morning!" Their mother was frail, with white skin and thinning hair. Misty was tempted to push her but controlled herself.

"We were out at the runway with Logan." Morbidly, Misty gunned for reaction and got it. Their father was a pilot. She knew her mother hated it when they'd go out to the runway to watch planes land.

"Don't have a cow, Mom," Drew added.

"It's a school night!"

"Nobody says we're gonna miss school," Misty muttered, perusing the refrigerator. "Besides, it's only community college."

"Did you forget about my A.A. meeting?"

"Oh," Drew nodded. "The cake thing."

"The *cake* thing," Misty remembered. "Sorry, we forgot!"

"I waited and waited. I finally had to ask a complete stranger to give me my cake."

"A newcomer, right?"

"We do it for the newcomer," Misty mocked her. Drew laughed. "My name is Betty *B,* and first, I'd like to welcome the newcomer."

"The newcomer is the life's blood of the program!" sang Drew.

"I'll drink to that!"

"Don't you have any respect for me at all?"

Misty smiled at her. "We weren't taught respect, Mother."

"Oh, I get it. You're angry at me, right? You have unresolved issues—"

"Issues," smirked Misty.

She pressed close to her mother's face, making Drew uncomfortable. "Mist," he admonished her, but Misty didn't pull back.

"Do you really think a few Alateen meetings will make up for the shitty job you did when we were kids?"

"Mist." Drew, again. "Back off, already."

"Misty," her mother grimaced. "You're hurting me."

"Mist," Drew took her by the shoulders. "You're hurting her."

"Well, she hurt me!" Misty whirled on him.

"I can't keep saying I'm sorry Misty! I've had a hard life! I had a crappy mother too."

"And now you have a crappy daughter!"

"Yes! Now I've got a Goddammed crappy daughter! I wanted to break the cycle with you Misty, but guess what!" She hurled herself past her daughter, completely outraged. "You're probably already a drunk. What are you on now that you think you can talk like this to me? Cocaine? You're both reeking of vodka. You think I can't smell it? You've been driving around like this? I hope the cops get you!"

She turned suddenly, shoving Misty. "You think I can't push back, Misty?" She pushed her again.

"Cut it out." Stunned, Misty started to cry. "I'm warning you."

"You kids think I can't get in your face? You think I'm so weak I'll just stand here and let you *threaten* me?"

"Mom," Drew tried to intervene.

Betty slapped his face. "And you're even worse! You're supposed to take care of her. She's your sister. You haven't had good parents, but at least you have each other. Is this the best you can come up with? You don't want to be my kids? OK. I gave you what the law said I had to give you. Food and a roof over your head. That's more than I could ever count on! But I swear to you both, if you ever come crawling through a window in this house again, I'll shoot you myself." She hesitated as Misty's grip tightened on the hook of her cane. Misty, of course, had already been shot once.

"Once is enough. Real nice, Mom. Fucking bitch."

"I mean it!" Betty reacted, pushing both of them with her hands. "I mean it! *I mean it!*" She stomped wildly from the kitchen, screaming, and didn't stop screaming till her bedroom door slammed.

Whenever Sister Agnes suffered a sleepless night, she took her pillow and blanket and crept across the parking lot to the main sanctuary where she curled up at the feet of the statue of the Blessed Virgin. This Madonna was particularly comforting, and Sister Agnes had seen much magnificent statuary in her travels. Father Gene, too, had expressed his admiration for her. The expression in her eyes was complex. She seemed both compassionate and guilty at the same time. Was her guilt because she lacked understanding? Sister Agnes wondered. Did she ever undercut God's will for her?

Sister Agnes had set everything in motion. *Vengeance is mine,* says the Lord. She had prayed, fasted and flagellated herself over these plans. She had seduced innocents to do her bidding, but she couldn't sit idly by. Not after seeing the crushed baby of Judi Romero. She knew God would punish her. Sister Agnes feared only one thing. The one way He could.

Before making her little nest, she fell to her knees on the hassock, and prayed the same prayer she always prayed:

"Bless my mother and father, sweet Jesus. Thank you because I'm not alone in this world. Thank you for my baby brother. Bless his life with your spirit. I pray for the day we can be together. In your Holy name . . ."

She poked at her pillow and blanket like a tenuous old cat. Finally she felt calm enough to sleep. "Please," she urged her Heavenly Father, moments before she fell to sleep. "Don't be mean."

18

Misty and Drew

They both lived in terror of Logan since Cathedral City. Not Cathedral City the town. Cathedral City the moment. The event. The night Misty got shot. Cathedral City. The owner of Nick's, looming out of the shadows from the side entrance to the bar. Surprising them. Startling them. They were only there because they were high and feeling a little ghoulish. Returning to the scene of the crime. And out he'd come. Cathedral City.

"Hello, young lady. It's a beautiful night, isn't it!"

He smiled. Waited. Didn't make a run for it. Had to know what was coming. She felt Drew behind her. Then Logan. Saw the flash of the bat. Heard it too. It whizzed by her head. She heard the sound of teeth smashing. A grunt was all she heard from Nick.

You stop right there or I'll shoot you bastards! Where'd he come from? One minute they're standing alone, minding their own business in a vacant parking lot, and then it's crawling with people. Where had the old guy been hiding? Why was he late? Why hadn't he stopped them in time?

Fuck you! The sound of her own voice screaming, *You're fucking next, you old Jew!* She could remember the sensation of her own drool, seeping from the sides of her mouth. Like black bile. Ugliness. Satanic. Acrid. Why hadn't he stopped them in time?

Who was that back there?

In the moments before Misty got shot, she was thinking about breaking it off with Logan. He'd gotten so intense. Intimidating.

Before, Misty always called the shots—pushed them around. She liked showing them who was boss. Cathedral City was just something to do when they got bored. And they were always bored. Drew was a fucking sheep. He did whatever she wanted. Probably because he grew up in a house with only women. He was older by a year, but for as long as she could remember, always did whatever she told him.

She didn't even really have anything against minorities.

Some nights, as she lay against Logan's hot, muscular back, she wanted to talk to him about it. Why did they do the things they did? Was it the meth? Was it boredom? Was it their upbringing? Betty B had never uttered a racist remark in her life. She had gay friends. She was liberal. Even when she was drinking and popping pills.

Where had the lingo come from?

Her little outbursts hadn't been easy on them. Her precious sobriety hadn't cured her violent temper. She still screamed. Smashed things. Lost control with the velocity of a plane taking off. You could never predict it. The dog could sometimes tell. He whined a little. He could feel the tension. Then, *kaboom*, off went Betty B. This last one, well, Logan wanted them to move out to Sky Valley. How could they keep taking the abuse?

Logan liked fucking her after she got shot. He didn't mind the scar, which was all she could think about. Her fucking bikini line as blood gushed from her abdomen. He thought it was sexy. Gave her a mystique. Where would she find another guy like him? Plus, the kid thing wasn't a problem. He didn't want kids. He just wanted Misty and his freedom.

He'd kill for both of them and she and Drew knew it.

The night Misty had been shot was their fourth trip back to Nick's, and they were only casing the place for a possible robbery or maybe just another night of mayhem. They marveled that they hadn't been caught on the previous assault. The alley had been packed with patrons of Nick's for some kind of grand reopening. Marcella, the vicious little black bartender, hadn't warned them there'd be so many people.

When they'd charged the alley, faces disguised by grisly Halloween masks, in Logan's cousin's black Mustang convertible (borrowed for this purpose without his cousin's knowledge) and paint pellet guns at the ready, they were too drunk to have the good sense to abort. They just went for it and started shooting.

It was over in sixty seconds, but the damage had been done. They had orders to scare a few locals. Instead they incited the wrath of a Jewish senior citizen's home, the local Mexican American Chamber of Commerce and the desert Gay Business association. Not to mention Sam Singer, who stirred up the local press. It had the effect of galvanizing the communities. Even the priest at St. Louis Catholic Church got into the fray.

Instead of scaring business away, the notorious club was packed every night for months. And still they hadn't been caught or turned in, and there was a very good reason for that. They'd been hired to make the hit by a local real estate attorney wanting to scare customers off so Sam Singer would be forced to sell his property. He protected them to protect himself. But he didn't get his way. Nobody ever successfully bullied Sam out of anything. Sam Singer had been a bully's bully.

Then came the night Misty got shot.

They hadn't even intended to stay, but out came the proprietor of the place, the namesake, Nick, for Chrissakes. He was alone in the empty parking lot, fumbling for his keys. There was only one car in the parking lot, a vintage Lincoln Mark IV, which they mistakenly assumed was empty and belonging to Nick.

Nick was friendly, and Misty remembered being bothered by that. "Hello, young lady," he'd smiled at her. "It's a lovely night, isn't it!"

And then Logan smashed his smile with a bat. Misty continued to have nightmares about the sound of his teeth shattering. He'd been proud of his smile, that was plain. Misty said it was an evil thing to steal someone's smile. Her smile had been stolen by her mother when she was just a little girl. Misty knew the high cost of a lost smile, and she was sorry Logan picked that one thing to take from the thin, grinning friendly guy.

The old Jew took them completely by surprise. One minute they were kicking the shit out of Nick and the next they turned and found themselves looking into the barrel of a .45.

"You stop right there or I'll shoot you bastards!"

But Drew came out of nowhere and tackled him from behind, causing the gun to fire.

Misty said that when you get shot, it feels like piercing heat, and your body reacts in shock, protecting you only briefly from the promise of true pain.

"Jesus, he shot me Drew," Drew remembered her saying, and

then she remembered slumping against the door of their white Blazer. Her leg had given out. With that, Logan and Drew threw her into the truck and they roared off, Drew driving and Logan applying pressure to the wound.

Logan explained calmly that they couldn't take her to a local hospital or they'd all be arrested. They'd take her to Mexico and have her stitched up there.

"She'll fucking croak before then," Drew had complained.

"We're gonna stay calm, drive south to the border and in two hours she'll be good as new. I know a doctor who'll take care of her. Can you hold out till then Misty? You aren't bleeding much. Can you hold out?"

Misty was already passed out.

When Drew complained, Logan placed his paint-pellet pistol to a delirious Misty's temple and thus implied the only other option he was prepared to offer. Drew drove as fast as he could. That night, a famous Mexicali abortionist performed emergency surgery on Misty.

They were indeed aware of Pablo's existence in Sky Valley. They knew everything about him. They knew he was a gay Mexican who worked in the very same restaurant they'd assaulted multiple times, over four years ago. They left him alone because they were never caught. They also knew, from perusing his mailbox that this particular Mexican was shockingly, unpredictably rich.

They saw the bank statements to prove it.

Pablo might be useful to them later on. And so might the gay border patrol guy who fucked him in front of the campfire, in full view of every coyote east of Desert Hot Springs.

On a hot windy Cathedral City morning at the kiosk waiting for a bus, Soila lost her scarf and in minutes found herself surrounded by wailing believers, all weeping and kneeling at the apparition of the Virgin of Guadalupe, embedded in her cheek. Anita had been with her, and upon their reaction, stormed off, pissed off that all the attention wasn't being paid to her.

Shortly Anita returned with Ruby, huffing and puffing down the sidewalk, demanding to know what all the fuss was about.

"The Blessed Virgin," someone whispered reverently.

"On her cheek," someone uttered in ecstasy.

"It's nothing but a disgusting birthmark that's changed," Ruby retorted, grabbing Soila by the chin and pinching it roughly. "It's probably melanoma."

"Fear not, for I am with thee," the birthmark advised her, and Ruby jumped back and screamed, but it wasn't the birthmark who spoke. It was Sister Agnes, who appeared from nowhere more miraculously than Soila's Blessed Virgin.

The crowd had swelled to twenty or more, and when passing cars saw hordes of people on their knees, weeping and counting the beads of their rosaries, they, too, stopped to see what was going on. Within a matter of ten minutes more, cars were jamming the intersection of Date Palm Drive and Ramon Road, the drivers craning their necks to see what could be going on.

"Sister Agnes," Soila whispered, "what should I do?"

Helping her up to stand on the kiosk bench so believers could get a better look at her, Sister Agnes surveyed the crowd, considered the gravity of the situation, mused for a moment after considering all of the consequences, looked Soila directly in the eye and said, "If I were you I'd get representation and go for it."

With that, Sister Agnes dramatically fell to her knees and kissed the toes of Soila's favorite red sneakers.

The crowd responded in full throttle frenzy, now that a representative of the local Catholic Church was confirming the miracle. The Virgin of Guadalupe had come to Cathedral City.

"What message does she have?"

"What can she tell us?"

Some began to pray passionately in Spanish. Then a Cathedral City police car pulled up. Two Latino officers swaggered up, wondering what all the commotion was about.

"Step down, young lady," they motioned to a red-faced Soila. Soila really didn't want any trouble with local law enforcement. Her father would kill her. But when Soila made a move to climb down from the bench, the crowd roared its displeasure. The cops looked uneasily at each other and told her to stay put for now.

"What's going on, Sister?" One of them recognized Sister Agnes from his church.

"We have what appears to be a bona fide visit from the Blessed Virgin," Sister Agnes admonished him.

The cops examined Soila's cheek.

"I've seen this girl before," one cop whispered to his partner. "It's a birthmark."

"It was a birthmark," Anita overheard him and protested. "Now it's a vision!"

"Where do you live, young lady?"

"Just around the corner," Soila answered, as a news van pulled up.

"Would you consider asking the crowd to peacefully disburse, go home and wait till we can get an expert or two to confirm your condition?"

"God is the only expert to make such a determination."

The cop loomed up to whisper in Sister Agnes' ear. "I can take you away for inciting civil unrest. How about that, Sister?"

Sister Agnes, who hoped to make it to Happy Hour at Maria's didn't want her afternoon habits derailed for anything.

"Do as the officer suggests," Sister Agnes admonished Soila.

The crowd quieted as Soila Quintero raised her hand, high over her head. Others followed suit, thinking she was about to lead them in prayer.

Instead all she said was, "I have to go home to have my lunch."

With cameras trained on her and reporters shouting questions, people reached out to touch her cheek, recoiling as if shocked, in some form of mass hysteria. The cops escorted Soila, followed by Sister Agnes, then Anita and Ruby, through the crowd to their street.

Thomas Quintero glanced out his window in time to see his daughters and his girlfriend striding solemnly up the walk, followed by an amassed crowd of over two hundred faithful.

Sitting in the bar, talking with Maria, Pablo glanced up to see Betty B enter. "Please," she whispered, taking her seat. "I have to find him. I have to find him to apologize."

"Would you like your regular?" Pablo asked her kindly, reaching for the spigot of Coca-Cola.

"No. I want a hard drink. Vodka. Gin. Anything."

Pablo and Maria exchanged a concerned glance.

"Maybe you should tell us what's on your mind before you drink anything," Maria advised her.

"I know who tried to kill Nick. I know the kids who came to your alley. I think you're in danger."

"Nothing could ever hurt me again," Maria replied. "Don't worry about frightening me."

"Let me have the drink first."

Pablo shrugged. "If you're sure."

He poured her a weak gin and tonic. She took one timid sip, her hands trembling. "There. I've done it. Now I can speak out loud. It's been eating me up."

"Who, then?" Maria asked firmly. "I was in the alley one night when they came! Friends were hurt badly. Who?"

"My son and daughter." And Betty downed her drink. "I wasn't sure before but they've moved out. I just came from home. All their belongings are gone. They're involved with a terrible young man. He leads a white separatist group. I knew Nick at Betty Ford," she admitted, "I was his drug and alcohol counselor."

Maria remembered only too well when Nick had checked into Betty Ford.

"Where did they move?" Pablo asked gently, but his knees were trembling.

"Somewhere to an enclave in the high desert."

"Where?" he persisted.

"Sky Valley," Betty told him.

Behind Pablo, Maria shook her head and smiled. The little nun was right.

19

The Call

"We don't have any beds," Inez heard a volunteer say. She was speaking through the locked mesh screen door to a small woman standing at the gate outside. Maybe it was the defeated way the woman's shoulder slumped. The look of longing toward Avance. The dirty street behind her. The homeless camp on the other side.

"Let me talk to her," Inez came to the door. She buzzed the gate.

The woman, Lucy, had been tiny, tinier than Inez. She was so short Inez thought she was a mature looking prepubescent teenager. In fact, she was in her late twenties. She was married, and had two daughters. Pregnant with a third, complications had developed. Lucy had agreed to a routine HIV test. It had come back positive. When it was suggested that her husband also agree to be tested, he naturally refused. A test for the two small daughters revealed her worst fears. Both had tested positive.

Her husband was *un machista,* and his family declared her a whore. He was the only man she'd ever had sex with. There was no occurrence of a blood transfusion in her medical history. No other way to trace the infection to her, other than through him. He kicked her out of the house. Her daughters had been taken away from her by her mother-in-law, and now were not getting the much needed medical attention they needed. Her mother-in-law believed with great prayer that any illness would be expunged by the Blessed Virgin herself.

Now Lucy was eight months pregnant, homeless and ill.

"I'm sorry, but we don't have any room at all," Inez told her.

"But where will I go? Am I to have my baby on the street?"

Inez hesitated. It was unbelievable. How could anyone so tiny even carry a baby to full term? She was perspiring. "Give me a glass of water for her," Inez ordered. An aide bolted for the cooler.

"She can have my bed," a voice spoke behind them.

Inez turned. Gracie had been listening in the hallway.

"And where will you sleep?"

"I can go home."

"No!" Inez leaped to her feet. "No, you cannot!" Several other volunteers voiced their concern. A small group of women surrounded Gracie. She'd come so far, since arriving at their doors with a bag over her head. Her eyes were clear. Her wounds had healed. The KS was gone.

"I'm healthier now. He wants me back."

"You're a fool! He'll probably kill you this time."

"If I get frightened, I'll come back. Maybe you'll have another room by then. She needs my bed more than me tonight. I'll go home. He'll take me back. All I have to do is call him."

They all waited for Inez to make the choice. "What can I do?" She shrugged. "Call him."

Gracie called her husband, who arrived drunk several hours later, to come and pick her up.

Thanks to Gracie, Lucy was sleeping soundly in her cot when Inez left tonight.

"Gracie gave up her bed at the shelter," Inez told Freddie. "For someone worse off." It was early evening, after her dinner. Her brother Fredrico, a dancer, was getting ready for the night shift at El Cid. Inez was ironing his dress. Tonight, the red satin. Inez had personally made the dress for her tall willowy brother, copying the pattern from a doll, handmade and given to her daughter Anita, five years ago. The doll had long since been lost.

Freddie was the transvestite brother of Inez. Without Freddie and her other brother, Nacho, Inez' return to Mexico would have been a miserable mistake. She might have been terribly homesick for Cathedral City's gay sub-culture. As she smoothed out the folds in the skirt of the red dress, Inez chuckled at the irony.

All the nights she sat bitterly at her bedroom window, listening to the sounds of men's laughter, the raucous show tunes, the whispers of ecstasy in the shadows of the alley she shared with Nick and Kenny's gay bar—she hadn't admitted that without that influence, her life then might have been doubly bleak. Only now could she acknowledge how much they entertained her. The priest had inadvertently challenged her to think in that direction. She wondered if Father Gene was actually homosexual. If not, what motive did a true heterosexual male have to be tolerant of such aberrance?

Of her six brothers, two turned out to be gay. All the femininity—the tall, willowy legs, the luxuriant black hair, the luminous skin—had skipped the lone family daughter. Fate awarded Freddie with all the beauty. And humor. No one was funnier than her brother Freddie. Nacho was the youngest, the baby of the family. Inez only knew he was gay because Freddie told her. Also the most serious, Freddie was studying to be an architect.

Affiliating with Freddie and Inez had incurred the wrath of his father. Nacho had been terribly distressed by the reports of Inez' failing health. HIV infection was spreading rapidly among ignorant, trusting Mexican housewives, who were contracting it from philandering husbands, many who frequented prostitutes, female and male, and refused to wear condoms. Nacho knew that some Mexican men would rather catch AIDS and die than ever wear a condom. They certainly could not be expected to wear a condom with their own wives. It wasn't masculine. And think of the questions their wives might start asking. No. It was unthinkable. A few deaths were inconsequential to the overall picture in their minds.

To Nacho, this was unthinkable. He moved from his father's house into a crowded little apartment with Freddie and Inez. After her move, Inez started as a client with a woman's help organization called Avance. Soon she was receiving free medical care and prescriptions, but funding for the program was always in danger. Because she was accustomed to the high quality service she encountered in Palm Springs area programs like the AIDS Assistance Program, which focused its attention on serving the financial needs of the desert's most needy HIV population, or the Desert AIDS Project, which in addition to HIV testing and prevention also had a strong community outreach program—Inez saw quickly what the Mexican programs were lacking.

Quickly she became a volunteer. Then ascended to the position of counselor, often the first stop for the timid, frightened and often ignorant new clients of Avance. Today a particularly sad case had come across her desk.

Freddie appeared. He knew Gracie's story.

*   *   *

Over the sound of the blaring television, and Freddie's pounding boom box, the telephone began to ring. Nacho was just coming in. He winced from the cacophony. So much energy exuded from his older sister and brother, but he smiled when he saw that Inez was ironing Freddie's dress. Tonight he was debuting a new act.

Nacho reached for the ringing telephone. "Bueno?"

He motioned for Inez to turn down the volume on her television set. Irritably she consented. It was probably one of Freddie's crazy girlfriends. She kept ironing.

"It's Soila. She sounds upset."

Soila was still grieving over the death of Ruthie Singer. And Maria's little girl. Inez had tried to contact Maria, but Soila advised her that she hadn't given up on the possibility that Conchita was alive. It made her mad to even discuss her. Inez sent her a Catholic bookmark instead.

"What's wrong? Why are you crying?"

"Daddy's sick," Soila whispered. "Ruby's leaving him. And Anita's going with her."

"She can't take Anita! You stop her."

"Anita wants to go. She says she hates us."

"Let me talk to her."

After a long silence, Ruby came on the phone. "You should be grateful that I'm taking her at all! You don't know what I've been through with these people. You can have your fucking husband back! You shoulda warned me! He owes me half of this house, too."

"You can't take my daughter."

"I can't *lose* your daughter," Ruby shouted into the receiver. "I couldn't leave without her if I tried. You have any idea what's going on over here?"

Inez had no idea at all.

"I got people camped out on my lawn, lady. All night long, nothing but moaning."

"What people?" Inez demanded impatiently. She was getting sick of Ruby, but happy to hear how fat she'd gotten.

"These fucking religious freaks. Hasn't your idiot daughter told you anything?"

And Ruby told her about the blazing transformation of Soila's cheek. The apparition. The Blessed Virgin. The hundreds of parishioners who'd turned her front lawn into a crazy freak show.

"They killed my fucking roses," Ruby shrieked. "And Thomas just lays around in bed all day."

"Has he seen the doctor?"

"He won't go back."

"What about his boss?"

"He called today to say he had to let him go. He doesn't go to fucking work."

How sad Inez felt to hear this. "Where will you take Anita?"

"We're going to my sister's place in Monterey Park. She's got loads of room."

Inez hesitated. She had to think. "Ruby, what about you? How do you feel?"

"What the fuck business is that of yours? I feel like shit, what can I tell you. After all I've been through? Like freaking shit."

"Let me talk to Soila."

When Soila came on the line, Inez spoke to her in a firm, caring voice. "I want you to let Anita go with Ruby. Just make sure you know how to reach her."

"But what about daddy?"

"I'll come to take care of daddy."

"What?"

"I'm coming back. I'll come back to Cathedral City. Now what's this thing about your cheek?"

"Your boyfriend keeps hassling my ladies," Maria informed Pablo, in an early morning call to Sky Valley. "I want you to put a stop to it."

"Your ladies? When did you get so butch?" Pablo queried wondrously. He was hiding under his blanket. The knowledge of his new neighbors was still particularly unsettling to him. He still hadn't confided what he knew to Bob.

"Since they killed my parents. Since they tossed my dead grandmother into the arroyo. Since they drowned Ruthie. Since they stole my daughter. Get him to stop."

"Nobody drowned Ruthie."

"They could have built a bridge. Every year the wash floods."

"Mija, he didn't have anything to do with those tragedies," Pablo murmured gently. Mornings were particularly bad for her. She couldn't stand the silence of a house without a happy child waking inside of it. Conchita had been a very cheerful and amusing early riser.

"He pulled 'em over three times in the last month."

Pablo knew she meant Bambi and Madonna. "I think he's dropping the case. I don't talk shop with Bob."

"You don't or you *won't*," she replied, all the life in her voice draining away.

"He's not a bad guy. If you'd get to know him, you'd see what I see."

"It's harassment. I know the law. I'll hire a lawyer for them."

Pablo knew that the first thing Maria did when she came into her money, after chopping off all of her hair, was to hire lawyers. Lawyers to threaten the Cathedral City planning department. Lawyers to set up her charitable foundations. Now lawyers to defend Bambi and Madonna.

Pablo had never discussed the Judi Romero case with Bob. He got all his information from Maria, who often fell to rambling ruminations about the afternoon that she died. He could tell she probably thought there was more to the story than her two friends were admitting to. How could anyone so pregnant have survived such a violent crash, even cushioned by so many other bodies? She would have suffocated before she crawled to safety. And Maria knew the back of Bambi's delivery truck was treble padlocked for security. If they were transporting Judi illegally, how had they come to know her?

Bob, Pablo knew, had limited resources. As one of twelve investigators in the El Centro division of the INS, Bob's hands were always full.

"Maybe you're right," offered Maria, who had been talking this entire time Pablo had been daydreaming. He hadn't heard a word she'd said.

"Right about what?"

"If this man is important to you, I should get to know him. Your mother wants to meet him, too."

"You told my mother about him?"

"I assumed you already would have. You hardly have any secrets with her."

She was right, he reflected. Why hadn't he told his mother about Bob? She was so clairvoyant she probably already knew, but she alluded to nothing in their last conversation. She was grieving deeply about Conchita. He knew that. She'd been present at her birth. Pablo was particularly intrigued to know that his father, according to his mother, was inconsolable.

They offered to come, but Maria, through Pablo, asked that they wait. It was too hot in the desert. They normally would never plan to travel in such oppressive circumstances. It smacked of grief. Maria would not entertain anyone grieving for Chita at present. Chita was alive, she reasoned tearfully to Pablo. There was to be no pronouncement or consensus otherwise. Anyone who did so would be cut out of her life.

Hence, Pablo was intrigued to hear that Maria and her mother had been talking. "What else did she say, *mija?*"

"She said she wished you'd start using your college education."

"I'm happy with what I'm doing for now."

"You're a smart boy, Pablito. I don't need you to baby-sit for me."

"I'm not baby-sitting for you. I like my afternoon regulars."

"I think Sister Agnes has a crush on you. I've only ever seen her smile at you."

"I wish you'd smile at me, *mi amor.*"

"In my heart, I do all the time, Pablito. Give me time," she asked. "Make a plan with me and your boyfriend."

"I wish you had a boyfriend."

"I've had more than my fair share in that department," she replied softly. "That much I'm smart enough to know."

"I worry about you."

"Don't." Her voice sharpened. "I'd hate to be pitied by anyone."

"I don't pity you."

"We understand each other now."

When Pablo hung up, he placed a call to Bob's cell phone. He'd started working at midnight. His shift didn't end till noon.

"It's me," Pablo whispered when Bob answered.

"Can't talk. I'm in pursuit."

The line sputtered and went dead.

Like the other border patrol wives, Pablo worried about Bob. He worked alone, without partners, in 120 degree heat. Although he carried a firearm, Bob told Pablo he never had to use it, let alone bring it out. The tight green uniform was his best insurance. Border jumpers had an unquestioning respect for the Migra uniform.

When Bob came upon them, traversing the cool desert floor, the first order of business was to call in his location and alight from his vehicle. They rarely took flight. Most were docile from heat and fatigue. A large group would be ordered to assemble in more manageable columns. If they were hungry or thirsty, Bob carried bottled water and candy bars. They were used to the drill. They'd sink to the ground and wait for transport. They'd daydream about tomorrow or next week, when fate would afford them the chance to try again.

"Hello, this is the Betty Ford Clinic—Personnel Division."

"Yes, I'm wondering if you still have a counselor called Betty B working with you?"

"Well, we did. She's on leave."

"Leave? A medical leave?"

"Who's calling?"

"I . . . I was a client of hers. I was hoping to talk with her."

"I'm afraid I can't give out her number."

"If I leave you my name, could you phone her and let her know I called?"

"I can't make any promises."

"I'd really appreciate it."

"Okay, sure."

And Nick gave his name and number.

Within five minutes the telephone rang. He was sitting in his robe with his feet propped up. He was hoisting a Campari and soda to his lips. He'd wanted to drink since they attempted the phone call to Ruthie. The disappointment that her number had been disconnected had thrown them both into deep depression. It was a sure sign, Kenny thought. They were better off not knowing.

Privately, both thought of a thousand ways to call Cathedral City and ask about her. Kenny made Nick promise not to call. Now here he was, about to take his first drink in five years. This kind of call was legitimate, he snarfed.

"Is Nick in?" A woman's voice queried.

"This is Nick. Who's this?"

"I'm Betty B. From the clinic."

"That was fast."

"The girl in the office is a friend of mine."

Nick stared at the receiver. Now what?

"Actually," she spoke first, "I've been wanting to talk to you too."

"Yeah?"

"Not about drinking. But you should know I have been drinking."

"I'm sorry, I guess . . . I'm no one to judge."

"I owe you an apology."

"An apology. For what?"

"On behalf of my children."

"What do they have to do with anything?" He was more interested in his untasted cocktail. He could barely hear her for the loud popping of the soda's effervescence.

"It's like this. They were the ones who assaulted you behind your bar."

"Describe them to me."

"My daughter was pretty. Blonde. Just sixteen. Her brother looks like her twin, but he's a year older."

Nick took a deep breath. "What about the third one? The older boy."

"I know who you mean. But he's no son of mine."

"Well, it's relatively minor in the grand scheme of things," Nick told her kindly. "But he gave the orders. And he swung the bat. Definitely. I think they were manipulated by him. Afraid of him."

"You've known all this time? I read that you didn't remember."

"I wanted to put it behind me."

"Why?"

"I didn't want to lose my friend."

"I know you loved Cathedral City. You talked about it so fondly in your group." She hesitated.

"What happened wasn't Cathedral City's fault."

She hesitated. He sensed she wanted to tell him something else.

"There's more."

"Yes."

"Involving your kids?"

"No. Unrelated, but horrible. Do you want to hear?"

He didn't answer so she told him.

20

Thomas Quintero

He could hear Ruby packing. Perhaps after she was gone, he might have some peace and quiet. That's all he wanted now, the quiet life he'd had before he met Ruby. Inez was plain, yes, and without humor, but she'd respected him. She worked hard and gave him all her earnings to save toward the purchase of their little house in old Cathedral City. He had no complaint about her on that score. Plus, she was quiet, practically nonconversant.

He hated this house. It was new, and cheaply built in the windy north end of Cathedral City. At night he could hear the trucks on the interstate. He could hear his daughters gossiping through the walls, which meant Soila and Anita could hear Ruby during lovemaking. The noises Ruby made during lovemaking had excited him at first. He mistook her vulgarity for passion. It was such a change for him. Now he missed the quiet submission of his first wife. With Inez, his mind could freely wander in fantasy as he rocked on top of her, his strong, thick toes, pivoting in even thrusts against the baseboard of their old wooden bed. His feet were like rudders, in the calm, quiet surface of the mattress. Ruby was always pulling him into her reality. She even resented his closed eyes.

Thomas and Inez' little rented house in Cathedral City was as nice inside as the showroom where he worked. Thomas would accept nothing less. He had personally replastered the living room ceilings and walls, and repainted them the soft buttery yellow Inez remembered from her father's comfortable home. With his own hands he had tiled the bathroom and the kitchen counters. Andy, his boss, had given him boxes and boxes of beautiful pale blue tiles which a spoiled client had returned, paid for, favoring something far more ornate for her Rancho Mirage pool house.

The antique furnishings had been old, simple and polished beautifully. When Andy visited his family for a Christmas get together, Thomas could tell how impressed he was by the understated taste of the Quintero *casita*. Outside, in the small, tiled front courtyard, Thomas had placed a small bubbling fountain. He and his family spent every weekend for a month planting the area, with flowering desert trees and shrubbery. Night blooming jasmine perfumed the sultry evening air.

Every bit of work had been painstakingly born of his own two hands. His landlord had made a promise. Thomas could one day buy this house if he saved up the down payment and continued to pay his rent. One thing he knew for certain, then. He would always work hard. If he worked hard, and if his wife worked hard, nothing was impossible in the United States.

Hadn't it all gone well until Inez became ill? And until the trouble in the alley with *la mojada* and his son? Thomas was too tired to even blame Maria for his misfortunes. God had evened the score with her. He took her baby girl.

Now Ruby was taking his.

"We're leaving, shithead," she stood in the frame of the bedroom doorway. She was so squat and big from his haze he thought she was the bottom half of the door swung closed. "I'm getting a lawyer. I'll get my share of the house."

"You don't need a lawyer for that," he whispered, drawing difficult halting breaths. "The house is yours, anytime you want it back."

That's how much he hated this cheap, wind-driven house.

"Bye, Dad," Anita waved to him cheerfully.

Ruby had already slammed out of the house. He could hear her shout one last admonition to the supplicants kneeling on her lawn. "You stupid lame-brained idiots. It's only a fucking birthmark that's probably cancerous!"

At last, she was gone.

In another moment Thomas felt Soila's presence. She had a cool wet rag, which she applied to his forehead. "Daddy, I think you need to go to the hospital. Mommy thinks you might have pneumonia."

"Good. I'll stay here."

"You need pills, she says."

"I won't take them. I want to die."

"Don't say that," she pleaded with him. "She's coming back."

"Who's coming back?"

"Mommy."

"They'll never let her in the country. Not with la SIDA."

"She has ways," Soila whispered. "She's coming back."

And for some reason, this comforted him enormously and he gave himself up to a deep, blissful sleep. Before he did, he muttered something Soila found sweet and very sad. "No matter how I acted, I wanted America for all of us."

Soila patted his hand and sat with him.

Nick resisted the urge to have his drink. She had given him too much information to disseminate, all of it awful. All of it dangerous. It was his fault for breaking the rule. For making the call. He cried for a solid hour over Ruthie. He had never asked for her forgiveness, which wasn't why he cried. He cried because she had selflessly shouldered all the blame. It had been his responsibility as much as hers.

How Maria now figured in the whole scenario was even more tragic. Betty B had called to absolve herself of her guilt over those monstrous children. He could see them as clearly as if they stood before him now. But the truth of their identity, and whereabouts, and even Ruthie's death were nothing compared to Maria's fresh tragedy. And Kenny's. His daughter had certainly drowned. Two babies lost. Ruthie had suffered in isolated, tortured silence. She shut herself off in her life with Sam.

Maria didn't even have that. Now that Nick knew, Kenny had to know. The impact would change their lives forever.

Would Nick have the courage to tell him?

He padded into the kitchen to empty his untried Campari. The ice had melted. Without hesitating, he dumped his glass in the sink, reached for a clean one, preparing a fresh cocktail; and dumped that one, too.

"You know," Maria smiled conversationally, "I'm a wetback."

"Oy," Pablo muttered, an expression he had picked up from Ruthie. He said it exactly as she always had, a rush of hurried exasperation. The perfect way to tap built up pressure.

"In fact, you aren't. You have a valid green card," Bob answered pleasantly.

"I was. Can't you arrest me for that?"

"I think we already did arrest you."

"*Ninos,*" Pablo implored them. "Let's be nice."

"You put me over the border, pregnant without any money. No resources whatsoever."

"I'm sorry," Bob studied her. "But we didn't drag you illegally into our country. You were willing to cross our borders without re-sources. Tell me how sending you back home made you worse off than when you arrived?" He was evaluating whether she was crack-ing up or still in control enough to finish dinner. He knew more about her possibly than any other living human being. He knew who her parents were. How they died. He had inspected her arrest record.

They were dining on Pablo's desert terrace. It was quite hot, but they were drinking cold beers. Pablo ran nervously back and forth to the Airstream refrigerator. It wasn't going well at all. Her attitude was highly aggressive when she arrived. Just when Pablo thought she was going to start growing her hair again, he could see she'd just gone at it again with her scissors. She'd lost weight from a vigorous training program she'd instituted. She was running eight miles a day, sometimes during the hottest part of the day. Pablo saw her working out at Gold's with a trainer. It had hurt him that she hadn't asked him for advice.

He paused to study them through the porthole of the galley kitchen. Their body language said it all. They were openly hostile to one another and only a modicum of civility for Pablo's sake kept them from exploding into an all-out bitterly political argument. Pablo recalled an observation she'd made the day Bob had come to investigate the Judi Romero incident. She'd been annoyed with her-self that she'd found him somewhat attractive.

Chagrined, Pablo shook his head. This was also fueling her fury about him. The first man she'd expressed interest in since Kenny was also gay.

"What do you think we should do? Step back and allow our bor-ders to be overrun?"

"Look around. The Latino population of California is now forty-one percent. More than whites, Asians and blacks. Face it. We're al-ready the majority. We're already here."

"You're making border politics a race issue. It's a security issue. An economic issue."

"That's bullshit, man. How many Canadians get beat up or killed, trying to border jump?"

"The Canadian economy is considerably stronger. Canadians have considerably less incentive to illegally infiltrate our borders. If they do, it's usually drug-related. The way to minimize border violence is to bolster the economy of Mexico."

"Without Mexico, California's economy would be in the toilet. California, Arizona and Texas owe Mexico."

"I somewhat agree," Bob replied pleasantly. "Who wouldn't want to immigrate to the United States? It's the most wonderful country in the world."

"Now that's bullshit."

"Whatever," Bob replied airily as Pablo returned. Bob pulled Pablo down next to him, perching him on his knee.

"Everybody getting along?" Pablo queried.

"We have strong opinions."

"But he has a badge and a gun," Maria interjected. She and Pablo exchanged glances. In an effort to be nice, she reached forward and patted his boot. "I'm glad you found each other," she acknowledged. "As creepy as the whole thing is."

Pablo allowed his body to sag against Bob's. He sank to the ground between his legs, and drew his knees up to his chest. He scanned the horizon above the crest of his encampment. "It stays lighter and lighter."

"What are you gonna do about the murderers who live over the ridge from you?"

Bob, who was hard to fluster, reacted by spitting out his beer.

"He tell you who they are?" Maria asked.

Composed now, Bob smiled at Pablo. "No. We know they're rough characters. We haven't known to what extent."

"We don't know if it's the same ones," Pablo told Maria.

"Well, they were involved in the gay bashing of our friend Nick, the guy who used to own my club before me."

"How long have you known?" asked Bob.

"We just found out. Their mother is a new customer."

"And she's been talking?"

"Drinking and talking," Maria told him.

"There weren't witnesses," Pablo asserted. Pablo didn't want them to be the same kids who were his neighbors.

"Yes, there were. There was Nicky, for one. And Sam." For Bob's benefit, Maria explained that Sam was Ruthie's husband. "Died of a heart attack, trying to protect Nick."

"I know the history very well. They were all questioned. Like Pablo said, Nick lost his memory. And even if he hadn't, without someone to back him up, they couldn't win the case."

"I bet I know of another witness."

"That so?"

"You're drunk," Pablo told her. "Stop."

"If you're thinking it might be the little Quintero girl, she was questioned too. I told you, I know the details of the case backwards and forwards. You need two viable witnesses. Nick without his memory or the little girl afraid to testify—you can't make the case."

21

Stacked Deck

A new secretary from a Reno escrow agency phoned to tell Nick when his closing was. Nick was out. Kenny had come home early with a migraine.

"You have the wrong number," Kenny laughed.

She repeated the telephone number listed on her computer.

"There's a mistake."

"Are the last four digits of your Social Security number 8989?"

She thought she was talking to Nick. Kenny had to fill out so many forms after Nick was assaulted, he knew Nick's Social Security number by heart. He hesitated. "What property are we buying?"

She gave him a nearby address. "Are you sure I have the right telephone number?"

"Yes," Kenny asserted. "We're in escrow on several buildings," he lied. "And I'm a little under the weather."

"This is the old bar on State Street. The Four Aces. If you don't mind me saying so, I think it's a wonderful opportunity. The whole east side of town is coming back. My great-grandfather used to gamble there."

"Thank-you. Do you need anything else?"

"Let me scan my checklist. We have your deposit. It's all cash. You've signed the escrow instructions. Your lawyer's sending the change-of-ownership announcement for the windows. We'll just need the balance at closing. You can have the funds wired or bring a cashier's check drawn on a local Reno bank."

"How much is that again?"

"Two hundred and forty-thousand dollars. Not a bad deal. Not with the property and the liquor license. Lucky guy."

"Thank-you," Kenny whispered. He hung up. His head was pounding so bad he could hear his heart. The radio waves in his vision were causing the room to disappear. He ran for the toilet to throw up.

Later that afternoon he started tearing the apartment apart. He turned the mattress, searched the toes of every shoe, rifled through all of Nick's coat and pant pockets. Then he reached for Ruthie's little suitcase. He pulled it down. For years he'd avoided looking inside. He didn't want to be reminded. When he snapped it open, he saw it was empty.

He searched the elastic inner pockets. He thumped the sides and top, looking for hidden compartments. He tried, without success to pry the lining on the bottom loose. Then he held it up to his nose and took a big whiff and he knew. After years of handling cash, he could smell it. Money had been stored inside. He remembered Ruthie begging them to let her help them.

Kenny had refused. They needed to make a clean break. Start fresh. Take their chances. Trust God.

Where had Kenny's faith gone?

He finally found a telephone number with an account number next to it, written lightly in pencil near the inside lock of the suitcase. He called it up.

"You have reached the Merrill Lynch automated account line. Please enter your twelve digit account number, followed by the pound sign . . ."

When Kenny was given the option to speak to a customer service representative, he pressed the star key.

The clerk asked him for his Social Security number and mother's maiden name. Kenny, who for years had filled out all the tax forms, knew Nick's by heart.

"Are you still holding statements to my account?" Kenny always had the bank hold statements for pickup. That way Nick wouldn't lose them and he could deliver them personally to the accountant at the end of each quarter.

"Yes, sir. Did you want me to forward them?"

"No. Hold onto them and I'll be by to pick them up. Can you tell me the balance in my account?"

"Stocks, securities or cash?"

"How about the bottom line?"

"Three hundred, twenty-eight thousand, four hundred thirty dollars."

"Thank-you."

"You're welcome."

Moments later she called back. "I've made a terrible error. I could get fired for it."

"What seems to be the problem?"

"A special instruction on your account states that under no circumstances are we to discuss your statement over the telephone."

"Yes?"

"I'm so sorry. I'm new. I didn't read my notes carefully enough. Please don't report me. I'm a single mother."

"You have nothing to worry about," Kenny reassured her. He gazed sadly into the living room. Nick was dozing on the sofa.

Maria came with less frequency to the café. So did her customers, but she didn't seem terribly worried about the business. Her crew, however, thought otherwise. Less customers meant fewer tips, and for the kitchen crew, fewer hours and no overtime. Miguel and Gabriel voiced their concern to Pablo.

"Kenny would never just ignore us," Gabriel told Pablo. "She worked in the kitchen before she became the owner."

"She knows how little we have to support ourselves with, even when business is steady," added Miguel. Miguel had seven children. Gabriel had five, but his wife was expecting twins.

"She doesn't make customers feel welcome," Gabriel said. "I've seen them. They're tourists. They want to feel at home. To talk to locals. Nobody was better at that than Nick."

"Nick was the best at it," Miguel nodded. "No stranger ever left Nick's front door."

Pablo manned the bar six nights a week. The dwindling business, he figured, was due to the pall that had fallen over the place because of Ruthie's death and the disappearance of Chita. The curiosity seekers stopped coming when an article in the desert newspaper appeared about the Cathedral City Café. It chronicled the checkered history of the location. From speakeasy to gambling casino to jazz club to gay bar and now, a Mexican café. It profiled the tragedies that in recent years continued to plague the location.

It reminded readers of all the terrible things that had beset Cathedral City during the years that the place had been Nick's, its flamboyant previous owner: The violent unsolved assaults on Nick's clientele in the alley between the bar and Latino barrio. The hate crime attack on Ralph Zola, a Cathedral City renewal attorney, mistaken for being gay as he walked from the lounge to his car. Then the major assault on the customers in the alley the night of Nick's grand reopening that debuted Ruth Harris, the desert's own glamorous cabaret singer and wife of the principal property owner in Cathedral City.

Lastly, a final incident culminating in the savage beating of the owner of Nick's and the death of Sam Singer, an apparent victim of a heart attack brought on by stress. The location stayed closed until three years ago, when it was reopened by Maria Castillo, the adopted daughter of Ruth Singer, as the Cathedral City Café.

The article then cited the discovery of Judi Romero's body found in the back of a produce truck making a delivery to the café, coincidentally while the funeral of Loretta Young was being held only two blocks away. An emergency delivery was attempted by a local Catholic nun who was known to frequent the café's lounge, but the tiny infant had been stillborn.

The entire matter was still under investigation, said U.S. Border Patrol investigator, Bob Roberts, from the El Centro division of the INS.

"So when you visit Bob, down in Imperial County, does he ever take you on ride-alongs?"

"Ride-alongs?"

"You know what I mean." Her voice sounded strange. Slightly thick.

"A ride-along is a VIP thing. Reserved for senators and reporters. Not boyfriends."

"I'd like to go on one. We could watch him arrest *mojados.*"

"*Mija.*"

"Sorry, sorry. I was only joking, *novio.*"

"Bad joke."

"Still, aren't you a little interested?"

"Interested in what?"

"What he does for a living?"

"In the first place, he's like a detective. He doesn't usually do sweeps. Unless they're shorthanded."

"But he used to do it all the time. Before he was a detective, I bet."

"Yeah . . . So what are you driving at?"

"I want to go. Can you make it happen?"

Pablo hesitated. Her vulnerability made it difficult to refuse her outright.

"He'll want to know why."

"Maybe we can invite your father. He'd certainly qualify as a diplomat."

"They want to come. They say you've refused them. They're very hurt, *mija*. They love Conchita. And they love you." He was careful not to use the past tense when referring to Chita.

"You dodged that one, didn't you?"

"I want to believe she's alive."

"She is."

Pablo fell silent.

"If you have anything to ask me," she told him, "now might be a good opportunity."

"I don't want to hurt you," his voice caught.

"You've never hurt me, Pablito. I've been selfish. I know how sad you are. I never allow you to express your feelings. Tell me."

He cleared his throat. His eyes welled with tears. "I'm sorry," he whimpered.

"Go on."

"Why are you insisting that she's still alive?" There, he asked her. He braced for her anger.

"I feel it. I just do. Why didn't they find her body?"

"Sometimes they don't," Pablo shrugged.

"Alex Quintero has been missing since he got out of jail. He could have arranged it from inside. Maybe he had himself arrested so someone else could grab her."

"So you really think he has her?"

"No. But the authorities should think he does."

"He's hiding in Mexico. He's obviously afraid, since nobody found her. Soila loves Chita too. She doesn't think he has anything to do with it."

"But still, to them, the possibility should remain."

"But if you don't really think he has her, what makes you think she survived?" Pablo proceeded carefully. He didn't want to distress her. "Where would she be?"

"Maybe she wasn't in the car. Maybe Ruthie left her somewhere. She's alive. I know it. A mother *knows*." Now Maria hesitated. "I need your help, Pablito."

"How so?" he asked warily.

"I want you to get some information from Bob."

"Such as?"

"I've read that coyotes plan their routes according to the antici-pated focus of the border patrol's activities in any given week."

"Why do you find that so interesting?"

"I want to know which routes are more heavily patrolled."

"And if you did know?"

"Then I'd know which areas weren't being watched as much. I'd know where the coyotes were planning their trips."

"I can't ask Bob that."

"You can keep your ears open. You hear his walkie-talkie. You're always complaining that you can't sleep because of it."

"What are you up to? What good will it do Chita if she's found and you're locked up in jail."

"What good will it do Chita if I have the power to help people and I'm impotent? I want to set an example for her, like my mother set for me."

"Well, I'm not using Bob to help you."

"Fuck you, then."

"What?"

"You betray us all by refusing to help."

"Betray who?" he demanded.

"*Mojadas,* that's who. Mexican women."

"I'm not betraying anybody!"

"Yes," Maria said sadly. "Yes. By your continuing involvement with this man. You are." And gently she hung up the phone.

When he told her, she was silent, and he could imagine her sitting on her porch with Jo-Jo huddled in her lap, thinking about what he'd just said, and mulling it over in her mind. The park would be active, just before sunset. Marilyn's neighbors would see her, wave hopefully, and just after she lost the light, she and Jo-Jo would move inside where she would watch the evening news and prepare their supper.

"If he makes you happy, Bobby. That's all that concerns me."

There it was. Her blessing.

"Thank you, Mom."

"For what it's worth, I never suspected in a million years." Marilyn chuckled. "I wonder what your father would say. You know, your second cousin, Donna's son. He was like you. Karl, I think his name was."

"I know, Ma."

She chuckled nervously again. "It's all over the television. My neighbor has Showtime. She watches . . ."

"I know the program. That show doesn't speak for all of us."

"*Queer As Folk*. I should hope not. But she says its fascinating. She doesn't miss an episode."

"Hmm," he said disapprovingly.

She laughed. "You were always so conservative. I still haven't forgiven you for voting for George Bush, but this helps."

"Nothing's changed."

"And your friend. He's a Spanish fellow?"

"Mexican. From Mexico, I mean. He has a college degree." His voice trailed away. "I didn't mean that the way it sounds. He's very smart."

"This is new to all of us, Bobby. Don't be self-conscious. I want to meet him if he's special. If he's important to you. Now I'll have two kids."

Bob laughed, but tears welled in his eyes. He choked up.

"Bobby, I think I'd better go fix Jo-Jo's dinner. You tell Pablo he's welcome at my humble abode."

"He lives in an Airstream trailer."

"Does he know you grew up in a double-wide?"

"Yes, Ma. It only made him like me more."

Later that evening, Bob heard a knock at his door. A worried looking Pablo stood on the other side.

"I should have called."

"I'm glad you thought you didn't have to. I'm glad you felt you could just show up." Bob pushed open the screen as Pablo eased past him. In the bright living room light, the concern on Pablo's forehead was even more pronounced.

"This is very hard for me to say."

Bob didn't reply, but he knew what was coming.

"I can't see you anymore."

For some reason, Bob wondered what his mother fixed Jo-Jo for supper tonight. Her menus were extravagant, now that he'd grown so much older. He told her often that she shouldn't spoil the old dog.

"It's your girlfriend, isn't it?"

"Yes. Well, my friend who happens to be a girl. She's obsessed about it. You saw her hostility. She was never like that. And she had good reason before she lost her baby. But now . . ."

"I understand."

"I think I'm in love with you," Pablo blurted out.

"I believe you. I know this is hard. You understand that I can't change my career to suit her," Bob spoke matter-of-factly. "I'm proud of what I do, as I made perfectly clear on the street the night we met."

"Yes. You did."

"Then I think you should probably take off. I appreciate that you drove all this way. It was kinder than a phone call."

He waited for Pablo to move toward the door. Stricken, Pablo touched his hand as he passed. After he was gone, Bob remained standing where Pablo left him. After a long moment he managed to take a deep breath, to lower his head, and noticed that the empty bowl of cereal he was holding trembled.

22

The Most Beautiful Girl in Cathedral City

To annoy Father Scolia, Sister Agnes convinced Soila Quintero to convene a group of her faithful in the empty vacant lot between Maria's restaurant and the Catholic Church. Soila was growing increasingly agitated at having to deal with the apparition embedded in her cheek. She had confided that a doctor was offering to remove it. Sister Agnes suggested that before she had the procedure, she might use her fame for some good.

Without Soila's permission, Sister Agnes circulated flyers announcing that Soila would address her followers in Cathedral City, across the street from the Cathedral City Civic Center. This would most likely be the Virgin's farewell appearance. Sister Agnes personally sewed Soila's garment of a long white robe with a pale blue mantilla to wear over her face.

"Like Jennifer Jones, in *Song of Bernadette.*" Sister Agnes smiled approvingly. "Only she didn't have a birthmark."

Word of her appearance spread through the desert cities. Soon over a thousand people had gathered in the open plot of Cathedral City desert. They came with picnic baskets. They draped colorful blankets on the sand. Some smoked marijuana. Others held rosaries and chanted. Inside Maria's restaurant, Soila was nearing hysteria. How had she allowed this to get so far out of hand?

Finally Sister Agnes cajoled Soila outside to make her appearance. When Soila was escorted to a chair, placed on a plywood box covered with white fabric, she began to cry. People were moaning in ecstasy, throwing flowers at her feet. They threw themselves on the ground, prostrating themselves before her.

Pablo appeared. He and Maria hadn't spoken since their conversation about Bob. They watched in amazement from Maria's windows.

"Is she safe? Does the crazy old nun know what she's doing?"

Maria shrugged sadly. She followed him outside.

Deftly, they came up behind Soila's podium. Soila, as she surveyed the masses, had composed herself. She seemed to be in some sort of ecstatic trance.

"I've come here today with a short message from the Virgin," Soila soothed them, "who will be leaving shortly. This is what she has to say."

The crowd began to moan softly. Many raised their hands in prayer, waving to the heavens in the clear desert morning. Soila spoke in a strong, clear voice. Her mantilla draped gently over the birthmark on her cheek. It was as though the Virgin coached Soila from behind a tiny lace curtain. Soila would make a statement, then wait politely, as if she were listening.

"The Blessed Virgin says that as a community we have developed the habit of gratuitous cynicism. We have forsaken the custom of kindness, of love, for each other," Soila gently admonished the crowd. A collective moan rose up from the crowd.

"Where words have been expensive, we spend them cheaply, we scatter them like seed. We claim to speak for God, when none can claim to even understand God. We worship material possessions. We esteem false prophets who make us comfortable with our prejudices and our conspicuous consumption. We live our lives without respect or gratitude. We have lost the habit of patience. We are frightened of solitude. To be silent. We don't avail ourselves of books and art, which truly are the earthly manifestations of meditation and prayer. We no longer value education. We feast on rumor and gossip. We only see tin, ignoring rubies."

In the distance, sirens could be heard. Police cars roared into Maria's parking lot. Two police officers cautiously approached the podium. They threatened to cite Soila for inciting civil unrest. Enough was enough.

"Until we wish to change, the Virgin will not show her likeness in Cathedral City again," Sister Agnes admonished the crowd.

"Where did you find the words to speak like that?" Maria later asked Soila.

"It was very beautiful," Pablo added.

"It was an old homily written by Father Gene," Soila acknowledged happily. "Do you think he'd mind that I used it? He wrote it after you all left, after Nick's closed. He gave it to me for safekeeping. He never got to use it."

"I think he'd be so pleased," Maria smiled.

"I think now it's time for me to go to confession," Soila whispered. Her hands were shaking. "It's been so long to carry such a burden." Dressed in her regular clothes, they watched her pick her way through the desert to the church.

"What burden is she talking about?" Pablo asked Maria.

The doctor's office called Soila, wondering when she wanted to come in for pre-op. How could she explain what was happening to her? Didn't they read the local newspaper? Hadn't they been watching the news? How could Soila Quintero, in good conscience, allow them to excise the Virgin of Guadalupe from her cheek, when she was clearly bringing everyone so much joy. Everyone except Soila.

It was now impossible to slip away unnoticed by her followers. She could no longer escape through a small hole in the backyard wooden fence. They'd wised up to her. Worse, everyone wanted to kiss or touch her face, and sometimes their hands were grimy with cheese and condiments local vendors were selling from hot dog carts on the street outside her house.

Father Scolia asked her not to come to work for a while. Her followers camped in the desert between the café and the church. The police were constantly arresting them and hauling them off to jail. They'd return once they posted bail.

First the local throwaway newspaper had picked up her story. The *Desert Sun* wouldn't touch it without verification by an authority from the local archdiocese in Riverside. But then rags like the *Globe* and *Star* ran stories. Soon the daily supplicants outside her house swelled from ranks in the hundreds to a thousand people, all kneeling, praying, and speaking in tongues. Agents and lawyers, wanting to represent her, called and knocked on her door at all hours, sometimes slipping business cards through torn window screens.

At first the neighbors were terribly irritated. Then they got in the act and started selling T-shirts and mugs with unflattering photos of

Soila taken randomly of her crawling under her fence or waiting bored at the kiosk for her bus to come. They sold lemonade, and charged to use their bathrooms. Soila Quintero had become a cottage industry.

This all took a terrible toll on her father, Thomas. The crowds were noisy and he couldn't rest. It became increasingly difficult to get supplies, and it fell to Maria and Pablo to brave the throngs and force their way, loaded with groceries through the garage. Thomas could never know they were in his house. He unfairly associated Pablo with Inez' HIV, because Pablo had confirmed her illness to Thomas in an unfortunate encounter in the alley behind his house.

Maria's arrival in Cathedral City connoted the beginning of the end of his sweet American dream. After she came, Inez got sick, the Anglo teenagers began their reign of terror on the alley behind Nick's, his son Alex had to go into hiding and Sam Singer was killed, thereby ruining his chance to buy his Cathedral City dream house. As far as Thomas was concerned, Maria, a *mojada,* had stolen the entire town from him and his hardworking neighbors.

"Sister Agnes, I have to hide somewhere," Soila frantically called her at Maria's café. Sister Agnes spent more time with Maria than at the church. "You have to come and take care of my father. He won't eat unless someone forces him."

The computer generated photograph Dr. Hansen had given her the day of her first consultation was torn and smeared by her constant nervous folding and unfolding of it. She called to make an appointment to begin her treatment.

"You should have come in earlier, sweetheart. I could have saved you loads of public scrutiny. Now *everyone* is going to guess that you've had work done."

The mass on Soila's cheek extended from just beneath her right eye, gracefully cascading down her cheek like folds in a robe, all the way down to her jawbone. When she entered his office, she half expected him to fall to his knees when he saw her. Instead, he snapped on the halogen examining light and examined her again.

She hesitated. She wanted to ask him if he noticed anything different.

"Am I going to need bodyguards?" He smiled at her. "Will the crowds tear me from limb to limb for desecrating a shrine?"

"I don't think they followed me here," Soila smiled worriedly. She liked Dr. Hansen. His wit was biting, but she sensed he was kind. She knew from his book of photographs that he'd performed miracles on hideously deformed poor third world children who suffered severe physical, as well as emotional, pain. She thought he was wonderful, and seeing him again, realized that she had a crush on him, something she found she enjoyed. What would he ever see in her? It was harmless and completely safe.

"You're worried about disappointing everybody, aren't you?" Soila nodded.

"It's clearly a case of mass hysteria. You aren't killing the Virgin of 'Guadaloop' with this operation. She can take care of herself. Nothing has changed about your birthmark. It's exactly the same size, shape and color as when I first examined you. Here, I'll show you on the computer."

He sat down and rapidly pounded at his keyboard. Her image appeared. She winced. It was horrible. Nothing holy about something so hideous.

"Now, I'm supposed to give you the speech."

"Speech?"

"It isn't done much anymore, but I'm rich and old-fashioned. Also," he winked at her, "I'd like to think I have a little integrity."

"Go on," she giggled.

"When I remove your birthmark, you won't be any different inside." He touched the center of his chest with immaculately manicured fingers. "It won't necessarily change your life. Plastic surgery can become habit-forming. Addictive. I have clients who page me demanding that I meet them here in the middle of the night because they want collagen injected into some imaginary wrinkle they found in the mirror just then. It's a sickness. I have no respect for it. Not when I've seen what I've seen in my travels. You," he motioned to Soila, "are already a very pretty girl."

"Maybe inside," she whispered wistfully.

"No. Outside, too."

She sagged. He was going to tell her the operation was off.

"Okay." She eased herself up out of her chair.

"Where are you going, sweetheart?" he asked quizzically.

"Home," she shrugged sadly.

"Why? Have you changed your mind?"

"No. I thought you had."

He shook his head and smiled at her.

"No honey. That was just the speech. It won't sink in now, because you're excited. But later, just remember what I said. I'm happy to perform the procedure, but I don't think you'll be a better person ultimately because of it. You're swell, just like you are."

She smiled at him. He was telling her he liked her.

"Okay then, shall we begin? Let me get the nurse in here. She's going to give you a slight sedative and help you change into a very stylish sterile paper dressing gown." He moved to open the door to call her.

"Wait," Soila cried. "Let me see myself again!"

Dr. Hansen flipped on the bright makeup lights surrounding the examining room vanity mirror. He steered her to the chair, where she sat submissively. "I'm going to leave you alone for a few minutes, sweetheart, so you can say goodbye to her." He patted her shoulder and closed the door behind him.

Soila studied herself in the mirror. Her thoughts whirled inside her head. Gently she traced the outline of the birthmark, as she'd done countless times in her life, usually on bad days, when boys had made rude remarks, or when lucky, pretty girls had hurt her feelings. She thought of Ruby's cruelty. Anita's and Alex's.

All she ever wanted was to be rid of this cruel joke of God's. What irony. Now passersby fell at her feet at the sight of it. Made the sign of the cross. The doctor was right. The apparition was merely that.

Now she found herself grateful for the person the birthmark had forced her to become. She was no longer bitter for what she imagined it had cost her. She was apprehensive now that she'd miss it. By removing the top layer, would she be altering the divinity that lay beneath?

For a brief instant the birthmark transformed itself into the image of the Blessed Virgin, startling her, but in the glowing moments which followed, Soila felt consumed with peace.

"Fear not," she heard the Virgin tell her, but it was the nurse, gently, giving her an injection. Soon the image began to fade.

"Soila," Dr. Hansen patted her hand. "Honey, can you hear me?"

"Yes," she answered.

"It's all done. It's gone." He eased her up to a sitting position. He offered her a hand mirror. With a quivering hand she held it up to her lovely new face.

23

The Sacrifice

"Maria."

She recognized the voice at once.

"I'm coming home to Cathedral City."

"I'll help you however I can."

"They tell me it's dangerous."

"I already know the way," Maria said with assurance. "I'll help you. I'll call you when I've set the details."

Every ten days or so, Bambi and Madonna would be stopped by a green and white U.S. Border Patrol truck, and Officer Bob Roberts would stroll to Bambi's window and ask to see her license and registration.

"This is gettin' real old, man. We know our rights."

Bob would say nothing. He'd examine her license, scan the truck, but never ask to inspect it. He'd hand her back her papers. Smile at her. Walk back to his vehicle.

"What a dick!" Bambi would jam her paperwork inside an old leatherette portfolio she kept in her glove compartment. "We lose half an hour, every time he stops us."

"I think he knows everything. But he can't prove it, " Madonna observed early one morning. The traffic rushed past them on Highway 86. "I think he stops us because he likes us."

"Funny way of showing it."

"He's curious about our relationship," Madonna observed,

watching him climb up into his truck. "And lonely since Pablo broke it off with him."

"You think he wants a threesome?" Bambi demanded incredulously.

Madonna laughed gently. "No. I think it interests him that we seem to love each other so much."

"I see where this is heading. You want to invite him over to Florencia's for Sunday dinner." Bambi burst out laughing. Then she hauled off and kissed Madonna, right on the highway. "I love you, baby. You've got a special heart."

"Can I go ask him?"

"My mother is an illegal alien. You want her to get deported after she feeds his pie-hole?"

"He won't lay a finger on her."

"Baby, you're the craziest girl. You're my girl, aren't you Madonna?"

"I'm going to ask him." Madonna grinned, popping open her door and hopping down to the side of her truck. Bob watched her curiously. She trotted to Bob's window. Inviting him to dinner.

"Why?"

"You like Mexican food?"

"Yes."

"Wait till you taste Florencia's cooking. We do it every Sunday. There'll be lots of people. They've been wonderful to me," Madonna's eyes were shining. "Why don't you come?"

"My mother's visiting this week."

"Bring her."

"She has this old dog. She won't go anywhere without him. Jo-Jo the Basset Hound."

"Jo-Jo, too."

Bob hesitated. He weighed the decision.

"You don't fool me for an instant," Madonna patted his arm. "Call us later. I'll give you directions."

"I already know where she lives."

"Thought you might."

As she walked away, a hint of a pleased smile curled his lips.

Maria surprised her crew with the purchase of a Winnebago. They knew she'd come into money, but this was the last possible example of anything they might have thought she'd indulge herself on.

The twenty-eight-foot coach had satellite television, state-of-the-art navigational equipment and featured two tiny staterooms and a faux marble bathroom with a Jacuzzi. She could have afforded real marble but she didn't want to burden the horsepower with unnecessary weight.

She heard about an Internet site that offered top-of-the-line spy equipment, satellite video and audio surveillance equipment complete with highly sophisticated recording devices. She could pick up police radio frequencies anywhere in the United States, Canada and most interesting to her, Mexico. All she needed were the coordinates, which were available on any Rand McNally map.

She could store a week's rations of food and water for fifteen people.

She had enough guns and ammunition to defend herself and her friends against a small army. In short, Maria had a survival vehicle that rivaled any government agency or smuggling cartel operating in the Mexicali/Calexico corridor.

To make everything work, she had to pretend to form a strange alliance. She hired her own coyote, a survivalist Sister Agnes referred her to, living in the high desert. One could imagine Pablo's surprise, not to mention the U.S. Border Patrol's special unit investigative supervisor, Officer Bob Roberts, when on the same evening, on opposite ridges, both noticed the arrival of Maria Castillo at the Sky Valley compound where Misty and Drew had moved in with Logan Delacourt.

Pablo and Bob were equally surprised to notice each other. Inasmuch as Bob was in uniform, accompanied by other agents, Pablo recognized his interest as official government business and retreated.

For his part, Bob didn't care if Logan knew the INS was investigating him. It might slow him down or scare him off. Since Tim McVeigh, every petty white separatist anarchist would be taken seriously until proven otherwise. Bob had notified the FBI of his whereabouts, partly out of concern for Pablo and also, by sheer coincidence, had noticed a high degree of activity at the International Border Station in Calexico. He was crossing at least five times per month that they knew of. Young, clean-cut Anglos were routinely recruited by smuggling cartels. They made perfect coyotes.

An FBI investigation revealed that Logan had no prior arrest record. He'd inherited the Sky Valley compound from his grand-mother. All he did was add the chain-link fence, the stadium lighting and the patrol dogs.

Bob had to weigh his motivation. His department was seriously taxed. He had limited manpower and finances to spend time and money to follow a whim. Maria's arrival tonight justified all. Although he held her responsible for the breakup with Pablo, he compassionately understood the grief that might be driving her here. She couldn't possibly know what she was getting in to, but her des-peration was clouding her judgment. According to Pablo, she now had the resources to buy some serious revenge, but against who? What faction?

The Border Patrol? The smuggling cartels?

"That Jo-Jo's the oldest dog I ever saw," Bambi reported to Madonna as she watched Bob help his mother down from his 4-Runner. Then he rounded the back of the truck and pulled some-thing from the back. "She's even got a baby carriage for it." They watched as Bob gingerly passed Jo-Jo down to his mother. Jo-Jo was wrapped in a blanket. Nearly blind, she howled when Bob placed her in the carriage.

"I gotta call my cousin Beatrice!"

"Her pitbulls!" Madonna screamed.

"Shit. Anything comes down bad with Jo-Jo, Florencia would be back in Mexico before dinner."

Beatrice had two fierce pitbulls named Rosie and Sandra. Family joke. Both were old girlfriends of Bambi's. Short-lived and long ago, Beatrice reassured Madonna. "She was dating them at the same time. One Sunday she forgot and invited both of them to Florencia's. We had to get the hose!"

"Why do you think we love you so much?" Florencia mirthfully patted Madonna's hand. "You're such a well-behaved lady. Such a relief."

Beatrice showed up late with her dogs. She hadn't gotten Ma-donna's message. All night long, Sandra and Rosie circled Jo-Jo's bassinet like sharks. Marilyn wanted to introduce them.

"I don't think that's such a good idea, Mom."

"There are babies crawling on the lawn. These precious dogs aren't dangerous."

Bob looked helplessly at Madonna. She shrugged warily.

Marilyn reached down inside the carriage for Jo-Jo.

"Was that your baby carriage?" Madonna asked Bob.

"Of your mom's two sons," Bambi quipped, "which one's the dog?"

Bob laughed. Beatrice had already leashed Sandra and Rosie for the introduction. The entire party fell silent. They all watched in silent, bemused horror. Someone's video camera started whirring.

"Dogs love Jo-Jo. I think it's good to mix things up. And you may not know it, but my son agrees."

All eyes fell on Bob. "Mom, maybe I should hold him."

"Bobby?"

"Yeah?"

"Your mother knows best." Marilyn shrugged at a nervous Florencia and her guests, as if to say, "when will children ever learn?" She lifted a baying Jo-Jo out of her blanket. Rosie growled a little. From tail to choppers, Sandra's body wagged in anticipation.

Marilyn knelt down, just as Beatrice lost control of the leash. The crowd screamed. The dogs lunged for Jo-Jo. They lapped her face in welcome.

Later, Bob helped crank the homemade peach ice cream. In a final toast to the evening, Florencia raised her drink in a toast.

"While we're all together, I'd like to remember a family member we recently lost."

"Shit," whispered Bambi.

"I'd like to drink a toast to my baby third cousin, Judi Romero."

"To Judi," Marilyn raised her glass. As he was exchanging a knowing glance with a shrugging Madonna, his mother leaned over to Bob. "What a wonderful family they are!"

"Yes," Bob agreed.

Maria decided to consult with Sister Agnes that afternoon, who was hunched over the bar on her usual stool, drinking her tumbler of bourbon. Maria noticed that after Sister Agnes heard about the inheritance, she began to order Maker's Mark instead of Jim Beam.

"You've been careless. It could ruin everything."

"You sent us to him," Maria replied tersely. "How were we to know he was being watched?"

"He's a very well-known coyote. You've made yourself too obvious. The shorn hair. The army fatigues. The military boots. Go home and put on some makeup. You look ridiculous."

Maria's face blushed hot. "I think maybe your drinking is affecting your judgment."

"You're a woman who could use a drink." Sister Agnes clutched her glass tightly with both hands. "My poor judgment is assuaged by drinking."

Maria shook her head in exasperation. "You have to get past your mistakes."

"Cut off any further contact with him."

"I've already done that. Everything's set."

Pablo was chatting up customers at the end of the bar. He'd been exceptionally cool with her since he broke up with Bob. She allowed that she hadn't adequately acknowledged his sacrifice, but the loss of Conchita and her newfound wealth had made her self-righteous—and somewhat arrogant. She decided to invite him to dinner.

"How are you, Pablito?"

"I've very unhappy, *mija*," he answered coldly, and took a sip of his beer. "I miss Bob very much."

They were seated on the patio of her little house. Chita's toys were still scattered in the yard, as if Maria expected Ruthie to return with her any minute. As angry as Pablo was with her, he found this moving and it made him emotional. Because of Sister Agnes' admonishment, Maria had softened her appearance with a little makeup. She also wore a bird's egg blue cotton dress and simple silver sandals.

"I'm sorry," and she patted his hand. He pulled away from her. "Pablito!"

In the months after she left Kenny and Nick's house, she had lived in Sky Valley with Pablo and then Inez, after Thomas had kicked her out of their house when she got sick. Together they had slept side by side in the small front cabin of his trailer. They had never been lovers, or even tempted, but they knew one another intimately, almost like twins.

It was inconceivable that a break could be possible by two friends as close as these. Pablo had been her Lamaze coach when Chita was born. Chita had spoken her first word to him. They had baptized her, together with Ruthie and Father Gene in Kenny's old kitchen, under the *retablo* he'd bought the day they'd met.

"I'm thinking very seriously of leaving Cathedral City."

"Leaving!" Had he punched her chest?

He nodded, his eyes flickering with sadness at her reaction, but hardening again.

"I've lost much here too. I don't think you appreciate it. I also don't feel that I'm needed anymore. I only came here because of you and Chita."

"And now Chita's missing," Maria began bitterly.

"She isn't missing. She's dead."

She reached across the table and slapped him. The beer bottle shattered across the patio.

"Hmm," he shook his head sadly. "I might have expected as much. It only makes it easier." He quickly brushed back a tear and stood up. "I'm only crying because it stings. I won't stay for dinner. If the appetizer is any indication, I'm passing."

"Please don't go."

"What were you doing? At the house below my ridge."

"It wasn't me."

"I saw you with my own eyes."

"You never saw me. Was her hair long or short?"

"Long."

"It was Soila."

"I certainly know Soila when I see her."

"If you mistook us, I'm flattered. It was an innocent business matter that has ended."

"You had the nerve to tell me I was betraying all the women of Mexico by seeing Bob, and you associate with those vermin? And send Soila? Knowing what they did to Kenny and Nick? To Ruthie's husband? Knowing that they destroyed old Cathedral City?"

"I needed something quickly and they provided it," Maria sniffed. "I'd never have sent Soila if you'd agreed to help me. If you'd only asked Bob to help."

"Well," he worked his jaw, "I'm sure he's aware of your activities. Whatever they are."

"Maybe so. But what I do in Mexico is no concern of his."

"I need to know something."

"What?"

"Judi Romero. Were you involved?"

Maria hesitated. Then she spoke.

"Not at first. But we're all involved now."

"Who?"

"Bambi. Madonna. Soila . . . Sister Agnes."

"What went wrong then, with Judi?"

"Judi was Bambi's niece. Very poor. You saw how young she was. She got pregnant. A neighbor boy. Her mother talked her out of an abortion. Bambi and Madonna wanted to adopt the baby."

"How did they get her into the United States?"

"A coyote they thought they could trust recommended by Sister Agnes." Maria shrugged. "They transferred Judi at Bambi's warehouse in Imperial. She told them she wasn't feeling well. They had to take the chance. Get her to Cathedral City. Why do you think they all happened to be waiting at the café at the same time? Soila, Sister Agnes . . ."

"Bambi and Madonna."

"The accident blew their timing. Judi went into premature labor. She was too afraid to say anything."

"Who else is involved?" He studied her intently. "My mother?"

Maria laughed. "No, Pablito. Not yet."

"Then who?"

"You know too much as it is, but this coyote is very dangerous. And evil."

Pablo studied the shimmering lights across the desert. "Was it worth it?"

"Was what worth it?"

"Judi's death. Her baby."

"It beat her options in Mexico. We've all taken the same chance she took. Some of us make it," Maria shrugged. "Some don't."

To Pablo, her tone was simply breathtaking. "I can't be friends with you anymore."

"I'm sorry you feel that way."

"Your losses," he shook his head. "Your losses have simply ruined you."

"You don't understand anything," she said simply. "You've never been a poor woman."

"Does it justify everything?"

"Yes."

"Why are you going to so much trouble? Why not climb my hill and just kill him?"

"There's no death penalty in Mexico," Maria reminded him. "Remember what he's done. Who he's hurt."

"Who chose you to avenge these pitiful souls?"

"Kenny did," Maria smiled proudly. "By example, he taught me everything I know."

"Who picked him?" Pablo asked.

"God," she whispered. "Kenny was dead, lost in the water. My grandmother offered to trade places with him. She was cast into the water so he could rise."

Maria stood, indicating that it was time for him to go. She walked him to her gate. He turned, wanting to say something. She gently touched his lips with her finger.

"Goodbye, then Pablito. I'll always love you. I don't know how or when, but all of us, including Chita, will be together again."

PART THREE

Return to Cathedral City

24

New Money

"I'm thinking of offering a reward for the return of my daughter."
Maria called her lawyer when the bank verified the first large transfer from Ruthie's trust.

"The result would break your heart. If someone has her and wants money, you would have already received a ransom note. You should consider yourself lucky you haven't gotten several already."

"What would be heartbreaking about that?" Maria demanded. "It would prove she was alive."

"There are cruel people in the world, Ms. Castillo. It wouldn't prove any such thing. Do you know what you'd get if you offered a reward?"

"What?"

"Among false leads, and requests for money to be left in obscure locations, you'd get poor families offering to sell you their baby daughters."

Maria was so sickened she slammed down her telephone.

They began in the same way: *Like you were once, I am a poor woman trying to make my way in this cruel world.* They were heartbreaking. The details of Ruthie's will had been published in the paper because the bequest was so fantastic and due to the tragedy associated with Ruthie's death and the disappearance of her daughter. People acted as if she'd won the lottery. Lately, a number of tragic requests for financial assistance began to deluge her mailbox.

When she casually mentioned to her attorney that there were several sad cases she felt tempted to accommodate, he vehemently advised her against it. Most requests were hoaxes. She'd be opening herself up to a floodgate of pariahs. She'd never have a moment's peace.

"A foundation in Chita's name might be preferable."

"Foundations are usually named for dead people! When are you going to get it through your thick head that Chita is not dead! If you make that mistake again I'll fire you!"

And he apologized all over himself for once again hurting her feelings.

Maria was surprised to receive a personal note from Father Scolia, inviting her to tea. It was hand-delivered to her by Soila Quintero. It came on the priest's personal stationery cards, and was sealed with his stamp.

"Only the most important parishioners are invited to tea by Father Scolia," Soila assured her. Maria had yet to notice her face.

Maria hadn't been to confession since she and Kenny made love in his pool. The night Conchita was conceived. "It's been almost five years. The last time I confessed was to Father Gene. That never felt like confession at all to me. It just felt—sweet."

"This new priest doesn't care if you worship Satan." Sister Agnes was sitting on her usual stool at the end of the bar, nursing her bourbon. "He knows you've come into a little cash."

Maria carefully peeled the wax seal away from the envelope and studied the card. "He isn't the only one . . . Look at his handwriting. It's very stern."

"It isn't an invitation," said Sister Agnes. "It's a summons."

"I'm not going," Maria shrugged. "Not after the way he snubbed Conchita with that cheap Mass."

"That's what he has up his sleeve."

Sister Agnes winked at Soila.

"Tell me," Maria asked her coldly.

"He'll trade you the prayers of the Archdiocese of Riverside for a new wing on the rectory."

"The Archbishop will say a Mass for Chita's return?"

"I never said a Mass. Maybe a novena."

"Oh, only a novena?"

"It's all negotiable," Soila offered kindly.

"Even the Pope's prayers are nothing compared to my desire for Chita to come home, safe and sound."

"I'd like another cocktail," Sister Agnes tapped her glass. Maria's sacrilege needn't get in the way of Happy Hour. Maria sighed. Since Pablo quit, she was the bartender. Business was too slow to warrant another employee.

"Can I do it?" Soila asked.

"You're underage."

"Nobody's here."

"I resent that." Again from the little nun.

"No paying customers, Sister Agnes." Maria chided her.

"You've become very rude," Sister Agnes scrambled down from her stool. She was genuinely offended. "You think because of your personal pain and your newfound wealth that you can say anything that occurs to you without thinking!"

"Sister," Maria shook her head. "Sit back down. Of course you can have as many drinks as you like."

"He means to ex-communicate me," Sister Agnes said, climbing back on her stool. "We've had words about his approach to the local community."

"He won't ex-communicate you. He has no grounds." Maria sighed. She enjoyed Sister Agnes, but when she drank, she became maudlin and self-pitying. "Soila. Go ahead and pour her a drink. I'll lock the door. No laws broken."

"Since when do you worry about breaking the law?"

"Since I had a child," Maria replied. "And I wanted to set a good example."

Soila studied Maria. She still spoke of Chita as though she was only away at day care. Or spending the day with Ruthie. She spoke of her with no hint of sadness. Her voice never choked. She no longer could be seen, wiping tears away. She acted the part of the satisfied mother of a happy, healthy, and most importantly, safe little girl. She moved to go lock the door. Behind her, Sister Agnes was urging Soila to not be so stingy with her pour.

"Maybe I should go," Maria reconsidered. "How many *mojadas* is the old priest inviting for tea these days?"

Maria sent a note back with Soila accepting the priest's invitation.

Misty awoke to find Betty B sitting next to her bed. Her face was troubled. Not angry, but troubled—filled with love for Misty.

"What's *wrong?*"

"Nothing, Misty."

Misty sat up. "Then what?"

"It's nothing. I'm sorry I frightened you." Betty B stood up.

"Well, what are you doing then?" Misty's voice sharpened.

"I was watching you. Like when you were a baby. I'm just glad to have you home. If only for a day. Are you all packed?"

"Jesus Christ!" Misty swallowed. Her mother's face was filled with sadness. "I don't get what's eating you."

"I'm afraid for you, Misty."

"Don't be."

"Promise me something, then."

Misty yawned. "What?"

"Promise me you're as tough and mean as you pretend you are."

"I'm not an ax murderer, Mother."

"But you and your brother can take care of yourself."

"Oh," Misty smiled. "If that's all you're worried about, yeah."

"Deep down you aren't frightened."

"No."

"I am."

"I thought you had God, or something."

"I do."

"I'm kinda tired."

"I'm not afraid of being afraid for me. I'm afraid if you're afraid for you."

"Mom."

"Are you, Misty?"

"I can take care of myself."

"Promise?"

"I promise."

Betty B stood, smoothing out Misty's blanket. "Okay, then. I love you." Misty didn't answer her. Misty loved her, too, but she wasn't ever going to tell her.

The tea with Father Scolia was brief and to the point. He expressed his sadness for her. Told her he prayed for her and Chita.

"And Ruthie Singer?"

"Who's Ruthie Singer?"

"My daughter's grandmother."

Father Scolia blanked out.

"Not your mother. You mean your daughter's father's mother?" He knew Maria had never married Kenny.

"No. Chita's biological paternal grandmother lives in New Mexico. I mean her other grandmother."

"Your mother?"

"No, my mother died in Mexico when I was eight. She was murdered by Mexican guerrillas."

"Then who is Ruthie Singer?"

"My daughter's grandmother."

Father Scolia shook his head in confusion. "Sure. I'll pray for her."

Soila appeared with a silver tray laden with cookies and hot tea. Again Maria didn't recognize her with her new face. Soila smirked at her. Maria looked up. Why was this pretty young woman making faces at her in front of the priest? Then it dawned on her. Maria started to cry. How self-obsessed she'd become.

"I had it done weeks ago," Soila chided her. "You never noticed!"

"You're beautiful!" Maria took the tray from Soila and after setting it down, hugged her sweetly. "Is it what you wanted, *mi vida?* Are you happy?"

"Yes," Soila nodded. "Yes."

"Let's resume," Father Scolia interrupted them.

Soila quickly composed herself to pour the tea.

"I never expected you to wait on me," she chided Soila. Maria waved her away to help herself.

"It's her job," Father Scolia explained.

"Soila is my sister," Maria rebuked him. "My sister doesn't serve me like a waitress." For the lunch, Maria had gone to great lengths to dress for the occasion. She was wearing Ruthie's best jewelry. A thin, magnificent diamond bracelet glinted in the sunlight. She noticed Father Scolia gasp when he saw the quality of the stones. It was easily worth fifty thousand dollars.

"Do you like the bracelet?" Maria grinned at him. "I inherited it from Chita's grandmother."

She had commandeered Soila's tray and was busily pouring Father Scolia his tea. "Soila. Sit down with us."

"I can't," she whined to Maria. She was embarrassing her. "I have book work to do."

"I thought you said her job was to serve tea."

"Her job is to serve at my pleasure," Father Scolia barked back.

"Oh," Maria shrugged. "By all means. She should go back to work."

Soila shook her head and rushed from the room.

"She's angry at me," Maria observed. "I'm sorry if I was rude, Father. I was raised with better manners. Why have you invited me to tea today?"

"As you know, the church could not survive without the generosity of its more affluent members."

"Not in a certain fashion, I expect not."

"Tithing at any level is always appreciated."

"But doesn't always cut the nut," Maria finished his sentence.

"That's not quite how I'd have said it, but okay. We've benefited from the generosity of some very illustrious parishioners. You know about the generosity of the Sinatra family. And more recently Miss Young."

"I do. Father, before you go on, you should know something about my background." She leaned forward, knees pressed together, clasping her fingers over her chin, blinding him with Ruthie's two carat engagement ring from Harry Winston. "When I came to Cathedral City, I had nothing. I had just entered this country illegally. My only grandmother died a terrible death as a result of that journey. Ruthie Singer saved my life, on a hot, dusty road only miles from the Mexican border. I was running from men who wanted to kill me. Coyotes. And along came this big white car, with a very pretty woman driving it. I remembered, as I was running for my life, thinking how pretty she was. I could see this ring, sparkling, from where I was running down the road. Isn't it absurd," Maria smiled, "what can go through your mind in times of terrible danger and stress?"

"I've often observed the same phenomenon," Father Scolia replied sincerely.

"Ruthie saw I was in danger and stopped her car. She didn't judge what I might have done to find myself in such a position. What my share of the blame or responsibility might have been. She didn't question my guilt or innocence before she stopped. I didn't have to negotiate for her to unlock her door. It was already open to me. No questions asked. Her act was unconditional."

"Go on," Father Scolia said coldly.

"If I had been driving, and I saw myself on the road, or someone who looked like me in the same position, I have often been haunted about what I would have done in the same position."

"What conclusion have you come to?"

"That's not for me to answer, sir."

"What?"

"I'm asking you. And this new church."

"This church has been here for decades."

"Without Father Gene, it's become another place." Maria sat up. "All kinds of people are running on roads, as I sit with my jewels, and you sit in this comfortably appointed room, they're running in fear for their spiritual lives. My daughter's father was one such man."

"I know who he was."

"Father Gene was very kind to us. We weren't, all of us, an easy fit. But we were made to feel welcome. The spire of this church was extremely comforting to me in the first days when I came to Cathedral City. I met Conchita's father in a very beautiful church in Mexicali. Did you know that?"

"No."

"We met on a hassock, lighting candles under a statue of the Blessed Virgin. He and his friend later took me in, after I'd lost everything. No questions asked."

"I don't think this is going anywhere."

"Then you don't understand Cathedral City." Maria stood up. She was frustrated, and momentarily without composure. "I'm so sorry, Father. I could have done some good here, but Sister Agnes is right. I've become arrogant. I failed my interview. I can't even pass the prerequisite tea. How could I possibly measure up to any higher scrutiny. You invited me here to ask for money in exchange for prayers for my little girl. Really, don't you know how despicable that is? Aren't you praying for her already?"

Father Scolia stood up. "This is a bad mistake you're making. Coming here, to lecture a priest. The church has considerable power. I had options I could offer you."

"What options?"

"Priests hear things."

"Confidential things."

"Not if one were to go back to the confidante."

"Someone has told you about the whereabouts of my daughter."

"No. Definitely not. I never meant to imply such a thing. "

Her disappointment was palpable. She reached for her small handbag. She removed the diamond bracelet. She held it up briefly. For a moment it appeared that she considered handing it over to him. Instead she popped open the clasp of her purse and dropped it in. "I've already designated my charitable contributions for this year. I'm planning to bequeath a considerable sum to the AIDS Assistance Program. They do good work, no questions asked, for the desert's poorest sufferers of AIDS and HIV. Good day, Father Scolia."

As Maria walked across the open desert to her café, Soila watched from the front windows of the rectory. Had Maria turned, she would have wondered why Soila was crying so hard.

When Maria returned to the café, she was surprised to find Betty waiting nervously, perched on a stool at the end of the bar. They were alone.

"I just put them on the plane. I'm closing up my house. I came to say thank-you."

"You promise me you'll never let them hurt anyone again?"

"I promise." Betty hesitated. "I believe you, if it matters."

"What are you talking about?" Maria asked wearily.

"I think you're right about your daughter."

"Thank-you," Maria replied, but without any animation in her voice. "Good luck to you."

"He's a very dangerous man. He's threatened to kill my children. And me. Be careful of him."

"You should tell him the same thing about me."

25

The Return of Inez Quintero

"You'll never get a visa," her priest told Inez after she confessed.

"I know."

"How will you manage?"

"I've been referred to a coyote."

"It's not an easy trip. You aren't strong enough."

"I'll have to be."

"You could be arrested. Thrown in jail. The desert is dangerous. Even with a trustworthy coyote."

"God will protect me."

"How much will it cost? A thousand, now? Two thousand?"

"I'll have the money."

"Where will you get so much money?"

"God provides."

Due to its horrific discriminatory policies against foreigners with HIV/AIDS, it became necessary for Inez Quintero to illegally cross the border of the United States of America under highly dangerous conditions, just so she could be with her husband, who had infected her with the virus, her two daughters and her son, whose whereabouts were unknown. No one had heard from Alex in six months.

Although each member of her immediate family was a naturalized American citizen, with her AIDS diagnosis, tiny Inez could not legally be permitted to join them unless she posted an enormous bond as proof she could pay for health care.

Thus, U.S. policy restricted her from the bosom of their loving care. Each year, since its inception, the International Conference on AIDS condemned the United States for its exclusionary polices, and steadfastly refused to hold its annual meeting within American borders. With all its enormous generosity, the United States remained biased, intractable and unbending in this vital area.

Nacho and Freddie drove her to Mexicali. She had been given the name of a park, Los Niños Heroes. It was there she would meet her coyote. The park lay sweltering and dusty in full view of the International Border, which ran on the other side of the All American Canal. It was flanked by two one-way streets—eastbound Avenida Francisco Madero and westbound Avenida Cristobal Colon.

Mexicali was a pleasant, prosperous Mexican city with a population just over a million. Thousands of Mexicali citizens legally crossed the border each day to shop in Calexico and El Centro discount stores or to work in the Imperial Valley's verdant agricultural community. At night they returned, with no questions asked if they flashed their hologrammed ID cards, proving they had legal status to do so.

If Inez had the time, she might have attempted to apply for the necessary paperwork to reestablish her green card, but she didn't. Thomas was gravely ill and Soila was left alone to care for him. There was also her fear of computers. The one Pablo warned might contain details of her HIV status. She wasn't worried for herself. They could deport her. She had nothing shameful to hide. But now her husband and her daughter needed her.

Cruel and ruthless as Thomas had been to her, as his wife, Inez intended to keep her vows. Secretly she'd been pleased that he'd made no attempt to annul their marriage. Ruby, accordingly to Soila, had been bitterly resentful of his refusal to do so. At the time Father Gene had been the parish priest. Even if Thomas had tried, they never could have gotten around him. The new priest, Inez understood, might be another matter.

Freddie, weepy at the prospect of his sister returning to Cathedral City, came in full drag, and he and Nacho walked arm in arm down the sidewalk. Freddie always got catcalls and stares. Only an expert ever detected his true sexual identity. Because Nacho was so typically macho, they seemed like nothing more than a happy husband and wife, taking their homely sister out to lunch.

Inez allowed that one indulgence. Today her stomach had been uneasy. Many neighbors had counseled her about the dangers of the coyotes. They were vicious and untrustworthy. But it seemed to Inez that if thousands of people per day tried this, how bad could it really be? Besides, Maria had arranged for everything. This coyote had an established reputation.

Nacho had rigged up a backpack with water, protein bars and candy. Inez was uncustomarily sentimental today. She had mixed feelings about going back to Cathedral City. She hadn't told Pablo about her plans. Soila had to promise to keep the secret as well. If Pablo knew, he'd interfere, and to do so would place them in jeopardy.

Inez knew that Maria had come into a great deal of money. When Soila reported that she didn't seem to be doing anything extravagant with it, Inez understood. Under the circumstances, such affluence must feel like blood money. If Maria really believed Chita might be alive somewhere, raised by coyotes, the four legged kind, she certainly wouldn't test fate for more fantastic retribution.

She heard Maria had cut off her hair. Her beautiful hair, which Inez had coveted the moment she first clapped eyes on her. They got off on the wrong foot. Whatever was up was down in Cathedral City. No alliance could be predicted. Foe became friend, as was the case with Maria. Could the same be true for Inez and Thomas?

Without her brothers to verbalize her concerns, Inez might have given up and died when she returned to Mexico. The life she left behind was in shambles. The husband she had married when she was only fifteen, and pregnant with Alex, had kicked her out of their house. To add more insult, he took up with a local cantina waitress.

What was God trying to tell her? Inez mulled day after day. All the greatest kindness shown her in her life had come from his gay constituency. Inez had no doubt that God loved homosexuals as much as anyone else, without the usual set of caveats imposed by organized religion. No gay bigot ever won a battle of public opinion with the homosexual community. She herself was a prime example.

She felt extremely guilty about abruptly leaving the shelter. The women of *Avance* were her true sisters. Day after day her own story wandered painfully through the front door. Ignorant women who steadfastly maintained the fidelities of their marriage; arrogant in their pieties; only to realize on the food chain of fate, they had now descended to the bottom rung. Day after day, week after week, Inez had been trained to wade through the quicksand of their superstitions, guiding them to accept the hand they'd been dealt without prejudice so they could begin medical treatment and maintain or improve what health they had remaining.

It was never difficult for Inez to summon feelings of gratitude. For Freddie and Nacho, for her daughter Soila, for Maria and lastly Pablito, her best friend in the entire world. Without him, without the divine intervention of Pablo into her sphere, Inez Quintero would certainly be dead now.

He was her Eskimo, her angel of mercy, sent to her in the form of compromise—she first saw him in the alley behind her house, receiving fellatio, pants around his ankles—God apparently had a great sense of humor. Pablo's life had been saved that night too.

As for what she was about to do, cross the border back home, there, she'd said it, whatever inconvenience it might prove to be, it was a small price to pay. She had experience to offer her husband. And insight. The courage of the survivors at *Avance* had proven as much to her. If Thomas would accept these gifts was up to him, but at least her children would see, and be forced to acknowledge, that Inez had changed for so much the better.

Freddie and Nacho located the gentle looking older man, sitting under a tree where they were told he'd be. He introduced himself as Señor Joel Ramirez. He would take their sister to the reputable young man who would look after her and have her safely across the border in a matter of an hour. He was trustworthy and professional. Ramirez would drive Inez to him. A group was leaving tonight.

"We have to go with you," Freddie winked at Ramirez.

"It's not necessary," Ramirez protested gently.

"We have no deal if we don't," Nacho murmured. "If we like what we see, you can bring us back to the park."

Because it was late, and Ramirez wanted to end this business day, he finally acquiesced. There were hundreds of potential clients in Los Niños Heroes, but this had all been prearranged. The little woman seemed determined, and fit. She probably wouldn't pose any trouble to his nephew, José. He led them to his big Chevy sedan near the park.

Nacho sat with Inez in the back, while Freddie sat perched next to Ramirez in the front. Ramirez had no idea Freddie was a man. They flirted and giggled the entire drive through the migrant barrios of eastern Mexicali. The car pulled into a gated yard. Inez studied her new surroundings with no trepidation.

"Okay. You can take them back," she told Ramirez. José came from the house. He saw Ramirez and nodded.

"You gonna be okay, sweetheart?"

"I love you," Inez affirmed.

Satisfied that Inez felt comfortable, Nacho and Freddie drove off with Señor Ramirez.

"When do we leave?" she demanded. José just shrugged and ignored her. Maria promised it was all arranged. She didn't even need to pay. Now she sat waiting in a Mexicali safe house for others to be assembled. Inez was growing increasingly irritable. Her husband was dying. Her children needed her.

Inez had listened compassionately to the stories of grieving, lonely women, who, cruelly fated with HIV, had been torn from their families, now established in the United States, never to be allowed to rejoin them, all because of a wicked American law. They cried because they would die alone, and to a mother, a death could not be more shameful than one unattended by her children. What, ultimately were they for?

Although Maria offered to post Inez her bond, Inez refused it. It was her turn to walk the desert, to swim the river. It was her turn to prove how much she loved her family.

On her person, in a small pink backpack, Inez had amassed over forty bottles of pills, to accommodate her fifteen pills per day regimen—enough for three months. She also carried the provisions which Nacho had sweetly provided because often the pills required that she take them with food.

Sometimes the pills were old, or had gone bad—this was the scary part. She'd recently had a violent reaction to a medication, which, she admitted later, looked a little suspicious, but she had so few left she couldn't be choosy.

If you asked Inez now, sitting in the cramped bedroom of the dirty little shack with these other women, all hot, hungry, frightened of being arrested, leery of the shifty little coyote and his crew, some on their periods, some pregnant, some desperately needing to use the filthy backed-up toilet—if you asked Inez how she interpreted these circumstances, she would tell you she felt lucky.

Even with the complications of her health, Inez had her optimism and dignity. She had surpassed expectations—of others and even her own. Instead of a meek little wife of an overbearing, sometimes cruel *machista,* Inez was her own woman now. She was a survivor. She had skills. Her consciousness had been raised. It had to be in order to survive.

Now she found herself encouraging her companions.

"It won't be long now. You'll see, *chicas.*"

To José, the little guard, lurking in the tiny main room with a sawed off shotgun, presumably to keep them intimidated, she was considerably more formidable. "We need water back here! You want us to die the first five minutes of the trip?"

"Shut the fuck up!"

She stood up, staring him down. José wasn't much more than an inch taller than she. He had a mother complex, and her matriarchal air was intimidating to him. "Say that to me again and I'll slap you. I'm a mother and you can't speak to a mother like that. I'll slap that dirty mouth right off your ugly face."

"Try it," he replied, but his tone sounded more worried than insolent.

"If you don't get us some water and food, we'll all walk out of here. We'll find another way."

José wavered the gun at her. Her reference to motherhood made him uneasy. Who was he kidding? He didn't have it in him to gun down a room filled with desperate women.

"Just do it, *mijo.*" She cajoled him with a term of endearment. He returned several moments later with a canteen of water that they all passed around, greedily emptying its contents.

His boss, the main coyote was another matter entirely. To her surprise, he was Anglo. Inez saw craziness in his eyes. This one was dangerous. A murderer. When he came around, Inez shrank back, blended in, kept her mouth shut.

Just as Inez found herself at her wit's end, Señor Ramirez arrived with four more passengers, all women. Two, immature, oversexed and giggling teenage girls, a tall somber woman who wore a bandanna over her face, as if she were disguising a deformity, and her companion, a short, overtly masculine woman who Inez initially assumed to be a man, until she heard her feminine voice. They now had enough passengers to warrant the trip.

"We'll leave tonight," José announced. "No pagers, no cell phones."

When the young girls snickered, the coyote leered at her. *"La Migra* can detect the signal and get us all thrown in jail."

There was something familiar to Inez about the tall woman's eyes. When she noticed Inez staring at her, she looked away. Her friend did all the talking. They were probably girlfriends. Inez had seen her share, sunbathing topless at the gay hotel where she worked in Cathedral City. Lesbian *mojadas*. Hmmph. It took all kinds. They looked tough. Like they wouldn't take any crap from the coyote. Mentally Inez noted to stick close to them.

The coyote herded them out into the yard, where a big rumbling cargo van awaited them. It was beat-up and unsafe-looking.

"The tires are bald," Inez complained.

"So are you and I'm not complaining," the coyote smirked. He was insulting her thinning hair, a lifelong malady complicated further by the side effects of her HIV medication.

Just as he started to load them into the van, the Anglo coyote stepped into the yard. He said nothing. The woman with the bandanna seemed intrigued. After they were all loaded up, he scanned all the faces of the van. His was the last face they saw.

He rolled the door shut, slamming them into darkness.

The teenaged girls never stopped gossiping, even in the darkness, the combined fear of their fellow travelers failing to quell their youthful exuberance. They talked and giggled the entire two-hour drive, though twice José threatened to kick them out.

"I mean it you bitches. I can drop you off right here! I will, too." This from the guard who had only served them all cool water three hours ago. The Anglo rode silently, ignoring them, the situation. He acted like he was better than all of them.

His head was shaved and it looked like he was powerfully made. He reminded Inez of the skinheads she'd see occasionally in Palm Springs. He had hard eyes, and even in the dark, Inez could tell he had scoped out the passengers pretty intensely.

The teenagers had been met with amused smirks by all the workers in the yard of the safe house. One of them supposedly had a rich Anglo boyfriend, who was paying for both of them to cross.

"We're going to L.A.," the taller one advised the group. "My boyfriend already has jobs lined up for us."

"Yeah, as hookers," the butch girl commented to her serious, bandanna-covered girlfriend.

The shorter girl heard them. "Hey, we aren't whores."

"Shut the fuck up back there," José cautioned.

"Shit, we're paying you," the smart-aleck tall girl told him.

"Yeah. You can't talk to us that way."

"Hey," said the Anglo, glancing over his shoulder. "Keep it zipped if you know what's good for you." His tone was considerably menacing. He sounded like he meant business. They ignored him and kept talking, but much lower.

In the group of women, most ranged in age from eighteen to forty. Together they probably had nearly twenty-thousand dollars stuffed in their bras, or inside their panties.

Inez studied her watch. It was nearly ten o'clock. She should take a set of pills before they started walking. She opened up her pink backpack.

"That's a cute pack," the lesbian nodded.

"Take your pills, little monkey," her girlfriend added.

Inez gasped. With that, Maria lowered her bandanna and smiled at her old friend. Then she quickly tied it back up again.

"What are you doing here?" Inez demanded.

"I'm here to protect you," Maria whispered.

"Protect me! Protect me from what?"

But Maria didn't answer. Instead she hunkered close to Bambi.

26

Guest Workers

"What's happening to me?" he demanded of his doctor.

"Well," the doctor pounded his back and listened with his stethoscope, "I think you're having trouble with your heart."

"My heart?" Bob asked incredulously.

"Have you experienced a loss recently?"

"What kind of loss?"

"A loved one perhaps?"

Bob didn't reply.

"You've suffered a broken heart." The doctor patted Bob's muscular shoulder. "It'll heal, but only in its own time."

To a man like Bob, who couldn't easily give up his heart, the loss of his darling, sweet, kissing Pablito was more painful than anything he could have ever imagined. He'd read about the experience in books, saw it in movies, heard about it in the twining lyrics of love-lost country songs, but hadn't yet experienced it personally. Until now. And worse, he now associated sex with love. He couldn't even masturbate to any satisfactory conclusion.

He complained to his doctor about a high, radiating pain under his rib cage. He suffered shortness of breath, and needed, on occasion, to pull over his green and white border patrol vehicle, only to curl up in the backseat and sleep soundly for at least twenty minutes. His head often felt heavy and fuzzy inside. He lost nine pounds without even trying. He needed to alter all of his uniforms.

On occasion he fell to weeping. One particularly embarrassing incident happened when he'd just detained a small group of border-jumpers while patrolling the East Mesa Sand Dunes, halfway between Calexico and Yuma. The group was as ratty and tired as he could remember. Older too. All in their forties and fifties. They'd been abandoned by their coyote just inside the U.S. border. He'd driven back across the Baja Norte California desert with their meager bags, including food and water. And over fifteen thousand dollars in combined savings.

If Bob, who wasn't really even patrolling the area, just driving crazily along the border to work off some steam, hadn't come upon them, they most certainly might have died. One woman even hugged him in her relief. He offered them paper cups filled with water from his big plastic water jug off the tailgate of his truck. He handed out protein bars. He even set up a sun tarp he kept for just such a reason. While he called for a pickup team, and watched them settle under the tarp with guilty, tearful relief, when the tall somber woman impetuously hugged him, *gracias, gracias,* Bob too, started to cry.

He thought he was losing his mind, but instead of taking advantage of his diminished capacity, the woman and several others patted his back, squeezed his hands, and then sat down to wait obediently until the transport van arrived.

Much to the private chagrin of many of the already naturalized Mexican citizens remaining in Cathedral City, the administration of George Bush was planning to offer citizenship to three and a half million *mojados* living in the United States. The implication was staggering. Three million new voters, plus the potential voting block of the already wildly reproducing Latino population born in the United States, or already naturalized. Of those, many were staunch Catholics and therefore, pro-life, anti-gay and stridently conservative. What a brilliant concept! And the Democrats thought he was dumb.

How should liberal forces be expected to respond? The big tent was becoming a reality. Other than lip service, what could the Democrats offer now? Mexico would be to George Bush like China was to Richard Nixon, thanks to the manipulating skills of Presidente Vicente Fox.

With rights they could vote. They could organize. They could push their own agenda. They could send for more family members. What they didn't realize was it would also allow an iron fist when it came to border control. We did the right thing. The three million are already here, working jobs no Anglo would touch, but now they'll have to pay taxes on them. Or, their employers will. Think of the gushing coffers. Enough for another tax break. Another check from the kinder, gentler IRS.

The proposed amnesty program had considerable impact on the morale of border patrol officers manning the U.S./Mexico border. Immigrants were amassing at the border, more desperate to get across than ever before. Once the plan was first announced, those Mexican citizens too meek to have tried to cross before started packing their bags. Now was the time to get across. It would take months for Washington to iron out the details. Maybe even a year.

After that, the iron curtain. The conservatives would demand it. Tougher enforcement. Tighter controls. More border patrol agents.

Well, maybe not. Work the ones they have even harder.

The threat to the smuggling cartels would create a backlash from them. This would cost organized crime on both sides of the border billions of dollars. It was as if the government was offering free airline tickets during the peak of the summer flying season to all resort destinations. The desperation would dissipate. New controls would be implemented. The scramble to cross the border began the moment the words left his lips.

Bob and his fellow agents were worried. And tired.

While Bob threw himself into the stepped up smuggling activity— arrests jumped from five hundred a day to over sixteen hundred within two weeks of the Bush amnesty announcement. U.S. Attorney General John Ashcroft visited the El Centro division of the U.S. Border Patrol. Pablo didn't have the same options.

When he broke off his friendship with Maria, he also quit managing the restaurant, and he felt guilty for the kitchen crew because business was so bad and for all her assets, she didn't seem to be making up the difference from her own pocket. She just cut back their hours. She didn't replace Ruthie. She didn't even play CDs. She seemed to be letting the place run out of steam by attrition.

And now, because of her planned getaway, she announced that she would close the place while she was gone. She had no one to manage it, or tend bar. Why shouldn't they all have a few days off. She'd present them with a plan when she had time away to think things over. She surprised and pleased them with envelopes stuffed

with cash—more than they'd earn on the busiest weekend. This re-
deemed her somewhat, but Gabriel and Miguel still missed Kenny. It
didn't settle the future for them. It only made them more anxious.
Miguel spent all his money on beer.

As for Pablo, he was free to leave the desert. So why didn't he?
Because of her.
Because of him.

Pablo gave into a few bad habits. He started haunting the clubs
on Arenas in Palm Springs. He cruised the freewheeling grounds of
the Warm Sands hotels. His favorite was the Bacchanal. He rejoined
Gold's Gym that overlooked the runways of the Palm Springs
International Airport and after working out, within a month, his old
musculature popped out. Pablito was back. His trust fund kicked in.
He didn't have to work if he didn't want to. He started back on all
the party drugs. GHB. X. Special K. Tina.

Pablo fell into his old sexual acting out. He picked up weekenders
from L.A., but never brought anyone over to Sky Valley. He'd go to
their hotel rooms, or rented condos. He feared running into Bob,
wherever he went. He felt so guilty. He missed him more than that.

His mother called, sensing things were bad. Elena Seladon was always so insightful.

"Pablito. I haven't heard from you."

He'd been smoking a joint by a small campfire. He no longer
cared if the lunatic separatists were spying on him or not.

"I've been pretty busy," he lied to her.

"You haven't made up with her. Mijo, she's suffered the worst
sort of loss a mother could ever endure. The worst imaginable. Why
do you think I was so frightened for you?"

She referred to the night she'd called him, sitting in the very same
spot and told him she suspected him of selling his body. She'd been
right. She'd begged him to come home the next day. Instead he'd remained in Cathedral City, befriending Inez and Maria.

"She's changed," he whimpered.

"Of course she's changed. But it doesn't mean she doesn't still
need you."

"Have you talked to her? She cut off all her hair."

"We're lucky she didn't cut off her hand. She's lost her child,
Pablito."

"Mamita. You don't harbor any belief that Maria and I will ever be together romantically, do you?"

"Never."

"Then why were you so kind to her? Helping the way you did. Papa thought you were crazy."

"He loves Maria as much as I do."

"Now," Pablo warranted.

"He did it for me. And I did it for you."

"You'd never even met her."

"You called me and told me she was your friend. That was enough." She paused. He allowed himself to imagine his mother's exquisite bone structure. Always an extraordinary looking woman, she had aged with such dignity. She allowed herself the vanity of not going gray. She dyed her hair, but didn't need a facelift. The tiny lines around her eyes were proof of her maturity. If she smiled, which she did often, they disappeared completely.

"Pablito. Do you think we don't really accept you?"

"I think you want to. Culturally, I think it's probably impossible."

"Listen to you. You've been at Stanford too long. Who are you? Margaret Meade?"

He laughed.

"I think we've all done very well. At times I've longed for a grandchild. I'll admit it. We never provided you with a brother or sister. We were selfish. We both agreed to one child. We loved you so much. The three of us was enough. Laying the responsibility of future generations on you alone was an unfair burden. But the experience of Conchita's birth was a privilege. I know Maria felt oppressed by my fervor. I wasn't her mother. I owe her an apology for that."

"You gave her a home," he objected.

"She wasn't a slave, Pablito. Listen to you. We could never accuse her of being ungrateful. Still, I grieve for the baby. And if I feel this badly, how much worse can it be for her?"

"I loved Chita too," Pablo whispered.

"I know you did, *mijo*. I know you're hurting too."

"I've met someone," Pablo ventured.

"I figured."

"She didn't approve. Asked me to give him up."

"Oh."

"He's a border patrol agent. A good guy. She couldn't get past his job. I hurt him. He hadn't really allowed himself to be involved before."

"Maybe she'll come around."

"You know, I haven't really allowed myself to become . . . attached either. You know what I'm really ashamed of?"

"Tell me, Pablito."

"He'd just told his mother about me."

"And about him too, I suppose." She paused. He could picture her sitting at her desk in the elegant study that opened off her bedroom. She had a small Picasso in her study. A gift from her father when Pablo was born. Someday she planned to give it to her only son.

"Mamita?"

"Yes, Pablito."

"Why are you always so far away when I need you?"

"I'm not far away, my love. Your mother will always be inside your heart. I know everything. See everything."

"Hopefully not everything."

She laughed. "When things resolve themselves for you and Maria, I think this fellow will probably be waiting. You're special enough, Pablo. Someday, perhaps, we'll all meet each other."

"It isn't impossible," he conjectured gently.

"I know. Frankly I hope that it won't be. You'd like to have a child someday?"

How could she guess what he was talking about?

"Maybe someday."

She'd known, even before his own heart had told him.

"I miss her . . ."

"Don't give up on her. Did I ever tell you her first words to me? After she was deported and the agent introduced her to me?"

"No."

"It meant more to me than anything anyone has ever said to me. I was so worried about you. Your future. What would become of you. Do you know what she said?"

"What?"

"She looked me directly in the eye and told me that my son was a wonderful, wonderful boy."

"She said that?"

"I know she still means it, Pablito. Give her more time."

*   *   *

Two days ago, as Maria finished packing her motor home, it gave her time to clarify her motives. What was she really hoping to accomplish? What, ultimately would this plan of action resolve? Would it get Chita back? No. She was clear on that. Chita was alive somewhere. Maybe someone sold her in Mexico. She was so pretty. Some lonely wealthy woman would pay for her. Was Chita living on a mountain somewhere? In an elegant hacienda surrounded by magnificent gardens? Chita was strong. Her character too rich to ever forget her mother. No matter how they tried to bribe her.

The drive south toward the Salton Sea always evoked strong, emotional memory in Maria. The last time she had driven south on Highway 86, she was a prisoner in an INS transport van. She was six months pregnant with Conchita. She'd been arrested in a surprise U.S. Border Patrol raid on the alley behind Nick's, after dropping Soila off at her small house across the alley.

She nearly escaped unnoticed until her nemesis, Carmen, pointed her out to an arresting officer. Carmen, for so many years Kenny's favorite kitchen crew member. Carmen, who Kenny had sponsored in her bid for citizenship. Carmen, who knew that the baby Maria carried was probably Kenny's.

Jealousy was the most powerful of all emotions. More powerful in its own way than love, Maria reflected. Equal to revenge.

All the hatred Maria had built up inside had to go somewhere. It couldn't just dissipate into the air. Every member of her immediate family had died an unnatural, violent death. Her parents, murdered in the mountains of Mexico. Her grandmother, tossed in a river like a bag of old clothes. Now her daughter?

Maria glanced down at her speedometer. She'd better slow down. She didn't need a speeding ticket at this stage of her trip.

The motor home purred along the highway that ran along the western border of the Salton Sea. She was below sea level now.

Daddy in the pool.

Who, she reflected, did she hate most for what?

Kenny? For allowing her to fall in love with him? No. Never.

Ruthie? For messing around with her medication and putting Chita in harm's way? How could she ever hate Ruthie? No.

Then who?

Alex Quintero. Definitely. As much as she loved his sister and his mother, how could she avenge herself with him?

And she hated the coyote who threw her grandmother in the river.

These two for starters. Alex was missing. The coyote was a different matter. And one was just as good as another.

Logan Delacourt had three strikes against him. He had a proven history of deserting trusting *mojados,* after he collected their money. He was responsible for the death of Judi Romero and her baby. Lastly, it was Logan and those monstrous children of Betty B's who assaulted Nick, causing the death of Sam Singer and the ultimate ruination of Kenny and Cathedral City.

Maria, in all of her grief-stricken insanity, believed she could go through with this because she *didn't* really know him. In the nights after her first meeting, with the Radical Sisters, when Sister Agnes laid out her case against Logan and made her request, Maria's motivation justified itself as she pounded screaming through her house or dashed off one more frightening *retablo.* She was filled with justifiable rage. It had to go somewhere. It wouldn't get her daughter back, but at least it would make her proactive.

The Imperial Valley cities of Brawley, Imperial, El Centro and Calexico all ran together in long, boring, flat, dusty blocks. The homes were nondescript. Nothing opulent. Primarily Latino. Neat little yards surrounding two-bedroom stucco houses, with canals and small rivers snaking through the neighborhoods. The entire area foreshadowed Mexicali, and the nation of Mexico below it.

Maria drove past the El Centro Border Patrol station, across the street from a huge Wal-Mart shopping complex. Discount stores, Mexican cafés and seedy motels flanked the main drag of El Centro. She remembered this border patrol station. It was here she was processed first, then transferred to a holding cell in Calexico, near the Mexican border.

The Calexico holding facility was pentagon-shaped. She was placed in a pie-shaped cell with long metal benches and an exposed toilet at one end. They kept her alone because she was pregnant, but she wasn't certain if that was for her protection or theirs. Every so often, a female border patrol agent would come to a cell, call several names, and those prisoners would be taken from the facility through a door and out the back to a waiting INS van.

Next stop, Mexico. It beat being kept in El Centro. Maria knew there were lifers being detained in the jail behind the main station. Political prisoners, most from Central or South America. Some even Asian. From Korea or Vietnam. Not so many Mexicans. It could take forever to be processed once they detained you. You had no rights if you were not an American citizen.

She knew she would be called soon, and taken to the border turnstile and tossed back onto Mexican soil. Frankly, she was looking forward to it. What a weird place California had ended up being. How horrible and cruel. What kind of a freakish Oz journey had she just taken? Still, she didn't have a single idea what she'd do once they put her across.

She had no money, no ID. No family in Mexicali. What did the border patrol expect her to do? Where would she sleep that night? What would she eat? How would she sustain her prenatal care? Of course she'd call Pablo, collect. She had him. Surely Soila had told him by now. But what of all the others?

There were old people, and children in the transport van. She could see them now, cowering in frightened huddles. They weren't given the opportunity to call loved ones. Collect their belongings. At least a wallet. It was humiliating. Depersonalizing. What did they expect them all to do? They were nonviolent, hardworking people. To be treated like murderers and thieves? Was this civil? Was it decent?

No, she shook her head. It was monstrous. She didn't regret intervening between Pablo and that Nazi boyfriend of his at all. It was a betrayal that he'd been too blind to see. His sexuality, once again, had clouded his judgment. Someday he'd thank her.

Maria arrived in Calexico early in the evening. She continued driving the motor home toward the signs directing her to the International Border checkpoint station. She found a parking space a block away from the main entrance to the walk-in border crossing. It would be heavily monitored with television cameras. Border patrol agents. She felt slightly nervous.

She reached behind her for a simple backpack, which she donned once she was outside the motor home. She studied the street. She trotted past the Calexico marketplace toward the main drag, where she turned left.

In a moment, Maria strode efficiently back into Mexico, a bandanna tied trimly over her nose and mouth. She didn't want anyone to recognize her. Not Inez. Not the Anglo coyote. If questioned, she'd simply say she suffered from allergies. Of course no one stopped her. She was a Mexican returning to Mexico.

What right did they have to stop her?

27

The Lounge Act

"An owner who wants to sing is a lounge act's worst nightmare."

Out of memory he heard it. "New York, New York."

Was Kenny imagining things?

"Oh shit. How can this be?"

Kenny thought he was going out of his mind. Was that Nick singing in the lounge?

"Why don't you all join me?"

Was he *drunk?*

"All right, all right, gimme back my microphone."

In a word, yes.

Kenny came bursting through the lounge, empty except for two old lushes holding up the bar at the far end. The lounge manager, Margie, was a heavyset old broad with frizzy carrot hair. Sometimes when it was slow, she liked to play the badly out-of-tune upright piano, which sat dusty in the corner overlooking the casino room.

The dining room only sat forty-four people, and Kenny had yet to work a rush. It was a tapped-out kind of place. Most fools had lost their money in Reno. Those with a few extra bucks always wanted to hold out for the last chance. Why stop at the second-to-last chance? They were gamblers, after all.

Margie liked Kenny, even had a crush on him, though he was half her age. She wised up when Nick came one night to pick him up. The pair of them hit it off real great. Margie was a sorrowful drunk. The nights were awful quiet without a drinking buddy.

"If I'd drink with anybody, it'd be you," Nick always told Margie.

Well, he'd been truthful there.

When Kenny entered the lounge he saw Margie and Nick, tugging at the microphone. "Just lemme finish one song."

"But I'm in the middle of my set!"

"Set! All the customers left an hour ago."

They surveyed the room and laughed until the outline of Kenny filled the door frame into the kitchen. How many nights in Cathedral City had the silhouette of Kenny cast the same long shadow as he watched Nick commandeer some poor lounge act's microphone, and take over the set.

It all came rushing back. Nick drunk and flopped against the piano, the customers in the lounge held hostage as he half-sang, half-cajoled the hit songs of Frank Sinatra, of which there were so, so many. When he'd forget the words, he'd snap his fingers, grinning extra wide and plow through, till finally the poor piano player just ran out of steam. Then Nick would call out another song, *Satin Doll*, maybe, or *Summer Wind*. The piano player would gamely play, because the night was still young and they were yet to be paid.

The customers would hurriedly finish their drinks, exchange nervous or sympathetic glances, vowing silently to never allow their own drinking to get this bad. They usually escaped when like now, Kenny, the chef from the kitchen, or as in tonight's case, the fry cook, would intervene, stopping the madness, and guiding Nick through the kitchen to be driven home by one of Kenny's kitchen crew.

Only tonight there wasn't any crew. Just Kenny. He'd have to do the driving. Just as Kenny was stuffing a snarfing Nick into the front seat of his truck, Margie appeared in the alley behind The Second Chance.

"There's some kind of a detective in the front, asking for you."

"For who?"

"He's asked for both of you. I can tell him you've already gone." Margie studied them cheerily. This was Reno, after all.

Kenny glared at Nick. What had he done now? Nick avoided his eyes.

"No," Kenny shook his head. "I'll go talk to him." He took his truck keys. "Stay put till I come to get you," he ordered. "By the way. I know all about the Four Aces."

"The Four Aces is ours. Yours and mine. I never touched a cent of that money till I bought it. It was Sam and Ruthie's. I didn't tell you because of exactly this reason. I agreed to your terms."

Kenny's back stiffened as he edged past Margie through the back door to her lounge.

A tall slender man in a black suit sat hunched over a cup of coffee in the back booth. He glanced up, nodding for Kenny to take a seat. Kenny slumped across from him. The detective flicked a business card across the slick surface of the table. Kenny picked it up.

"You're a private detective."

"Yes."

"Who sent you?"

"Can't say. I don't even know. I received my instructions by e-mail. I was paid by wire transfer." He eyed Kenny with curiosity. He hadn't expected someone so beaten. "I'm hoping I can talk with your partner. He around?"

"He's around. Why are you here?"

"This is difficult. I have bad news to give you. You were friendly with Ruthie Singer."

"Yes." A cold chill shuddered down Kenny's spine.

"I'm sorry to tell you that she's passed away."

"How?"

"It's complicated," the detective offered. "She drowned in a flash flood."

"When?"

"At the end of August."

"That's months ago."

"They tried to locate you."

"They?"

"The Cathedral City authorities."

Kenny shook his head. "Why would they be the ones to notify me?"

"Admittedly, they didn't try very hard. I found you. Your name was on the birth certificate."

"Why would they want to talk to me?" Kenny insisted again.

"It's believed that your daughter drowned with her. She was in Mrs. Singer's care at the time. At least, that's what the Cathedral City police believe. They've closed the case. Her car seat, a few personal articles were found near the car. They haven't recovered her body, however. Ms. Castillo is holding out hope that her daughter is still alive." He studied Kenny's reaction. Kenny was clearly stunned. Tears welled in his eyes.

"Does Maria know that you've located me?"

"No. That's why my client wants to remain anonymous."

"Why didn't Maria call me herself?" The words strangled from his throat. A look of fresh horror flickered in his eyes. "Does she think I have her?"

"No," the detective raised his hands. "Don't go there. Not at all."

"Then what are you doing here?"

"I actually came on other business. I was retained about another matter."

"There's *more?*"

"I need to speak to your partner. It involves him. It's a pretty crazy coincidence."

"He's in the alley. He's drunk. Good luck."

"I know how you must be feeling."

"You couldn't possibly know how I'm feeling."

"She's devastated."

Kenny contemplated his words. "And what do you think, Detective?"

"What do you mean?"

"My daughter. Is it possible she's still alive?"

"There was no evidence of foul play. The little girl was dropped off with Mrs. Singer that afternoon. Ms. Castillo spoke to her right before she left her house to bring the baby to Cathedral City. A heavy rain began to fall. They never arrived."

"She lives in Cathedral City?"

"I thought you knew."

"I don't know anything. I don't know if she's married, or how she makes a living."

"She was formally adopted by Mrs. Singer. She owns a restaurant."

"She owns *our* restaurant?"

"She mentioned you had the place before."

"You didn't answer my question. Is it possible she's alive?"

"I don't think so. I'm sorry."

"I'll get Nick for you."

"I'm sorry to tell you this way."

Kenny disappeared into The Second Chance parking lot. Moments later the detective was surprised when Nick returned. His face was lined with fading scars. He knew Nick's history. The attack behind the bar.

"Kenny told me you wanted to see me."

"Isn't he coming back inside?"

"He's gone. Drove away."

"Is he coming back?"

"Would *you* come back?" Nick shrugged. "What else could he stand to hear? He told me you had something to say to me. What is it?" Nick's intoxication had worn off slightly. He didn't sit down. He just stood in the shadow by the lounge door.

"What I'm about to tell you is very amazing. Unbelievable."

"Spare me the editorial comment. My lover of twenty-three years just drove off. Left me. Tell me what I need to know and let me go home."

"I was hired to find you."

"You mean Kenny."

"No. You. That's the irony."

"I've known about Ruthie and the baby."

"You have?"

"I contacted an old acquaintance from Palm Springs. She told me two months ago."

"But you didn't tell your partner?"

"No."

"Why?"

"Because I knew how he'd react."

The detective waited for Nick to explain.

"He's left me, don't you get it?"

The detective sighed. He hated finding people in Reno. There was always a sad, long story. "Do you want to know why I came here or not?"

Nick slumped in the booth and let him talk.

A few minutes later, after the private dick was gone, Margie cautiously entered the lounge.

"What went on in here?"

"Kenny's gone. Past caught up."

"Everybody in Reno has a past, waiting to bite 'em in the ass. You bought the old Four Aces?"

"Yes."

"I'll buy you out," she smiled, "if you need a little sudden mobility."

28

The Crossing

"If I want to be insulted, I'll go home to my husband in Cathedral City," Inez smiled at Maria.

"This is my friend, Bambi," Maria nudged Bambi, who smiled from the shadows at Inez.

"Hey, Bambi. So much commotion made over me," Inez whispered. "So unnecessary."

"Only the best for you." Maria stroked Inez' cheek.

"And these two sluts play on our team too," added Bambi. Patti and Lupe nudged each other. "And wait till you meet my girl Madonna."

"That's sacrilegious," Inez clucked. "Talking about the Blessed Virgin like that."

"No," Maria giggled. "Her girlfriend's name really is Madonna."

"Shut up back there!" José turned. "They got surveillance equipment so sensitive they can read your lips!"

The van was rumbling west after stopping for gas in Progreso on Mexico Highway 2. While it was stopped, the coyote stayed in the passenger seat while the Anglo filled the tank with gas. He leaned, his right arm draped nonchalantly over the driver's seat. What any casual observer couldn't see was the pistol he was holding, hidden from view by the headrest of his seat. It was meant to intimidate his passengers into silent submission.

"Okay," José grinned, when the Anglo climbed into his seat. "We'll be driving thirty more miles west till we take the turnoff toward the border. It's bumpy, and I don't want any complaining. Okay?"

One of the teenage girls whined to use the bathroom.

"You gotta hold it, beauty. Hold it or piss your pants. Either way, I don't mind."

The group of women clucked.

"It's ladies night," Bambi observed in hushed tones. "A real coyote buffet."

Inez sneezed. The coyote turned and waved his gun in annoyance. He kept driving.

It was no different than five years ago, Maria noted. If possible, this was the very same van which had transported her, her grandmother and Kenny through that terrible night.

Her *abuelita* had been so excited. Completely guileless, Maria recalled with emotion. Her dream was coming true. They were going to California. Concha was only doing it for Maria, because she was worried about Maria living alone in Mexico after she was gone. She wanted her only granddaughter to be safely established in the United States, but as a student or an artist. Maria was intelligent and cultivated. Concha knew that once they made it north, everything else would fall into place. Maria's future would be set. Her safety assured. To Concha, Kenny had been an added bonus she never would have allowed herself to wish for.

They met him in the park, Los Niños Heroes, where he intervened after they were swarmed by hordes of coyotes, competing for passengers to smuggle. He'd fought them all off, and Maria, thinking he was just one of them, began kicking at him to get away too.

"No, I saw you at the church. Just now? Remember? The candles? *Recuerdas?*"

Of course. The dark-haired Anglo from the cathedral. He'd shared a taper, in order for her to light a candle. He'd been praying at the statue of the Virgin of Guadelupe, where she had insisted they stop before continuing on with this ridiculous adventure concocted by her grandmother.

She'd been so frightened in the park that when he offered to take them for a cold drink while they gathered their wits, she'd agreed. Only because she thought it would buy time to change her *abuelita's* mind. In fact, because of the blue-eyed stranger, her grandmother became more resolved that absolutely, this was something they were going to do.

Kenny had explained he was only in Mexicali for the day, that he lived two hours north, near Palm Springs, in a little town called Cathedral City. He said he owned a restaurant. He asked a few questions. Where were they headed? Did they know what they were up against?

She must have seemed so naïve, in over her head. The belligerent old woman led her around by her nose. Now, in the darkness, riding along with Bambi and Inez, she reflected that he only offered to come along because he was concerned about their well-being. It was a kindness too good to be true, and Maria became suspicious. She even accused him of colluding with the coyote.

"What do they pay you to hide in the church?" she'd charged.

He'd been so hurt. Blue eyes like his couldn't have summoned umbrage like that if he were the best actor in the world.

"He only wants to help," Concha had cajoled.

And seeing his expression, Maria knew she was right and relented. Besides, they had more to worry about than him, she'd thought at the time. He was only a tourist. He could leave the caravan anytime he wanted to. All he had to do was hitchhike back to Mexicali and walk back across the border into the United States.

When the coyote and his partner finally popped open the back of the van, Kenny, who'd been the last to be loaded, fell back in surprise, the wind knocked out of him when he hit the hard desert floor. While the rest of their companions disappeared wordlessly up the *bajada,* the rising, cactus studded plain that led into the mountains, Kenny nearly couldn't catch his breath.

When they were finally able to revive him, they realized he had no water, no food. Nothing to protect him against the elements. She'd been so angry to think that instead of helping her, he was now a liability. In addition to the old lady, she now was obligated to worry about him as well.

When they finally got him standing, they found themselves face to face with a weathered tin sign, posted at the foot of the *bajada.* A warning sign to the pilgrims who passed here.

Desierto Peligroso

"What's that mean?" Kenny had asked.

"The desert is dangerous," Maria had translated for him.

"So am I," admonished her grandmother. "Let's go."

* * *

"How's Pablito?" Inez inquired.

"He's been busy. We don't see much of each other."

Inez shook her head. "You're lying to me. You think I can't tell?"

"We've had words. Sometimes friends fight."

"When we get back, you can make things right with him."

"Why is it automatically my fault?"

"You're very opinionated. And given to hysteria." Inez laughed, explaining to Bambi. "She once chased me down the block. Slapping at my head like a mad old crow."

"You're lucky I didn't catch you," Maria grinned.

"Does he know I'm coming?"

"I'm sure Soila told him."

"So it's that serious. That's not right, *chica*. He loves you."

Maria's hand fluttered up as if to say, lay off. She only knew too well. Inez studied her.

"I pray for the baby," Inez offered tenderly. "Every night."

"I haven't prayed since we baptized her. Do you think God is punishing me?" Her mouth twisted with cynical bitterness.

Bambi noticed and patted her knee.

"Why should he? Clearly you're punishing yourself enough without him."

"Spare me the philosophy!" Maria snapped.

"Shut the fuck up back there!" José glared through the drape.

Dismayed, they all looked away. Now wasn't the time. Several moments later, the van pulled to a halt. After a few hurried instructions, the coyotes rounded the back of the van and popped open the sliding doors.

Maria gasped. They were out in the middle of nowhere. The stars shone so bright they reflected in the eyes of her friends. It was dizzyingly bright. And moonless. A warm Santa Ana poured down the *bajada* and enveloped them.

Maria tightened her bandanna. Then she slid her backpack over her shoulders, but only after removing a small fanny pack which she fastened around her waist. Bambi equipped herself with a similar rig. To Inez they didn't look like average *mojadas*. They'd decked themselves out like action film commandos.

They sized up José, who was busy flirting with the young girls. Inez struggled to open her small bag. The zipper was stuck. She needed to take her pills. Finally, she forced it open and pill bottles exploded everywhere. Her precious medication fell to the sand.

As Maria and Bambi watched, Inez knelt, madly scrambling for all her pills. Not all the bottles had opened but she must have dropped over fifty colored pills. It was an unmitigated disaster. José was coming their way.

Bambi knelt to help her.

"Hey, what's with all the pills?" he said to Inez. "You smuggling? You some kind of mule? What kinda shit you carrying? That could add five years onto any sentence we get if we're caught."

"It isn't her shit. It's mine." Bambi explained. "She's only trying to help me."

"What is it?" He opened his hand.

"They aren't narcotics. It's just regular medication," Bambi protested.

"You sick? You don't look sick. I only take able-bodied passengers. You can't come."

Bambi shot to her feet. "I'm coming. I've got to get across."

"If you don't need the pills, dump 'em and you can come."

Bambi and Inez exchanged a hurried look of despair. These pills could extend lives back at her clinic. Certainly Maria could replace them, but the idea of tossing them into the sand made Inez physically ill. They'd probably already been smuggled into Mexico, at great personal risk to the mule, who was only doing it to help women like Inez.

"Let her take them," Inez clucked.

"You don't give orders on this trip. You can stay behind with her, if you like."

And Inez popped him, gun and all. Astonished, he involuntarily took several steps back. What he didn't notice was how quickly Maria and Bambi unzipped their own fanny packs.

"Pick up your pills and let's go," Inez ordered Bambi. Bambi knelt obediently and recovered as many dusty pills as she could.

The chagrined coyote took his place at the head of the group. They marched wordlessly up the path into the canyon.

Laurie was cold again on the telephone. Madonna had to practically beg to see her. She was home for the weekend in La Jolla, staying with her father. Since Madonna had moved into Bambi's house in El Centro, Laurie had been barely civil to her mother. Burton wouldn't even talk to her. When she called, asking for Laurie, he simply passed the phone over without saying hello.

"I really don't see the point. We'll only have an hour before I have to leave."

"I'd just like to sit with you for a few minutes."

"It's a two-hour drive for you."

"Laurie, please."

Finally she agreed.

"Do you think Daddy might be home when I get there?"

"Are you for real, Mother?"

"I haven't seen him. It'd just be nice for the three of us to be together."

"So where does that leave Bambi?"

"She's spending time with her family." Madonna hated to lie to Laurie, but she was so hostile to Bambi she felt she had no choice.

"Dad doesn't want to see you," Laurie told her. "He'll go out."

"Well, okay then. I'm leaving now."

Gently Madonna flipped her cell phone closed. She was sitting in Maria's Winnebago, which Maria painstakingly taught her how to drive on those hot afternoons on the back roads of Desert Hot Springs. She felt comfortable with it now. The big rig was much easier to handle than Bambi's old produce truck. She eased it up the westbound Interstate 8 on-ramp to San Diego. The timing would work out. A three-hour round-trip. An hour with Laurie. Madonna would be well in position. Bambi even taught her how to flood the engine. If she was questioned, she was just another San Diego retiree having engine trouble with her motor home. As the rig purred along the El Centro Freeway toward the coast, Madonna passed the turn-off to Highway 98, where later this evening she would veer east to the Yuha Desert Freeway and then south on Mt. Signal Road.

Given the circumstances, the risk, it was important for her to see Laurie tonight. If things went wrong, if she was arrested, or worse, she'd want to have this hour with Laurie. Laurie would never understand. She was too much like Madonna had been before she met Bambi, before her consciousness had been raised.

Laurie played tennis, shopped at Nordstrom's, had her legs waxed and thought of little else other than herself. She was a junior at UCLA and had yet to declare her major. She'd been dating a wealthy MBA student, who Madonna had not met. The lesbian mother with a short butch Mexican girlfriend wouldn't look good on Laurie's resume. She just told him her mother traveled after her parents split up.

It wasn't her fault. She'd learned everything she knew from Madonna. Madonna had swam in the shallow end of the pool of thought and social conscience since she uttered her first words. Oddly enough, her considerable height had always thrown everything somewhat askew.

She didn't know where it came from. Her father was of medium height. Her mother, petite. Her brothers were no taller than their dad. Madonna towered over them in family photos. She was always the zenith of the photograph. The point at the top of each photo dynamic. She thought her height contributed to feelings of being different. An outsider. Certainly she was pretty enough. Very feminine.

Just so damn tall. It was lovely to now be in a community where her height made no difference. Many of their girlfriends were as tall or taller than she. If anything, they ribbed Bambi for being so short.

All the introspection started to tire her. What they were about to embark upon was crazy, but other than raising her daughter, probably the most important undertaking of her life. At face value, these weren't her issues. What did she care if poor Mexican women were being abused or even dying while trying to illegally cross the border into the United States? What were they to her?

But two things stuck with Madonna, at the time seemingly insignificant, which now it occurred to her were informing this choice, this huge risk she was taking. The first was the film *El Norte*, directed by Gregory Nava. Madonna loved foreign films, which Burton and Laurie refused to see because they both hated subtitles.

She'd been visiting a college girlfriend who lived in Beverly Hills, and didn't want to head back to La Jolla till after traffic. She noticed the film playing at a small Beverly Hills art-house theater on Wilshire Boulevard. It was a perfect way to kill two hours. It was Sunday. Maid's day off.

She knew because the theater was filled with Latino housekeepers, many in uniform. To Madonna, *El Norte* was both a sweet love story between two siblings and a border drama. It told a story of two poor immigrants, a brother and a sister, who are forced to leave their civil war–torn village or be killed. They decide to make a break north, to the United States, where maybe they can work hard and earn a living wage.

As Madonna and the maids of Beverly Hills watched and wept, the brave brother and his sister finally make it to the northern

Mexican border, where they are forced to crawl through a vermin infested drainpipe to cross into the United States. His sister is badly bitten by rats. Later they find refuge in a dirty, halfway house for illegal immigrants. They find jobs. Evade the INS. Because of his hard work, the brother is offered a job in Chicago if he can go right away.

He comes home to tell his sister, only to find her seriously ill, and near death because of her rat bites.

Madonna would never forget the deep sorrow she felt in the theater.

The second incident occurred fifteen years later, during a televised INS chase that resulted in a Mexican woman being dragged from the passenger side of the suspect van and beaten in full view of TV cameras for no apparent reason. The country reacted with outrage. Marlon Brando offered to give the woman twenty-five thousand dollars when he learned that her children had watched the same incident on television, their mother being beaten by U.S. Border Patrol agents.

Madonna never knew what came of the offer. But she remembered the savagery of the beating. She remembered the crying of the Beverly Hills maids. And these two events made her reexamine the absurd shallow life she was leading. So here she was. About to commit a felony. She told herself she was doing it for Bambi and to some extent, Maria.

But in truth she was doing it for selfish reasons. She owed someone something for the easy life she'd led, even with the anger and humiliation she'd endured in the breakup with Burton. She understood so much now. Was grateful for her joy in finding Bambi, which had been hard-won, even selfish. But without regret.

Of the group of immigrants, Patti and Lupe were the only redeeming factor of this particular trek for the coyotes. At seventeen, Patti was six months older than her cousin Lupe. They were both voluptuous and heavily made-up, with big teased up hair. Lupe frosted hers. Between them they carried one small backpack, which they made a big deal bickering about whose turn it was to carry it; with a single liter bottle of Arrowhead Spring Water, two Baby Ruth bars, a fresh T-shirt and panties apiece, and lastly, taking up the bulk of the space, melting makeup and hair care products. Their combined insipid demeanor at least provided comic relief to the others. And it kept the coyotes off their guard.

"Hey, how much longer?" Patti demanded. They'd been walking

in the late afternoon sun for nearly three hours. "It should be right over the next hill."

"Just over the next hill, beautiful," José winked at her.

"My boyfriend's waiting in El Centro. He'll be pissed off if we hold him up."

"We should be right on time," José grinned and stroked her face. He scanned the horizon. "Just over the next hill, I think."

"We're nearly out of water."

"I have a little water if you run out," he smiled at her. "So, does he know how to treat you right? Does he make you feel like a woman? Do you have a grown woman's orgasms. Or are you still just a little girl? Are you a virgin?"

The girls giggled nervously.

"Does he kiss you before? And after? That's how you know he really loves you."

Bambi and Maria watched the exchange warily. Would he lay off or keep harassing them?

He shoved to the front of the group.

"You old ladies have to move quicker. We can't hang out here all day."

Maria took a sip of water after forcing Inez to do the same. Inez had aged in five years. The HIV and the toxic medications that kept full-blown AIDS in check conspired against her body. She looked much older than her years. Maria wondered if she'd been lying about her age.

An older woman took a moment to challenge the two girls. "You should stop flirting with him. You'll get yourself into trouble."

"You're just jealous," Lupe tossed her hair. "Because you're old."

"Lupe," Patti admonished, gum cracking. She shook her head in mock dismay.

"We're just kidding around with him. We don't have all the money we promised," she whispered. "We want him to go easy on us. We spent it on new clothes."

She shrugged, the others would automatically see the natural humor in this. She was actually trying to bait him.

"He's gonna want to collect when we get to the border," Bambi cautioned.

"He's okay," Patti reassured Lupe, who pretended to act a little alarmed. "We're good for it."

Bambi shook her head. "You'd better be good for something."

She and Maria exchanged a glance. Maria knew that would all change the instant they crossed into California. From what she'd learned in her talks with Pablo and Bob, they'd most likely get picked up on heat sensing surveillance equipment. It would depend on how much activity was concurrently out there.

If there were a hundred groups of twenty, that was two thousand people trying to cross the border only today. Those numbers were too great a match for the limited resources of the border patrol. They'd go after the bigger groups. And also the one seemingly the most threatening to U.S. interests. A small bank of women wouldn't attract much attention. José had been glad for an all-girl group. They would be more compliant and vulnerable.

The heat always made his balls churn. He always got lucky on women's groups. He saw to it. Today, with Patti and Lupe, he'd be doubly so.

Of any illegal activity, the border between the two countries is the line of demarcation. You didn't want to murder in the United States. They had the death penalty. They went easier on rapists in California if the victims were illegal. If you couldn't resist, it was better to wait till you got out of Mexico. A *mojada* was less likely to make trouble in a country where she had no rights.

Maria knew about these two considerations only too well. She, like the others, was most interested to see what would go down once the marker for the U.S. border appeared.

Wasn't that what the trip was all about?

29

The Virgin Has Left

Her father was too delirious to recognize his own daughter. She came home to find him collapsed in a pool of sweat, next to his soiled bed. First she called Pablo, who told her to call 911. He'd be over right away. Soila did exactly what he told her. She tried to lift Thomas back to the bed after she hurriedly tore the sheets away. This was it. This was her punishment. Now God would take her father because she'd done away with the vision, the apparition of the Virgin of Guadalupe.

She had no idea he was this ill. She'd pretended to go to Monterey Park to visit Ruby and Anita, but in fact had been staying at Maria's house. Maria had invited her to stay over. While she was away, she wanted someone at the house in case a call came about Chita. Soila gladly agreed.

Her father waved her off. He didn't care if she came home or not.

Of all her siblings, Soila was the only one who managed to maintain her relationships with both her mother and her father. And neither seemed to mind. Both felt that in the grand scheme of things, Soila had gotten a raw deal. Alex was handsome and overconfident, making friends easily and bullying his way through life. Anita was too pretty for her own good. She could be bought, and later on, would believe that the desertion of her by her mother justified all sorts of acting out. Ruby was like a mother to her. The five years since Inez left Cathedral City had been formative for Anita. She didn't remember much from their old house. She remembered her mother's sighs when she came in after a day of cleaning motel rooms.

This was unthinkable to Anita. Her mother a motel housekeeper. What could be lower than that? It justified her father's behavior with Ruby. Ruby had filled her with bad thoughts about her mother. She deserted her hadn't she? Anita didn't understand, as Soila did, that their father had turned her out for being sick.

One night, shortly after her AIDS diagnosis, Soila and Alex woke to the sound of her father moving their sick mother from their bed to the couch in the living room. The next morning Inez was packed and inching her way down the sidewalk, toward Mexico.

"This was your father's dream, not mine," she told Soila.

And like today, Soila had called Pablo to come and make things right.

After her treatment, Soila had planned to surprise Thomas with her new face but he didn't even notice. He now had two beautiful daughters, if her trip to the Ralph's market at Date Palm and Palm Canyon had been any indication. People continued to stare at her, just as they'd done all her life. But not because of her deformity. They stared at her the way they contemplated Maria.

Soila used to love following Maria as she made her way through a public space. She guessed then what it would be like to be beautiful. Men dropped their jaws when Maria passed them on the street. Soila made it a practice to lag behind, like an obedient Japanese wife, trailing a respectful distance behind her husband, something which annoyed Maria. Maria was sensitive enough to know what Soila was up to. She didn't want Soila envying her for her looks.

"Soila, hurry up," she'd insist.

"You walk so fast," Soila would say.

"Then I'll slow down. We're friends. I don't want to keep looking over my shoulder to talk to you."

"I like to watch them," Soila admitted one day in the plaza as they pushed Chita along in her stroller.

"Who?"

"The men. The way they look at you."

And Maria became very annoyed. "They want one thing. It isn't admiration. It's only lust. They want sex. It isn't flattering. It's obnoxious."

"I'd love it if a man looked at me that way."

And then Maria felt bad. She'd turned around and hugged Soila tightly. "Someday a man will look at you that way. He'll see what I see. You're very pretty. Even with the birthmark. You have to learn to accept it. If they aren't looking at you, it's because you're uncomfortable with yourself."

And Soila gazed at her sadly. "It's easy for you to say."

"Yes," Maria warranted, "I know. I really do. But I also know what it's like to be loved for what's inside of me. I've had that experience and I'm lucky. In all my life, if I never have it again, I'll have had my share."

"Do you mean Kenny?"

Soila had never dared ask her about Kenny.

"Yes," Maria admitted. "I mean Kenny. He didn't love what I looked like. He loved who I was in here." She patted her heart.

"How do you know?" Soila asked simply.

"Because of who he was, it was difficult to love any woman."

"Why?"

"It isn't easy to explain."

"Nobody ever explains anything to me. They act like I'm too delicate to hear the truth."

"I guess we think it's because you go to Mass all the time."

"I have the same feelings everybody else has."

"I know, Soilita. I know you do."

"I don't want to marry God. I don't want to give my life up for the church!"

"Who says you have to?" Maria grasped her hand. Soila was growing increasingly agitated.

"My mother always did. My brother and father always told me I was too ugly to ever get married." And Soila burst into tears. Seeing her prompted Chita to start crying too. Maria shook her head in annoyance at her little girl. Chita, even so young, was already trying to upstage everyone else.

Maria knelt down by her carriage. "Stop crying. This isn't about you. Stop it at once!"

And Chita had fallen obligatorily silent, allowing Soila to have the spotlight.

"I've been to a doctor."

"Yes."

"He says he can get rid of it."

"Which doctor?"

And Soila confessed to the proposal offered her by Dr. Hansen.

"You don't have any idea who offered to pay?"

"I think it was Loretta Young."

"Nick always loved you."

"Really?" Soila asked doubtfully.

"But he could never afford it."

Soila hesitated. "It wasn't you, was it?"

"No, *mija*. I would never want you to think I thought it was necessary. But I'd give you anything you ever wanted if I could. You know that, don't you?"

Soila smiled. "The doctor called right after Ms. Young died."

"And he's a good doctor?"

Soila nodded.

"Then do it!"

"I don't know if it's right. I've prayed about it."

"Just do it!"

And that night Anita first saw the apparition in Soila's cheek.

What had Maria meant when she said Kenny hadn't loved her outward appearance? That he was only capable of loving who she was inside. One day she hoped to ask him. Kenny and Nick had always been so kind to her. She'd watched Kenny come and go through the kitchen door to his restaurant ever since she could remember. He always seemed so long-suffering, hunkered under the hot sun. But he was handsome, and very kind. She wished she could tell him so.

Now, as she opened Maria's front door, she apparently had her chance. A man with startling blue eyes smiled uneasily at her. She hadn't given him a chance to knock. Kenny held up his hand. He didn't recognize her. "I'm sorry to disturb you. I was told Maria Castillo lives here."

"She does."

"Oh," he replied nervously. He hadn't changed much. A few lines around his blue eyes. Soila always loved Kenny's lapis blue eyes. They were like finely polished turquoise stones.

"Don't you remember me?" Soila asked him brightly.

"I'm afraid I don't."

"I'm Soila. Soila Quintero."

And he grinned broadly. She fell into his arms and allowed him to hug her. Other than Pablo, this was the first spontaneous hug from a man she'd ever experienced, but Kenny didn't let go so quickly. She realized that he was trying to control his emotions. Because she was responding to the affection, she gave him all the time he needed.

"Is she here?" he asked worriedly.

"No," Soila shook her head. "She's away for the weekend."

Then the import of his visit dawned on her. "You've heard."

"Yes."

"I'm so sorry. Come inside."

"You were just leaving."

"I can wait. Come inside."

And Soila ushered a humbled Kenny into the home of Maria and his daughter.

"She doesn't change anything. She won't allow it."

Kenny studied a recent photo of Maria and Chita with nothing less than reverence.

"When did it happen?"

"In August of last year."

"August," Kenny whispered disgustedly.

"It's changed her," Soila observed solemnly.

"Ah," he replied. "It would."

"They never found her body. She doesn't believe Chita is dead. She's hired investigators. She's given everything in her being to try to find her."

"Who does she think might have her?"

Soila was afraid to answer.

"Soila?"

"For a time, my brother."

Kenny tried not to react. He hated Alex Quintero.

"It's hard to understand, but my brother has changed. He'd never do such a thing."

"So they questioned him?"

"He disappeared. He was afraid. He knew they'd blame him."

"What do you think?"

"He found God. He's had his epiphany. He doesn't have her. He had nothing to do with it. Maria doesn't really think so either."

"When do you expect her back?"

"Not for several days. If you want to stay, I'm sure she'd be happy."

He hadn't even considered such a thing.

"If you don't mind, I'd like to sit here for awhile. If I feel comfortable, maybe I'll spend the night."

"If you do, it would be helpful. My father is sick. I should probably spend the night at his house tonight. She wanted someone here, for Chita, you know, in case."

Kenny nodded.

"How's Mr. Nick?"

Guilt flooded through Kenny. "He's recovered nicely. Almost a hundred percent."

Relief flickered in her brown eyes. "I think about him so often."

"He says you probably saved his life. He told me. By holding him. He thinks he would have died if he'd lain there alone. Without the benefit of touch."

"I wouldn't have left him. I thought he was dying." Distress filled her eyes. A tear rolled down her new cheek.

"What is it?" Kenny asked her.

"I feel so guilty. I couldn't tell her, and now that she's gone, I'll never have my chance to ask her for her forgiveness."

"Who?"

"Mrs. Singer."

"Why do you need her forgiveness?"

"I didn't call the ambulance. Her husband was dying. Mr. Singer begged me to leave Nick and get them help. But I thought Nick was dying too. I thought he was worse off. His blood was draining into the street. I didn't want him to die alone. If I stood up, if I'd left, even for a moment, he might have died with no one to love him at all."

"When I got there, the ambulance was already coming. Someone called. Nicky lived. They did their best to save Sam."

"But Mr. Singer died because of me." Soila gazed up at Kenny. "This is the awful part. I was glad. I was angry at him."

"Because he wouldn't sell your father his house."

"Yes," Soila whispered. "He ruined my father. He destroyed our family. We never would have had to move. My mother might have come back. Ruby would not have won."

Breathlessly Kenny stood, studying Soila as she wept quietly in Maria's living room. She sank to a stool at the foot of a chair.

"I was angry at Sam, too." Kenny told her. "You saw them, the ones who did it."

"Yes. Through the peephole in our fence."

"Why didn't you tell the police?"

"Because Nick didn't remember. And Pablo and Maria thought I'd be harmed. Maria promised me that in exchange for my silence, she'd get revenge."

"Revenge? For who?"

"For Nick. For you."

"Is that where she is?"

Soila didn't reply. After a long pause, Soila moved to hug him again. "I'm sorry," she said again.

"For what?" he asked in bewilderment.

"Her eyes. Blue like yours. Maria loved her so much. She feels terrible guilt about hurting you. It's doubled her pain. She's not the same. I'm so sorry."

After Soila left, Kenny's curiosity got the best of him. He scoured every framed picture and photograph album, searching for images of Chita. Would this be his only experience of his daughter? She was exotically beautiful. The best of her mother and father. She had his eyes, with the gravity of her mother's brow. There were photos taken of her in Cuernavaca, with Pablo and a very elegant woman who was probably his mother. In each group photograph, Maria, if present at all, never smiled. She only smiled when she was alone with Chita.

There were several framed photographs of Chita and Ruthie. Poor Ruthie. She looked radiant, holding Chita. What a sad ending to her life. Kenny fought emotion. His nerves were raw. He hadn't called Nick, but he was still furious. He hadn't even called Margie to tell her he'd quit. In Maria's house he felt like an intruder. If she'd wanted him here, all she ever had to do was ask.

Kenny wandered down the hall to Chita's room. The door was open. It was small, with a tiny, frilly pink bedspread and curtains. A bookshelf was crammed with children's books, some in English, some in Spanish. A number of toys—dolls, erector sets, building blocks, apparently she had eclectic taste—lay where Chita had last left them.

On a small table, with a lamp and little clock was a framed photograph. Kenny knelt to inspect. It was of him, standing in the door frame of his kitchen, looking out into the alley. Maria had taken it from a shelf the day she left their house. That and a doll Kenny made for her. The doll lay on Chita's bed, next to her pillow.

She hadn't erased him from their lives. Chita apparently had at least seen the photograph, perhaps asked about him. Maria saw to it that she knew she had a daddy somewhere. But how had she explained that he wasn't in their lives?

How could Kenny ever justify it, later, when she'd probably ask?

The last days in Cathedral City had been so chaotic. Maria had disappeared, deported, Kenny was told by Ruthie, long after the fact. He and Nick had finally decided to separate, to take Sam Singer's offer to buy them out. Kenny would go to Mexico, to be with Maria. Nick had been uncertain about his plans, but it was mutual. They both wanted out.

And then came the savage assault on Nick in the alley. And Sam's death. The resulting collapse of Ruthie's mental health. And on top of that, Maria's refusal to see him. Not if it meant Nick would be left alone. Kenny reflected, sitting on the edge of his lost baby girl's bed, that she'd made it easy for him. How could she ask him to choose under such horrific circumstances?

Had she wanted him to come, and sacrificed her wishes to spare him the anguish of leaving Nick? Or did she have what she wanted? A little girl. A new family to replace the one she'd lost to such tragedy.

Did she really love Kenny after all?

With that, Kenny felt uncomfortable about remaining in her house. He stood up and walked down the hall to the living room. Just as he opened the door, the telephone began to ring. It might be Soila, he reflected. Should he answer it?

It continued to ring. There wasn't any answering machine hooked up to it. Kenny decided to pick up.

"Hello?"

"Yes, this is the San Bernardino County Sheriff's office. Is Maria Castillo available?"

"No," Kenny shook his head.

"We already tried her place of business. Is there any other way to reach her?"

"What's wrong? What's happened?"

"I can only speak to Ms. Castillo, sir. Who are you?"

"I'm the father of her daughter."

Silence on the line. Kenny heard the officer conferring with a fellow cop. "Can you prove it?"

"How do I prove such a thing?"

"The birth certificate. What's your name?"

Kenny told them.

The officer referred again to his notes. "We tried at length to find you."

"I'm here, now. Tell me what's happened."

"Well, we have officers coming to Ms. Castillo's home. They'll explain when they arrive, which should be momentarily. Please wait, sir."

Kenny sank to a chair near the telephone. What were they coming to tell her? And him. Moments later, a police car pulled up in front of Maria's windows. Kenny stood up to open the door.

When Pablo arrived at the house of Thomas Quintero, attendants were already loading him into the ambulance. A few neighbors were gathered on the lawn. A very pretty, tearful young woman stood helplessly nearby. Out of the corner of his eye, in the midst of the unfolding events, Pablo noticed a large, handmade sign in the corner of the living room window, in both Spanish and English.

La Virgen Se Ha Hido! The Virgin Has Left!

The emergency crew was shouting questions to Soila. "Is he on any medication?"

"No," she shook her head.

"Did he complain of pain in his chest? His arm?"

"He's been having trouble breathing."

"Any known health complications we should be aware of?"

Her father looked gray on the gurney. A tight white sheet, pulled up under his chin, exacerbated his pallor. Soila shook her head.

"He has HIV," Pablo shouted across the lawn. Then, upon the startled reaction of Soila's neighbors, regretted it. He rushed up to the ambulance. "Where's his daughter? Where's Soila?"

The attendant studied him quizzically. They placed an oxygen mask over Thomas' face. He was unconscious.

"His daughter is standing right next to you."

Pablo turned in amazement. It was her. "Soilita!" Then he turned back to the attendant. "Can she ride with you?"

"Not if he's infectious. Can you give her a lift? We're heading to Eisenhower Medical Center. Take Frank Sinatra Drive to Bob Hope. Turn right."

"We'll follow you."

The attendant climbed up next to her father, and they pulled the gate to the ambulance closed in Soila's face. When she saw it reflected back, she didn't recognize herself. Sirens wailing, the ambulance took off.

Pablo urged Soila up into his Jeep.

"I hope she makes it in time."

"Who?"

"My mother. She'll know what to do."

"When do you expect her?"

"Any time in the next several days. Depending."

"Depending on what?"

"Her coyote," Soila replied innocently.

"Your mother is crossing the border with a coyote?"

"They won't let her in this country with la SIDA."

"When was all of this decided?"

"Maria decided."

"Maria?" Pablo was furious.

"Yes. She's gone to Mexicali. She arranged for the whole thing. She's coming with her. To protect her."

"Chinga tu madre!" Fuck your mother, Pablo shouted.

Soila was appalled. "It isn't her fault. She's coming to help my father!"

"I'm sorry, I'm sorry. She's just so stubborn. Why doesn't anybody tell me anything?"

"Because of your Migra boyfriend," Soila retorted. She fell silent, worried now about her father.

Pablo drove in furious silence. Finally he erupted again. "Anything else you haven't mentioned?"

Soila smiled at him defiantly. She was beautiful now when she got angry. "One more thing." Her hair whipped around in the hot wind.

"What?"

"Kenny's back. He's waiting at Maria's house. He's angry nobody told him about Conchita."

30

La Migra Bueno

"Hello, Bob?"

Bob was cautious but elated when he heard Pablo's voice on the line. Cautious, with elation ready to be checked at a moments' notice. He was sitting in his office at the El Centro Border Patrol. In front of him, a well-worn topographical map of the Imperial County deserts. He was analyzing field reports of officers patrolling the barren eastern Creosote Flats (the quadrant south from the All American Canal to the border) and the Yuha Basin, west of Calexico. The surveillance equipment had been buzzing all night. His transport vans reported a record one-hundred-twenty-three sorties in one night. Over eighteen hundred arrests. Ninety-two percent returned within eight hours of apprehension. His officers were exhausted.

Many reported high ratios of repeat attempts. They'd turn groups back into Mexico only to catch them again, twelve hours later. It was a nightmare. When activity was high like today, tempers flared and mistakes were made. The combination of intense, high heat and a tired, overworked border patrol agent could be deadly.

It also meant that nearly a thousand people were roaming the California deserts, ill-prepared for the 118 degree heat, guaranteeing unnecessary deaths. River crossings could be especially deadly, particularly at night. Swiftly moving canals spider-veined the Yuha Buttes.

Dead air. Bob didn't reply to Pablo.

"Bob?"

"Yes."

"It's Pablito."

"I know."

"I wouldn't call you but it's an emergency. Can you talk?"

"I'm pretty busy," said Bob, as he continued to chart the past night's arrest pattern.

"It's about my two very best friends in the world. They're in danger. I'm begging you to help them. Begging."

Bob's fist clenched the receiver of his telephone. "Why should I help *her?*"

"Because you understand her. Someone else is involved too."

"I'll only do this face to face." At least he should have that much. Pablo near him for fifteen minutes. He was owed that.

"Good. I'm across the street at the Fed Co. I'll meet you at the coffee shop down the block."

Cement obelisk monuments commemorating the boundary of the United States and Mexico gleamed in the moonlight of the arid desert floor.

Maria remembered the obelisk from before, or one like it. Now it loomed in the distance, down the valley floor, ahead of them like a miniature Washington Monument, beckoning the band of immigrant women into the land of George Bush, and his nephew, half-Latino heartthrob, George P.

If she was going to act, it must be now.

For the duration of the seven-hour desert hike, Maria studied Logan with such intensity, he and the little coyote were already suspicious of her. Shortly they would be demanding the balance of the agreed upon fare. Two thousand from each woman. Having lived in the United States, Maria had grown accustomed to the conspicuous consumption of the average American woman. She saw them in supermarkets, department stores, nurseries and even airports—always in endless pursuit of quick gratification.

She couldn't fairly judge them. She herself, without such a personally tragic history would most likely do the same thing. But it hurt her to imagine the sacrifice each and every peso about to be transferred represented to the proffer. Coyotes could argue that they risked a five-year prison sentence if caught. Was two thousand worth five years of his life? No, Maria allowed. Was twenty thousand? Was two hundred thousand?

Getting interesting.

Maria had offered him ten thousand to personally supervise this crossing. She would have paid more, but she didn't want him to get suspicious. Soila simply arrived at his gate, with a letter from Sister Agnes, who he knew. She made the offer as Pablo and Bob watched from above. If they were being observed, Maria wanted them to think Soila was her. The resemblance, from a distance, was probably uncanny. Soila wanted to be certain he was the same man she'd seen in the alley five years ago.

Logan wasn't the coyote who'd caused the death of her grand-mother. She would never be that lucky. That coyote had simply been inept. Logan was something much different. Her sisters had done their homework. He had brutalized several women as recently as a month ago when they came up short with the money. He was infamous on both sides of the border. He was rising fast in a small but treacherous smuggling cartel. His ethnic background was reportedly holding him back. He made up for it with increasingly high receipts—hassling *mojados* for more than they agreed. Sometimes holding them hostage for weeks or months till relatives would pay.

It was believed that he'd deserted several small groups last spring, after robbing them of their savings. Of the two groups, one band was never found. The desert simply swallowed them up. Of the other group, all perished but one small boy who survived and described Logan to both Grupo Beta, the Mexican border security police, and to the U.S. Border Patrol in El Centro.

He was wanted by both agencies. Only the U.S. Border Patrol knew of his whereabouts.

Maria had been grieving the last several hours. Many times tears welled in her eyes, causing Inez to tug at her arm and insist on knowing what saddened her so.

"I miss them," was all she'd confess. "I miss them all."

And Inez, who was used to sad stories at the clinic, didn't have a cheery reply to muster whatsoever. No hope to offer at all. On Maria's case she was stumped. She was completely and utterly alone. Inez privately hypothesized that perhaps her friend was jinxed. Bad luck to those she loved.

"Thank-you," Inez whispered to her.

"For what?"

"For coming along. For arranging the trip."

"I may not have done you such a favor," Maria studied the pointed boundary marker in the distance. "No matter what happens, keep going."

"What? What's going to happen?"

But Maria fell to the back of the group with Bambi.

Several moments later, Logan and the little coyote stopped marching. Logan turned to face the weary group. He spoke for the first time. "Okay, okay, time to collect the rest of your cash. See that marker? It's El Norte. You've made it. Time to pay me what's due."

The women began adjusting clothing, some turned modestly so they could reach inside their undergarments to remove bills, rolled and hidden in bodily cavities. Some had their money taped to their bellies. Others had lined their shoes. In the case of Patti and Lupe, both simply reached for their handbags.

After a long silent exchange between Patti and Lupe, they eased their way forward to the head of the group. The little coyote grinned at them. He shuffled over. They both made exaggerated efforts to dig around in their bags. Patti pulled out a wad of cash and handed it over. José quickly counted it.

"You're short, beautiful."

He glanced over at Logan, who watched with interest.

"I'm nearly five-ten," she wisecracked.

"C'mon. We agreed on two grand."

"I had two grand when we started," Patti proclaimed. "Right, home girl?"

Lupe nodded gravely. She cracked her gum.

"What about you? Same story?"

"No, I got it. Lemme take you somewhere private so I can give it to you." Lupe shifted sexily. She yawned.

José glanced to Logan for reassurance. He grinned okay. If she was so hot. They headed up the short hill and over the ridge. They heard shouting. The quick report of gunfire. The sound ricocheted down the canyon. The women began screaming, dropping to their knees, holding their heads, as if bullets were flying everywhere.

Logan told the others, "If we wanted what she had, we'd have taken it before this. Gimme your cash."

"Why should we?" Patti demanded. "We're already where we wanted to go. Just a short walk down the hill. And we're home."

"*Home?*" he repeated.

"That's right. We're U.S. citizens."

He whistled for his partner. Looking around, he found himself now the only man, surrounded by women.

Bambi and Maria studied each other.

"Maria?" Inez queried.

"All of you drop to the ground," Bambi ordered.

"Do as she says," Lupe called from the top of the ridge. She was holding the semiautomatic rifle, belonging to the little coyote. It was aimed directly at a surprised Logan's head. She trotted down the hillside.

"Hey!" Logan called into the canyon. "What'd you do with him?"

"He wanted to see what I had for him," Lupe smiled. "So I gave it to him."

"José! José!" Logan drew his pistol.

"Not so fast," Bambi whispered in his ear. He felt the cool metal of a gun barrel at his side. Looking around, Logan saw he was surrounded by Bambi, Maria, Patti and Lupe. Lupe disarmed him. Bambi handcuffed his hands behind him. He shook his head in disgust.

"This is a terrible idea, ladies. You'll regret it."

"I bet you wish you were back in Sky Valley, tending your little homestead," Maria told him.

"Who the fuck are you?"

She nodded, insolently. "I'm your client. You want to be paid, don't you?"

He relaxed slightly. "Sure thing. Can you loosen the cuffs?"

"This is only for the benefit of the others," Maria whispered. "I'll free you once they've gone ahead."

"Maria! What's going on?" Inez scrambled to her feet.

Bambi addressed the group. "Because they know where they're going, Patti and Lupe will lead you all down the trail to the border marker. You're perfectly safe. Everything will go forward as you hoped that it would. A transport vehicle will take us north shortly after we cross the border. We've planned this mission for months."

"And then the three of us are gonna have a chat," Maria found herself grinning into Logan's face. "About Judi Romero."

"Who's Judi Romero?" he demanded. "You bitches will never get away with this."

"Maria!"

Maria turned to face a concerned Inez. "You go with Patti and Lupe. You aren't far from home. We'll catch up."

"What do you think you're doing? You aren't a murderer."

"He is," Maria motioned to their hostage. "He's also the guy who beat up Nick. Shot Anita in the alley that night. He raped and killed a little girl."

"This is wrong. I won't allow you to do this. I'm not going anywhere."

"Soila needs you. So does your husband. You're wasting precious time. He may not make it. Please go with them."

"I can't save my husband's life. You still have a chance, *mija.*"

"You don't know who he is. What he's done."

"He killed my cousin," Bambi screamed. "Our baby."

"I didn't kill anybody!" Logan shouted.

"All of you keep walking," Bambi ordered the remainder of the group. "Patti and Lupe know the way. We have transportation waiting, just a half hour away. Go, or you'll be part of this. Is that what you want?"

They surveyed the frightened faces of the women. Many of them whimpered.

"C'mon," Patti urged them. "It's only a mile away. We know where we're going."

One of the women offered her a roll of cash.

"No," Patti shook her head. "We don't want your money. You keep it. Just come. You've done nothing wrong."

"Go!" Maria screamed at them.

Frightened, the women began to move down the hill. Patti and Lupe trotted after them. Maria, Bambi, Inez and the coyote watched them descend to the desert floor. None of them looked back.

"So what do you think you are, some kind of commandos?"

"We're the Radical Sisters of God."

Logan chuckled. "The Radical Sisters of God. I guess we should'a seen it coming. Fucking dykes."

"Shut up," Maria told him.

"Why don't you shut me up with one of those big tits of yours."

Bambi pistol-whipped him in the side of the head. Stunned, he dropped to his knees, blood gushing from his mouth. "Fuck," he muttered.

"Inez. Please go ahead."

"I'm staying. I'm a witness to this crime. You'll have to kill me too."

"Jesus," Bambi muttered disgustedly.

"She's little," Maria said. "Take her forcibly."

"I have *business* here," Bambi reminded Maria.

"I promise I'll take care of it," Maria smiled radiantly. Her eyes were shining. "We're still in Mexico. Go."

"She's gone insane," Inez murmured.

"I don't want to hurt you," Bambi threatened Inez.

"This is nothing compared to what faces me ahead. Maria! *Mija!* If you go through with this, your daughter is probably dead for sure. You'd never kill him if you thought there was a chance Chita might need you."

"I managed without my mother," she replied dully.

"Did you?" Inez asked her.

"Let's go," Bambi yanked her arm. Inez resisted. "Let's go!" Bambi roared. She dragged Inez, who made herself go limp, all the way to the bottom of the hill.

Logan watched them go. "It's just you and me, beautiful. Now we're alone like you wanted us to be."

"That's right," Maria nodded. She removed her bandanna.

He responded to her beauty.

"Tell you what. I'm gonna try to change your mind. I think you should follow your girlfriend, and I should go back the other way. Did you already kill José?"

Maria didn't answer.

"What'd I ever do to you?"

"You exploit dreamers."

"Oh. A poet. Well, poet? You know how many folks I've led across?" He could see the group, just as they reached the marker. Some of them turned to look nervously back up the throat of the *bajada*. Bambi urged them forward. Inez now walked dejectedly on her own.

"We're gonna go back and find José."

"I guess the old lady got to you," he snickered.

"She isn't an old lady. She looks old because she's got AIDS."

"Lotta spunk. Once she gets on the American side she'll get her drugs easier. I transport meds to clinics in T.J. and Mexicali. See, I'm not all bad, am I beautiful?"

"Hey, home boy. You didn't tell me. How many people you take across?"

"Hmm. I've been in the business now about four years. I make three trips a week. Sometimes more, but lemme be conservative. Maybe six thousand? Six thousand who got across. I'm special, cause I've never been arrested. My people, they make it."

"That's not what I'm told. I'm told that chances are, you'd probably desert us once we got past the marker."

"I *never* did that."

"Well, I'm sorry to disagree, but you have."

"What'd she mean? The part about your daughter. You have a daughter?"

"She's right. I had a pretty baby girl. She drowned in the Cathedral City flood last summer."

He smiled curiously at her. "I checked up on you. You own the bar in Cathedral City."

"Yes."

"Shit, you're loaded. You can have anything you want."

"So it would seem. I was a friend to the men who owned the bar. Nick's. Sam Singer's wife rescued me on the road. After a coyote killed my grandmother."

"That wasn't me."

"But it was you behind Nick's. We have witnesses now who say it was."

"Fucking Misty and Drew. Who got to them?"

"Their mother."

"Drunken slut." He grinned at her.

"You don't have to worry about them. She moved them away. Canada. They'll never have a chance to say a word against you. Now, about Judi Romero."

"What about her?"

"You personally delivered her to Bambi and Madonna the morning she died."

"She was lucky. Everybody else burned up. Remember?"

"She wasn't so lucky," Maria shrugged sadly. "She'd just had intercourse. Sister Agnes tried to save her baby. She could tell she was raped. She knows about these things. Sister Agnes referred them to you. She blames herself for everything. That's how I come in. She sent us to Sky Valley to see you. To arrange for Inez."

"I never raped her."

"She was thirteen."

"It's bad at any age."

"I know," Maria nodded. "But whoever forced themselves on top of her killed the little baby. The baby's blood probably killed Judi. Her head was crushed."

"It wasn't me."

"Then someone in your crew. Maybe we should do a DNA test. Nah. Takes weeks. You don't have weeks."

"So what's this, you a vigilante now? If you like this game, I can connect you to the best people on both sides of the border. You think America has gone to hell? With your cash? Do you know how much money you could create with your kind of wealth?"

"I don't care about wealth. I just told you, my daughter's dead. I have nothing left to live for."

"You might feel that way now." His eyes gleamed.

"I feel dead. Since she was taken, I never felt dead," Maria shook her head in controlled amazement. "Now, I do. They told me I'd have to accept it someday. Now I have."

"That isn't so good for me," Logan bowed his head. "Can't we work something out?"

"Yes. You for her." When Logan lunged for her gun, Maria shot him.

The Winnebago purred against the backdrop of the muted desert dawn. The sun was just coming up. Madonna slept amazingly well. Her conscience felt clear for the first time. She studied the sleeping figures of the women, draped in various positions in the sleeping quarters of Maria's Winnebago. Only Inez was also awake.

They'd arrived shortly before three. A vote had been taken. It was decided unanimously to wait for Maria, but Bambi was fearful about her well-being. She'd fallen asleep with her head in Madonna's lap. They couldn't risk waiting much longer. The others had been through so much already.

Madonna shook Bambi awake.

"She here?"

"No, baby."

Stricken, Bambi stood up to survey the horizon. Nothing. Soon the sun would rise. So would the temperature.

"We may as well go," Inez whispered. "She isn't coming."

"We'll wait."

"She never went through with it. He probably killed her."

"Shut up," Bambi cried.

"I know her better than you do."

"We're her best friends."

"Friends. Huh."

The other women stirred awake. Patti stepped over dozing bodies to find her way to the bathroom. Lupe began to brush her hair. Madonna flipped on the coffeemaker. With the morning sun streaming through the windows, it was almost cozy. The questions started up almost immediately.

"How am I gonna get to L.A.?"

"I'm supposed to hook up with my daughter to take me to Bakersfield."

"He promised us a place to stay till we got on our feet."

Bambi shook her head. Damn that Sister Agnes. So many details yet to be ironed out. And now they didn't have Maria. Or her disposable income.

A plane buzzed overhead. A lone motor home parked in the middle of open desert would invite curiosity. It was probably a border patrol surveillance plane.

"I don't know how much longer we can safely wait," Madonna confided in Bambi.

"I need to get to my family," Inez asserted. "If we don't go, we'll be arrested for sure. It isn't fair to the rest of them." Inez waved her hand at the intimidated woman who waited meekly in line to use the toilet.

"We have to go, babe," Madonna urged Bambi.

"There's a car coming," Inez muttered, shaking her head.

In the distance they could see a fast-moving vehicle roaring toward them, dust spewing out behind it.

"It's green and white." Bambi said. "Shit. Everybody in back." She yanked the curtain closed. "Nobody say a word. Madonna can handle this."

And Madonna found herself sitting alone in the front seat of the motor home. When the INS vehicle pulled up, she was casually applying lipstick, tying her hair back into a ponytail and reading a *Vanity Fair.* A border patrol agent climbed down from the driver's side of the truck.

"Goddamn it." Madonna swore softly. "It's Border Patrol Bob.

Somebody's with him." She was surprised that she recognized his passenger.

Pablo hopped to the desert floor. While Bob waited by his truck, Pablo approached the Winnebago.

Madonna rolled down her window.

"He wants Maria. She comes with us, you can leave, no questions asked."

"We don't have her," Madonna shrugged.

"What do you mean?"

"She stayed behind. She hasn't come back."

"Is she alone?"

"She was with the coyote."

"Oh shit!" Pablo scanned the barren desert slope which gently rose toward the distant mountain range of Mexico.

"I'll go with them," he heard Inez' unmistakable voice behind the pulled curtain. "I'm tired. I want to go home."

"Fucking bitch," he heard Bambi whisper.

"I've gotta go talk to him." Pablo trotted back to where Bob waited. "She's not in there. She's up in the mountains."

"I don't want to know anything else until this vehicle is out of my sight."

Pablo ran back to Madonna. "Go. Now. You never saw us. You're on your own."

And Madonna started her engine. Shortly, the gleaming white Winnebago began rolling up the dusty desert road toward Highway 98, shortly to head east on Interstate 8 toward El Centro.

Pablo and Bob contemplated the shimmering *bajada*. The temperature was probably 113 degrees. Pablo waited for Bob to tell him what they should do. Bob was clearly very angry. The tendons in his temples and jaw were contorting.

"I'm sorry!" Pablo told him. "You go. I'll hike up and find her."

"Do you know how hot it is?"

"She's my friend. She needs me."

"For me to cross the border into Mexico would be breaking so many major laws, I could be thrown in jail for the rest of my life."

"I'm not asking you to go."

Bob hesitated. Bitterly he surveyed the scene.

"If I could have a canteen with some water. I'll just hike up to the crest of the hill. They could see the marker when they separated. She can't be far."

The radio squawked in Bob's truck. He moved to answer the call. Pablo could hear him confer in hushed tones to the border patrol dispatcher. When he came back, he was visibly shaken.

"What is it? What's happened?"

"Her daughter. She's been recovered."

"Chita? Is she alive?"

"I'm going with you," Bob told him. Bob strode to the back of the truck and quickly packed a day pack with survival supplies. Water, freeze-dried foods, a medicine kit and reflective blankets.

Quickly he stripped out of his uniform. For a moment it was just Bob and his Jockeys standing before Pablo against the backdrop of the open desert. A rush of sexual desire jolted through Pablo, which he checked out of sheer decency, but Bob noticed and smirked.

"I've been working out," he said, yanking up a pair of hiking shorts and a clean white T-shirt over his head. "It was all I had to save my sanity." He tossed Pablo the backpack. "You carry it. And put on a hat."

"Thank-you," Pablo said tearfully.

Together they crossed the border into Mexico, and quickly made their way up the hillside to find Maria.

31

Return to Cathedral City

Soila tried in vain to convince Ruby to return from Monterey Park to sit with Thomas Quintero in the Eisenhower Hospital ICU. At least Anita agreed to take the bus and would arrive in Rancho Mirage this afternoon at three. Soila would borrow Maria's car to pick her up, but first she had to pick up her mother at St. Louis Catholic Church, where Madonna had dropped her off earlier, glad to be rid of her.

Inez waited sadly in the sanctuary. Nothing felt familiar to her now. Father Gene was gone. Her little house and surrounding neighborhood had been torn down. All vestiges of the old gay bar had been stripped away. Cathedral City was a cold, sterile, concrete city, and not the quaint desert village it had been before. She had vowed never to return, and here she was. At least the inside of the church was the same, but in addition to Frank Sinatra memorabilia, there were plaques commemorating Loretta Young, the most famous Catholic in the world.

In the foyer of the church, Inez had run face to face into Sister Agnes. They remembered each other from before, two formidable little women, but they'd never spoken, and neither knew the important role the other had played in the drama that was soon to unfold.

Inez was furious to discover that electric candles now replaced the beautiful flickering votives of the past.

"Fire regulations," Sister Agnes muttered, taking the prayer stool next to Inez and reading her irritation.

"God would protect his house against fire," Inez clucked.

"Unless he wanted to burn us out," Sister Agnes observed, which caused Inez to chuckle.

After they quieted, Sister Agnes asked what Inez intended to ask of God.

"I'm praying for the soul of my husband. And my friend."

"What's wrong with your husband?"

"He's very ill. I've just come from Mexico. My daughter is meeting me here to take me to hospital."

"Maybe I know her. What's her name?"

"Soila. Soila Quintero."

Sister Agnes gasped. "Are you Inez?"

"Yes," Inez nodded.

"I've heard much about you." She struggled for words. "Did you just arrive?"

"Yes." Inez studied her intently. Her face grew grim. She struggled to her feet. "I'm here also to pray for the soul of my friend. You know who I'm talking about."

"Where is she?"

"Ask God. I don't know. She's lost. We left her behind. She's probably been devoured by buzzards by now!"

"What can you mean?" Agnes grabbed her sleeve. Inez yanked her arm away.

"Pray for her. Pray for yourself!" Inez stormed out the side door of the sanctuary.

When she emerged, a small red station wagon waited at the curb. A pretty young girl sat behind the wheel. Inez scanned the parking lot for Soila. Where was she? It was so hot, but she'd never set foot in the church again.

The driver of the red car honked. Who was she waiting for? The church was empty. She honked again, waving at Inez.

Cautiously, Inez approached the car. "Who are you?" she peered into the open window.

"Mommy. It's me!"

Inez recoiled. "Soilita?"

"Yes, Mommy. Get in. It's hot and we have to go. The hospital called before I left."

Inez opened the door and climbed in. She contemplated her beautiful daughter. She reached over to touch her cheek.

"It's a miracle."

"Do you like it? Do you approve?" Soila's eyes flooded with fear.

"I still see the same beautiful girl," Inez smiled and patted her hand.

Soila started the engine and together they raced down the highway toward Rancho Mirage.

The grocer at the Pioneertown general store called it in to the San Bernardino Sheriff station in Yucca Valley and they went out to investigate. It had been like clockwork with Gloria. The Friday walk into town to buy her provisions and get her mail. She'd grown increasingly less conversant. More distant, but she seemed to be selecting healthier items. No more TV dinners. Good grain cereals. Milk. Spaghetti sauce and noodles.

When she hadn't appeared by closing time, a call was made. A car was dispatched to investigate.

Gloria was found stretched out at the end of the driveway where she'd dropped. A heart attack. Died instantly. A small stuffed bear sat perched upright. As if to guard her, or keep her company. The deputy who found her knew Gloria, felt bad, and quickly covered her with a blanket from the trunk of her car. He'd been startled as he scanned the blank windows of her cabin to find a pair of eyes staring out at him. Had Gloria acquired a pet of some kind or was it a play of light in the old glass? He moved carefully forward to investigate.

That's when he discovered the little blue-eyed girl. Perfectly well groomed and cared for. The match in the computer came up immediately. Plus, Chita informed him in perfect English, then Spanish, what her first and last name were. She told them that she missed her mommy.

From her vista in the valley of the high, flat plain descending at the crest of the foothills of the Superstition Mountains, the blue sky looked like the cool, clear pool behind Nick and Kenny's house in Cathedral City. The white vapor trails of the jets practicing maneuvers from the nearby U.S. Naval Test Center were like candles floating in the distant desert over California.

In the sky Maria saw the comforting faces of her loved ones, holding hands in heaven. Conchita first. Then her beautiful mother Pia and her father Hector. Her *abuelita* Concha. And now Kenny's image was rising from the north, in clean white robes, holding out his hands as if beckoning her to join them all in the sky.

Thoughts of Kenny kept appearing and reappearing in her mind.

What had possessed him to come along? Where was he now? Had he managed to clamor to safety or had he perished, submerged in the muddy water? She could still see his eyes as he fell back into the water; beatifying Kenny for all time in her thoughts.

His outstretched muscular arms, a calm swan dive backward into the water; graceful even in chaos and then gone. She had known him less than twenty-four hours and she would never close her eyes again without first seeing his image flicker briefly before fading; Kenny would always be in her mind. But then the image distorted.

When her grandmother learned that Kenny had been swept away in the flooding waters of the arroyo, she had begged God to exchange herself for him. "Me for him! He was so young! He only came because of us! Me for him! Me for him!"

The wind changed and Chita began to disappear.

"No," Maria whimpered now. "Not again. No. Me for her. Me for her." Then she passed out.

"She's alive."

"Drink some water, baby," she heard Pablito say.

"Don't take her from me again," she moaned.

"Shield her from the sun." A quiet command from a strong voice. "We've got to get her hydrated."

"Maria," Pablo patted her hand. "It's me. Pablito. Wake up."

The beautiful image of her family became distorted by that of Pablo, gazing with concern into Maria's face.

"Sit her up. Ms. Castillo! Can you hear me?"

She knew that voice. Border Patrol Bob.

"How are we gonna get her out of here?" Pablo asked.

"I'll carry her."

"No," she moaned. "Let me die. There's nothing to go back home for."

"What about the guy?"

"It's your country," Bob told him. "You handle it."

"He's dead."

"Leave him." Bob pulled out his handkerchief and picked up Maria's pistol. He tossed it far off into the desert. "Nothing we can do."

"Really?" Pablo was astonished.

Bob leaned down and scooped Maria into his arms. "Can you

carry him? Let's go. We have to get her to a hospital. And I want to get back on U.S. soil."

Pablo watched as Bob lurched down the path toward California with Maria in his arms, looking for all the world like King Kong.

Pablo surveyed Logan's body already infested with desert insects. "Collateral damage," he shrugged, and trotted down the desert slope after his boyfriend.

Maria revived enough to insist on returning to Cathedral City. With Soila at the hospital, and no one answering Maria's phone, Pablo couldn't find anyone who could tell him the status of Conchita Castillo. Without knowing for certain, he thought it best to get Maria home without giving her any false hope. In El Centro, Pablo and Maria said goodbye to Bob and Pablo drove them north in his Jeep.

They were detained at the Salton Sea Border Patrol checkpoint because both of them were Latino. They were allowed to leave after the Jeep was searched. Neither mentioned Bob's name once.

When they returned to Cathedral City, Pablo noticed SOLD plastered over the FOR SALE sign of the Seven Palms.

"You should have left me there," Maria observed when she saw her café. It was open, but there were few cars in the parking lot. "Inez was right. I killed any hope I had back there. My baby is gone," she gulped back tears.

Pablo rounded the corner past the restaurant and headed up the hill to Maria's house. The Jeep came to a halt in her driveway. He hopped down and went around to her side to help her down.

"C'mon, *mija*. We'll face this thing together. Like always. I'm always here for you."

But she didn't reply. Her eyes were riveted on the front door of her house, which stood ajar. She couldn't believe who she was seeing. Kenny!

He gazed at her gravely. A hint of a shy smile on his face.

She couldn't move. She remained rooted in her spot. "No . . ." she whimpered, fearing the worst. "He's come back to tell me himself."

Pablo bolstered her up.

Kenny spoke calmly from the frame of Maria's front door. "She was found by an old hermit in the high desert. The woman had Alzheimer's. They think maybe she pulled her from Ruthie's flooding car."

"And?"

"Well," Kenny, stepped to the side, revealing a smiling Chita hiding behind him. "See for yourself."

"Abuelita left me," Chita observed. "But Gloria was nice."

Maria's knees buckled. Her baby daughter rushed to hug her.

32

Pioneertown

Chita had spent most of the hours she sat waiting for Maria to come home staring at Kenny. She had known right away who he was. Surprisingly, the cops who found her left her alone in his care. He was her legal guardian. Her bona fide father. Chita was so fascinated when they presented her to him that concern about wondering where her mother was took a back seat to her keen interest in him.

As much as she resembled Maria, Chita favored Kenny more. She had his blue eyes and his lips. When the police passed her over, Kenny closed the front door and allowed her to get her bearings. He sensed that according to her, nothing had changed much about her house. From what Soila told him, if it took another twenty years, nothing would be touched until she returned. That was how great Maria's faith had been, or insistence, that her daughter was alive and would be returned to her.

"It looks smaller," Chita observed.

"You've probably grown an inch or two," Kenny suggested.

"You're taller than your picture."

"The one by your bed?"

"Yes." She studied him with neither restraint nor animation. She had a frankness about her. Kenny worried that she might be slightly in shock.

"Was that okay for me to look inside your room? I didn't touch anything."

"It's okay."

She seemed troubled by having to choose whether to re-acclimate herself to her surroundings or memorize him, as her eyes darted from familiar objects and quickly back to Kenny.

"Do you want to go back to your room? I wouldn't mind. I'm not going anywhere. I'll be here when you get back."

She pondered this suggestion. "Okay."

She made her way down the hallway toward the bedrooms. She paused first to take in her mother's room. Her chest cavity heaved with a sigh, but she controlled her emotions. She lingered in the doorway. She didn't step inside. For now, it was enough to know that it still existed. She turned, catching Kenny's eye. She checked a relieved sigh.

"That's how I felt when I saw it," Kenny admitted.

Chita didn't reply. Instead she moved resolutely to her own bedroom. She lingered hesitantly.

"What's wrong, Chita?"

"My Mommy's doll. Did you move it?"

Kenny shook his head.

"Who did?"

"Maybe she did. Maybe she wants you to have it."

"She'd never let me play with it before."

"No?" Kenny smiled kindly. "Maybe she missed you so much she changed her mind."

Chita considered this. "I should put it back on her bed."

"If you want to. I could make you one of your own," Kenny offered. "If it's okay with her."

"It better be," Chita blurted out. Kenny laughed. A smile curled up from Chita's lips.

Kenny found enough odds and ends to make them an early dinner. How the old woman had managed to clothe and feed her was a mystery to all the social services personnel combined, but she had. Chita had been examined by a Yucca Valley pediatrician and been pronounced in perfect health. Her weight was normal. Her teeth and gums healthy. Her hair was unmanageably long. It was thick and black like Maria's, Kenny noted. Slightly curly like his.

As they ate a light supper of tuna salad and Trader Joe's Organic tomato soup, Kenny and Conchita fell into an undeniably poignant sense of ease with one another. They both shared an unspoken sense of uneasiness as to what might happen once Maria finally returned.

Soila had called, subdued, from her father's hospital room. Had he heard from Maria?

"No," Kenny informed her. He should tell her about Chita, but selfishly did not. He didn't know who he could trust in Cathedral City, with exception to his daughter, the only other living entity who truly understood his position.

"My father is dying," Soila blurted out.

"I'm sorry," Kenny murmured sincerely. He didn't want to alarm Chita. "Can I do anything?"

"No. My family is with me. My brother and sister. My mother."

"Inez?"

"Yes. She just came from Mexico," Soila whispered.

"Give her my regards," Kenny told her. "If Maria comes home, shall I have her call you?"

"My mother says Maria may not come home at all," Soila observed tearfully.

"What?" Kenny shot a glance at Chita who suddenly grinned up at him from the table.

"I'll explain later."

"But how does she know?"

"She just saw her recently."

"Where?"

"It's too difficult to explain right now."

"Soila," Kenny whispered. "She's back!"

"Who? Maria?"

"No. Chita." He covered the mouthpiece of the telephone to muffle her cries. After a moment he ended the conversation by telling her: "Do what you need to do with your family. I'm so sorry about Thomas. Chita is happy and looking forward to seeing her mother. As am I."

Chita continued to eat, knowing fully well he was talking to Tia Soilita about her. She already knew if she pretended to mind her own business, there was much to be learned by listening to the adults around her. Gloria had been different. Gloria never talked to anybody but her. Chita had basked in her attention. Like Abuelita Ruthie, Gloria seemed a little off kilter at times, but she was always caring toward Chita. Toward the end, Chita just had to remind her who she was every day.

Gloria didn't have a television, and rarely listened to the radio. Chita knew on the days she went to pick up provisions to hide in the house and not answer the door. Nobody ever knocked anyway. Gloria explained that her mother would come for her, as soon as she figured out where she was.

In the meantime, would Chita like to learn how to square dance? Or would she like to hunt for trapdoor spiders in the muddy walls which reinforced the rocky hill behind Gloria's cabin? Gloria taught her how to recognize the horseshoe shaped hinge to their tiny cliff dwellings. Gently Chita could pry it open without damaging the earthen door. Inside, a surprised spider peered out into the world, snatching the door and yanking it closed, much to Chita's delight.

When asked later why she didn't try to run away, Chita knew she wouldn't have an answer. She was so stunned to wake up and find her *abuelita* gone, and so immediately intrigued with Gloria's strangeness that it was a day or two before she decided something was really amiss. She would cry for Maria at night, but she was so concerned about distressing Gloria that she buried her head under her pillow. Her mother would come tomorrow, she would console herself. In the meantime, Gloria needed her. And before she knew it, another day, and another day, and many other days had come and gone.

Pablo had filled out, looking more serious, more grown-up than Kenny remembered him. At first, Kenny didn't even recognize Maria. He thought she was possibly related to Pablo, a sister perhaps, or a cousin. With her hair cut short, and her arms tanned and sinewy with muscle, she, like Kenny, had aged handsomely in the last five years. Both of them were mud-streaked and dusty, like they'd walked all the way from Mexico.

His relief when he realized it was her drenched any deep-rooted resentment he'd been harboring. He'd seen this dark, deeply grieving look on her face before, the night he walked into his old house in Cathedral City and found Ruthie sitting at his piano, gently humming while she softly played. Ruthie had nodded in the direction of a corner side-chair, and there, miraculously, was the young woman he'd befriended only days earlier in Mexicali.

Then, like now, her face hadn't been like a window thrown open wide with happy coincidence that he was now standing before her again. In that case, a roaring flash flood. Then, the last time she saw

Kenny he was falling back into raging water, in the moments following his rescue of her grandmother. Concha had complained to the
heavens on the rain-soaked muddy banks of that arroyo that God
should take her for him.

He heard her prayer. In less than twenty-four hours, Concha
asphyxiated in a cramped, stinking van, overloaded with border-
jumpers, only hours on U.S. soil. And then Maria herself was running for her life, only to find herself rescued by Ruthie, out driving in
her big white Cadillac, down an isolated desert highway.

In a series of serendipitous miracles, God could not have made
himself plainer. An atheist would have been convinced, and the only
feeling Maria could summon was outrage, her sorrow was so acute.
How could she feel grateful to be spared a life without any living
family member left alive?

Kenny saw all of it ticker-tape across her brow, as she contemplated his presence on her doorstep. In the seconds that followed,
Kenny could see that she believed he would try to take her daughter
from her again. He was the only one now who could. He saw murder in her eyes, masked deceitfully when Chita playfully stepped out
behind him, explaining in one sentence with frank child candor that
Ruthie had left her but Gloria, whoever she was, had been nice.

The realization that Maria thought, even for an instant, that he
could and would claim her, was out on the table. He knew it. She
knew he knew it. Even the ecstasy of once again holding Chita
against her pounding heart was tainted by her shame about this. To
make matters worse, Kenny had two witnesses. His own daughter
had been affronted by the madness in her mother's eyes.

Pablo, already knowing more than he ever cared to know about
her, read her betrayal as reflected in Kenny's eyes.

"Abuelita left me, but Gloria was nice."

An exoneration for Kenny but the damage was done.

"She's not herself," Pablo whispered as he hugged Kenny. "I'm
not sure if she ever will be again."

Maria gazed up from Chita's shoulder. She saw Pablo, clearly
aligned with Kenny. There was nothing she could say now to either
of them. Chita straddled her waist. Maria pushed through the door
of her house, closing it to them, to the outside. After five years, she
had nothing to say to Kenny.

Kenny and Pablo gaped at each other.

From the other side of the door they both heard Chita proclaim: "I want my daddy."

Although Pablo offered to let him stay in Sky Valley, Kenny opted to check into a cheap hotel. Pablo suggested the Seven Palms Inn. The Seven Palms Inn was offering rooms for $29.99. It was little more than a flophouse, but all Kenny needed now was a room with a bed and a lock on the door. So much had happened so quickly. He needed to regroup, to clarify in his own mind what he should do next.

Pablo suggested that Kenny get situated and later they could meet for dinner. Kenny reacted stiffly to the suggestion. Did he know about Pablo's brief interlude with Nick? If he did, could he possibly be jealous?

Later, as they sat across a table in the Dates Bar & Café, a former Wells Fargo pony express station, now a charming gay restaurant situated in the date palm grove of The Villa, Pablo inquired about Nick's well-being.

"Well," Kenny said. "The last I saw him he was barely standing in the parking lot behind a Reno café called the Second Chance. It was snowing and he didn't have a coat. He was wearing white slacks and red espadrilles with no socks. His arms were folded and his hair was dusted with snow. He's probably still standing in the same spot, waiting for me to come back."

"So he started drinking again, huh?"

Kenny tossed back a shot of tequila in disgust. Pablo hadn't recalled ever seeing Kenny take a drink. This was his third shot in an hour. He was still striking, Pablo noted. His black hair was shaggy. Even by candlelight his eyes were blue. Just like Chita's. Tonight, his frustration and anger made him more appealing. His nostrils flared slightly whenever he spoke.

Why had Pablo never reacted to Kenny's physicality before? He had big hands and feet. He didn't work out, but his shoulders were square, his neck thick. As a cook, Kenny was basically a laborer. Years of standing on his feet, maneuvering heavy pots and pans around a hot tight kitchen was more legitimate exercise than Pablo's workouts at Gold's.

His intellect and enormous humility made him extremely attractive. No wonder Maria closed the door on him, Pablo mused. He smiled as this notion occurred to him. Kenny noticed. His eyes darted around the room. The restaurant was expensive. It was also cozy and tasteful. Fresh flowers adorned each table. The patrons were upscale gay men and women.

"They've done a nice job," Kenny commented. "No lounge act. It's quiet here. I like that. No offense to Ruthie," he added quietly. Tears glistened in his eyes. He pushed his shot glass away. A waiter zipped over to ask if he wanted another one but he shook his head. Too much indulgence.

"I'm sorry you had to come back to all of this."

"Seeing my daughter makes every bit of it worthwhile."

"She's very special," Pablo agreed. The import of Kenny's words resonated through Pablo. Now that Kenny had met her, he'd never let Chita go again. Even with her wealth, if she wanted to, Maria couldn't fight him off. He had rights. Her letters. Would she want to? Pablo wondered.

This afternoon it moved him to watch Kenny appraise the Cathedral City floor, stretching out before them.

"It's all gone."

"Yes," Pablo agreed.

"The barrio. The small shops. Just a vacant lot."

"Only Nick's and the church are still standing."

Wonderingly, they'd scanned the empty patch of desert between Kenny's former church and restaurant kitchen.

"I came back hoping to recreate what I'd had before. I feel guilty saying so, but I regret it," Pablo whispered. "I've grown up."

"At least one of us has." Kenny studied the old bar, now with a face-lift, new paint. The Cathedral City Café. Closed again. And then Kenny examined his old church. The new community hall dwarfed the old sanctuary.

"I tried to call Father Gene," Kenny murmured. "They told me he'd had a stroke. I sent a note, but I never heard back."

"Without Nick and Father Gene," Pablo acknowledged, "Cathedral City is a much different place."

"I'm not going back to Reno," Kenny announced abruptly. "You can tell her that."

"Will Nick come here?"

"Nick is not part of my plans."

Pablo chuckled. The busboy cleared their plates.

"What's funny?" Kenny demanded. The tequila had made him slightly aggressive.

"Nick won't ever let you go," Pablo said gently.

"How do you know so much about Nick?"

Instead of admitting their affair, which he happily guessed Nick had never confessed to Kenny, Pablo simply replied: "Because you're too special."

"I'm a fucking fry-cook," Kenny snapped, loud enough that heads turned.

"Let's go for a walk." Pablo folded his napkin. He reached for the check folder, and without looking, tossed a hundred dollar bill on top of it.

Once on the grounds of the Seven Palms, Pablo steered Kenny gently past the oleanders toward his room. Kenny staggered slightly, and Pablo gripped his upper arm to help his balance. Men were cruising the bushes. One shirtless man loitered when he saw them approach. He massaged his crotch. Pablo winced in amusement. This is what he used to do. Kenny hadn't even noticed.

They arrived at Kenny's door. Kenny fumbled for his key.

"You must wonder about me," he said.

"Wonder?"

"Yeah. What my trip is."

Pablo didn't understand.

"What my sexual preference is," Kenny spelled it out. He was sobering up. Or so Pablo thought. Doors were opening and closing up and down the exterior corridor of the rooms below them. The sexual tension distressed Pablo. Kenny was very vulnerable right now. He could invite himself in to talk about Kenny's confusion. His sadness. His need for comfort. Then Pablo noticed Kenny's room number.

Suddenly Pablo flashed back to five years before. He'd tricked in this very room once before. Number 18. When Inez had stepped on the needle.

"But this is amazing!" Pablo said.

"What's amazing?" Kenny asked, but it was too complicated and sad to explain. Pablo struggled to collect his thoughts.

"I once asked Nick, after you moved to Desert Hot Springs, if I could ever have what the two of you had."

"What, a co-dependent, alcoholic relationship?"

"No," Pablo replied. "A lifelong mate. Has it really been all bad?"

Kenny softened. "Yes."

But Pablo knew he wouldn't change a day of it. Surprising them both, Pablo leaned forward and kissed Kenny passionately. From the dark lawn, someone whistled appreciatively. Kenny didn't resist at first.

"What are you doing?" He held up his hand. It was too unexpected.

"I just always wanted to. Thank-you! I've just had a revelation."

"What are you talking about?"

"I have my chance," Pablo said, his face lighting with joy. "I need to make a call."

"To who?"

"To my lover," Pablo smiled, rushing toward the stairs. "I'll call you tomorrow. Things will work out!"

That night, at Pablo's word, Kenny slept peacefully, while men prowled the date palm groves, looking for something Kenny already had; comfort, contentment, familiarity, release, for most of his adult life.

33

Paying Respects

When Inez entered her husband's hospital room, she didn't have the luxury to fully embrace the enormous change she saw in each of her three children, assembled by his bedside. She'd already had the opportunity to spend time with Soila. Soila, because of her deformity, had always been her favorite—for the wrong reasons Inez freely admitted—but still it was true. Soila was a manifestation of all of Inez' former superstitions, which evaporated since her work with Avance.

She'd been marked, and therefore punished by God, in an act of retribution against Inez. Now the mark had been removed. Soila was a beautiful twenty-year old girl. The curse had been lifted. Much significance would be made of this fact, but for now, there wasn't time.

Under Ruby's tutelage Anita, once considered the prettiest little girl in the extended Quintero-Sanchez family, had grown into an angry, cheaply made-up teenager just barely fourteen. Nothing Inez remembered about her was visible in this gum-snapping, insolent girl who deeply resented having to be here at all.

"Who's that?" Inez pondered when she followed Soila into the room.

"Mamita, it's Anita," Soila whispered. Anita didn't seem to notice the gaff. She was stunned by the removal of Soila's birthmark. If pressed, Anita might also admit she was privately terrified of catching anthrax. What other explanation could there be? No one explained that her father had AIDS, which wouldn't have made her any more secure. She'd been borrowing his razor to shave her legs for a year.

Lastly, Inez was startled by the marked change in her formerly lusty, good-looking son. This boy looked like a twin who had died, but continued to walk the earth in ghostly purgatory. His skin was sallow, and he'd easily lost twenty or so pounds. He was missing a front tooth, the product of his recent time in jail. Rumor had spread quickly he was suspected in the abduction of Conchita Castillo. No child thief had a chance in a Latino prison population. His life would be vastly improved once word got out about Chita's remarkable return.

So these were their children. This was the end result of their father's American journey. Thomas was so drugged he possibly didn't recognize any of them.

"Leave me alone with your father. Come back in ten minutes with a priest."

One look at Thomas, and Inez knew she had very little time to accomplish what she hoped she could, so she had to ask them all to leave, to wait in the family lounge. They filed past her, Soila patting her shoulder.

Inez moved close to his bed, gently grasping his hand, bruised with IV markings.

"Thomas. It's me. Your wife. I'm here. I came back to say goodbye. We're all here. Me, Alex, Soila and Anita. We came to pay you our respects. Your family is around you. You can die with dignity."

He surprised her by squeezing her hand. Good. He knew she was here. God had answered her prayer. Because of her experience working with AIDS infected men, usually the husbands of her clients, she knew what he needed most to make his transition easier. His primary emotion would be guilt.

In the end, looking an infected wife in the eye, or worse, their infected small children clinging to her skirt, always produced enormous sorrow and guilt in these men. It was rare that early in their diagnosis, any of them accepted counseling or medical advice and treatment.

They usually disappeared when symptoms began to erupt. Shingles, herpes outbreaks, thrush—then pneumonia, TB, Kaposi's sarcoma. They refused to get help—not because of pride, Inez believed, but guilt. They were getting what they deserved, even if they'd never been devout a single day in their lives.

"Thomas, can you hear me?"

He squeezed her hand.

"You need to know that I'm healthy. I'm doing really well. Do you understand?"

Again, his finger twitched.

"It's time for the truth between us. I want you to die peacefully. I know how you feel. We made mistakes. Both of us. I abandoned you and the children. I left you in Ruby's clutches. I didn't fight, and I should have. I'm so sorry," she said. The enormity of emotion inside overwhelmed her. It was true. All her life she'd been contrary, a hell-cat, and when Thomas put her out in some foolish display of *machista,* she selfishly saw her opportunity and left them all behind.

It had been more fun with Pablito and Maria. They were handsome and kind. They took care of her when she was so sick. They talked to her as if she were their contemporary. They loved her, in a different way than her own children, but they'd had the benefit of sophistication. They'd enlightened her. Challenged her prejudices. They treated her as an equal, and she justified those days in Sky Valley, joking with Pablo and Maria, sitting around the campfire under the desert stars with merely a shrug, as if to say her own family didn't really want her, so what was the harm? What could she do about it?

Her family didn't know any better.

"I was selfish too," she whispered to Thomas. "It wasn't just you. Can you forgive me, *esposo?"*

He nodded, so discreetly she could barely discern it.

"Thomas," Inez then said. "This is important for you to know. I've made a good life for myself. I've learned so many wonderful things. I wouldn't be who I am today without you. I have no shame. I've earned my dignity. I forgive you, *mi vida.* I will always love you. Do you understand? Please forgive yourself!"

His body trembled. He was suffering a small seizure.

"Mommy!" Soila cried from the door, where she'd been eavesdropping.

"It's okay, *mija,"* Inez stroked his face. "He isn't suffering. Look how peaceful he looks now. Is the priest with you?"

"Yes, Mommy."

"I'm here, Señora." A man's voice reassured her.

"Niños," she beckoned them. "Come here. Soila, stand by his head. Hold his face, very gently." Soila pressed herself above her father's head. Gently she clasped his forehead. It felt surprisingly cool.

"Alex. Take your father's foot. Anita, the other one."

Anita whined. She was freely weeping now.

"*Mija,* don't be sad. He isn't in any pain. Take his foot in your hand. Hold it like your brother is doing." Alex, caught up in the rapture of his father's passing, was already aflame with murmured prayer.

The priest quickly moved to the other side of Thomas's bed. He smiled at Inez.

The family of Thomas Quintero had managed to assemble at his bedside moments before he died. Present were his wife Inez, his daughters Soila and Anita, and his son Alex. It was not certain what the configuration of the family would be after Thomas made his transition. But for this important moment his family presided.

Although his eyes were closed, he felt the presence of each of them. His children cried, each kissing his lips in turn. Inez placed a rosary in his hands while the priest issued last rites. Moments later, Thomas Quintero, a forgiven son of Mexico—died his American dream.

34

For the Sake of the Children

In addition to the deep emotions she suffered over her daughter while she was missing, Maria was surprised to be revisited by the equally powerful phenomenon of what it was like to lose her own mother. Cruelly, that old sadness returned. It felt like yesterday. A parallel nightmare.

Maria Castillo was a woman who'd lost both mother and daughter; in addition, her maternal grandmother. Her father's mother had died before she was born. The family women were all stolen from her. Who would teach her about life? What example could she follow? Who knew the family stories, the history, the traditions? The recipes? Who would corroborate the existence of the Castillo women? She didn't care if anybody remembered her, but agonized deeply that her beautiful mother would be forgotten. And if Chita never returned? Impossible. *No.*

She spent her nights painting *retablos.* As a little girl the nuns tried to foist her off on the *Virgin of Guadalupe.* "She'll be your mother," they told her. Maria didn't buy it, but it fostered her interest in the art of the *retablo.* The colorful *retablos* were painted with such primitive emotion, the supplicants begging the Blessed Virgin to grant them their wishes, answer their prayers, or thanking her profusely for having done so.

Since Chita's disappearance, Maria prayed through the tip of her paintbrush. With passing months, the images grew increasingly disturbing as faith dwindled. Where in the beginning Maria might depict Chita hiding playfully from her behind the fountain statue in

Cathedral City's Civic Center plaza, the latter *retablos* reflected a grave need for Chita's rescuers to hurry:

Chita trapped in a sinking car, her tiny face pressed into a diminishing pocket of air as the Virgin floated benignly in the clear sky over the river. Chita, running for her life, lost in the desert, pursued by *coyotes;* the four legged kind, as the Virgin gazed away in the wrong direction. The most distressing image, painted the night before Maria departed for Mexico, depicted a mother and her small daughter encased in an open wooden coffin, on display in Cathedral City's plaza while townspeople passed, selfishly ignoring the tragedy.

It was early morning. Chita slept soundly in Maria's arms. Through the French doors in her bedroom, Maria could see hummingbirds dart from flower to flower on the back wall of her small stucco patio. No one called last night. Not Soila, or Pablo or Sister Agnes. Not Inez, Bambi or Madonna. Not the press or the Riverside County Sheriff's Department.

Not Kenny.

His silence was deafening.

The others were waiting compassionately, allowing Chita to acclimate to her surroundings; giving them a chance to normalize. With the exception of the press, which her attorney could handle, they would wait for Maria to call them.

She'd phoned him briefly. "My daughter is home. Seems well. Find out what happened. Handle it. I'll call you." And she hung up.

With Chita's assurance that *Gloria* had treated her kindly before she died, Maria could wait several days for information. Chita might need counseling. If anything, Conchita's interest in meeting her father seemed more important than her return to Cathedral City.

Now, Chita murmured something in her sleep. Maria studied her face.

Kenny hadn't appreciated being shut out like that, and as she stroked their baby girl's hair, Maria wasn't thinking only about yesterday. Sister Agnes' admonition rang in her ears. Sister Agnes was the only person with enough insight to call Maria's bluff. Maria was a survivor, not a victim. Chita's return was another notch on her belt. What were the odds after she'd been given up for dead? What price would fate set for Maria?

The answer would lie with Kenny. He saw her. Saw her eyes. Spent some time. Saw firsthand what he and Maria had created.

Wherever he was, Maria knew he was awake and thinking about his daughter.

Chita stirred, awakening to the fast grip of her mother. "Let go," she whined.

Appalled, Maria released her. "What do you want to do today, baby?"

Chita didn't answer but her blue eyes said it all.

When Sister Agnes had been summoned to Father Scolia's office, she assumed he knew everything and would be asking her to leave Cathedral City. A new girl sat at Soila's desk. Mr. Quintero must have died. Sister Agnes crossed herself as she pushed her way into the stern priest's office.

"Sister Agnes," he nodded.

"Father Scolia."

"Several matters of importance to discuss with you."

Sister Agnes had been interrogated with an M-16 pointed at her temple in El Salvador. This priest couldn't break her. She perched at the end of a chair without being invited, and folded her hands.

"You never come to confession, Sister."

"Is that what you wish to discuss?"

"It wasn't my intention, but it occurs to me that it's been months."

"Clean conscience."

"You're lucky. The first item is a sad one, I'm afraid. Father Gene passed away last night in his sleep."

She hadn't expected this. She blinked, her eyes tearing up. She kissed her crucifix.

"He's with God, Sister."

"I'm happy that you accord that certainty to his memory, Father. It comforts me, particularly, coming from you."

Father Scolia hesitated, unsure if she was insulting him by innuendo. If he asked for clarification, she'd surely rise to the bait and today he felt somewhat benevolent toward her. "You must be very happy about the return of Miss Castillo's daughter."

Again Sister Agnes blinked. He'd managed to surprise her twice. Why hadn't she been informed? Where was Maria? Was the priest trying to trip her up? Had one of the Radical Sisters ratted her out?

"I'm very pleased," Sister Agnes nodded.

"I never took advantage of her tragedy," Father Scolia remarked. "In deference to your concerns about my ministry tactics. We ended up insulting each other."

"Too bad. You probably cost the church a big reward."

"Perhaps."

Sister Agnes stood to leave. She was anxious to compare notes with Maria.

"I'm not quite finished," the priest told her. "For this, I think you might sit down."

Sister Agnes searched his face for insight into what other mystery he had to report. At the same time, he was scanning her face, as if to suggest that her potential reaction might be of concern to him.

"Sister, many of us leave our families behind when God calls us into service. Some of us adjust more easily than others. I've remained quite close to my family."

Agitated, she tugged at the folds of her sleeve. Where was this going?

"You've never discussed your childhood. Is there any particular reason?"

"I was orphaned. Raised by nuns. Nothing fantastic."

"Were you ever curious about your birth parents?"

"I knew my mother."

"Did you ever wonder if you had siblings?"

She stiffened. She'd only discussed this matter with Pablo the night he walked her back to the church. How dare he come to the priest about it! He was probably going to suggest spiritual counseling. Some new coping program the church had cooked up. More unnecessary coddling. Why didn't they mind their own business? You take the cards God deals you.

"I hired a private investigator to find someone important to you. You have a brother who wants to meet you. He asked me to approach you, to gain your consent. If you aren't comfortable, he won't bother you. I've seen the paperwork. Seems legitimate."

Emotion welled up inside her. Tears began to flow. Of all people she had to cry in front of, why did it have to be Father Scolia?

"Sister Agnes," he rushed to comfort her. "I'm sorry to have taken you so by surprise."

She fought for composure. "Where is he?"

"He's in Cathedral City. The coincidence is remarkable."

"You mean he lives here?"

"He did once."

"Yes," she uttered.

"Yes?"

She clutched the sleeve of Father Scolia's suit. It amused her that he'd be disgusted by her runny nose and tearing eyes, staining the fabric. Instead he compassionately allowed her to compose herself.

"I'll make the arrangements. He's on his way to Cathedral City. He'll contact me when he arrives."

Bambi and Madonna had been informed by a hurried cell phone call from Pablo of Maria's return to Cathedral City and that her daughter had been safely found. The two of them were reunited and in seclusion. Their joy for her was tainted by the rancor of Inez Quintero, the very woman they'd risked their necks to help across the Mexican border into the United States. In front of the other cowering border-jumpers, she'd called them criminals and accessories to murder.

"There'll be consequences," she promised, as they expelled her in front of St. Louis Catholic Church in Cathedral City.

"What a pain in the ass you are," Bambi railed at her. "Get outa my rig!"

Madonna tried a more moderate approach. "Go take care of your children. They need you. We'll figure this all out later. Right now, we need to find Maria."

"She's probably already dead!" Inez was yelling so loud construction workers could hear her over the din of their jackhammers.

Without Maria to talk sense into her, all they could do was drive away and hope for the best. The other women in the group had been released in El Centro. None of them posed a problem. They wanted to be as far away from this ill-fated ship as possible. They all knew they were lucky to be alive.

Although apprehensive, Patti and Lupe proclaimed the mission a success. Inez Quintero had been safely transported back into California to be with her family, where she rightfully belonged. A wicked coyote was certainly disposed of. Maria, who'd masterminded this entire odyssey, was on her way to becoming a folk hero. If God saw differently, why was she rewarded with the magical return of her daughter? The Radical Sisters crowed their promise to follow Maria anywhere!

Madonna, more than Bambi, felt particularly bad about Border

Patrol Bob. She didn't press for details from Pablo for fear of compromising them all, but she had a gut-level feeling he had been key to rescuing Maria from Logan Delacourt. Bob was such a good square egg. Madonna had been so touched by his gentleness at Florencia's Sunday supper. She knew how much he'd been hurt by Pablo.

They were all culpable. All because of Judi Romero.

The night they learned Maria was safe, Madonna caressed Bambi after the two of them made love. The lovemaking was still so powerful. How happy Madonna was to live with Bambi. For all her bravado, Bambi was not as fierce as her persona indicated. In many ways, probably because she was the mother of a young adult, Madonna's maternal instincts came out with Bambi. She tried to fight them, wanting to maintain an equal partnership with her lover. After years of feeling subordinate to a husband so many years older than she, Madonna didn't want to reverse roles with her younger girlfriend. Still, having been integrated into Bambi's family and having personal experience with Florencia's capacity for maternal nurturing, Madonna now saw nothing wrong with mothering Bambi when she seemed to crave it. She was good at it, and in the grand scheme of their life together, Bambi did more than her share of the heavy lifting.

She had offered Madonna an equal partnership in the delivery business. After her long marriage to Burton, Madonna didn't need to worry about money. Bambi's offer created tension between them. Why wasn't Madonna accepting? Madonna had to gently explain that while she wholeheartedly saw an unlimited future with Bambi, she wanted to unify in traditional terms, at which time hearts, assets and families would merge.

Her daughter Laurie was the sticking point. On her quick trip to La Jolla in Maria's Winnebago, she knew Laurie was happy to see her, but out of loyalty to her father, tried to act detached. Madonna quizzed her about her boyfriend. Her classes. Her new friends at school. When the subject fell to Madonna, Laurie cut the visit short and made excuses about needing to get back to her dorm early.

"You didn't ask me about my life at all, Laurie. We only talked about you."

Laurie had blushed in embarrassment. She could be self-centered, but she wasn't unkind.

"I'm seeing a therapist," she blurted out. "She'd like you to come to a session."

"I'd agree to that," Madonna told her. "But I'd want to talk to her privately first."

"This isn't about you, Mother."

Madonna found herself checking a rush of anger. She took a moment to calm herself.

"You're wrong, Laurie. It is about me, just as much as you. I want to be sure your doctor understands that I'm not up for a session where I'm recriminated for my sexual orientation."

"Nobody recriminates you for being gay."

"You won't ever visit. You never acknowledge Bambi. It hurts her. Her family has been wonderful to me."

"So you have a new, wonderful family! Lucky you!"

"Yes. I'm very lucky, frankly. Your father is getting on with his life. You're nearly out of college. None of us can hang onto the past, Laurie. I told you I was sorry for hurting you both. I don't expect your dad's forgiveness, but I deserve more from you. I never left you."

"I have to go."

"Bambi and I have been putting off a commitment ceremony. It's just family and friends in her mother's backyard."

"What are you waiting for?"

"You, frankly. I want you to come."

Laurie's eyes darted around the kitchen countertops, looking for her keys. She found them finally, snatching them and heading for the door.

"Call me with the name of your doctor."

"Don't count on it."

"I'll set a date with Bambi and send you an invitation."

"I won't come!"

And she was gone. Madonna gazed around the family kitchen. Burton would be home soon. She, too, should dust off her shoes and go.

"I'd like to set the date," Madonna told Bambi as she stood at the stove, frying eggs for their Sunday breakfast. "Think Florencia's offer still holds?"

"Laurie come around?" Bambi tried to act all casual, but inside her heart was pounding. She'd have never been prouder of Madonna than she was yesterday, so calmly negotiating the big motor home up the freeway toward El Centro, loaded with frightened women from Mexico, at more risk to herself than to them.

Bambi could only imagine her fear, but Madonna remained calm and loving, so as not to scare their passengers. The drop-off had gone flawlessly, and because they were spared the payment to the coyotes, the women had more money than they counted on to start their new lives.

"Laurie will be invited. If she comes, she comes. I just want a party. No ceremony. No tuxedos. Do you mind?"

"Babe, every day I have with you is a party," Bambi grinned.

"It isn't that I don't want to say the words in front of our friends—I just think its redundant at this point."

"I'm not complaining, babe. Everybody knows you're my girl."

"And I know this is touchy, but I want to invite Bob and his mother. I think she'd make the trip from Prescott. I don't know if he wants anything to do with us, but I want to invite him. Do you mind?"

"It's your list, babes."

"It's our list."

"I just trust you to do the right thing."

Madonna turned from the stove, holding the frying pan with a hot pad holder. She scooped Bambi's omelet onto her plate. "I have quite a bit of money. We can save it, or use some of it. I thought I might buy us a new truck. Something with a hidden compartment."

"I thought the delivery service might incorporate. I'll be needing a co-president."

"How do you like your eggs, Madame President?"

"Just like my women. Easy . . ."

35

Father Gene

When Father Scolia announced the passing of Father Gene in the weekly calendar, an outpouring from local grieving parishioners overwhelmed him. He decided it would be appropriate to hold a special funeral Mass in his honor. Father Gene had comforted so many residents of Cathedral City, particularly during the massive demolition of local homes and businesses. Although many of the seniors he ministered to had died or were infirmed in outlying nursing homes, arrangements were made to find transportation to the Mass for as many unable to travel on their own.

With all the clucking going on about the new community hall, Father Scolia realized many hadn't been back since Father Gene left. What were they complaining about? The hall provided additional meeting rooms, a nursery, and a large kitchen to better serve the needs of the desert's hungry. Over a thousand meals per week were prepared and delivered to anyone in need.

This constituency was different from Father Scolia's, as the curious priest observed, watching the congregation assemble. They came in buses, or transport services, or overloaded older cars. There wasn't a Mercedes to be found in the parking lot. A large portion of the sanctuary was filled with Latino parishioners. A hush momentarily fell over the room when Maria Castillo, in sunglasses, entered through a side door with her little girl.

They knew who she was. Flushed, she took her seat near an exit, but close to an alcove with flickering electric candles, because they were amusing to Conchita. On the opposite side of the sanctuary entered Inez Quintero and her daughter Soila. Inez scanned the assembly, noting Maria with disdain, and huffed into a pew near the altar. Soila, beautiful but miserable because she couldn't get her mother to be civil to Maria, reluctantly took the seat next to her mother, but waved extravagantly to Chita, who giggled in her mother's lap. No one had confirmed Inez' suspicions about Maria. She was especially furious with Pablo, who she thought knew the truth. Without denials, Inez convicted Maria and anybody who collaborated with her. She was a murderer, and Inez had stayed in Cathedral City only to bury her husband and pay respects to Father Gene. A private Mass for Thomas had been held several days after he passed away. Without telling her mother, Soila had borrowed the money for his funeral from Maria.

Sister Agnes was already seated on the front pew several rows ahead of Maria, opposite Inez. Inez approved of her about as much as she did Maria. She nudged Soila, scowling at her.

"Don't be so mean," Soila admonished her. "After the Mass, she's to be reunited with her lost brother in Father Scolia's chambers! Look at how excited she seems."

Sister Agnes was indeed ebullient. Father Gene's spirit had overtaken St. Louis. The generous flower arrangements, contributed secretly by Maria and arranged for by Soila, overflowed in their urns, perfuming the sanctuary. Before the Mass was to begin, a wonderful photo of Father Gene was moved ceremoniously to an easel, just to the right of the altar. His smiling image caused a rush of emotion to his congregation. Murmuring could be heard. Here and there, noses were blown, eyes dabbed.

A tear rolled down Maria's cheek. What would she do without Father Gene to console her?

As a young girl stood to sing the *Ave Maria,* Chita twisted in her lap. *"Tio Pablito,"* she cooed, her body shaking with pleasure. Pablo entered the sanctuary. She hadn't been reunited with him yet, the fault of him and her warring mother. Maria and Pablo hoped to reconcile for her sake after the funeral.

"Hush, baby," Maria patted her. The singer had completed her song. "The priest is about to speak."

Just as Father Scolia began the liturgy, Chita shrieked, causing all heads to turn in Maria's direction.

"Papito!"

Moments after Pablo entered, Kenny followed, dressed in a dark shirt and black pants.

"Papito! Papito!"

The congregation laughed, embarrassing Maria and Kenny.

"Conchita," Maria begged her. "Please be quiet."

"*Papito!*" she cried again.

Father Scolia smiled benevolently at the excited and very rich little girl. "Jesus said, 'let the little children come unto me.' She wants her daddy," he grinned at Maria. Patronizingly he added, "Can her mother make room for him so we can start over?"

The congregation applauded, waiting for Maria to make a move and allow Kenny to situate himself in the pew next to her. The parishioners sitting near Maria expanded, giving wide birth and isolating her further from her fellows.

Pablo helplessly shrugged at Kenny. This was Kenny's defining moment.

As old friends watched, Kenny strode confidently down the carpeted aisle toward his daughter, claiming his seat next to Maria and Chita. Chita quickly scrambled onto his lap, quieting happily. Stoned-faced, Maria and Kenny stared directly ahead.

From the front of the sanctuary, it seemed that Father Gene was smiling down at them with approval.

"I am the resurrection and the life, says the Lord. Whoever believes in me will not die forever."

After the Mass was ended, it was announced that refreshments would be served in the Loretta Young community hall. Because Father Scolia didn't know Father Gene well, much less approve of his ministry, the homily felt hollow but Kenny and Maria didn't really notice. Their minds were on other matters. As the congregation began to file out, they had to negotiate the matter of Chita in the moments following the Mass.

During the service, those seated nearby had accommodated more room for Kenny than proved practical. Gradually they crushed back toward him, forcing him to sit knee to knee and shoulder to shoulder with Maria. Chita was delighted. For several moments as the congregation filed forward to receive the host, Chita spent her time first kissing the cheek of her mother, then her father and back and forth until she tired of it.

When the church began to empty out, they were forced to decide what to do. Pablo and Soila surprised them both with an answer.

"We want to borrow our little niece. People are asking about her. We'd like to show her off."

"You won't let them hold her," Maria said.

"She'll never be out of my arms."

"My mother wants to meet her," Soila said. "She's going home tomorrow."

"I don't know if it's a good idea," Maria protested. "This is the first time we've been out in public. She may be uneasy."

Chita cackled as Pablo tickled her.

"*Mija*, please," Pablo cajoled. "We want ten minutes with her."

Maria shot a glance at Kenny. Did he concur?

"I'd like to sit with Father Gene for awhile."

"Oh. Then I'll go with them," Maria offered. She stood up, struggling with her protesting little girl. Chita's spurt of growth had given her more strength, which Maria hadn't gotten used to.

"I'll be out soon," Kenny smiled up at Chita.

They left him alone, Pablo and Soila bickering over whose turn it was to hold Chita. Maria followed them, wistfully glancing over her shoulder to where Kenny remained seated, Father Gene's prodigal son, sitting alone in a sea of empty church pews.

The last time Kenny had been inside this sanctuary, he confessed to Father Gene. It had been twenty-one years since his last confession. Now, five more years had passed since then. He studied the gentle face of the old priest in the photograph. Father Gene had never compromised his vows, at least if he'd told Kenny the truth, but Kenny believed him. On that occasion, he commended Kenny for honoring his commitment to Nick. Kenny had been spared a premature death, Father Gene conjectured, as evidence of God's love for Nick.

What would Father Gene think of him now? Kenny still hadn't called Nick. When Nick checked himself into Betty Ford he'd asked Kenny to not call or visit until he completed the program. In the same spirit, Kenny felt justified in taking these weeks for himself. He hunkered into the pew, his foot resting on the hassock.

Where had faith gone? Did it die at California's borderline? They'd been so filled with hope. The promise of something new. Yes, much had yet to be answered for. They'd turned their backs on old

Cathedral City. They hadn't pursued Nick's attackers. His crew members, Carmen, Miguel and Gabriel, were out of jobs, though what little they could scrape up out of the sale of the house Kenny had split between them.

And then the matter of Maria and their baby daughter.

That.

Kenny shook his head, astonished by his selfishness. He'd never considered that Chita eventually had a say in these matters. She was as much entitled to know him as he, her. On this, Kenny was clear. Maria had borne the brunt of responsibility the first several years of her life, but she'd also experienced the elation. While Kenny had only suffered a mere few days knowing of her disappearance, Maria had lived in agony for many, many months.

She was owed time to get used to Chita, to reintegrate her back into a day-to-day ritual that both Maria and Chita could trust. But so, too, was Kenny owed the same opportunity. More than Nick, or Maria, or Kenny himself, Conchita was his priority now. All choices he made from here forward would have her best interests at heart.

The dearth of faith he'd experienced shortly after he and Nick left California could now be explained. Without a relationship with his daughter, his life had been worthless. Now he had something to pray for.

Kenny scanned the small prayer chapels, searching for an unlit votive to light. To his dismay, they were all illuminated, and electric. He routed around the sanctuary perimeter until he discovered an unlocked cupboard, decided to investigate and was delighted to notice two real votive candles, unlit and forlorn, nestled far back in the cabinet. He pulled them both out, wondering how sensitive the fire alarms might be.

He placed them on the carpet in front of the easel which supported the photograph of Father Gene. They'd be safe here. He reached in his pocket for his matches. He struck a match, allowing the first candle wick a moment to catch fire. He sighed, heavily. He was already on his knees. Behind him, the door to the sanctuary creaked open. He didn't turn around. He only wanted a few more moments of privacy with Father Gene. Whoever it was could wait, or complain to the priest that some stranger was lighting real candles in the church. Instead, he could tell by their approaching footfalls they intended to reprimand him.

*   *   *

"I wish he were here to tell us what to do," Maria spoke from behind him. He turned and she smiled sadly. She removed her dark glasses. She was alone. "Inez has Chita. She's showing her off, now that I reminded her that Inez is Chita's middle name."

"You never asked me what I thought about her name. You just wrote and told me what it was."

"I didn't think you'd mind about the Concha part. Inez is still so angry at me I'd be happy to drop her name altogether."

"Why's she mad at you?"

"Everyone is angry with me. Including you, I know."

Kenny felt silly, kneeling in front of the flickering votive. He moved to stand up.

"No," she told him. "Stay. I'll join you. I see you have another one."

She knelt beside him. He struck a match, handing it to her so she could light the dark candle. He stole a glance at her, and saw her much the way he remembered her from that first afternoon in the cathedral in Mexicali. The wick illuminated. She placed it gently next to his.

"She's wonderful," Kenny murmured.

"Yes. People say she looks like you." Maria hesitated. "Things are different between us. What should we do, Kenny?"

"Wait till we get used to each other again."

He didn't know if now was the time to start making demands. It felt good to be near her again. Comfortable, in fact. He resented it and tried to fight his emotions.

Maria, too, seemed to be struggling for the right words. She'd been thinking deeply about the right thing to do over the last week. With Chita back in her life, her flooding hysteria had receded. She still had the events of her trip to Mexico to mull over. In the moments and hours which followed her return home and the discovery of Chita, she explored every possible option, including leaving Cathedral City in the night and disappearing to any foreign country which didn't have the death penalty or an extradition treaty with Mexico. Her actions would have ramifications. Pablo and Bob had saved her life, and by placing them at the scene, she'd made both of them accessories. Kenny, standing on her front step had been the topper.

She concluded that the last thing she wanted to do was fight for her daughter again.

* * *

Kenny sat back wearily in the front pew.

"Only the hypocrites sit in the front of the church."

He patted the bench. She sank next to him.

"How's Nick?"

"I haven't spoken to him since your detective told me about Chita."

"I never sent a detective to find you."

Kenny believed her. "He knew all about you. He told me about Ruthie. And Chita."

"I have no idea who sent him. What did he say about Chita?"

"That her body wasn't found and he thought she was dead. So I got in my truck and came as fast as I could."

"I would have found you if I thought she was dead," Maria began. "I couldn't call you not knowing where she was. I was too ashamed for not taking better care of her." A silence fell between them. "I was ashamed for keeping her from you."

"You must not have a very high opinion of me," Kenny said. "I didn't fight you at all."

"I lived with you and Nick," she smiled. "You didn't have any fight left, Kenny."

"I didn't come when she was born. I didn't come for her first birthday. I only came when I thought it was too late. It's his fault." Kenny motioned toward Father Gene.

"Why?"

"He told me the right thing to do was stay with Nicky."

"I'm sorry about what happened to Nicky. I never called him. I'm sorry about other things, too. Especially Ruthie. I knew she was in trouble. I ignored it."

"Are you sorry about Chita?"

"Never. Or anything else between you and me. I've thought it all through. Chita loves you. I have resources. Ruthie left us very well provided for. I'll share everything with you, but I want you and Chita to have each other. And I need one more thing."

"What?"

"Your friendship, Kenny. And your forgiveness. I'm not the same person I was. Before you decide to become involved, at whatever level, you have to know the truth about me."

"What's the truth?"

"I believe, in retrospect, I took advantage of you. I think I purposely seduced you, hoping I'd get pregnant." She shrugged. "At least that's what Sister Agnes has me believing. I wanted a family of my own, to replace the one I'd lost. A blood relative. You made it all so easy."

Kenny listened, taking everything in. "I really only want one thing in return and you've already agreed."

"What's that?"

"I want to participate in my daughter's life. I'm moving back to Cathedral City."

"What about Nick?"

Kenny threw up his hands. Maria laughed. She leaned over and kissed him gently on each side of his face. "I've missed you, Kenny."

"I've missed you too . . ."

A commotion in the lobby caused them to look up. People were returning to the sanctuary.

"It's a miracle! *A miracle!*"

"That's Sister Agnes' voice," Maria turned.

To his astonishment, Kenny gazed up and thought he was seeing a mirage. Sister Agnes barged into the sanctuary. He recognized the man behind her.

"Maria! Father Scolia hired a private detective. I want you to meet my brother," she exclaimed. She was clearly drunk. A nervous Pablo appeared. Soila and Inez followed.

"I think we've all met." Stepping from the shadows and holding a laughing Conchita, Nick appeared at the top of the landing. Uncertainly he surveyed Kenny and Maria. A joyful Sister Agnes rushed into Maria's arms.

"Isn't it wonderful?" she whispered to Maria. "God doesn't intend to punish us. You have your daughter. I have my brother. We aren't alone anymore!" she proclaimed.

"It's true," Inez acquiesced, surveying the disparate faces assembled at the altar of God. "It's a miracle! None of us has to be alone anymore. How that will work, remains to be seen!"

36

Sunday at Florencia's

The Winnebago was stopped heading south on Highway 86; a routine check courtesy of the United States Border Patrol. Searches were commonplace now, since racial profiling was socially acceptable. It made Maria's blood boil, but she kept her tongue. As a permanent resident, they could detain her, no questions asked, for any length of time. She was bitter about the stalled amnesty negotiations for the 3.5 million undocumented Mexicans living in the United States, working jobs and paying taxes on jobs no Anglo would touch. Kenny kept urging her to apply for United States citizenship. She could keep her Mexican passport, but she continued to put off the decision.

More than once she was mistaken for being of Arab descent and stopped for no good reason doing errands around Cathedral City. Anyone with black hair and olive skin could be hassled. So now when the INS truck pulled up fast behind her, she just pulled over and the whole troop piled out: Kenny, Nick, Soila, Inez, Pablito, Sister Agnes and Chita. They were driving to El Centro for Sunday supper at Florencia's. Afterward they intended to drive Inez to the border, where her brothers Freddie and Nacho would be waiting on the other side of the turnstile. Maria had to beg Bambi to allow Inez to attend.

"She's family."

"She threatened us."

"People threaten you every day, homegirl," Maria reasoned. "You gotta let it slide. She's my daughter's godmother. I want Chita to have a solid foundation in the Catholic Church."

"I gotta check with Madonna."

She called back in five minutes. "It's only because Madonna is cool, but you gotta show us your tits."

"I've been wanting to," Maria cooed.

Bambi howled with laughter. "Bring a gift, you fucking rich bitch."

A lone border patrol agent approached the vehicle. He was backlit by bright afternoon sunlight. Something about his swagger seemed familiar. Pablo's heart raced.

"Why'd you get out of the vehicle?" he asked them. It wasn't Bob.

"It's routine," Maria mocked him.

The agent scanned their faces. He winced when he came to the sour puss of Sister Agnes. "You're free to go."

Maria noticed that the stop had subdued Pablo.

"You miss him. I'm sorry, *mijo.*"

Pablo had called Bob right away to let him know that Chita was home. All he got was Bob's voice mail. When Bob didn't call back, Pablo decided he should give him time. Weeks later he called the U.S. Border Patrol in El Centro. After asking for Agent Bob Roberts, he was informed that he'd been transferred to the Canadian border at his own request.

The group had not reassembled since the funeral of Father Gene. Inez stayed on later than she planned, wanting to help Soila with all the necessary arrangements required after the death of Thomas. Ruby was demanding that the house be sold. When informed by Inez the cause of Thomas's death, she quickly got tested for HIV. She was no fool. They had drugs for that sort of thing.

"If that bastard infected me," she railed. "I'm suing for the whole goddamned property!"

"For all we know, he got it from her," Soila countered defiantly when Inez repeated the conversation. "Ruby is such a whore."

"No, *mija,*" Inez corrected her. "How any of us contracts HIV is nobody's business. That's the thinking that delayed help. Many wonderful people died because of that very reason."

"But she's blaming Daddy."

"Let her," Inez said calmly. "And pray that she doesn't have it at all, because if she does, you'll have to take care of her."

"Why me?" Soila asked.

"Because no one else will, *mija*. Look at her. She's so awful." And both of them laughed. Inez also wanted to reacquaint herself with Anita. Anita was worrisome. She needed to have the facts of life explained, that life was more than *cholos*, hair spray and Ricki Lake. She was deeply disturbed by her father's death, and had resisted knowing the truth about what caused it. She also needed to know about her mother's health.

Inez made a call to Freddie and Nacho. "I want to bring Anita back to Mexico. I've got to get her away from Ruby. She needs her own family."

"Bring her on, girl," Freddie shrieked. "I need a maid. Can she sew and iron as good as you?"

Ruby's test miraculously came back negative. Soila could stay in the house, she agreed. Property values were rising in Cathedral City. Curiously, Anita did not resist when her mother proposed the move. She was a U.S. citizen but had kept her Mexican passport. She could come back and forth whenever she liked. She's begun to read the old pamphlets her mother sent her on la SIDA. She was worried herself, about the razor she shared with her father. Although she was too afraid to express her concern, somehow she felt safe with Inez. Anita was proud of her mother and impressed with her growth. If any bad should happen, she wanted Inez nearby.

After Father Gene's funeral, when Kenny remained inside, Maria had a moment to make peace with Pablo. Together they watched Soila introduce Conchita-Inez to her mother. Chita cried when Inez wanted to hold her, but finally the little gnome won her over with a fuzzy piece of hard candy.

Maria whispered to him. "Didn't I tell you?"

"Yes," he nodded, his resistance wavering. "We're all together again. You're clairvoyant like my mother."

He watched Chita rush happily among the mourners. It was difficult for Maria to let her guard down. Without telling anyone, she'd hired a bodyguard to watch over them for the next several months. He now stood discreetly among the crowd, a lean, smart-looking man in a tan suit.

"Who's that?" Pablo asked, his sexual antenna picking up a signal.

Maria glanced over. "Shit."

Chita's bodyguard.

"What, you like him too?"

"Yeah. Hands off. He's mine."

"Okay, but you owe me."

"Thank you, Pablito. You didn't give up on me."

"Things gonna be okay with you and Kenny?"

She nodded happily. "Chita already loves him."

"Just Chita?"

Maria smiled, watching Kenny and Nick stroll to the edge of the church lawn.

"*Corazon,*" Maria whispered to herself, as Chita reached up to her mother to be held.

Father Scolia had been so moved by Father Gene's funeral and the affectionate happy way the St. Louis congregation had celebrated his life, that he announced a personal fast. In his prayers he prayed for wisdom. For love. The introduction of Sister Agnes to her brother Nick was the most significant event of his long career. He couldn't exactly explain why. What were they to him? An alcoholic homosexual and a surly little nun with highly questionable scruples.

At the end of his fast it came to him. The presence of Christ could be felt when he witnessed their first tearful embrace. A brother and sister, separated by fate—reunited years in God. Old grudges could be put away.

Father Scolia had been privileged to watch such wretched loneliness subside, and their lovely reunion spawned his own renewed commitment to the community of his church.

"Father," Sister Agnes later came to him. "When I've fully collected my thoughts, I'll be finding myself in need to confess."

"I look forward to it," Father Scolia replied. "I promise to be gentle."

"Don't make promises you can't keep," she'd eyed him warily. "I think you'll find, as you come to know a few of Father Gene's constituents, that more of them may be seeking spiritual advice and forgiveness."

"I absolve you now," the priest told her. "I don't want to know the details."

"Maybe you're right, Father." Smiling, Sister Agnes wandered into the sanctuary to say her prayers.

*   *   *

Florencia outdid herself today. She'd been cooking for days, roasting chickens and pork, and Bambi's favorite green corn tamales. When Maria's motor home pulled up, the yard, festooned with beautiful balloons, was already crammed with Bambi's family and the friends she shared with Madonna. True to her word, Bambi resisted wearing a tuxedo. Instead she wore the ornate Mexican wedding shirt her father had worn on the day he married Florencia. Beautiful in a long gauzy green dress, Madonna wore orchids in her hair. She was thrilled to see Maria and Conchita enter the gate.

A *mariachi* band began to play, as keg after keg of beer emptied into the bellies of Florencia's guests. Kids and dogs chased through the legs of the adults, including Sandra and Rosie, Beatrice's barking pitbulls. Chita had a marvelous time. Nick, Kenny noticed, had refrained from drinking. They were both staying at the Seven Palms, but in separate rooms.

Much had to be decided, negotiated between them. Kenny explained to Pablo that until he and Maria came to a legal understanding regarding Chita, which wouldn't be difficult but time-consuming, what happened between him and Nick remained secondary.

Nick was too busy catching up with Sister Agnes. With a bona fide family member to call his own, the considerable pressure he placed on Kenny had already eased. Maria had offered them the restaurant as an outright gift, and both of them refused. They didn't want to go back there.

For normalcy, Maria kept it open. It provide consistency for Chita and employed Miguel and Gabriel, who she'd slighted badly during her grief-stricken blindness. She even allowed Carmen to make her amends. Carmen approached her as if Maria was the head of Cathedral City's Mexican Mafia.

"Why is everybody acting so funny toward me?" she asked Sister Agnes in Florencia's backyard.

"They're afraid of you. You have their respect."

"I don't want people to be afraid of me," Maria said.

"Nevertheless, you'd be a fool not to appreciate that they are. There's more to be done," Sister Agnes swilled her drink. "People are still suffering."

And just as she said so, Kenny gazed up and caught Maria's eye.

"I've been speaking with him. You have a willing partner if you ever need one."

And around the yard, Soila, Bambi, Madonna and Inez all gazed over at her at the same time.

Only Pablo was at odds tonight. He missed Bob. He'd missed his chance, probably the only chance he'd ever have to love someone; to be patient. As he watched the ballet of avoidance between Nick and Kenny, he knew they'd get back together. What would life have in store for Pablo?

"Sandra! Rosie!" Beatrice hollered near the gate. "Jo-Jo's back."

A baying basset hound could be heard over the throng. Jo-Jo was Bob's mother's dog. How many basset hounds could be named Jo-Jo?

"I think you might be interested in this," Madonna whispered to Pablo.

"Who is it?" he asked, unbelieving.

"Well," Madonna smiled, "I'm tall, taller than anyone at this party, and from up here I can see an old lady with a bassinet being unloaded from a Toyota 4-Runner by a very muscular man. He's holding a dog wrapped in a baby blanket. Who'd treat a dog like a baby, I wanna know."

"Did he know I'd be here?"

"He came *because* you'd be here, sweetie."

Pablo watched as Bob assisted Marilyn while surreptitiously scanning the faces of the partygoers. Pablo noticed Madonna deflate, somewhat.

"What's wrong?"

"My daughter. So many reunions, today. I was hoping she'd come."

"Night isn't over."

"No, she isn't coming. I'll just have to be patient with her. Excuse me, but I need a hug from my girlfriend." She wandered over to where Bambi stood kidding her cousins. When Madonna approached, Bambi stopped whatever she was saying and reached out for her hand. She pulled Madonna close and kissed her.

"*Cholos,*" she barked. "This is my girl! Any of you have a girlfriend as pretty as mine?"

"Pablo?"

Pablo turned around. Bob studied him wistfully. "I don't like Canada. Too cold."

"It's warm here," Pablo assured him.

"That's what I hoped," Bob smiled.

Across the yard, Sandra and Rosie joyfully circled Jo-Jo's bassinet while Jo-Jo howled happily at the new moon.

EPILOGUE

The Best Is Yet to Come

"What *now?*"

Maria and Sister Agnes were in quiet, earnest conversation when a group introducing themselves as the Cathedral City Preservation Society entered the restaurant and asked for the proprietor, Ms. Castillo. Sister Agnes summed them up:

"They're just typical suits trying to fake you out in resort wear."

Maria scowled at her and stood to greet them. At Sister Agnes' suggestion she had resumed her former, more feminine mode of dress. Her hair was long again. Her daughter loved her mother's long, luxuriant tresses. She wanted long hair when she grew up, Chita informed her. Just like Maria's. Just like Kenny's.

Why did the mind wander the way it did? Maria wondered in exasperation.

She was only crossing the room to find out what this group of somewhat ingratiating Anglos wanted from her. Was it another attempt to convince her to change her location? To sell the business and the building to the city so they could build a parking structure to service the needs of the empty city hall?

Where did they keep finding the money? Maria wondered. There was more new construction going on across the street. The local papers warned of dire financial consequences if the madness continued. Now here they were, Leslie Mason, the city planner; Peggy Lane, the president of the Chamber of Commerce; Scott Travers, the smiling burly president of the Cathedral City Preservation Society, who was a good customer and for a short time, wanted to sleep with Pablo.

Pablo was so vain, Maria shook her head. She checked her smile when she remembered that Pablo, too, was gone now, no longer a constant in her life.

In the short distance from the end of her bar to the foyer of the restaurant, Maria realized her face must have presented a wild card of emotion. Was she talking to herself as she approached them? Lately, as in the time at Mass when Sister Agnes got her hooks into her, Maria worried that her thoughts were so noisy she must be walking around muttering to herself. Everybody knew who she was anyway.

Scott Travers reached forward to shake her hand. "We came in for a late lunch. And, we were wondering if we could talk with you."

He had a sweet smile, Maria mentally noted. It was little-boyish, almost goofy, but he was anything but immature. He was smart, had lived in Cathedral City for twenty-five years and loved it. He had aspirations to be mayor, it was generally believed, but here he was now, making a round of introductions. First Leslie, then Peggy, and then the mayor of Cathedral City, Harry Hills.

"I'm very pleased to meet you. My wife loves your fajitas."

"Swell," Maria replied flatly. "Where would you like to sit?"

"Anywhere at all," Scott grinned at her. "Do you have a moment to talk with us?"

Maria glanced down the bar at Sister Agnes, who openly gawked at the group while she downed her bourbon. She was impatient for Maria to finish their discussion. Tonight Maria, Kenny and Chita were leaving town. Their first road trip in the new motor home. Nick was invited but he wanted to watch the bar.

"Well, I am a little busy."

"It'll only take a moment of your time," Mayor Hills pressed.

"Only if it isn't a financial matter," Maria acquiesced.

"Nothing of the kind," Leslie assured her. Peggy smiled magnificently.

"Perhaps if you could just tell me," Maria urged them. "And I'll buy you lunch."

They studied her.

Scott made the request. "We want you to serve on the board of the Cathedral City Chamber of Commerce."

"And the Cathedral City Preservation Society."

"And the Friends of the Library."

"The Rotary Club."

"*What?*"

"Look," Scott took her hand, which she recoiled from, instantly. "We'll be straight with you. With all the uproar from the unfortunate news leak—"

She knew what he was talking about, but made him explain it to her just the same. "You heard about the Chamber of Commerce brainstorming meeting."

Maria folded her arms.

"When a list was leaked to the press about the positive and negative public perceptions of Cathedral City."

His companions began to bleat in unison.

"It was a closed, informal meeting."

"We were shouting out ideas."

"It was never intended to leave the room."

"They weren't our perceptions."

"I'm sorry. I guess I still don't know what you're talking about," Maria smiled.

"You're gonna make me say it," Scott shifted on his big feet.

"Yes."

"As reported in the newspaper, top on the list of negatives was that Cathedral City was perceived as too Hispanic."

"You're even making a mistake by using that word now," Maria pointed out.

"Hispanic?" Scott wilted a bit.

" 'Latino' is preferable. Hispanic is a divisive term. It's a bureaucratic word. It appears on forms, and refers to Spain. It leaves other nationalities out. Whole continents, even. Like Central and South America."

"Look. That's why we need Latino board members."

"There's already a Mexican American Chamber of Commerce."

"Are you a member?"

"No."

"Why not?"

"Well, I'm not much of a joiner."

"We need you," the mayor admitted. "You're a symbol."

"A symbol of what?"

"You're a success story to the large Latino community of Cathedral City."

"There are many successful second and third generation Latinos in Cathedral City." She wasn't friendly with any of them, but she knew they existed.

"They want Cinderella. Better press," Sister Agnes spoke into her drink.

Scott laughed. "Actually, we want *Evita.*"

Maria checked a smile. Anything to get the best of the churlish old nun.

"I'm not a political person," she shrugged.

"You could be," Leslie Mason observed. "What's to stop you?"

"Interest," Maria replied airily.

"And are you?" Peggy queried.

"Am I what?"

"Interested."

"It's always flattering to be asked," Maria noted. She led them to a large booth with a window that looked across the street to the Cathedral City Civic Center. "I'll give it some thought. What were some of the positives?"

"Positives?"

"About Cathedral City?"

"Diversity," Scott smiled.

"For starters," Maria handed them their menus, "why don't we forget the bad publicity and just focus on that?"

"Welcome to the Seven Palms Inn and Resort Retirement Community," said Dom, the silver-haired maitre'd. "Relax outside. Later in the afternoon, the new owner/manager is planning some very special entertainment." The rehabilitation had gone smoothly. The developer, a Nevada restaurateur, was very knowledgeable about the history of Cathedral City.

"Why would I want to have drinks at a place with so many bad memories?" Inez griped at her friend, Sister Agnes. She was visiting Soila. She made regular trips back and forth, thanks to Maria.

"Because drinks are free," Sister Agnes reminded her.

She charged out on the patio and up to the bar. They were all invited to a small party held on the terrace of the grounds of the newly refurbished old Seven Palms Inn. The legacy would continue. The Seven Palms had been saved again, but this time with the help of the Cathedral City Preservation Society. The hotel was beautiful. The atrocious lobby had been scaled down to a more hospitable size. The rooms were redecorated in authentic mid-century decor.

Phase One of the retirement condominiums had already been completed and occupied. They'd gotten very favorable national press. Phase Two and Three were already sold and ready for construction to begin. The hotel would close next summer to accommodate its completion. It was rumored *Architectural Digest* planned to photograph it. The first gay hotel and retirement community to ever grace its pages. It was the pride of Cathedral City.

Pablo and Bob luxuriated in chaise longues by the sparkling pool. Maria and Soila sunbathed nearby, reading magazines. Soila wore a large hat. Her boyfriend, famed Palm Springs plastic surgeon Tim Hansen had warned her that too much exposure to sunlight could cause a shadow of the apparition to return. Sometimes Soila missed the Blessed Virgin.

Chita came screeching onto the patio, darting from table to chaise.

"Conchita!" Maria clapped her hands. "Be quiet, *mi vida*. We're trying to relax. Go play with Daddy."

"Where's Daddy?"

"He's inside."

"No," Kenny corrected her. He was laying on a raft. "I'm in the pool."

Chita ran as hard as she could and cannonballed into the water, splashing all the adults. Kenny rolled off the raft to intercept her.

From inside the cocktail lounge overlooking the pool, a piano started up. Inside the unmistakable strains of Nick could be heard singing.

Kenny gazed worriedly over at Maria. "It's *The Best Is Yet to Come.*"

"It's his place. He can do what he likes," she smiled.

Kenny tossed his laughing daughter high into the air over the cool aqua water.

Please turn the next page for
an exciting sneak peek
of Gregory Hinton's next novel
THE WAY THINGS OUGHT TO BE
coming in September 2003.

Gregory Hinton's wonderfully evocative, lyrical novels transport readers to a time and place as magical as a favorite film and as real and immediate as our own lives. Now, in THE WAY THINGS OUGHT TO BE, he chronicles one man's erotic coming of age among the activists, intellectuals, hedonists, friends, and lovers of 1970's America . . .

Life is good in Boulder, Colorado, in the heady hey-days of the 1970s. Ginsberg and Burroughs are in residence, and gay sexual liberation is both a political statement and a feverish, carnal dream lived out fully in the baths and the bars, in college dorm rooms and parks, in furtive looks and increasingly bold public statements. The world is alive with a new promise. And sex—glorious, abandoned, intense sex—is there for the taking. For everyone except King James.

In addition to having the most ironic name ever for a gay man, King is saddled with other troubles. Young and beautiful, he can't seem to follow the only ground rule of his new life: anything goes but falling in love. Instead, the sensitive writer is constantly searching for that elusive connection. It's something he doesn't find in his secretive family, where he feels compelled to protect his controlling mother, depressed, alcoholic father, and gay-and-out-there older brother. It's something he feels in fragments with his pregnant, bohemian, best friend, Jen, who has tapped him to be both Lamaze coach and surrogate partner for her illegitimate baby. And it's something he's looked for in every man he's ever slept with—the cruel, hypocritical Lex; hunky, closeted quarterback, Barry; the charismatic gay-rights leader, Sam; tragic Tim; erotic Matthew; and the uncompromising Theo who reminds King that "It's just sex, remember?"

As his friends and lovers fight for their rights, twenty-one-year-old King embarks on his own mission—a journey of sexual and spiritual liberation that takes him into the steamy, dark voyeurism of the bathhouses and into the rarified world of intellectuals and poets who hold court at the *L'Bar* . . . to the hotel rooms of men who want to please and be pleased and into the arms of a few willing to hold on . . . from the fantasies and confusion of his own painful past to the quiet, calm peace of a place where he can watch men swimming naked, "their tight bodies shimmering like marlins in the blue, blue water." And finally, his search will take him to the most surprising destination of all—himself.

In this sensual and beautifully written novel, Gregory Hinton captures the decadence and hope of the disco era, when sexual freedom was both a pledge and a battle cry, and creates in King James an unforgettable hero—an everyman whose poignant, triumphant voyage of self-discovery mirrors the small victories we all experience along the way.

He was surrounded by a small group of good-looking guys holding court. A few King recognized from around campus, some from the Denver bars. He looked up when King came in, but King gave himself no credit for his interest. He stood against the window, his face in shadows, but he was tall, a head taller than they were, than King was, surely. Behind him, outside, the snow was falling gently. The soft light from the church floodlights illuminated the white snow, and it seemed brighter outside than in. Inside, the only light came from the flickering table candles, the dimmed lights from the nearby church hall kitchen.

Backlit by the glow of the snow, Sam wore a dark sweater, blue jeans, boots. His dark hair was shaggy-long, just shy of ponytail length, and he had a subtly hawklike nose and dark, important eyes, though why King could see his eyes, he now couldn't say. It was too dark to make out his eyes, but there they were still. He was framed by the gently falling snow.

Sam was tall and he was handsome and looking at King. He felt new to Boulder, that was for sure. King would have surely remembered him. Sam was new and interesting for that reason, interesting for all the basic reasons. Interesting because he was surrounded by several others King had found interesting at other times.

King sized up his odds and looked away.

It was early October, and snowing softly that night, the first snow of fall. King was wearing a parka. The roads were slippery and he'd been told he didn't need snow tires because his new car had radials; his first new car, the silver Mercury Capri. The car was beautiful and handled well in the snow. Still, the roads were slippery.

The car handled well in the ten-minute drive along Broadway Avenue, capably rounding the perimeter of the softly lit flagstone buildings of the University of Colorado campus. King proceeded slowly down the hill, past the eclectic campus housing of old Victorian houses and flat, postwar apartment buildings. At Arapaho he turned right, continuing past Boulder High School till he made another right on Folsom Avenue. Then King proceeded up a short hill, parking on the street instead of in the parking lot.

Friday night and too snowy to make the drive to the bars in Denver. Not till he got the feel of his new car. They had no gay clubs in Boulder. This was the weekly Friday night Gay Coffee House. They charged a dollar cover.

King crunched his way up the sidewalk toward the entrance to the recreation hall of Boulder's A-frame Wesley Chapel. It was probably around eight-thirty. He could see his breath in the cold air. He could smell snow and the faint comforting scent of smoke from someone's nearby chimney.

If it was slow inside, King might be willing to attempt the drive to Denver. He came in through the side entrance, and several men were hanging around a table where a guy named Theo was selling tickets. He'd seen Theo around. He was one of the original founders of the Boulder Gay Liberation Front. He was lanky, intellectual looking, and wore thin, round glasses. He always dressed in black.

King peered inside the rec hall. Busy enough. The overhead lights were off. Candles flickered on tables pushed off to the side. Maybe fifteen or twenty guys hung around the edge of the room. He recognized a few of them and decided to stay. He nodded hello to Theo and gave him his dollar. He walked into the cloak room and hung up his parka.

It felt strange coming to the church for this reason, in light of what it once meant to King. On the walls of the rec hall, children's artwork depicted stories from the Bible. *Jesus loves the little children of the world.* The liberal elders of the church had offered this space to provide a safe place for gay men and women to gather. Make alliances. Like-minded friends.

King had no gay friends. He didn't know the first thing about how to go about making them. For him, being gay in and of itself wasn't enough of a reason to base a friendship. As he looked back, he better understood his thinking. Coming out had been a personal and social disaster: the *Titanic* of any coming-out story he had ever heard, due largely in part to his considerable naiveté. King once believed that with family support, his trust in God, and lastly, the fact that he was living in Boulder in the mid-seventies, no harm would come to him.

Free love, alternative lifestyles, *Saturday Night Live*. The collapse of the Nixon White House and the end of the Vietnam War. The antiwar movement had won. When King came to Boulder, the campus was in a state of flux.

Whereas only a year before, the Colorado National Guard had tear-gassed Kittredge Commons, the upscale, country-clubby dormitory complex where he lived as a freshman; the fraternity and sorority system became so passé that many houses sought renters; there was no pressure at all to belong to anything. Boulder had no specific identity, at least as far as he was concerned, except for once being rated by *Playboy* magazine as the number one party school in the nation.

King's parents allowed him to attend the University of Colorado only because it was one of three affordable in-state universities. This pissed off his brother Neil, who several years before wasn't even allowed to apply because their parents thought Boulder was too radical and dangerous for him. They dispatched him to a teaching college in nearby Greeley instead.

Boulder was a beautiful city, sloping up along the front range of the Colorado Rockies, and in his time, King watched it evolve from a quaint university town to a bastion for smart and entrepreneurial money. In the mid-seventies, Boulder offered many options: political, spiritual and sexual, it had become a melting pot for innovative thought. An antiwar activist, the Reverend Daniel Berrigan, was rumored to be in hiding there. Influenced by Chogyam Trungpa Rinpoche, wealthy Eastern religious sects were buying up old buildings in downtown Boulder.

Poets Allen Ginsberg, Gregory Corso, Diane Di Prima, and Peter Orlovsky formed the Jack Kerouac School of Disembodied Poetics at Boulder's Naropa Institute. Radical Christian groups, such as the Children of God, had established a foothold among Boulder's burgeoning Christian movement.

At some level King never knew what he had and would regret leaving. Had his emotional circumstances not thwarted a more speedy departure, he might have missed out on the very best time of the five years he lived there.

He would have missed out on Sam.

After standing off to the side and watching several lame attempts by a few coffee-housers to dance, King felt like an idiot. No one approached him. Often his shyness got mistaken as arrogance or conceit.

His body began to feel like so many loose pieces of Lego. If King stayed a moment longer he would disassemble right down to the scarred and yellowing rec hall linoleum floor. He decided to leave. The room had filled to thirty or more. He was still alone. As he made his way along the perimeter of the room toward the cloak room door, a hand touched his shoulder.

"Leaving so soon?"

The voice was gentle, even slightly tremulous with the slightest East coast twang. King didn't reply. He was so nervous, he turned, staring in utter deer-in-the-headlights stupefaction. Of course it was Sam. He was hanging in the shadows, gazing down at King and smiling.

King was of average height, just shy of 5 feet 10 inches, but because he had long legs, he seemed taller. King didn't have a proscribed body type when it came to a sexual partner, but to be a male and looking *up* into the eyes of another extremely tall man was, to him, sexually charging. Small talk was clearly not his forte.

"Yeah," King mustered.

"That's a shame," Sam offered. "I saw you and I wanted to say hello."

"It's not too late." King brightened.

"No." He smiled. "I suppose not. I'm Sam."

"I'm King," King introduced himself.

Sam gestured King into the shadows, patting the wall as if inviting him in. King leaned in awkwardly, muttered a few unmemorable remarks, but Sam was clearly happy to be talking with him. They exchanged the perfunctory demographics. King was born in Montana and grew up in Denver. He was getting a degree in English. He was here on a writing scholarship.

Sam came from a small town in upstate New York. He was working on his graduate degree in city planning. He'd arrived in Boulder the previous semester. Sam was as surprised as King that they hadn't noticed each other before.

"A few of us are planning to walk over to the UMC," he said. The UMC was the University Memorial Center. The campus student union. "They're holding some kind of a monthly dance. We thought we'd crash it and dance together. I was wondering if you wanted to come along."

He grinned down at King, but his eyes were earnest. Sam was testing him.

King hoped he didn't look appalled.

"Sure," King agreed, and Sam laughed heartily in response and hugged him.

About ten or twelve of them left the church and headed across the snow-covered field behind the School of Engineering, toward campus. King knew most of the guys. Theo, of course. All of the sycophants King saw surrounding Sam earlier. A preppy-looking guy named Tim. His sweet boyfriend Peter. Rod, a tall, striking, smirking, short-cropped blonde who apparently, as much as King could gather through eavesdropping, had just broken up with his boyfriend, a sexy Italian stud he'd always admired named Tony. Rod owned a local gay rag, a Denver newsletter filled mostly with advertising, a few political articles, and photo teases. The usual shirtless skier advertising a gay ski weekend in Aspen.

King knew these guys because he'd tricked with a few of them. Tim, right after he and Lex broke up, in a bedroom at a party house on the outskirts of Boulder. King hadn't known about Peter. Tim had a cock that curved down instead of up, like a Japanese bridge.

Rod had only been an attempted conquest. King sat gin-drunk on his lap, probably at the same party, where Rod confided that he'd had a crush on King for years. They'd made out passionately. King had quoted a little poetry.

"In my Tanqueray recollections, I do not lament rejections, only mistaken identities . . ."

Rod laughed, made excuses, and left.

Had King come on too strong? He called Rod in the middle of the night. Rod told him he wasn't the marrying kind, which by implication meant that somehow King was.

If King had known how to make gay friends, he might have better understood that every smile didn't imply a long-term commitment; that sometimes sex was for fun and not always for love. He might have developed a sense of humor about the whole thing. Finally King might have known how comforting friends could be, that sometimes it was better to leave a bar with your friends than a strange trick. King personalized every encounter, every false hope, every letdown. The stakes he played for were high.

As King walked along the periphery of the amassed group, he felt very nervous about what they planned to do. His motives were not exactly pure, and the uneasy feeling that he hadn't just been picked up by Sam but recruited by him was beginning to creep into his mind.

Sam wasn't even talking to him. He was walking way out ahead and trying to talk sense into Rod. King's acute sense of survival was informing him to fall back, out of ranks, and slink quietly back to his new Capri and then home. He realized he could never trust anyone, least of all his own intuition.

At the very moment King began to slow down, Sam turned and anxiously searched the group with brooding eyes. Rod continued to march moodily ahead, but Sam stood off to the side, reviewing his troops. Would twelve gay men be any match for five hundred drunken heterosexuals?

Sam caught King's eye. Now King could never escape.

"Hi," he said, as King slowly approached.

"Hey," King muttered.

"Sorry I got hung up with Rod. You know him? He says he knows you. Says you're a great poet."

Terrific, King thought.

"Listen, are you still up for this? You look a little worried."

"I'll be okay," King murmured.

King didn't know what else to say. He'd had enough public humiliation to last a lifetime. So had his parents. It was all too intense and complicated to explain to Sam on the snowy streets of Boulder.

They crossed the campus in silence and began to approach the University Memorial Center. "Look, I'd be surprised if we had any trouble, but I can't guarantee we won't. If you're worried, you don't have to stay. I wouldn't think any less of you."

"I said I'd come and I'm coming."

Sam smiled down at King. "You won't be alone. You have us. Me," he corrected himself, humbly. The others were making their way up the steps to the lobby of the UMC. Band music blared out from inside. The snow was falling heavily now.

Sam waited patiently. He held out his hand. King took it.

They walked up the steps to the lobby where their friends had gathered. They all paid the cover. They entered the dance floor hand in hand. King didn't remember much about the band except the fact that they were local.

Sam led the group through the crowd to a small opening in the middle of the packed ballroom. The dance had started an hour ago, and the energy was peaking. Sam came to a halt and King looked around. The attendees looked mostly like Greeks. King thought he recognized a girlfriend of Jen's, Holly, dancing with a sorority sister nearby. Holly had been over to Teddy's once or twice. She seemed to recognize him, because she nodded just as the band started playing "Eli's Comin'."

Sam held out his hand. "Dance?"

Stepping out, King never took his eyes off Sam. The gay men and women began to dance. King, noticing Holly's shock, watched in amusement as she and her partner fled the floor, afraid of being mistaken as part of Sam's group. She glanced over her shoulder at King, as if to make certain he was who she thought he was. Teddy's roommate. Teddy. Jen's boyfriend.

The surrounding straight couples noticed, rippling away momentarily, but acquiesced to their presence without comment. They weren't scandalous. Only interesting, a mental bookmark event with which to amuse their friends. Boulder, after all.

That night King walked Sam back as far as Sam's room, a graduate school dormitory in the same direction as the church. Sam was enthused about the action, glad for the statement they had made. King, too, felt invigorated. The throngs didn't turn on them. They weren't hung up by their toes. The floor didn't open up and swallow them whole. They only danced a few songs and left. Outside, they all hugged each other. King felt like he had brothers and sisters. A new kind of family. The Boulder Gay Liberation Front.

As Sam and King walked back, King was laughing with relief. Now the sky was clear and cold. The storm had passed and the outline of the Flatirons hatcheted across the starlit sky.

When they came to Reed Hall, Sam's dorm, he stopped.

"This is it. This is where I live."

The end of the evening had come. King took in a deep breath. "You wanna come up?" Sam offered. "I'll make us some tea."

King nodded, expecting only tea.

Sam's room had a twin bed, a desk, a dresser, and a drafting table by the window. King feigned interest in a drawing Sam was working on. Behind him, Sam peeled off his coat and sweater. He wore a white T-shirt with dog tags underneath.

"Take off your coat," Sam ordered King pleasantly. "You aren't leaving anytime soon."

King smiled and unzipped his parka. Sam disappeared into his bathroom to fill a small electric percolator with water. When he came out, he plugged it in. King sat on the edge of his drafting stool and smiled at him. Heat pumped from a radiator under the window. The room felt cozy and warm.

Sam's body was lean and he moved jauntily, with joy. He fiddled through a box of herbal teas. Celestial Seasonings.

"Boulder's own," King said.

Sam looked up and smiled. "Sleepy Time okay with you?"

"Yeah," King whispered.

Sam dropped a bag each into two mugs. Then he walked across the room and kissed King from behind. Sam handed King his mug. "I'm feeling a little sleepy. You?"

They made love twice that night, once in the morning. Sam was the first uncircumcised man King had been with. He explained that as a baby his foreskin had been so negligible his doctors hadn't bothered with a circumcision. King had trouble getting the hang of it. Sam instructed him how to hold his cock, taught him where the most sensitive area was to arouse him.

They made love on Sam's single bed, facing each other, on their sides, Sam's arm around King protectively, cradling him as they gently rocked. He had long, dark eyelashes. He closed his eyes when he kissed, and King could almost count each lash as it feathered across his cheek. King liked kissing him. For a man, Sam had especially pretty, perfectly formed lips.

Outside it started to snow again.

They whispered through the night, in and out of sleep. They slept bound together by a flurry of arms, bedclothes, and legs; limbs tangled with limbs. Sometimes they'd drift awake kissing passionately, only to fall back on the pillow and float away.

They blurted out intimate details. They could remember how many men they'd slept with. They could remember names, ages, and the circumstances of how they'd met. They talked about childhood, of brothers and sisters. Of aged parents. They talked about favorite books, music they liked, colors.

They talked about future plans. King's desire to move back to California. Sam's longing to move back to New York. In the morning Sam wanted to fuck King. King had only tried it once, with Lex, unsuccessfully, and because it was Sam, wanted to try it again. King grimaced through the whole ordeal.

They made plans to meet at the gym later that day. Maybe they'd go to dinner after that. That night, King found himself back in bed with Sam.

"Listen, I'm sorry about this morning. Did I hurt you?"

"No," King lied.

"I found a drop of blood on my sheet."

"I'll get you a new one."

"No, King. I'm not worried about the sheet. It washed out. If you don't like being fucked, you should say so."

"I thought it might be different with you."

Sam laughed. "Fucking is a pretty outrageous thing to do. It didn't even occur to me till one night it was happening to me. I didn't know two men did such things! There are other things we can try," Sam smiled kindly. He kissed King on the top of his head. "This is all new to me, too."

King headed to the library with a smile on his face. Something clearly was developing between them.